LOVER, BETRAYER . . .

As Juana undressed, she hummed a tune from the nightclub. It was self-aware but not insistent, neither coy nor stupid. Under the brown hose, her long legs were brown; her body was strong and supple. She cried out with pleasure and laughed afterward and then hugged him as they spiraled down toward sleep.

"Do you have to go away in the morning?" she murmured.

"Not right away."

"Good." She smiled, her face against his shoulder, and he could feel the muscles move. "Go to sleep, then."

He had not slept for thirty-six hours. He let go, and his mind floated free.

When Tarp awoke, there was light coming into the room from the window, and the barrel of his own .22 was poked hard into the soft flesh just below the bend of his left jaw.

"Did you take me for an imbecile?" she said. She was sitting on the bed naked, the gun in one hand and his false papers in the other.

There are no accidents, he thought. Repin had been right.

Novels by George Bartram from Pinnacle Books

THE SUNSET GUN
UNDER THE FREEZE

UNDER THE FREEZE

GEORGE BARTRAM

PINNACLE BOOKS   NEW YORK

UNDER THE FREEZE

An original Pinnacle Books edition, published for the first time
anywhere.

First printing/November 1984

ISBN: 0-523-42055-2

Can. ISBN: 0-523-43314-X

Cover art by Paul Stinson

Printed in the United States of America

PINNACLE BOOKS, INC.
1430 Broadway
New York, New York 10018

9 8 7 6 5 4 3 2 1

UNDER THE FREEZE

Tarp went down the sun-whitened wooden stairs as carefully as if they were paved with gulls' eggs. He walked erect. Two buckets hung from his hands as if their weight were trying to pull him through the planking and into the scummy water underneath. In the buckets were dead fish, the last two loads he would have to carry aboard the *Scipio* before heading out into the Gulf. It was not yet seven in the morning, yet he was streaming with sweat and the sun was like an accusing finger that jabbed at him from the sky.

He set the buckets down and took a breath, and then he swung one leg over the rail of the sportfisherman, leaning far forward as he pulled a bucket after and then put it on the deck. He reached back for the other and then straightened, looking all the way around him as if he expected to find an enemy, his fingers digging across his palms to ease the hurt of the buckets' weight. There were birds circling over the bait barrels on the dock a hundred yards away, and farther out in the Gulf a line of pelicans lumbered along above the water. Fish made little swirls close in. *Ladyfish*, he thought, but he was not sure.

He stepped over into the boat and it rocked just a little under his weight, the way an elevator rocks when it comes to the end of its ride, slowly and heavily. Up on the flying bridge a piece of electronic gear crackled, saying nothing; forward on the platform, which was small and almost not a platform at all but simply a railed place forward where somebody could stand with a harpoon if he was that crazy, a gull had landed on the white neoprene-covered rail. It curled its cruel feet around the tubing

1

and looked at him with its head over on one side, the eye calculating, hungry; and as it looked him over it let a stream of droppings fall, missing the platform and landing in the water below.

"Thanks for being so thoughtful," Tarp growled. He moved forward but the bird did not fly. It had its greedy eye now on the bait buckets. Tarp stepped down into the shaded cool of the cabin. As he moved forward he saw the shadow of the gull pass across a port, heading for the bait. *We're all the same,* he thought. *Taking targets of opportunity.* There was a half-finished cup of coffee, cold now, on the galley sink; he drank most of it, threw the dregs away. He got a bait knife and a big cutting board and a section of yesterday's Miami newspaper, which he folded and put under his arm so that the word NU-CLEAR was visible in black letters but the rest of the headline (FREEZE OPPOSED) was hidden; he went up to the deck again, squeezing through the passage that separated his cramped bunk on the right from the storage lockers where there were charts and foul-weather gear and his few clothes and a twelve-gauge pump and a Weatherby .375 and, concealed behind a bulkhead, an AR-15 with the retaining spur removed.

Now there were two gulls on the bait buckets and half a dozen more coming in. "Go away," Tarp said quietly. He headed toward the buckets and they flew off, each with a piece of fish. He slid the buckets along the deck to the transom, clipped the cutting board into its holders, and began to slice the plump, smelly, red-sided fish into chunks, cleaning the knife on the newspaper. *Fish or cut bait. Me, just now, I'm cutting bait.* Most of the fish would be ground up for chum, and he dropped the chunks into the wire basket of the chopper, all but the big, meaty pieces, which went into an ice chest for bait.

He was still cutting bait some minutes later when a shadow fell over the deck. He had not heard anybody come, and he knew that nobody had come out along the dock while he had been cutting the fish because he could see it all the way to the gas pumps. His grip on the fish knife shifted.

Tarp swiveled his head slowly to the left. The sun was there, with the newcomer in front of it. Rays of brilliance shot out around the head and shoulders like the aura of a cheap plaster Christ.

"Going fishing?"

Tarp knew that voice. It sounded English but he knew that it

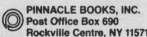

was not. He knew that the voice was being faked somehow and that it was really deeper and harsher. But he was distracted by the sound of an engine as a boat swung out toward the Gulf. He remembered hearing a boat come in sometime earlier, just after dawn.

"This isn't a charter boat," he said. He always tried to be polite, although polite people never found him so.

"May I come aboard, please?"

The voice had dropped a couple of notes and there was definite slippage in the English accent, especially on the word *please*. Tarp knew who it was now. "Are you alone?" he said quietly.

"Of course."

"Nobody on you?"

"I am tourist! Who would be on me?" A rich laugh erupted from the sunburst, and Tarp, still unable to see the face, imagined the old man's mouth opening, rather soft, almost flaccid, the small eyes crinkling in their setting of fat and wrinkles.

"Come aboard."

"The *Scipio* swayed a little again, for the old man weighed as much as Tarp although he was much shorter. He was clumsy in a boat, and he had to get his balance again before he could stand on the deck.

"Want to go below?"

The laughed rolled again. " 'Go below'! How very nautical! You sound, if you please, like Jack London. What is 'below'? Some crowded little place full of dead fish's stuffings? No. I sit here in the sun. I am tourist. I come for sunshine." He moved to the big fighting chair in the stern. "What is this throne?"

"It's a barber chair. I do razor cuts on the side."

His Russian accent fully intact now, the old man glowered. "What is this razor cut? Is way that black Negroes are fighting in Harlem, yes?"

Tarp almost smiled. "Russians aren't supposed to be racists. Want coffee?"

"Vodka."

"I don't keep vodka on hand, and anyway it's too early. I've got Scotch, if you have to have it."

"Coffee is bad for liver. Scotch is good. Bring the bottle, my friend."

Tarp went below and got a bottle of Laphroaig and one glass;

he washed his hands at the galley sink, but he was in a hurry and so a lot of the dried fish blood stayed on him. Coming out past the lockers he reached under a slicker and took out a battered little .22 Woodsman in a scarred holster and carried it up with him. He put down the bottle and the glass next to the fighting chair and put the pistol in the ice chest, then picked up the hose that ran from the water connection on the dock and began to hose down his hands and arms with a trickle of blood-warm water.

"So, Repin," he said quietly, "what are you doing here?"

The old man was pouring himself a full glass of the malt Scotch. "I am tourist," he said amiably. He drank off the whiskey neat, smacked his loose old lips, raised his eyebrows in an atheist's parody of a saint's ecstasy, and grinned. "Very good. Very, very good!" He poured himself another glass. "I was in neighborhood, I thought I drop in." He laughed merrily. Tarp threw the few remaining uncut fish overboard and the gulls came screaming down; then he hosed the knife and the table and the deck and wiped the knife and the board with the newspaper. "Cuba?" he said.

"The neighborhood. I was in the neighborhood."

"Bit of a risk."

"Why? If U.S. Coast Guard catches me, I tell him I am freedom-loving refugee from tyranny of Fidel Castro." He laughed some more and poured some more.

"I don't think they'd like finding a KGB officer in Florida."

"KGB? Ahh! Was a long time ago. All that, a very long time ago. I have not been to Dzerzhinsky Square in—seven years. Eight!" He waved the glass happily. "This is nice place, Tarp. I *like* it here!" He sipped, looked down into the glass. "Seven years, the body changes completely, eh? I am new man—no more the Repin of old days. All that is history."

"Everything's history."

Repin's voice fell to a growl. Suddenly he looked sly and ugly, his lower lip pushed forward and his eyes tiny and greedy like the gull's. "I remember. You never forget, never forgive. The American way." He spat over the side. He stirred the whiskey with a stubby finger and then looked at the finger, from which an amber drop began to fall, and he flicked the finger toward the water, sending tiny droplets seaward. "For the gods of the ocean," he said gloomily, his mood completely changed. He looked like a man with a chill now, indrawn and miserable; he looked at the horizon and glanced warily toward the sun as if he expected it to hurt him. "Will there be storm?"

"No."

"I can get back to Cuba tonight?"

"As far as the weather's concerned."

Repin massaged his forehead with his left hand, pushing his straw hat back on his head, the half-empty glass seemingly forgotten in his right hand. The fingers passed down over the eyebrows, went to the left eye socket, massaged the eye, and pulled down the lower lid as if he were a man trying to wake up. He sighed, and the left hand dropped lifelessly to his side. "I got big problem, Tarp."

Tarp said nothing. When people talked, he let them.

Repin lifted the bottle, poured more whiskey on top of that already in the glass. "Not so long ago," he said, holding the bottle on his left thigh, "Soviet submarine went aground in Swedish waters. You heard about it?"

Tarp nodded.

"Was very old submarine, but usable. What you call whiskey class—conventional, no missiles. You know. Going aground like that was big embarrassment. The damned Swedes made a lot of it; the peace movement, they made a lot of it; for once, even the U.S. looked good in European press. Still, everybody says, is only embarrassment. But—big surprise! Swedes announce there is atomic material on board. Uproar! Nuclear warheads, say the Swedes. They find radiation when they check sub from outside. Inside, they never go. But big uproar, big noise—more ammunition for peace movement, more embarrassment for Soviet government. The Swedes, they love it. They invite in press, television, all that. Private joke in Moscow: Swedes are going to keep submarine and rename it the *Raoul Wallenberg*. Funny, hey? But is only embarrassment after all; when damned Swedes have got all the attention they can, they let submarine go and send it home." He grunted, nodded, then shook his head as if in amazement at the story he had just told. He looked at Tarp. "Well?"

"Well? You got caught—so?"

"But that is point—we did *not* get caught! There was no nuclear missiles on that submarine!" Without ever taking his little eyes from Tarp's, Repin drank. He jerked the glass from his lips angrily. "You understand what I just say? There was *no atomic missiles*! *Not* atomic submarine; *not* a missile-equipped submarine. Eh?"

"So, the Swedes were wrong."

Repin looked at the horizon as if he wanted to wipe it away with his hand. "No." His voice was rich with disgust. "Swedes were not wrong. In forward torpedo tubes, there was enough weapons-grade plutonium to make eight tactical atomic bombs." He flattened his lips by pulling them down over the teeth like an ape; then he pushed them out, as if he were a clown expressing comic gloom. "That plutonium, Tarp, it was not supposed to be there."

Tarp waited again. Repin disliked his silence and glared at him, but Tarp did not make small talk. This all had a point, he was sure, and Repin would get to it without any chat from him.

"The plutonium was stolen," Repin muttered. "They think from plant at Semipalatinsk. Stolen plutonium, Tarp—stolen in U.S.S.R."

They were silent. The boat rocked gently on the wake of another sportfisherman that had just gone out. Tarp had been leaning against the side, and now he straightened. "I'm going to take her out." He could smell the last cool vestige of the night on the breeze; in minutes the air would be sticky and the breeze would shift. "Want me to put you ashore?"

"Why would I go ashore? I don't know anybody ashore."

"How're you going to get back to Cuba?"

Some of Repin's good humor returned. "You are going to take me."

Tarp looked over the boats, the marina, the oily swells that still heaved behind the distant boat. "Why am I going to do that?"

"Curiosity. Money. Your *fire*."

"Fire?"

"That fire in your belly. Always burning. I know you. It is like lust in some men—that fire to make things right. I know you. After I tell you this story, you will take me to Cuba and you will try to make things right."

Tarp did not look at him. "It must be some story."

"It is."

"What happened to the captain of the sub?"

"He died in the Lubyanka."

"Some of your colleagues must have gotten a little insistent with their questions. Did he say where he got the plutonium before they killed him?"

"He had deal with man he never saw, he said. For quarter million dollars in diamonds, he carries two packages in two torpedo tubes."

"Where?"

"He didn't know. Orders to come."

"How?"

"In Cuba."

"From whom?"

"He didn't know."

"Some businessman. What was the sub's legitimate mission?"

"Training and long-distance testing—through the Baltic, running some probes on Swedish defenses, that's how he went aground, stupid bastard; rendezvous with support ship off Narvic, then run to Cuba; then rendezvous with support ship below South Georgia Islands and run east to Indian Ocean. Rest stop at Zanzibar, waiting further orders."

"That's a hell of a trip for an old boat."

"Maybe."

"Who wrote the orders?"

"Fleet Undersea Central, absolutely in the usual way. Is normal mission, perfectly normal! There is program, very low priority, for testing capabilities of conventional submarines; this voyage was part of it. Is not so unusual."

"Precedent?"

"Yes."

"When?"

"Last year, two years ago. More planned."

Tarp eyed the intelligent, ruthless old face. "How many plutonium thefts have there been?"

Repin actually turned red. He grunted, shook his head as he had earlier. "You. *You!*" He shook a finger at Tarp. "All right, after they find this plutonium in submarine, they check. They think maybe four times as much is missing, but is very, very hard to tell."

"Plutonium gets lost in the cracks, I know. So, four times as much; the subs have been making this voyage for the last two years—how many of them?"

Repin smiled. "Four."

Tarp felt the breeze turn hot. Sudden sweat made crescents under his eyes. "It's not enough of a story to make me run to Cuba. Sorry."

Repin leaned forward, the whiskey bottle on his left knee like a gun butt. "One hundred thousand dollars. Gold."

Tarp was frowning. "Let Dzerzhinsky Square handle it." But it was Repin's turn to say nothing. Tarp turned on him and he found that the old eyes were weary. "What is it?" Tarp said. "What's the problem? Infighting? But that's normal. Something else? Because Andropov's new? But that's not enough; those bastards are all at each other's throats, but they get their work done. What is it?" He looked at Repin, and Repin's eyes bored into him.

Tarp nodded suddenly. "It's one of *them*, is that it?"

Repin had smiled, as if with relief. "That is the fear."

"Who?"

Repin really laughed now. He made it seem the greatest joke there was, and it made him quite cheerful again. "That is the trouble, Tarp! Nobody knows!" His pitch went up and he giggled. He poured himself more Scotch and drank. "There was a great meeting in Dzerzhinsky Square. Andropov came. All the way from his office as general secretary of the Party he came! Beranyi came—young, hard, called by many an idealist because it is thought he would hesitate for a second or two before knifing his mother. Telyegin, my personal friend of the old days, pal of Ho Chi Minh and maybe the man who poisoned Stalin. Strisz, the bureaucrat. Falomin, the wolf. Mensenyi, Szelyupin, Galusha—a dozen others! I was not there, this is all relayed to me by various of them individually and in secret, you understand. But—what a meeting it must have been! First, they are nervous because of Andropov, because *he* is nervous; second, they all want the job of Semyon Tsvigun, recently deceased, mourned by nobody. And third, they believe that right there in that room is probably the man who has stolen from his mother country enough plutonium to make so many atomic bombs the world could go insane. *Stolen it and shipped it out of the Soviet Union!* Can you picture it, Tarp?"

"Not a pretty picture."

"And what do all these heavy fighters do in the same ring? Eh? Do they punch hard and knock each other out? Oh, no,

Tarp! They *negotiate*. They agree that none of them would touch this problem with his fingertips with asbestos gloves on! Why? Fear—what else?'' Repin grinned and leaned forward and banged the bottle slowly on his thigh. "What if the thief is Andropov himself? Or what if the thief is Beranyi? Or what if it seems to be one man, and it is really another? Oh, no! Not with *two pairs* of asbestos gloves on! No, no, they say, let us go to an outside master; let us not bother the rest of the Soviet leadership with this matter; let us keep it among the brotherhood of the upper echelon of the KGB. Let us go to old Repin and ask *him* to deal with it.'' A great grin split his face, as if a melon had been slashed. "So—I deal with it! I come to you!''

"Was that their idea?''

"No, no, that is my judgment. They do not know about you—do not *want* to know about you.''

"All but one of them.''

"Well, maybe, yes—all but one. Yes, the plutonium thief will want to know. Hey?''

"And the money you offered?''

"That was voted in Dzerzhinsky Square. At the meeting. There is lots of money in Dzerzhinsky Square.''

Tarp took the cutting board out of its clips and rested it against his thigh, his narrowed eyes searching the white docks and the white boats around him. "Who knew you were coming here from Cuba?'' he said.

"Only three people in Cuban KGB.''

"Swell.'' He moved toward the hatch. "Come below.''

"But I like the sun!''

"I don't want blood on my deck. Come below before somebody starts shooting.''

Laughing, stumbling a little, Repin blundered his way down the narrow ladder and along the passage to the cabin. By the time he got there Tarp was pushing shells into the twelve-gauge from an open box on the room's central table. He slammed the last one in, swung the gun up, checked the safety, and laid it on the table. "You armed?'' he said to Repin.

"Certainly not.''

Tarp jerked his head toward the shotgun. "Safety right there. Push it this way. Pump it after each shot.''

"What am I shooting at, please?''

"Almost anything but me. I'm going topside to take us out.''

When he had reached the ladder, Repin called after him, "Will you do it?"

Tarp turned slowly. "I don't see yet what it is I'd do."

Repin held up a hand, fingers spread. "Find where the plutonium goes." A finger dropped. "Get back the plutonium or the bombs made from it." Another finger closed. "Find the traitor who engineered it all." The hand became an angry fist.

Tarp did not have to think for very long. He had no interest in the internal rivalries of the Kremlin or Dzerzhinsky Square: if they all killed each other with stolen plutonium, it would be fine with him. But when the plutonium passed the Soviet border and threatened the rest of the world, he got worried. Repin was right about that—he had a fire. Weapons-grade plutonium passing out of regular channels meant madness, just as Repin had said. Terrorism or oppression or an insane war. *Forty bombs worth of madness.*

"I want a quarter million bucks," he said.

Repin began to protest as a matter of form and then gave it up.

"Pegged to the New York price as of today," Tarp insisted. "Gold."

"Of course. One-third now. Where would you like it?"

"Half now. My bank in London. They can probably just wheel it from the KGB corner of the vault to my corner."

Repin shook his head. "So cynical," he murmured.

"I'll want three passports, all different nationalities. One with a diplomatic stamp so I can get in and out easily. I want a *sluzhba* courtesy card, first priority."

"Oh, now!"

"You know the game, Repin."

Repin shrugged. "Oh, well."

"A source of money and weapons inside the Soviet Union. And don't put me in touch with anybody's network, not even yours. And for God's sake don't try to use me—got that? No ploys to bust dissidents or any of that bull. If you try to use me, I'll get you."

Repin's head sank down, seemingly into his neck, as if there were a well between his shoulders waiting for it. His hard old eyes met Tarp's and his hands spread wide on the table, only inches from the shotgun. "No. Because right now, I need you." His left index finger came off the table. The gesture was a very small one, but commanding. "But do not threaten me, Tarp. Nobody ever threatened me and carried it through."

"Likewise."

They stared at each other. Tarp gave a little nod. He went up the ladder into the wet heat and the sunlight.

First Cuba, then Moscow, he thought, *what could be simpler?*

CHAPTER 2

Repin was wearing a suit that looked as if it had been made in Bulgaria for sale in Cuba to Russians, for its fabric was sleazily lightweight and its style was a decade or two out-of-date, even in Eastern Europe. Repin had probably picked it up in Cuba on purpose, Tarp thought; he was normally vain about his clothes, but he believed in protective coloration. In this case, however, the coloration was wrong, for he looked like exactly what he was—a Russian in the wrong part of the world.

"Put this on," he said tersely. He tossed a red knit shirt to the Russian.

"What is this?"

"It's a shirt. Somebody left it on board."

"What is wrong with clothes I am wearing? You do not like these clothes?"

"You look as if you're planning to offer Castro a cigar. Come on, put it on; this area's crawling with Coast Guard patrols. Drugs and Haitians are their big thing, but they'd take a Russian agent for the change."

Repin was fingering the shirt with distaste. It was short-sleeved and it had a press-on image of a small animal just above the pocket. He wrinkled his nose.

They had come out on deck and Tarp was steering from the flying bridge while Repin held on to the ladder halfway up, behind him. To their left the Caribbean sun was burning away the last of the morning haze, while to their right the water was green and then indigo and then a wonderful purple like the side of a dolphin when it is first caught.

12

"But I will look stupid in this," Repin said.

"Of course you will."

"I am a man very proud of his appearance!"

Repin had a great reputation as a womanizer. Even now, in his seventies, he was vain about it. The last time that Tarp had seen him he had had one bad eye and he had looked ten years older, but now he was more robust and the eye was healthy, as if he had grown younger. Repin was pleased, Tarp was sure, to have been chosen for this job. There would be schemes forming in his head, not merely for the recovery of the stolen plutonium, but for his own reinstatement to the KGB. No matter how old a man, he always schemed, hoped, desired. The body aged; the passions remained young.

Thinking of all this, Tarp was watching another sportfisherman that was cutting a wake in the water to his left on an almost parallel course, as if it meant to intercept him miles out in the Gulf.

"Is anybody expecting you?" he said, watching the other boat.

"Is very ugly shirt," Repin muttered.

"Put on the shirt, please. Is anybody expecting you?"

"Nobody. Was all done under tightest security."

Tarp saw the flash of binoculars from the other boat.

"What's your cover in Havana?"

"I am papa to Soviet dance company. KGB overseer. Very cute girls, those dancers."

"Not very original."

"But good. Dance company directress is my mistress."

"Truly?"

"Truly!" Repin scowled at him reproachfully. "It was part of story made up for cover, but Repin *makes* it true!" He barked out a laugh. "Repin is like actor—always truth, truth!" He shook the knit shirt as if it were a small animal that had tried to bite him. "Why I got to wear this?"

"It's camouflage. Put it on."

"I take off before we get to Cuba?"

"Yes."

"Good. Is very, very unfashionable shirt."

He emerged from the cabin some minutes later with the shirt pulled tight over his barrel torso like a sausage casing. His was a hard, convex abdomen that started its outward swell at the rib cage. Below the short sleeves his old arms were finely wrinkled but still muscular, with little fat.

"Wear your hat," Tarp said.

"Is Cuban hat."

"It's okay. The hat is okay." Tarp did not tell him that the same hat could be bought all over Miami. In that hat and the shirt, Repin looked just like a New York businessman on a holiday. Even his Russian pallor was right.

Tarp switched the control to the deck and went down and began to ready the fishing gear. From time to time he glanced over at the other boat, which kept its distance but stayed even with them. It was not a boat that he recognized.

He sewed big treble hooks up through chunks of cut bait and then wired the hooks behind big Kona flashers, one on each of the two rods that would feed from outriggers until a fish hit; then the outrigger would release the line and the fish would be played from the fighting chair. When he lifted the cover of the ice chest for more cut bait, he checked the .22 pistol to make sure it was dry and easy to reach.

Tarp tuned the radio to a Latin station and raised the volume in case they had a narrow-cone listener on the other boat. "Tell me what you think about the submarine again," he said. He looked at the other fishing boat, and Repin, always alert, followed his glance and turned back. "What is that boat?" he said.

"Don't know. We wait and see."

"You can go faster than them?"

"Don't know. Now isn't the time to find out. Tell me about the submarine."

Repin looked resentfully at the other boat and then took a cigar from the pocket of his Bulgarian jacket, which was hanging on the fighting chair. "Maybe submarine was bringing plutonium to Cuba. That is why I come to Cuba, so far as my old friends in the KGB think—I not tell them about *you*. Is very obvious and too simple idea, that plutonium comes to Cuba, but is worth checking because sometimes obvious ideas are right."

"Does Moscow think the plutonium came to Cuba?"

"I don't know."

"Well, what do you think?"

"I do not think. It was made very clear, Repin is not to think.

Repin is to be—good pimp: he is to find somebody to service Moscow. Repin is to stay pure.''

"A pure pimp."

"Yes—like homosexual, no? Homosexual, often he is good pimp, he stays pure from his whores. So, to you, I am your faggot pimp. You tell me so much, you service Moscow, I stay pure."

"I don't believe you."

"Is true."

"You live for information, Repin. You can't stay pure."

The old man spread his square-fingered hands on the deck. "If Repin learns too much, they kill him."

"Who will kill him?"

"Maxudov."

Tarp was watching the other boat. "Who's Maxudov?"

"Is code name of plutonium thief. Submarine captain spoke it just before he died. They say."

Tarp reached down into the locker beside the ladder and got a pair of huge old German binoculars. They had neutral density filters for sun and haze, and he could turn them against the morning glare and watch what was happening on the other boat. "Plutonium," he said with the glasses still at his eyes. "Who'd want it?" He slouched against the bulkhead so that the other boat could not see him.

"Who would *not* want it?" Repin shrugged. "Argentina. Brazil. Israel, maybe. India, Pakistan. South Africa. Maybe one of the East African nations—Kenya, Tanzania."

"Cuba?" Tarp was watching a blond young man work clumsily with the fishing gear, too clumsily for anybody who had ever done it before.

Repin hesitated. "Well—Cuba, maybe."

"Tell me."

Repin sighed. "Is only gossip. Stupid gossip, yes? But Beranyi—you know Beranyi, the shark?—Beranyi is Department Five. He is rising star. Not rising fast enough to suit himself, they say, but rising. So, he was in Cuba in nineteen sixties, is friend of Castro, they say. There is this idiotic gossip that Beranyi wants to move Cuba faster into a military posture than the Central Committee wants to move Cuba."

"To atomic weapons?"

"So they say. Is only gossip."

Tarp watched the young man bungle an attempt to attach a lure to a line with a Bimini twist, and he knew from the angle of the young man's head and from his concentration that he was trying to follow the instructions of a book that he had put down on the deck. Tarp lowered the binoculars. "So the idea is that Beranyi free-lances plutonium so that Castro can go into the atomic bomb business. Is he that kind of man?"

"Is very ambitious."

"Yeah, but is he crazy?"

"Not that way."

Tarp grunted. He turned to the wheel and swung the boat thirty degrees closer to the other boat's course so that he would pass close astern of it unless it took some action. After thirty seconds it accelerated and changed its own course farther to the left; Tarp swung back to his original course and increased his speed, then turned twenty degrees away from the other boat and really gave it power. When the other boat did not follow, he knew that they had decided to be cautious, and he went up on the flying bridge and watched them move away toward the east. A little later his radar told him that they had taken up a parallel course again about three miles away.

"What's Beranyi got in Havana?" he said now.

"Is not sure. Is believed he has penetrated Third of June Movement."

"Anti-Castro?"

"So they say."

"That's beautiful. Some bunch of nitwits with an uncle each in Miami and a contact each in the CIA. So Beranyi's into them, naturally, and it puts him right into the Florida Cuban community. It must be nice duty for an agent who's been working the Finland station, pulling Dade County. A condo, a pool, lots of girls in string bikinis—what's his defector rate?"

Repin shook his head. "I know nothing. Only the gossip. I am not in that work anymore."

Tarp looked at the Slavic face, the barrel torso. Despite its high cheekbones and its flat nose, the face could have been that of any retired old man along the beaches, any businessman who had gotten there by cunning and greed, a hard, driven, successful face—except that this one had gotten here because of torture and sabotage, subversion and death, none of which had left any more trace on it than if it had been in the hardware business all that time. When Tarp had been running networks in Southeast Asia, Repin had been in charge of agents from Singapore to Sri Lanka. Now he looked like a retiree from the garment district.

"You're always in that work," Tarp said almost bitterly. "It never gives you up."

Repin looked away. His face clouded for a moment. He sucked on the cigar, and the shadow, whatever it had been—anger at Tarp, perhaps; perhaps regret or even guilt—passed.

Tarp looked at the radar. The other boat was still keeping station on them.

"Okay. I take you back to Havana and then I go home and I start to look around—where or how, we don't know yet. How long do you think before they know it's me?"

"How are they to find out?"

"I don't know—you tell me. It's my guess it'll take them less than twenty-four hours. Who knows you came to Cuba?"

"All of them. That is, all of them who are suspect, and a few more."

"And they think you're here investigating Beranyi? What does Beranyi think?"

"He suggested it. To clear his reputation, he said."

"Gutsy. Supposing he told the truth, why does he worry about his reputation? Who's he afraid of?"

"Andropov. Telyegin."

"Eugen Telyegin?"

"Da."

"Old-time hard-liner. Friend of Lenin. Your patron—yes?"

"Da." Repin nodded, smoked, spat. " 'The Monster,' the Germans called him after Stalingrad. Very good to me, always." He looked at the ashen end of the cigar. "He has cancer. First the prostate, now the bowel." He exhaled. "I would kill myself."

"Is he still at work?"

Repin stared at the dying cigar. " 'Work is blood,' he says. I saw him three days ago in Moscow. A skeleton. Three operations, then chemical therapy. Everything has been burned away. He is like a man in the gulag. Like a man in religious fanaticism. His work has become his faith."

"Could he be the one? What's the name—Maxudov?"

Repin's head moved heavily back and forth, back and forth. "He is suspected, too. Yes. But is ironic, you see—even if he is not Maxudov, finding Maxudov kills him. Only fanaticism for finding the guilty one keeps him alive.''

"It's his project?"

"He has Internal Investigation Division now. So, it has become his blood—his truth. And I will say to you, my friend, only Telyegin, *only Telyegin*, had courage to say, 'This must be stopped! This traitor must be found!' " He struck a little lighter and a gas flame thrust up. Puffing out clouds of fragrant smoke that vanished on the wind, he said, "Maybe it is cancer that gives him that courage, having nothing to lose. But it was Telyegin that insisted, nobody else."

"Then you do know what went on in the meeting in Moscow!"

"I know what I know."

"You're holding out on me."

"Of course! But I hold out nothing that you need."

Tarp brought the boat into the stream and took a reading, then throttled down. On the deck again, he put the rods out for fishing.

"How many people are involved?"

Repin sucked in smoke. "One. Maybe two or three small ones, like the submarine captain. Maybe some more very small ones. But only the one matters: Maxudov. The others are like criminals anywhere—one who sells black market vodka, the manager who steals butter from his dairy, the woman who steals coupons from the company book. Little ones are nothing. They are typical Russians, good workers of the Soviet state." He laughed. "Good petty criminals. Good for making examples of."

"Is that meant to sound disloyal?"

"The Party tells me that self-criticism is a virtue." Repin braced his forearm between his thighs and leaned forward. "One man planned it all and one man did it all. It is a scheme so enormous that more than one man would never dare do it. A paradox, yes? But true. Trust Repin—I know. I know my Russia, I know my KGB. It is one man, giving out a little bribery here, a little patronage there, always to the small ones, who know so little that they cannot put things together. To one he says, 'Fix this report so such and such a thing has never happened, and I promote you over your superior'; to another he says, 'Change these figures so the different total is more to my liking, I see that your sister-in-law is not implicated when we prosecute that dissident she has been sleeping with.' And each one he tells something good. 'For the Party, Comrade,' or 'For the Central Committee, Comrade,' or 'So Dzerzhinsky Square will like your work, Comrade.' And each one does it and is grateful and says, 'Oh, thank you, Great One,' as if they said, 'Thank you for letting me kiss your bottom.' That is how it was. I know. I *know* how these things are done. I know my Russia.''

"Do you know how to steal plutonium?"

Repin blew out the smoke. "I do not, but I could find out. The method is not important, I think; in Russia, *anything* can be stolen. How is not so important; *why* is important. What I cannot imagine is the why. Why steal all that plutonium? Suppose I am already a high official in the KGB. Why do I begin this dangerous affair—and carry it on for two years, maybe more? What do I mean to do? Start my own world war? Destroy a nation? Take my personal revenge on the Western warmongers? What?" To Tarp, his bewilderment seemed real.

"Money?" Tarp said.

"What money?" Repin bellowed. "What money? KGB has all the money they could want already. Even when I was KGB, I was only commander, Southeast Asia Sector, what more money did I want?"

Tarp twisted a wire leader-connector around itself and snipped it off. "Freedom?"

"KGB upper echelon have power, my friend. When a man has power, what does he want with freedom?"

Tarp dropped a baited lure into the swirl astern and watched it swing into position behind the boat. "More power, then? Plutonium would give a lot of power."

Repin stood up, leaned against the fighting chair. "Maybe." He did not sound convinced. "Maybe, for more power, yes."

Tarp headed for the ladder. "I want a list of everybody at Dzerzhinsky Square who's suspect and who could have brought it off. Ages, positions, personalities—everything."

"You want to know more about them than CIA does?"

"You knew I'd be asking for it; don't try to kid me, Repin. They wouldn't hire you as a pimp unless they thought you'd find a whore who'd ask the right questions."

"I was given 'discretion.' ''

"Good. Use it."

Tarp pulled himself up to the bridge and checked the instruments. The other boat was still three miles east, keeping a parallel course; now, however, there was a third craft on a heading that would bring the two together.

"Company coming," Tarp said.

"Shall I get shotgun?"

"I hope it's not that kind of company."

CHAPTER 3

"Just keep fishing."

"This is fishing? I am not fishing; I am sitting."

Repin was in the fighting chair; in front of him, a big rod rode in the gimbaled socket. It had been an hour since the baits had gone into the water, and they had taken two small dolphin and had thrown them back.

Tarp swung himself partway down into the cabin where he could see the Weatherby in the cubbyhole to his right. He took the loaded clip from a drawer, slammed it in, and checked the safety. After a moment's thought, he took two steps down and grabbed the shotgun and took it up to the flying bridge, stowing it there in a scupper with a plastic tarp over it.

"Just keep fishing," he said when he came down to the deck again. "Let me talk." He trained the old binoculars on a bank of haze and waited for the new boat to emerge from it. The white glow of its bow wave was the first sign, like ice floating on the tropical blue of the water. Then the mass of the hull appeared above it, gray, seeming unnaturally high because of a trick of the atmosphere.

"Coast Guard."

"What will they do?"

"They usually don't bother me." He did not add, *But they don't usually make contact with another boat that's been shadowing me all morning, either.* "You got any ID?"

"Nothing."

"Naturally. All right, your name is Rubin. You're from Scarsdale, New York. This is your first day down here and you

left your wallet at your motel, whose name you've forgotten.
You chartered me for the day. Got it?''

Repin scowled. ''Rubin is Jewish name?''

''Probably.''

''I do not like being a Jew.''

''Role-playing teaches tolerance, they say.''

The Coast Guard boat grew larger. He recognized it now. It
had been seized on a drug raid a few years earlier and had made
its way through the courts to the GSA and then to the Coast
Guard. It was fast and fully adequate for ocean travel. It had
been given a gun forward and two light machine guns aft and a
tower of electronic gear.

When it came in close it throttled down, and Tarp, the binoculars still in his hands, waved. A sailor by the rail waved back
languidly, and in the wheelhouse somebody wearing sunglasses
lifted a hand partway to his shoulder.

''Name and home port?'' a voice blasted over the speakers.
Tarp picked up his bullhorn and said, ''*Scipio,* Boca Chica. It's
me, Tarp.''

''How're you doin', Tarp?''

''Good. Is it Lieutenant Martin?''

''Doing some fishing?''

''Charter. One customer.''

''Doing any good?''

''Baby dolphin.''

''You staying on this heading?''

''For a while.''

''What then?''

''Maybe put out a chum line and drift.''

The dark glasses looked at him. The lieutenant was holding a
microphone in his right hand, like an apple he was ready to eat.
''How long you staying out?''

''Maybe all night.''

Tarp's eyes were raking the Coast Guard boat, looking for an
explanation for this long conversation. There was a flicker of
movement among some equipment cases near the rail, and he
thought he had found his explanation—somebody with a camera.

''Gotta go, Tarp.''

''See you.''

''Good fishing!''

The big gray boat shuddered, swung away, then got up on its step and roared back toward the bank of mist that was moving slowly toward them. Tarp's boat rocked a little in its wake.

"So?" Repin said.

"They're on to you."

"Is impossible."

"You've got a leak already. They were waiting for you."

"Is impossible. U.S. Coast Guard?"

"Probably fed through some double into CIA and then down here. The two yo-yos in the other boat are probably Agency. Your Maxudov probably figured the easiest way to get rid of you was tip you to the perfidious Yankees."

"So what do we do?"

"We fish, just like I told the man. They're not sure yet, or they wouldn't be horsing around taking pictures. They'll try to get a confirmation, then they'll come in like gangbusters."

They took three more fish, one of them good, and Tarp gutted it and iced it down and rebaited. Repin asked no more questions. They were drifting southwest now, with Cuba far to their left and Florida behind them to the right. Three miles back, almost in their track, the other boat kept pace. There were fishing boats spread around them for twenty miles now, but Tarp was certain that the one behind him was the same one, and the same boat that the Coast Guard had had a rendezvous with.

Tarp got food for them. He cut thick, dark bread into big chunks and sliced quarter-inch slabs from a crumbly, honey-colored cheese, and he set out Dijon mustard and bottles of bitter English ale. Repin grinned at him around a mouthful of the food; Tarp nodded and made a fist and held it up like a gesture of triumph. Repin took great joy in food, as he took great joy in women and in victory. He emptied one bottle of the ale by holding it an inch above his open lips and letting it splash down into his pouting old mouth, laughing as he gulped it down, delighted that some of it ran down his chin and darkened the despised knit shirt.

"Good!" He slapped his powerful belly. "*Good* food, Tarp!"

"Better than I'd get in the gulag, ha?"

"Sometimes, you are not very funny, my friend."

"No, sometimes I'm not." Tarp sipped his ale. "But we need to remember who we are, you and I."

Repin tapped the faded khaki fabric on Tarp's left knee. "You have done your crimes in your time, my friend." His accent seemed thicker, his voice hoarse, the words slow, as if the emotion that clogged them were as painful as an emotion like love or grief. "I have done my crimes. I share in the gulag and that other excrement, yes. But you have the villages in Viet Nam. You share in Chile. All that." He sat back. His blue eyes looked like windows into Arctic sky, as if his old face had been pierced so that it was possible to look through into the ice of his curious morality. "We are not judges. We are policemen. We do what we have to do."

The executioner's creed. "We do what we choose to do."

"So, I am worse than you because I choose the KGB?"

"I didn't say you were worse. I said we had to remember who we are."

"Ah. It is *your* guilt you want to remind me of. How very American!" He laughed.

"This is a stupid conversation."

"I did not start it."

"Want another beer?"

"No. Whiskey."

Tarp brought up the Scotch and coffee and then he made Repin write down the names of the people who were suspected of being Maxudov. Repin had given up objecting and did it meekly enough; Tarp realized that he enjoyed doing it—giving away at last a fraction of all the secrets that had clogged his head for a lifetime. Repin whistled while he wrote, sipping the Laphroaig, licking crumbs of cheese from a finger. When the list was done, he sat back sleepily and smiled; Tarp went below and uncovered a computer terminal and a scrambler that were hidden behind a bulkhead. He typed:

ACCESS: FILTER BLACK SUN NINER SEVEN.
PREP: SEARCH MODE.
SEARCH: LIST.
ANDROPOV YURI/ BERANYI MIKHAIL/ TELYEGIN
EUGEN/ STRISZ FEODOR/ FALOMIN JOSEF/ GALUSHA
GEORGII/ MENSENYI KONSTANTIN/ END.
INSERT: DATA.
DATA:

He followed with a digest of what Repin had told him. The information would go to a program of his own design that was stored in a vast computer near Boston, in which he rented time; mostly the computer was used by large corporations and think tanks. He communicated with it by a scrambled telephone line, transmitted in this case from his boat to his shore phone by radio. The request for a search would go to his own banks as well as to those of three large computer services that were often as well informed as the government was and that were a good deal more discreet.

He looked at the terminal, glanced out the hatch at the drowsing Repin, and then typed:

SEARCH MODE.
SEARCH: NAME.
REPIN VLADIMIR PETROVICH AKA CODE NINOTCH-
KA.
DESIGNATE: CURRENT LOCATION AND MISSION.

The machine hardly paused. Letters spread across the screen from left to right:

REPIN VLADIMIR AKA CODE NINOTCHKA DEPARTED USSR AEROFLOT 1783 DEST HAVANA 3/27/ MISSION OVERSIGHT REGIONAL BALLET TROUPE ON OFFI-CIAL VISIT TO HAVANA FESTIVAL OF ANTINUCLEAR NATIONS FOR WORLD PEACE/ ARRIVED HAVANA 3/27 10:27 LOCAL/ RUMORED LOVER OF SYLVA TATANOVA ARTISTIC MANAGER KOMI ASSR BAL-LET/ REPIN RETIRED KGB 1977 BUT ATTENTION/ STILL RUMORED ACTIVE/ ATTENTION/ REPORTED TULA 3/21 AT KGB SAFE HOUSE/ ATTENTION/ AN-DROPOV, YURI REPORTED PRESENT SAME LOCATION SAME DAY ALSO QUOTE UPPER ECHELON KGB LEADERSHIP END QUOTE DETAILS NOT GIVEN/ AT-TENTION/ KGB REPORTED UNDERGOING MAJOR SHIFT OF UNKNOWN NATURE AS REFLECTED IN RE-PORTS LONDON, PARIS, WASHINGTON, TOKYO, TEL AVIV ETC/ QUERY IF DETAILS WANTED/ END.

Tarp told it, HOLD DETAILS.

The screen went blank.

Well, Repin checks out, he thought. *But then he would; if he was going to lie to me, he'd lay the groundwork.*

He stared into the blue rectangle of the computer screen. It was temping to believe that it was the outer eye of a mind playful and intelligent that waited only for the right question. He knew better. It was only a blue screen. Unlike Repin's eyes, it did not give insight to another world.

He typed:

SEARCH.
STORE FOR FUTURE ACCESS MY CODE BLACK SUN:
ALL REFS LAST THIRTY MONTHS COVERT MOVE-
MENT PLUTONIUM
DITTO SUBMARINES SWEDISH WATERS, USSR PROV-
ENANCE
DITTO SUBMARINES USSR PROVENANCE NEW LOCA-
TIONS
DITTO SUBMARINE MOVEMENTS CARIBBEAN AND
SOUTH ATLANTIC, USSR PROVENANCE.

I'm fishing, he told himself. *I'm asking the machine to do my thinking for me.* With an impatient gesture he turned the machine off. *Better to cut bait.*

Repin was awake and staring at the water as if it, too, were an eye that might give up an answer if only he could probe beneath it.

"Ready for some action?" Tarp said.

"Good. Yes."

"What happens if I get to Cuba?"

"Cuban navy patrol will meet us. I give you radio signal to transmit. Is all arranged. I go aboard, you return to Florida."

"Just like that. Cute."

The other boat was still on the radar. The Coast Guard vessel had joined it some hours earlier but had disappeared. Now, Tarp tapped the glass over the little green brightness. "They're going to have to do something soon."

"Because of me?"

"And me." He tapped the glass again. "The Coast Guard made contact with them, probably to drop off somebody who went aboard earlier—one of the two guys on the boat, probably a photographer. Getting pictures of you. Very exciting for him.

Probably had to use a fast shutter speed because his hands were shaking—never had a KGB major-general so close before."

"What will they do?"

"Try to pick us up."

"Bad business."

"Probably."

"When?"

"Before dark, if they have any sense." He switched to a wider sweep, and a scattering of other bright spots appeared. Most of them were to the north, closer to Florida; three were ahead of them; two were to their left. Tarp tapped one of them. "I think that's a friend of theirs. The other one's a commercial fisherman, judging from the course. Out of one of the west Florida ports." His finger came down the line of boats closer in to Florida. "Coast Guard is one of these. That's a fast mother of a boat. Can be here right quick."

He switched to a still wider sweep. The boats became almost indistinguishable stars in a green sky full of static. "Cruise liner," Tarp muttered, pointing to a bright blip out in the Gulf. "Oil tankers."

"Why do we not run to Cuba?"

"We probably wouldn't make it, and if we did, all the wrong people would know about it, and even if it worked, I'd be busted when I came back."

He studied the screen again. He switched it back to its smallest sweep. The other boat seemed a little closer now but a little to the southwest, as if it meant to come up on him on a curve. Tarp stared at the bright dot as if he were looking through it at the boat itself. "They've got a coded radar," he said carefully. "So they show up on the Coast Guard and the other boat as a special signal—a friendly. We don't." He folded his arms and stared at the screen. "They can call in air cover if they need it. We're about fifty miles from the Cuban coast. Very iffy if the Coast Guard try to follow us in. Aircraft's a different matter. As for the other boats . . ."

The sun was starting down. There would be two hours until darkness.

Tarp touched the ignition and the big engine throbbed; water gurgled throatily at the stern.

"Well?" Repin said anxiously.

"Diversion."

He put on enough speed to maintain headway and then began to turn toward Florida.

"I'll bring in the fishing gear and then we'll eat. We may need it."

He pulled in the big rigs and threw the baits over and stowed the rods in their upright holsters, like knights' lances at the ready, and then he went below. He put out salad, and he cooked steaks cut from the iced fish, and he opened a bottle of crisp Alsatian white from the refrigerator. There was more of the thick bread and, after it, mangoes and coffee and more whiskey.

"Well?" Repin said when they had eaten hurriedly.

"Right."

Tarp shut the engine down. The sky was lavender above them and a deep, gun-metal blue straight ahead. On the western horizon, a single cloud hid the setting sun and was rimmed with copper by it; on each side, the sky spread out in brilliant orange. Tarp opened the engine hatch and scattered tools around it; he poured a can of oil over the stern and watched it spread and stain the hull. He took black grease from the engine and smeared it over his hands and forearms. "You're still Mr. Rubin of Scarsdale. Lie down."

"I am tired?"

"You just had a heart attack. Or maybe a sunstroke."

He climbed up on the bridge and flipped the radio to the general channel. "This is *Scipio* out of Boca Chica calling any boat with medical personnel. I got a medical emergency here. Man of seventy, maybe more, he's down on the deck unconscious. Could be his heart. I've tried mouth to mouth and pressure and I got a pulse, but not much. Position follows." He guessed at his position. There was only one boat that he wanted to answer the call, anyway. *Irresponsible, Tarp. Crying wolf.*

"So lie down," he called down to Repin.

The tough old Russian tossed his straw hat to the deck and grudgingly sat, then lay flat on the deck. It was getting dark, yet he was very clear to Tarp, and the colors of the knit shirt seemed remarkably intense. "You like theatricals?" Repin said.

"If they get you off my hands, yes." He moved to the ladder but stayed where he could watch the radar. "If those are Agency people, they have several choices. They can come in now, or they can hold off and take a chance you really are sick and may die. If I'm a liar, they've done right to lie off; if I'm telling the truth, they're SOL. If they're from your side, they've got only one choice, and that's to get here just as fast as they can, because somebody else is bound to pick up that call."

Repin crossed his hands over his chest. "If it is CIA, I go to prison, *da?*"

"They'll probably trade you for some college professor got arrested for drunk driving in Tashkent. What are they going to get you on? You're in international waters; you haven't even got a gun. They'd put you up at one of their cushy places in suburban Virginia, then they'd send you home."

Repin raised his head. "I do not want to be taken by your CIA!"

"Neither do I. They're as big assholes as your KGB." He watched the green dot on the screen, brighter now in the gathering darkness. "We'll find out which they are real soon. They're coming."

He jumped down to the deck and bent over Repin, reaching forward to pull up the knit shirt as if he were skinning the old torso; Repin flinched and put his hands up. "I want you to look as if I've been going over you. Lie still and close your eyes." The eyes closed, then opened. Tarp looked into them, seeing only hardness now. "Can you hurt a man from that position?" he said.

"I can kill a man from this position."

"That won't be necessary. Or even advisable. Just wait for me to make the move."

CHAPTER 4

Tarp bent over the fish box and took out the little .22, which he laid next to the engine hatch with an oily rag over it. When he straightened, the other boat was coming toward them fast.

"Play dead, Repin."

He knelt over the Russian, who had made himself go limp and who was breathing in shallow gasps that sounded convincingly stricken. Repin had watched many men die, Tarp recalled; too, he had had major surgery the year before. He had probably rehearsed it all in his mind many times, like saying that if he had Telyegin's cancer he would kill himself. *More theatricals.*

Tarp thumped him on the chest. He pressed down with both hands. He thumped again. He looked up. The other boat was slowing twenty yards away. Between them the oil slick spread like a gleaming skin on the smooth water, rippled with crimson from the sunset.

"You got an emergency?" a blond young man called from the waist. He looked like a college boy on a summer job. He was big, Tarp noticed, with a neck like the base of a mast. *If he's Agency, they hired him for that California look. Too much television.*

"I got an old man down on his back!"

There was a second man at the wheel. He was shorter and older and had wary eyes. He also had a rifle that he held cradled under his right arm while he steered with his left.

"I've been working on him but I haven't done much good!"

30

Tarp shouted. "He's breathing. I don't know. Either of you know any medicine?"

The man at the wheel touched a control and the engine gurgled and his boat swung stern-in toward *Scipio*. He reversed and began to back slowly toward her through the oil. "Whyn't you take him into Key West?" he said.

"Engine trouble!"

"What a coincidence." He throttled it way down and the engine noise dropped to a rough purr. "You must be on a roll." He looked the *Scipio* over. It was a bigger and faster boat than his own, and its electronic gear was remarkable for a sportfisherman. "We can give you a tow," he said grudgingly.

"This old man can die!" Tarp bellowed.

The young blond looked at the older man. There was disagreement there. He knew the dilemma they were in: they had been sent out because of a rumor, and now they were confronted with a complication. A wrong judgment would mean newspaper stories, then internal investigations. It was the sort of dilemma that led to short careers.

"Take him on your boat and you take him to Key West," Tarp said. "You can't tow my boat at any speed at all. Take him in and I'll stay with the boat."

Their craft came very close and then bumped *Scipio*'s hull.

"I'll have a look," the blond one said. He stood on the gunwale, and Tarp saw that he was wearing a diver's knife and a .38 on a separate belt at his waist. *Feeling young and immortal. A sure way to get killed.*

He jumped to the *Scipio*'s gunwale and then to her deck.

Repin's shallow breathing was inaudible over the other boat's engine. His tongue stuck out a little between his flabby lips, and somehow he had managed to look pale. The young man bent over him. "Jeez, he's in lousy physical shape," he said. "God, it's a lesson in how you don't want to let yourself go, am I right?"

"That's right." Tarp looked covertly at the other man. He was holding the rifle loosely in both hands now. "Hey," Tarp said to the young one, "let me get rid of some of this grease and I'll help you with the old guy."

He knelt beside the rag. He picked it up with his right hand, picked up the gun with the left, still concealed by the oily cloth, and fired. There was a cry of rage and pain from the man in the boat and then there was a flurry of action on *Scipio*'s deck where Repin was lying. Tarp never took his eyes from the man with the rifle, however, moving quickly to his right and raising the .22 to fire again. He had hit what he had aimed at—the man's left knee—and the shot had made the man spin to the left and go down, but he was a tough man and he had caught himself, and he was trying to force himself erect again so he could bring the rifle to bear.

"Don't!" Tarp shouted. "I'll kill you with the next one." He stood at *Scipio*'s rail with the Woodsman pointed at the dark man, who slowly put the rifle down and then sank to a sitting position with his left leg stuck out in front of him.

"Mr. Rubin?" Tarp said.

"Well?" Repin's voice was deep and mocking.

"You okay?"

"What you think, I am beginner like this boy?"

"Get the rifle."

The dark man was stoic. Blood soaked his pant leg, but he made no sound. He looked at Tarp and then Repin with open hatred, but he wasted none of his energy in words.

Tarp looked down to *Scipio*'s deck and saw the blond boy lying on his back. He looked peaceful.

"Get yourself over here," Tarp said to the older one.

"You're a real sweetheart."

"It's a twenty-two, not a cannon. Come on."

"It's big enough."

He dragged himself to his feet and came down his own boat, supporting himself on the rail. Tarp put a line on the other boat and tied the two together, then he hauled them in tight, stern to port side, as the man put his bleeding leg over and then swung his good leg after and carefully slid to a sitting position on *Scipio*'s deck.

"They sent me a kid for a partner," he said glumly.

"He learned a lot."

The dark man squinted at Repin. "KGB?"

"No, he's a Polish aristocrat. Don't ask questions."

The dark man looked at him with an expression that showed both pain and disgust. "They told me you were a tough nut. I told that kid we should shoot you first and then find out who the old man is. I told him we could always make an accident out of it later, but he said I was cynical." He laughed. Tarp laughed a little. "Now I'm not just cynical, I'm bleeding. Christ, that hurts!"

"I've got morphine." Tarp reached down into the cabin without taking his eyes from the man and felt in the first-aid box. He tossed him the morphine kit. "Strictly do-it-yourself. You got another gun?"

"On my ankle."

"Don't get cute with it."

Repin had taken the pistol and the knife from the blond one; he put the gun in his own belt and threw the knife overboard, and then, when the older man had finished squeezing the morphine syringe, he felt over him, staying out of Tarp's line of fire. He stood up and backed away a step with a little revolver from the ankle holster and the two wallets from the two men. He tossed the wallets to Tarp. There was Agency identification in each one.

"That's pretty risky," Tarp said. "Tough if the Cubans caught you."

"The Cubans wouldn't catch me." The man smiled foggily. The morphine was starting to work. "I was going to throw them the kid as a diversion."

Tarp went aboard the other boat and killed her engine, then looked her over. She had been leased in Key West and was simply a decent sportfisherman with adequate radar and some fancy listening gear that the two men had put aboard. Next to the radar was a black box the size of a toaster, and Tarp knew it was the device that identified them with a friendly signal on properly equipped radars. It was on now, a red light gleaming like a bean-sized eye against the blue-black sky. All the friendlies would know that the boat was sitting here with *Scipio*.

Tarp went back to his own boat and removed the engine starter and threw it overboard. He took the shotgun and the rifle, then slid open the bulkhead compartment at the rear of the lockers and took out the AR-15 and the clips that were hidden there. He put the weapons on the other boat, then went back into *Scipio*'s cabin and removed his computer-signal scrambler and dropped it overboard; then he went down again and rummaged under his bunk and found a waterproof packet that looked like an electronic tool kit but wasn't.

Inside the pockets of the packet was money in three currencies and a set of identification—passport, driver's license, credit card, as well as three "details": a reader's card for the Bibliothèque National in Paris; a member's card for the Paris Jockey Club; and a journalist's pass issued by *Agence-Presse Europa,* all in the name of Jean-Louis Selous. The Selous identity was a deeply established one that was expensive for him to keep up; it was supported by a listing in the Paris telephone directory and two professional organizations, and by five articles that had appeared over the Selous byline in European magazines, paid for by Tarp and written by some rather high-priced talent. Tarp folded the packet and put it in a rear pocket and buttoned it down, then he looked over the cabin and decided there was nothing more that had to be taken, and he went up to the deck.

"I need your boat," he said to the blond one, who was sitting up, massaging his neck and shaking his head as if he had learned how to do it from an old movie. "The Coast Guard will pick you up soon."

The blond one looked helpless. He looked all of nine years old.

"Berth the boat at number thirty-seven at the Boca Chica marina. I'll hold you personally responsible."

The young man tried to speak, but whatever Repin had done to him had turned his voice into a gull's squawk.

"And take care of your partner. There's a medical kit just inside the hatch, to the right. There's a book in it if they didn't teach you what to do. The refrigerator's full. Help yourself to the booze—*after* you take care of your partner. I'll check it when I get back and submit a bill to the Agency."

The young man tried to squawk again.

"Your partner's a good man. Learn from him. Don't be so bright-eyed and bushy-tailed next time." Tarp stepped across the dark man, who was unconscious. "He's a got a twenty-two slug just above the knee; the kneecap's okay, but you ought to clean the wound and make sure he doesn't bleed too much. It's all in the book." Tarp swung a leg over and sat with a foot in each boat. "Never trust older men. And never trust an old man at all, even when he looks dead."

He went aboard the other boat and Repin followed and cast off; Tarp hit the starter and nosed the boat out into the Stream. Thirty seconds later they were racing for Cuba. On the friendly radars, their signal would show as a strange but not yet dangerous movement. By the time people understood what had happened, it would be too late.

CHAPTER 5

He had taken the boat in by dead reckoning without radar or sonar and with the radio giving a three-second signal every seven minutes on the frequency Repin had specified. They were off the Cuban coast above Viñales, sitting dead in the water now, with Latin music coming and going on the land breeze like a sound from another decade.

"It seems to be okay," Tarp said once. Everything was very quiet, except for the music. There should have been a patrol boat and a radar sweep, at least.

"Is all fixed. Is very efficient."

The ocean seemed endless with no lights. It was as if they were sitting in the sky, space above and below and all around. The air was salty and damp and warm; everything was strange and therefore menacing—the leap of a fish in the void, the random slap of a tiny wave on the hull. Because he had nothing better to do, Tarp slid the .22 into a plastic bag and taped it to the underside of the open hatch cover, then he went around the boat checking weapons: shotgun on the bridge, AR-15 in the scuppers, the Weatherby and the Agency man's rifle in the cabin.

"When the Cubans come, you talk to them. I'm staying out of sight."

"*Da,* is embarrassment for them to see you. To them, you are American paid to bring me back, nothing more."

"Your Spanish okay?"

"Good enough."

But not very good, Tarp thought. Repin was like the English

36

in the old days; in Asia, he had spoken the local languages in a guttural pidgin that the locals mocked. His Spanish was probably like that, too, serviceable but not tactful.

The radio crackled and a voice broke in clearly in Spanish. The volume had been set too high and they both jumped and then laughed.

"Large Bear, this is Rum Bottle," the radio said. "Large Bear, this is Rum Bottle."

"Talk to him," Tarp said. "Just press the button on the mike."

Repin put his mouth very close to the microphone. "Rum Bottle, is the Large Bear over this way." His Spanish was terrible.

"Identify, Large Bear."

Repin plodded through a string of numbers.

"Breaking radio contact and approaching," the radio said. "End communication."

Tarp waited until he heard the Spanish boat's engines, then he picked up the AR-15 and boosted himself up to the flying bridge with it in his hand. He squatted there, feeling suddenly how flimsy the spray rail was and how easily he and this rented boat could be blown away. They would never get a better chance.

I've gotten very pessimistic about this operation already, he thought. *It's tainted, for sure.*

"Large Bear, show your lights."

He reached up and flipped on the running lights. The engine noise was very loud now, a menacing growl, as if the other boat were stalking around them in the night. Then, almost with his lights, a bright beam shot across the water ahead of the boat and swept quickly over them.

They're good, he thought, and he ducked as the light came over the flying bridge. Repin was standing on the deck below him, and Tarp saw him in the white glare, legs spread, arms folded, seeming to dare the lights' brilliance. *You'll never get a better shot,* Tarp thought, but no shot came.

The patrol boat swung in close. The searchlight went off and a battery of small lights on her starboard rail shone down into the sportfisherman, which was lower in the water, with the flying bridge two feet below the other's deck. Tarp saw two sailors at the rail, and then they scuttled away and a man in an officer's cap leaned over toward his own deck.

"Large Bear?" he said.

"How?" Repin said in his clumsy Spanish.

"Come aboard, please, Citizen."

There was a ladder down the patrol boat's side with a platform at the bottom and a light shining on it. Repin stepped over to the platform, grabbed the metal rail of the ladder, and pulled himself across.

"The captain of this American boat?" the officer said.

"He is to be taking it home."

"Where is he, Citizen?"

"Of what is that the importance?" Repin was at the top of the ladder now. He and the officer were almost nose to nose, their heads silhouetted against the glow of the ship's lights. "Make you for Havana immediate!"

"Where is the American?"

"This is not of relevance! The arrangement is for me to be gone to Havana."

"Precisely, respected Citizen. I have orders to deal with this boat, however."

"This boat was not in the arrangement."

"Precisely, Citizen."

He called an order. His voice sound strange and faraway, like one of the sounds from the dark water. Repin wanted to protest, but the officer was drawing him away from the rail.

There was a thump, and Tarp's boat rocked.

Boarding me, Tarp thought. *Some arrangement.*

A hand light flashed a beam in his stern and then a second joined it and came swinging forward. Tarp waited for one of them to come up the ladder, but one of the lights disappeared into the hatch and he knew that the man holding it had gone into the cabin under him.

There was a narrow space between the spray rail of the flying bridge and the handrail just above it. He could look up through this gap at the patrol boat. Now, squinting up, he saw a black mass between him and the lights on the boat; it seemed to grow larger and to float above him. His boat rocked hard to that side, and a big hand gripped the rail right above his head. Somebody had jumped from the patrol boat to the flying bridge.

A silhouetted head rose above the rail next to him.

Tarp struck upward with the butt of the shotgun, thrusting up and out, taking the boarder just below the chin. There was a strangled rattle and a gasp, and then the man was pitching backward, the hand sliding off the rail and clawing at the throat as he went back and down into the space between the patrol boat and the sportfisherman. Tarp was on his feet as the man hit the water, and he fired once down into the waist of his own boat where the hand light was, then pumped the gun and twisted, firing again at the lights above him, three quick shots as fast as he could work the mechanism, the twelve-gauge booming into the dead-still night. The lights shattered. Tarp was moving then, twisting, crouching behind the spray bulkhead, and there was a clatter of automatic fire under him as the man down in the cabin fired up through the ceiling at him, firing wildly, firing in confusion, nervous, firing out of bravado and fear and instinct, firing a little off because he knew where the patrol boat was and he knew where his own people were supposed to be; and Tarp felt pain along his left calf (thinking, *Serves me right for gunning down the Agency man*) and he dove for the blackness of his own deck, dove over and beyond the flashlight that had fallen to the deck there and was stabbing its light toward the open hatch like an arrow.

And as he dove into the darkness he saw a figure on the platform where Repin had stepped aboard the patrol boat, and it registered: *Scuba diver; man in scuba gear on the ladder;* and he was leaping into darkness.

On the deck of the patrol boat there were voices, alien, faraway, the Spanish like a language he had never heard before. "Cast off! In the name of Christ, cast off!" And there was movement on the ladder where the scuba diver was.

He twisted through the air and landed on his right foot, but off-balance. He tried to turn his body back toward the hatch, but his momentum carried him toward the stern, almost over the transom, and he stumbled over something yielding and heavy and went down, his right arm and the shotgun turned under him, and his head ducked as if he were going to do a somersault; then his back came up against the transom with a concussion that almost knocked the wind out of him. Yet he got his legs down and slithered forward until his shoulder met the yielding mass he had fallen over, and then, hurting in his back and his shoulder, he had the shotgun up and ready to fire.

There was no light at all now except for the flashlight that had fallen on the deck and that had rolled almost over into the scuppers on the port side as the boat rolled. The patrol boat had put out its own lights; men were shouting and the engines were roaring and the black bulk of the patrol boat began to slide away as if it were sinking, but it was only moving a few yards away from him to get running room, and then the engines rose to a higher pitch and suddenly it was gone, and he was aware of a void to his left where it had been.

And, with the engine sound going away, he could hear now the quick, disturbing sound of a dying man's breathing. The breath came in little sighs, little whines of despair with a groan at the end of each one. The deck under his left elbow was greasy with blood and the man's breath came like the panting of a dog that has been out running.

He fired one shot toward the open hatch, and a string of shots came back at him. The dying man was pushed up against him as if he were cuddling up for warmth, the force of the bullets pounding the breath out of him so that there was no more panting, but only a long, dignified, quiet gurgle as he gave it up. Tarp fired another shot at the muzzle flash and waited until the rolling light stuck its finger into the open hatch and showed him the top of a head when he fired again; the light rolled on, but not before he saw movement, and he pumped and fired.

The patrol boat was going away at flank speed. Tarp was still watching the hatch, which he could almost see as his eyes adjusted; as he waited, part of his mind was thinking, sorting it out, and telling him, *There were two operations laid on here; one was Repin's with the Cuban navy and one was something else that Repin didn't know about, and now the navy's getting out because their part is over and they want to stay clean.*

From the hatch, a voice said, "Oh, Jesu, help me," and Tarp fired another shot at it and waited. The dropped flashlight rolled back the other way and showed the hatch empty. Tarp counted twenty and moved to the dead man's feet, from where he could reach far over to his left and grab the flashlight and shine it where he wanted. In that dead light, the hatchway looked as if it had been attacked by crazed carpenters.

Tarp got up on one knee. From there he could see the top of the man's head. By stretching, he could see part of his back.

The man was very still. A machine pistol was gripped in one hand, the arm twisted under him on the stair.

Tarp got up and went closer and saw that the man was dead. He forced the body down the ladder with his feet, sitting on the deck and pushing with both feet, and it went slowly down with the unwilling heaviness of dead weight.

Tarp started the engine and put the boat on a course that would take it westward, parallel to the coast and into the Caribbean. Heading straight for Florida would be stupid.

He was shaking a little. He sat at the controls and held on to the wheel and waited to run down. When he felt better, he lifted his left pant leg and shone the flashlight on it. An inch-long piece of wood from the flying bridge was stuck into the muscle like a spear. He found pliers and pulled it out and let it bleed.

He looked over the two dead men. Both carried machine pistols and diver's knives. Their flashlights were identical rubber-coated, heavy-duty marine lights. They wore identical dark T-shirts and dark cotton pants with cargo pockets, dark-brown canvas shoes.

He turned over the man on the deck. He was young, dark; he had grown a brave little mustache. Tarp pulled up what was left of the T-shirt and searched the abdomen, then opened the pants and pulled them down. There was a plastic-covered card taped below the man's navel. Tarp pulled it loose. It had been laminated; it was dark green, with a legend in black letters and a thumbprint but no photograph.

A get-out-of-jail-free card. There was one just like it on the other man. Other than the cards, there was no identification, no wallets, no keys. Nothing.

DGI, he thought. *Dirección General de Inteligencia.* The Cuban KGB.

Tarp squatted on the deck and scowled at the moonless sky. It made no sense.

He knew what had happened well enough: somebody had busted Repin's deal with the Cuban navy captain and the DGI men had been put aboard to deal, not with Repin, but with the man who had brought Repin back. The navy captain had divorced himself from all that as quickly as he could, so that, if there were repercussions later, he could claim to have done his duty both to Cuba and to Repin. And the DGI men had come aboard Tarp's boat to capture or kill him. But if they failed, then Tarp would go free.

That made no sense.

Tarp thought of the figure in scuba gear whom he had glimpsed on the patrol boat's ladder.

They planted a bomb on me, he thought. He wrapped his arms tighter around his knees and stared at the darkness. He knew it now as surely as he knew that he had killed two men. It would have taken only minutes for the diver to plant a limpet mine under the sportfisherman's hull. Then the DGI men would have killed him or captured him and they would have left the boat to drift and then blow up. There would have been no loose ends that way.

Tarp felt as if a gentle wind were blowing over his scalp. He was sitting on a bomb whose timer was running.

There was an inflatable forward of the cabin, and he raced to make it ready. Even with the help of the two flashlights, it took him valuable minutes to loosen it and get it into the water and pull the inflation lanyards. There was a small British outboard in clamps next to where it had been stowed, and he loosened those and screwed the little one-lung engine to the wooden transom with impatient movements.

He grabbed the .22 from its hiding place and climbed into the dinghy. The jointed oars seemed useless for moving the stubborn hull, which rose on a slight swell and seemed to go nowhere. Tarp pulled harder, waiting for the limpet mine to blow, imagining the inflatable lifting suddenly on the explosion and the fabric tearing, the floor erupting under him, ripping him apart, striking his legs and spine and genitals with the force of a runaway truck. He pulled as hard as he could. The inflatable coasted down the swell; when it rose again, the sportfisherman was fifty feet away. He rowed for ten minutes, when the fishing boat was a small silhouette against the pale light above the Cuban coast, and then he rested, his breath rasping, his arms weak.

He had brought the stainless-steel bottle of gasoline from the boat and he poured gas into the little motor's fist-sized tank. The motor was a noisy workhorse that would push the inflatable all the way to Florida if he would let it. *And if I had the gas.*

He started the engine and headed slowly up the coast. His watch told him it was half an hour since Repin had boarded the patrol boat. Eleven minutes later, there was a roar of fire behind him, and any doubt he had had about what the scuba diver had been doing was removed. The light trickled down over the water toward him like an oil slick as red fire went up like a ball, turned orange, then gold, and then sank quickly to a low glare of yellow. Gasoline was burning on the surface where the boat had been, but the boat was gone.

He went slowly westward, steering by the lights of the coast and the stars that showed through muggy haze. There was no use trying to get out into the Gulf. If the Cubans didn't get him, the Coast Guard would.

He turned in toward the Cuban mainland, and, a quarter of a mile out, cut the engine and went over the side, slashing the inflatable and letting it sink on the engine's weight before he struck out for shore.

Moscow here I come, he thought wryly.

CHAPTER 6

He lay on a sandy ridge twenty yards above the coarse grass that marked the edge of the beach, with broken butts of palm fronds around him like big celery stalks. Behind him were small pines, on which he had draped his clothes to dry. Now, in the daylight, he gathered the clothes and brought them down to the place among the palms so they would not be seen.

He cut the American labels from the clothes. He wanted Cuban identification and Cuban money, and for that he would have to find Repin. Moving around was going to be dangerous, because Cuba was a country as localized and as organized as a medieval manor; any stranger would be reported. Every city block, every rural crossroads, had its Committee for the Defense of the Revolution, which functioned as neighborhood council and intelligence center and which could put together anything from a party to a purge.

He was hungry. Today he could ignore hunger. Tomorrow would be different. He would have to get to Havana and make contact with Repin quickly. How long before Repin returned to Moscow? he wondered. More to the point, how long before the DGI put the military and the militia on him? Or would they know that the boat had blown up and believe that both he and their men were gone?

A helicopter came over at ten o'clock. Tarp, wearing only the dark-blue briefs that looked like swimming trunks, walked boldly to the water's edge and stood there, hands on hips, staring at the water. When the chopper passed over, he waved.

A few minutes later, he heard voices. He knelt by his clothes

44

with one hand under them, holding the .22. They came closer, and he could tell that one was a woman's. Then words—English words—became understandable. "Definitely not what I . . . Incredible! Night after . . . Betrayal . . . take me for, anyway?"

The word *serious* was used several times.

A male voice said, "Yeah." In very American English.

Tarp kept his head down. They passed on his left, going toward the beach.

"I'm really, I mean I'm *really* disappointed. I mean, I'm *disappointed.*"

"Yeah."

"Don't you think?"

"They're not *serious.*"

"It's *really* disappointing."

He peered through the palms and saw a young man and woman. She had very pale hair that looked almost white in the sunlight, but her skin was burned pink. She was wearing a dress that looked like a piece of Edwardian underwear, white, frilly, eyeletted, with a very full skirt. She was carrying her shoes in her left hand and just then she was digging the toes of one foot into the sand like a pouting child. The boy with her might almost have been a clone of the younger Agency man, for he had the same look of rather brutish innocence, that amoral California quality of brainless muscle. He wore shorts and a bright-yellow T-shirt with a decoration on the front.

"Nightclubs," Tarp could hear the girl saying. "Goddamn nightclubs just make me barf. Don't they, Rick?"

"They're sickening."

"And all this booze? I don't think they're *serious* about the freeze. Do you?"

"I think they've been corrupted."

"Bourgeois."

"Yeah."

Tarp wriggled into his trousers and slid the .22 under the shirt, which he left lying under the palm stumps.

"Do you think they've betrayed the revolution?" the girl was saying.

"Don't talk so loud."

"Well, do you?"

Tarp stood up. Even barefoot, he towered over them, the

low, sandy ridge giving him more height. The girl saw him first and her mouth opened in a perfect circle. It was small and soft and pink, like a baby's, and it stayed opened, looking astonished.

"Comrades," Tarp said. He walked down the sand hill toward them. "Comrades both!" He tried a Russian accent and it came out like Repin's voice.

"Comrade?" The girl had taken the boy's hand and they both looked terrified of him.

"Comrades," Tarp said again. His mind was jumping ahead: here he had two people who would not question his identification and who had no Committee for the Defense of the Revolution to which to report. "Comrades, I am not being able to help overhearing what you are saying next to me while I am enjoying the Cuban sunshine on my visitation to this lovely island." He smiled. His smile was never very jolly, and it sometimes was worse than his frown. It had the effect of moving the girl closer to the young man, and her mouth opened a little wider. She had no makeup on, except around her eyes, and she looked about fifteen. "You are Americans?"

"We're here for the freeze," the young man said. "The International Friends of the Nuclear Freeze Movement."

"Ah. Yes?" Repin had said something about the freeze movement as a reason for the ballet troupe's being there. "Ah. I, too."

"You're here for the freeze day?" the girl said with what seemed to be suspicion. It might simply have been disinterest.

"Ah, in a manner of talking. Yes. You have transport, have you, back to Havana?"

"The bus, yeah," the boy said. The girl frowned up at him. "Don't you have transportation?" she said. Now she sounded quite suspicious. Perhaps she had a CDR block group, after all.

"Of course!" *A bus.* What kind of bus would they take back to Havana? And how was he going to get on it without any money? "You took bus all the way out here from Havana, my friends?"

"It's a tour," the boy said.

"Everything's a tour," the girl added.

Tours meant tour guides; tour guides meant intelligence agents, or reports, at the very least. He began to regret speaking to them. "Well, I have to go, Comrades," he said. "I have an appointment." As he turned away, the boy said quickly, too loudly, "We weren't complaining, you know!"

"Oh, Rick!" the girl muttered.

Tarp turned back. "You are worried about what I will say I heard, my friend?"

"No, no. I just wanted to be straight with you. You know. We were just having a private, uh, conversation. About all the great things they've done for us. It's a great tour. Really."

"Oh, Rick!" the girl said. Her voice was nasal. She faced Tarp, pink with defiance. "Actually, we were bitching a lot!" she said. "You heard us, right? So why pretend? We've never been to Cuba before, we wanted to see how the revolution works, and they keep taking us to *night*clubs, and they keep giving us *booze,* and they keep showing us *apartment* houses, and . . . We just came to demonstrate for world peace, you know?"

At the edge of his vision, Tarp saw another figure approaching along the same route that the two Americans had taken to the beach. He wanted to kick himself for getting into such a stupid situation. Yet, being in it, he had to stay with it. He tried to frown as Repin did, and he tried to make his voice even more like Repin's as he said, "Comrades, is wrong to question the judgment of the people's representatives. Who are you, to reject nightclubs when workers all over Cuba dream of nightclubs? Who are you, but children of the bourgeoisie, looking for the titillations of playing at workers? Who are you, but decadent Americans, still hand in hand with Rockefellers and United Fruits, sneering at the nightclubs of the twenty-sixth of July? Who are you"—he said, his voice rising as he heard footsteps crunching over the palm fronds—"but the offspring of the middle class, trying to satisfy corrupted urges by playing at work while you sneer at the pleasures of the workers? Shame, I say. Shame, Comrades! Do not criticize until you have earned the right to criticize!"

"Bravo," a firm voice said behind him. Tarp turned slowly and tried to look surprised. "Bravo, Comrade." She was quite sincere. She was also tall, strong, dark, strikingly handsome. She put out a brown hand. "Juana Marino."

Tarp tried to think. He had already made a Russian of himself; the French identity was no good. *Too smart!* "Yegor Solkov," he said.

"You are Russian?" she said in Russian.

"Most assuredly."

"Thank you for what you said," she told him in lightly accented Russian. "These two have done nothing but complain since they landed." She smiled at the Americans as if she had said something complimentary about them.

"They are children," he said. "Your guests?"

"I am their guide. From the Bureau of Tourism and Solidarity."

"Of course. You have a group?"

She nodded. "Thirty. We are here looking at the cement plant. All but these two. It is hard to know what they want. Machine guns and urban revolution, perhaps. They do not seem to understand that Cubans like nightclubs and baseball, and that cement plants and furniture factories are necessary to us."

"Maybe they want to see spies and counterrevolution and another Bay of Pigs," Tarp said. He laughed. The woman laughed, too. It was a beautiful laugh, musical and open. She glanced at her watch.

"Time to wipe their noses?" Tarp said in Russian.

"You are a bad man," she said lightly. She was still laughing. She was very flirtatious, he saw, perhaps habitually so. It would have been flattering to think that she did it only for him.

"You must go back to the bus," she said to the two Americans in English.

"We just wanted to take a walk!" the girl protested.

"And you made the group lose time."

"Well, the group has made us lose enough time."

Juana Marino was very cool. "Individualism is an aberration," she said. She made it sound like a quotation. "Please go back to the bus now."

Tarp walked up the beach and squeezed his feet into his damp canvas shoes. He bent down and pushed the .22 into the front of the cotton trousers and buttoned his shirt so that the square-cut tail hung out all around. It was an old short-sleeved shirt with epaulets that looked vaguely military and that had been made in Africa years before. He thought it would pass in Cuba.

"Are you going back to the road, Señor Solkov?" the beautiful guide called to him. She was standing by the path that led away from the beach, just where she might have been able to see what he was doing if she had wanted to.

"I was waiting for a friend," he said.

"*Here?*" She sounded as severe as a schoolteacher. Tarp thought of the Committee for the Defense of the Revolution, and of tour guides, and of the intricate systems of surveillance that made everybody a spy on somebody here.

"No," he said. He gestured vaguely. "Out there."

"Well, won't you walk with me, then?" she said. She sounded flirtatious again.

Tarp reached her side in half a dozen running strides. The two Americans were ahead of them, and Tarp and the beautiful Cuban woman came behind like parents herding their children homeward after a day at the beach.

"You are visiting in Cuba, of course," the woman said in Russian.

"Of course."

"For the celebration of antinuclear peace?"

"Partly that."

The path led along a cut through the sandy scarp behind the beach; on each side of them was a head-high bank of sand and a growth of pine trees. Tarp saw an old tire track in the deep sand, as if the cut were used for vehicles that patrolled the beach, perhaps. He sensed the Cuban woman studying him, and as a distraction he said, "Americans are very young for their years, are they not? These two seem like children."

"You have been to America?" she said.

"I have met Americans before."

"Yes, they are very young. And very spoiled. They think they are the kings of creation."

"Many Americans think that," he said.

She laughed. "All Cuban *men* think that."

Up ahead he could see a paved road and a rather pretty circular road with benches and palms in the middle. There were two buses there and a crowd of people. "Are Cuban men different from Cuban women?" he said idly, thinking of how he was going to get to Havana and of whether he could get on one of these buses safely. The gun seemed very big and very visible just then.

She was looking down at the sand. "Cuban men are children, but they think they are very grown-up, and what they want their women to be is even younger children." She looked at him with a smile and then looked away. "It is called *machismo*." She shrugged. "Politically, Cuban men are all Communists now, but sexually they are still tied to the pope's skirts."

Tarp was looking at the buses, which were decorated with brightly colored posters celebrating peace and the establishment of nuclear-free zones. "Happily, we Russians do not have that problem," he said. She laughed. She was laughing at him, no doubt, and even though she was laughing at the stuffy Russian he was only pretending to be, he was piqued. She went right on laughing at him, and the annoyance changed to genuine amusement, then to sexual recognition. "You are very beautiful," he said.

"You even talk like a Cuban man!" she said.

"Men are men, at a certain level. You are *very* beautiful!"

"Well." She stopped. She took off a shoe to empty it of sand, and to hold herself steady she put a hand on his arm. "Well, I am enough of a Cuban woman to like being told I am beautiful." She blew out her breath in what seemed to be impatience with herself. He thought she would empty the other shoe, and to do so she would hold his arm again, but she started toward the road and the buses. He caught her shoulder. "Will you go out with me?" he said. He was not sure whether he had asked her as himself or as his Russian creation.

"Where?"

His hesitation was very brief. "The Russian ballet."

"You want to see the ballet?"

"Of course."

"Tonight is their last performance in Havana."

"Well, then—tonight."

She looked him over. He had a sick feeling that she could see the gun, even though the shirt hid it well. She folded her arms, which were brown and leanly muscled, like a swimmer's arms, and covered with fine brown hairs the color of a seal's. "I'm not one of the easy Cuban girls, Russki," she said.

"I can tell that by looking at you."

"Well . . . All right." For the first time she looked unhappy with herself, as if she disliked what she had done. Still, she said stubbornly, "I will meet you in front of the theater at seven-thirty."

"It will be a great pleasure for me."

"Don't count your chickens before they hatch." She looked at the buses and the crowd, her arms still folded, her face twisted by a frown. "How are you getting back to Havana?" she asked.

"A friend is picking me up."

"When?"

He lied. "Ten-thirty."

"But it is long past that!"

"It can't be."

"It is after eleven!" She held a brown wrist up for him to study. "See?"

Tarp frowned. He meant only to look like a man who was annoyed with himself; his frowns, however, inevitably looked far more serious than that.

"Don't be angry," she said softly.

"I am not angry."

"You look angry. Terribly angry."

"Not at all." He rubbed the lines between his brows. "Only at my own stupidity."

"Have you money?"

He frowned again. She winced. "I left everything in his car," he said. "A walk on the beach—no need to take anything—well, what a fool I am! If my superiors hear of this . . ."

"Typical Russian," she said.

"I beg your pardon!"

"You all go crazy in the sun. Well, come on." She grabbed his short left sleeve and tugged. "I will find you a ride, sunstruck Russki. Come along!"

"Can I ride with you?"

"Certainly not! These young Americans have antennae like oversexed roosters; they would giggle and gossip and I would lose my authority with them. What little authority it is possible to have with them! You will ride in the *other* bus."

"But I will see you tonight?"

"Yes, yes, in front of the Theatre of Revolutionary Culture."

"How will I find you?"

"I will find you. You are so tall, you will stick up like a signal for yourself. Come on."

There were two militia men in the back of the second bus, which was rather old and which put out a cloud of diesel smoke as it racketed down the highway toward Havana. The militia men were from a Havana suburb, and they carried holstered pistols, but they were less threatening than two American deputy sheriffs might have been. Tarp sat with them and chatted whenever the bus slowed enough so that they could hear each other.

"You like Cuba?" one of them said.

"Oh, yes. The finest country in Latin America!"

They smiled shyly, as if Cuba were their personal triumph.

"You are from Moscow?"

"No, no, the Ukraine."

"I studied that in school. I have been to school, of course. Before the revolution, a man like me, he would never have been to school. Now, I can write, and I read the announcements to my block committee. The Ukraine is the breadbasket of Russia."

"That's very good," Tarp said in his Russian-accented Spanish. He did not say what he really thought—that the breadbasket of Russia was in Iowa.

They passed through clean little towns, then through a development of semidetached concrete houses that would have reminded him of Moscow because of their sameness if they had not been painted in pretty pastels and if there had not been chickens and mules in the minuscule front yards. He waved a hand at them. "Cuba is very picturesque," he said.

"Cuba is very *clean*," one of the militia men corrected him. "All of it?"

"All except Buena Ventura." The man smiled shyly. Then he guffawed a little nervously, and his companion elbowed him and they both giggled.

"What is Buena Ventura, please?"

"Buena Ventura is the place that does not officially exist."

The man's companion looked disgusted. "He is a thug," he said. "He has no manners. He should not have said that."

"I see."

The first man was enjoying being bad, however. "Buena Ventura is more carefully hidden than Fidel's bald spot," he said. He giggled again. The other man shushed him, then turned away and stared out the window as if he were trying to disassociate himself from his unruly friend. Clearly it had occurred to him that Tarp might make a report of the conversation. (It had already occurred to Tarp that they might make a report on him. There was nothing he could do about that.)

"What is Buena Ventura?" he said. "Come, come, I am a man of the world."

The first man had gotten scared now. He closed his mouth very tightly and shook his head.

"It is very unfair to introduce a subject and then not continue it, Comrade," Tarp said. "A person would think there was something to hide."

The second man turned on the first. "You see?" he said loudly. "What a mouth!" He waved his hands at Tarp. "The first thing that comes into his head, he says it—out it comes, just like vomit. Disgusting!" He folded his arms and scowled at the other militia man. "See what you have done now, you and your mouth? Now a foreigner has formed a bad opinion of the revolution. What is that between your ears, a rock?" He swung back to look at Tarp. "Buena Ventura is a slum. Eh? That is very plainspoken, no? A slum—dirty, poor, mean, crooked—the works. The revolution has passed it by. Why? Because the people are incorrigibles. They should have been sent to the United States, but we could not get them to the boats fast enough. In my block committee, we have had a paper about Buena Ventura. As a bad example. Buena Ventura is famous. In a very bad sort of way."

"Maybe the revolution needs Buena Ventura to remind itself of what it triumphed over."

The man looked at Tarp with respect. "That is pretty good. May I repeat that at my block committee?"

"I am flattered. But let me be honest, my friend. Even in the Soviet Union, we have slums. One or two. Socialism is a stage, after all. It is not perfection. Eh? There are always backsliders who betray the best interests of the people."

The first man was grinning. He had round cheeks, like Ping-Pong balls. "You can get girls in Buena Ventura," he said.

"Oh, sweet Jesu," the second one said. "Will you ever shut up?"

"You can get *anything* in Buena Ventura." He swung an arm over the shiny, greasy metal tubing that formed a handhold over the back of the seat and faced Tarp. "Colombian cocaine, they say. Truly. Gambling. Cockfights. There are *degenerates* in Buena Ventura." He leaned back, looked around the bus, leaned toward Tarp again. "You can really have a good time, they say." He leaned back again, then again leaned forward and said, "Get me?"

"I get you."

The man grunted. He smiled at his friend as if he were sure he had done exactly the right thing after all, for now the Russian comrade would know the real facts of the revolution. He seemed quite pleased with himself.

The bus did not slow again long enough for them to talk, and they were all quiet. The two militia men got off near their suburb and then stood by the road, arguing with each other as the bus pulled out of sight.

Tarp went forward and asked the driver how close he went to Buena Ventura.

The black driver looked at him with cynical amusement. "About half-a-mile walk, man."

"Let me out when you are closest to it."

"Keep everything in your pants, man." The black man shot him a look. "I mean your money, you follow?"

Fifteen minutes later he waved to Tarp and brought the bus to a stop. "Don't believe the first kid tells you his mother's a virgin and you can have her for ten pesos," he said.

"Should I believe the second one?"

"I think he lies a little, too. Have a good time, man."

Tarp got down from the bus and the door folded up behind him. He waved, but the driver was already looking at the road ahead, and he roared away with a belching of diesel smoke that left Tarp coughing.

CHAPTER 7

Buena Ventura had been middle class long ago, and then it had
become a slum, and then the revolution had renovated it. Now
it was a slum again. The government had cleaned it up and
moved in the people of another old slum, perhaps believing that
a change of scene would make them good revolutionaries, and
they had managed to make it just like home. The architecture
could still speak of a great past, a past sometime around the
Spanish-American War. Decayed posters spoke of a revolution
that had tried and had then turned to more rewarding efforts.
One of the posters read "Exhort your men to—" but it no longer told the women of Buena Ventura what they were to exhort
their men to do. "Enlarge the—" read another. "Resist," instructed a third. Faded pink-and-gray letters, above once noble
faces that had bleached like poor photographs, warned, "Enemies of the Revolution surround us." Tarp believed it.

The first girl approached him just after he turned the corner
from the typically clean, typically spare streets of revolutionary
Havana into the first of Buena Ventura's alleys. He felt that he
was moving backward in time. The litter grew deeper. There
were dog droppings on the pavement. There were graffiti.

"Want to have a good time?" said a girl of fourteen. She had
a bored, professional voice.

In two blocks he counted five pimps and eight girls, and he
supposed that at least a few of them were police.

"Sell your watch?" a grinning youth said, pressing close to
his left side and falling into step.

55

"Go fornicate with yourself," Tarp said in his best Miami Spanish.

"I give you the best price in Havana."

"I will give you a permanent pain between your legs."

"A hundred ten pesos."

"Go away."

"A hundred twenty."

"Go."

"A hundred thirty."

"*Go.*"

"My last offer, absolutely, no excrement."

Tarp felt deft fingers lift the tail of the khaki shirt and feel for the wallet that should have been there. He caught one finger, twisted, drove the extended fingers of his right hand up under the young man's ribs. There was a sound as if the man had been sick; his face was very white and his little mustache seemed to jump from it because it was so black. He looked angry and desperate and frightened, and Tarp felt sorry for him, even while he despised him.

"Want me to break this finger?"

"No—no! I did nothing. . . ."

"You change money?"

"Yes—ah!"

"French money?"

"Yes."

"I want to change some French money. You want to do business, stop trying to rob me and show me your money."

"How much?"

"Four thousand francs."

"I have to get that much money. That is much money. I give a good price, but I have to check."

"Where?"

"Up that alley. Two minutes." He nodded toward an opening ten yards ahead.

"You think I am an imbecile."

"No!"

"You want to get your friends so you can rob me."

"In two minutes?" He was almost screaming. Across the street, a girl who had her hair piled up like a forties movie star watched them without expression. "I need to check the price and get money, that is all. Truly! You think in Buena Ventura I would carry that much money? I swear!"

"On the Virgin's cloak, I suppose."

"I am a good Christian. Two minutes."

Tarp let him go. "You had better be honest with me."

"I swear."

The girl sauntered across. A cat, pausing in its pursuit of a flea, sat down in the middle of the pavement to watch her.

"Want to go to paradise?" the girl said.

"No money, angel."

"Did he get it all?"

"There was none to get. How about taking me to paradise for love?"

"I save my love for Fidel."

"And the church, I hope."

"Are you a cop?"

"No, I am a priest. Good-bye, angel."

He went back down the street, looked into the alley, and saw the young man with the mustache. The alley was like a canyon choked with trash, sunless, smelly. There was a chain-link fence blocking it fifty feet down, and the paper had blown up against it into a pile half as high as Tarp was tall.

Tarp walked into the alley. The brick walls were windowless; there was one doorway that had been bricked in. The only place big enough to hide a man was a buttress to his right, but the space behind it was empty.

"The money?" Tarp said.

The young man reached behind his back as if he were going to get something from a pocket, and his hand came back with a knife.

"Stupid," Tarp said. "You did think I am an imbecile."

"Because you *are* an imbecile. This is Buena Ventura, not your farm, excrement head."

Tarp put his back against a wall. The buttress stuck out to his left now, ten feet away, partly blocking the street. There was enough space for him to see a big man there now, however—a huge man, one of the biggest he had ever seen. He had a timber in one of his enormous hands, and he carried it easily like a baseball bat, although it was three inches on its side and four feet long.

"Uncle Tonio and me are going to teach you a lesson, farmer."

Tarp waited for the big man to come into the alley. The young one was anxious, however. He moved close, flashing the knife back and forth in front of him, and Tarp broke his arm and flung him toward the rear of the alley. Then, as the huge man came toward him, he took out the .22 and pointed it at the basketball-sized face. "Drop the tree, Uncle Tonio," he said. The man puffed. "I'll shoot your eyes out first. Then your *cojones*." The wood thudded on the filthy pavement.

Tarp gestured with the gun. "Both of you against that wall. Strip."

"Naked?" Tonio was almost bald. He sounded as if he had emphysema.

"Naked."

"Are you a queer?"

"No, I am a policeman." He flipped out the green DGI card that he had taken from the dead man on the boat.

"Holy excrement," Uncle Tonio groaned.

"Just so. Get the little man on his feet and start stripping."

When the young man objected that he had a broken arm, the older one slapped him and told him to mind his manners. He muttered like a scold and called him a fool and told him to look at all the trouble he had caused.

"Naked?" he said again.

"Stark naked."

His skin was like dirty bread dough, and it enveloped great circles of fat that fell in cascades over his chest and hips. The young man, on the other hand, was painfully skinny, and together the two of them made a very sad picture.

"Put your hands against the brick wall and spread your legs."

"What for?"

"I want to see what you are hiding, what else?"

"Holy excrement."

Tarp went through their clothes hurriedly. He knew enough about the Cuban criminals who had been exported to Florida to know that they worked in big gangs and they were ruthless—made so, he supposed, by a ruthless Cuban police. He found another knife, several thousand pesos, and, sewn into the big man's jacket behind a pocket, a little bundle of identification cards, presumably from stolen wallets.

"You know the penalty for selling identification, Uncle Tonio?"

"I do not sell them. They are souvenirs. Of my relatives. Did I sell them? Did you see me sell them?"

"Do you know the penalty for hoarding identification cards?"

"There is a penalty for that?"

"There is a penalty for everything. You know that."

"They are not mine, I swear! I bought that coat used. I did not even know they were there. Truly."

Tarp pocketed the Cuban money and the cards and kicked the clothes down the alley. He dropped some francs from the waterproof pocket on the pile.

"We have our eye on you two. You have one chance. Cooperate with us, or it's the People's Court."

"Sweet Jesu."

"I will come back tomorrow. If you have said anything about what happened here, I will know you are enemies of the revolution, and I will arrest you on the spot. Understand?"

Uncle Tonio nodded. He elbowed the young man, who groaned. "It never happened."

"What never happened?"

"Nothing never happened."

Tarp shoved the pistol into his belt under the shirt and stepped carefully out of the alley. He crossed it quickly and turned a corner and went a block and turned again. Fifteen minutes later he found a street market where it was possible to buy used clothes without coupons, and he bought a dark suit and very shiny black plastic shoes and a white shirt and tie, and he put Buena Ventura behind him and found a public men's room. It was clean and almost restful after the slum; he changed his clothes and stuffed the clothes from the boat into the trash can.

He went to a barber shop and had his hair cut, and before he could stop the barber he had been doused with sweet-smelling lotion that plastered his hair to his head like a cap. He hated the way he looked, but at least he did not look like himself. He went to a little park where children and dogs seemed to be running back and forth without stopping; there was a small Ferris wheel and a booth for throwing baseballs and a portable instant-picture place where he got two photos of himself. He found a secluded bench and ruined two of the ID cards separating the laminations, then managed to pry a third open and insert one of the photos and then seal it again crudely with the heat from a match from a packet he found on the pavement with "Support the sugar cutters in their drive for productivity!" on the cover. The card was not very convincing, but he judged it to be somewhat better than nothing.

He ate standing up at a cafe back from the main streets, leaning on a wood counter between a truck driver and a black merchant sailor who insisted on introducing themselves and being friendly. It turned out they thought he was a policeman.

"Do I look like a policeman?"

"You look like George Raft. Who but a policeman would want to look like that?"

He wiped some of the lotion out of his hair in another men's room, but he still looked like a forties gangster.

At seven o'clock he began looking for the Plaza Marti, and he was there by twenty minutes after. He looked with real interest at the beautiful modern building that took up one side of the square and that was the Theatre of Revolutionary Culture. Somehow, a sense of human scale had been preserved despite its size. Three tiers of lighted windows were stretched like bright ribbons across its façade; inside, and outside on terraces with plain, waist-high railings, people were moving, looking at this distance like colored chips swaying on the ribbons. In the vast plaza itself, couples moved in a clockwise whirl with the slow and graceful gait of flirtatiousness. In a larger circle, bicycles moved around them, with one or two now darting through the crowd; at the outer edge, scooters and a few cars moved almost hesitantly, like animals that have wandered into an alien environment.

He crossed the square against the swirl of moving people. Many of the men looked as he did, slicked-down and suited, so he supposed that they were all policemen or else his two informants had been wrong. Then again, nobody else was wearing a white tie on a white shirt with a black suit. The women looked overdressed to him and too extravagantly made up. They affected dark lipsticks and towering hair and stiletto heels. Despite the revolution, it still looked as if Havana were the Las Vegas of the Caribbean.

Juana Marino found him in the crowd. He was looking the other way when he heard her rich voice say, "You have been to a Havana barber!" and she was giggling. She had spoken Russian, which helped to remind him that he was supposed to be a Russian named Yegor Solkov and not a French journalist named Selous (as it said on the packet of documents he had in a pocket), nor a Cuban named Ibazza (as it said on the doctored ID card in another pocket), or even an American named Tarp. "You smell like a Cuban," she said.

"Is that bad?"

"Oh, well . . ." She wrapped her hands around his left arm. "It is not yet time to go into the theater. Let us walk."

"Like the other couples."

"Yes." She was wearing a light dress of a lavender fabric that had a sheen like silk, and her hair was piled on one side of her face with a flower in it. Her makeup was sophisticated, rather highly colored, and she seemed to have accentuated the Negroid elements of her cheekbones and her lips.

"You are even more beautiful than I remember."

"Short memory." She relaxed her hold and put one hand lightly on his left arm. "Where are you staying, did you say?"

"I did not. I hoped that tonight I would stay with you."

She pulled her hand away. "Don't be like that," she said quickly. "I hate that."

"I was trying to be honest." He took her hand and put it in his arm again. "Now I will be less honest."

They strolled once around the plaza and then turned toward the theater. People were pressing into the lobby in rather happily messy lines. Tarp found them much noisier than an American crowd, and noisier by far than any in Moscow.

"Actually," she said as she watched him come back with tickets, "you look quite handsome. Even with the Cuban hair."

"I was scolded when I told you you look beautiful."

"No, you were scolded when you made what you thought was a sexy remark. Then you not only looked like a Cuban man, you sounded like one. Well, for me that doesn't work so well, because I am a new Cuban woman."

"One is not supposed to want to spend the night with you?"

"One is not supposed to say so as if they were giving prizes for such remarks."

The auditorium seemed as big as the plaza outside. There were two vast balconies above them, an orchestra like a football field; chandeliers the size of buses hung from the ceiling, dark gold and crystal and oddly old-fashioned in such a setting. Tarp felt shrunken by such space and by the thousands now moving into it. "Individualism is an aberration," she had said, and this theater said exactly the same thing. The only concessions to privilege were a row of loges along the front of the lower balcony, but even those were made subservient to the dominant scheme, having no private entrances and no privacy walls. They were, in fact, showplaces where officials and visitors sat, as much on display there as the performers on the stage. Now, Tarp watched them fill with men and women who were neither Cuban nor Communist.

"Foreigners?" he said to her.

She twisted her head to look up. A breath of perfume reached him. "From the embassies. And delegates to the antinuclear congress from South America."

He thought he could pick out the Russians and the French. He tried to pass the time by making a game of the nationalities, but finally he had to admit what he already knew too well— that, except for the obvious distinctions, national characteristics were not easily expressed in faces. The Africans were colorful and exotic; the Orientals seemed too pleased with it all. Many of them wore lapel badges that identified them as delegates, including a small, silver-haired man in a wheelchair who came in with two bodyguards, and an older man in a dinner jacket with military decorations that Tarp was sure were British.

"Who's that?" he said to her, pointing at them.

She shook her head. "I don't know them."

They took their places in a box. Tarp thought them an odd foursome, particularly when he saw the bulge of a weapon in one of the men's coats. *Some peace congress.*

There was a stir then at the back of the orchestra and they stopped talking, although Tarp glanced again at the man in the wheelchair and his thugs and found himself wondering if the man with the British medals could be English, and what he was doing there; and then, like Juana, he was craning his neck to see the group coming into the orchestra from the back.

"Who is it?" he asked her.

"Your Russians," she said. She was standing, unabashed by her own curiosity. A group of twenty people was coming down the wide aisle. Around them some of the audience were applauding politely. A heavy-jowled man came first, with a short, heavy-jowled woman half a step behind him; next came two men, one either drunk or feverish; and next, to Tarp's surprise and relief, came Repin. With him was a fortyish woman who had that rawboned look that dancers sometimes take on with age; Tarp thought she was the ballet manageress. Repin looked pleased and yet pugnacious, like Khruschev in his old photos.

Tarp stood up.

Repin was on the side away from him, and he was bowing a little this way and that, but he turned to say something to the tall woman with him and he saw Tarp. His face went slack momentarily and he turned rather red, like the man ahead of him. Tarp smiled and bowed.

"What is it?" Juana tugged at his arm.

"An acquaintance."

"In the ballet?"

"A friend of theirs."

He smiled at Repin again. The old KGB officer had composed himself and he bowed in return, and his head came back up to jerk toward the door behind him in a way that was impossible to misinterpret. He wanted Tarp to meet him in the lobby.

An overture played and the huge chandeliers dimmed and then the curtain rose on a lush, pretty, Romantic scene. People were still coming in, and Tarp watched for Repin's stocky body to appear in the aisle.

"Excuse me," he said to Juana Marino.

"It has just started!"

"I shall come back."

He found Repin in the shadow of a staircase, at the bottom of a lobby that rose up through the building's three stories. He seemed to be studying a program with care. When Tarp came up, he looked over the folded paper and said, "I thought you were dead."

"I need your help."

"They told me your boat had blown up."

"The boat did. I need to get out of Cuba."

"I was betrayed. You believe that, I hope? I did not try to kill you. Other times, yes. This time, why should I?"

"There are easier ways. What went wrong?"

"I made an arrangement with the navy; somebody in DGI finds out, maybe from Moscow. Eh? They do not kill me; that is too obvious; killing you is good idea."

"Do they know it's me?"

"Maybe not. They know is an American, obviously."

"Anything new on the submarine or the plutonium?"

"I have agent here looking at something. He has idea, he thinks. We will see." Repin pushed out his lips as if he might whistle. He was dressed in great style, not in a Bulgarian tropical disaster but in an expensive English suit, and he looked more than ever like a ruthless capitalist. "I leave Cuba in six days. Not much time." He tapped the edge of the program on his teeth. "You are with beautiful woman. How does that happen?"

"An accident."

"There are no accidents." He tapped the program some more and lifted an eyebrow. "We are being watched by the KGB agent sent to watch the KGB agent who watches the ballet troupe. He is one of Telyegin's, I think, so he is perhaps all right. Still, it is best I introduce you." He took Tarp's arm and turned him around. There was a mousy-looking young man huddled into himself next to a drinking fountain. They walked over. "Eugen Nemirovich, my young friend, I want you to meet one of our staunchest friends in the hemisphere. May I present Señor Picardo."

Good, Tarp thought. *My fifth identity today.* The Russian made a little bob of a bow. *"Enchanté,"* Tarp murmured.

"Señor Picardo is an internationalist," Repin said. He smiled. The KGB man smiled as young men do when the boss says almost anything. "We are all friends of peace," he said.

"Peace with honor," Tarp said.

"Indeed, oh, yes, surely." After some seconds, the young man backed away to another wall, where he stood uncertainly, still watching them. By then they were the only people in the gigantic lobby.

"I've got a passport, but it needs a visa and an entry stamp. Can you fix it?" Tarp said.

"Put it inside your program and leave it on the third urinal in the men's room. I will come in after you and get it."

"I'll need a way out of Cuba."

"I will work on it." Repin's face was troubled. "But it is very hard to trust anybody now. This young man who watches us, for example—who does he talk to? Who reads his report besides Telyegin? Bad, very bad. You need a place to hide tonight?"

"That's all right. I'll take care of myself."

"The woman?"

"I'll take care of myself."

"Maybe I should hide you. If I could find a place where it would not be handing you over to them to kill."

"I'll take care of myself. How do I contact you?"

"There is a promenade along the harbor. A cafe called Angolan Memories. Tomorrow night at seven, all right?"

"All right." He hesitated. "If you do find out something, you know, they will try to kill you next."

Repin's face slackened. "It has been tried before. I cannot prevent it."

"Your agent here. Is he secure?"

"Who knows?" Repin sighed. "Enjoy the ballet."

When he slid back into his seat next to her, she took his arm again. Her thigh was very warm against his, and the touch seemed not to bother her at all. Tarp looked at her instead of the ballet. She was taller than most of the women he had seen in Havana, her face angular but full-lipped, high-boned. She was a woman that many men would have made great effort to have. He put his mouth close to her ear and said, "Do you believe in accidents?"

"Shhh," she said, intent on the ballet.

Tarp stared at the stage and concentrated, instead, on Repin and the plutonium. That Maxudov had a network in Cuba was obvious; it was probably not the regular KGB net—it was silly to think that he would have corrupted a whole section—but was, perhaps, made up of a few well-placed agents and a lot of people who thought they were performing their patriotic duty to Cuba or the U.S.S.R. and were really serving one man. Such a situation did not mean that the plutonium had come to Cuba. Tarp was not convinced by the nuclear freeze posters that covered the walls of Havana, any more than he was convinced that the diplomats who sat above him at the ballet believed in peace; but he would need hard evidence before he would believe that Cuba wanted its own atomic weapons so much that it would deal with a Soviet traitor. No, that was senseless. What was far likelier was that the buyer was a terrorist or the PLO or a consortium of terrorist groups—yet it was hard to see why even they would risk the fury of Moscow.

But if it were they—or somebody like them—who, then, was Maxudov? And why was he willing to take such risk? Not for zeal. Tarp had only marginal belief in zeal. He believed more fully in human weakness—a woman, a man, money, ambition. But how was Maxudov served in any of those ways?

I'm in the wrong place, he thought. *Wrong city, wrong country, I need to get to Washington.* Ironically, the CIA would know more perhaps about Cuban ambitions toward atomic weaponry than the Soviets did, especially if the Soviets were being diddled by one of their own. *Then I need the gossip from Europe. I need to be in London. Paris.* He looked down the hall at Repin. *Then Moscow.* He would have to kill twenty-four hours before he could start. *Wrong city, wrong country.* He glanced at the woman beside him. *Right woman.*

She was applauding. He applauded. "Wasn't it brilliant?" she cried. "Wonderful. Wonderful!" She stood up and he realized it was over. "Would you like to go to a nightclub?" she said.

"What would we do at a nightclub?"

"Dance!"

"Do you like to dance?"

"Just now, I love to dance!"

"We will go to a nightclub."

It was like places in New York that people of his generation had dreamed about when they were adolescents, places that no longer existed—the homes of gossip columnists and "cafe society." There was a floor show of extravagant noise and glitter, and a remarkable show of bare skin for a Socialist country. There was lots of rum, and there was dancing.

"Where did you learn to merengue?" she demanded. "You *are* a Cuban man!"

"You are very beautiful."

"Dance with me again!"

When the nightclub closed at two in the morning, she took

him to her apartment. She carried her high-heeled shoes in one hand and held on to his arm with the other, and on the concrete balcony of the floor below hers, they kissed. They held each other's hands, nothing else; it was like the dance again, the dance impacted. "Come upstairs," she whispered.

Outside her door there was a bulletin board with notices and posters and a long cardboard sign that read COMMITTEE FOR THE DEFENSE OF THE REVOLUTION. BLOCK MEETINGS TUESDAYS SEVEN P.M. EMERGENCIES ANY TIME.

"I am the block chairman," she murmured.

As she undressed, she hummed a tune from the nightclub. It was self-aware but not insistent, neither coy nor stupid. Under the brown hose, her long legs were brown; her body was strong and supple. She cried out with pleasure and laughed afterward and then hugged him as they spiraled down toward sleep.

"Do you have to go away in the morning?" she murmured.

"Not right away."

"Good." She smiled, her face against his shoulder, and he could feel the muscles move. "Go to sleep, then."

He had not slept for thirty-six hours. He let go, and his mind floated free.

When he awoke, there was light coming into the room from the window, and the barrel of his own .22 was poked hard into the soft flesh just below the bend of his left jaw.

"Did you take me for an imbecile?" she said. She was sitting on the bed naked, the gun in one hand and the DGI green card in the other.

There are no accidents, he thought. Repin had been right.

CHAPTER 8

"Did you think I believed you, even on the beach?" she said. "Do you think that in Cuba we find men on the beach and think nothing more about it?"

"Take the gun away," he growled. He hardly dared move his jaw.

"Oh, no. It is a very nice gun. An American gun—what a nice gun for a Russian to have. Or are you a Cuban named Ibazza? Is your name Ibazza when you work for the DGI?"

"I don't like guns."

"Do you think I always bring men home to my bed because they are handsome and charming and because they dance like angels?"

Some of her hair had fallen and her makeup was smudged, but she looked wonderful. She looked intelligent and vibrant, and she looked as if she hated him.

"You are beautiful," he said. They were speaking Spanish now.

"Oh, yes." It seemed to make her sad.

"What in the name of God—may I mention God?—do you think I was doing on the beach if I wasn't doing what I said?"

"You are going to tell me that."

"It has no logic."

"Oh, but it has!" She waved the green card. "It is all logic."

Tarp thought he understood. It made him want to laugh. He did smile a little. "You are a subversive!" He looked into her eyes, trying to penetrate to the mind beneath them, but she was

68

tough and experienced and she held him out. "What are you, Juana?" he said. "Anti-Castro? A terrorist?" But an alarm was going off in the back of his head, which meant that something was very wrong, and he looked at the opaque eyes and the excited face and he thought she was too good to be an amateur. "Do you help people get to Miami, is that it?" he said, to play for time.

She waved the green card again. "You know all that or you would not be here."

By looking down and to the left, he could see the gun. It was old; its blueing was raddled; it was only a production gun intended for somebody's backpack. He thought of the Agency man he had shot on the boat, then of the two DGI men he had killed with the shotgun. *Staying alive is a matter of knowing when to shoot first.* Or at least of thinking that you knew when to shoot first, because you could never be sure—and if you shot first, you never found out if you were wrong. His eyes shifted to her face again. *Does she know when to shoot first?*

There was a knock at the door. She did not move, nor did her eyes leave his. "Well?" she said.

A man's muffled voice said, "Fernando is here, Juana."

"Wait for me."

She stood up very slowly and backed away from him, pulling the pistol away from his throat last as if she were disconnecting a cord. She felt behind her in a drawer for a pair of panties and then pulled them on one-handed, then got slacks and a blouse and put those on without ever looking away from him. She pushed her rather big feet into shoes by standing in them and wiggling the heels in, and then she said, "Come in now."

Two men came in. They were both young, both dark. One looked like a college student, the sort who would be intensely intellectual and who might call himself a poet. The other looked as if he had worked all his life to get where he was, so that he was thicker and coarser and yet jollier.

Juana gave the poetic one the pistol.

"I will be back at noon," she said. "Do not let him out."

She closed the door behind her and he heard her steps rapping over the concrete floor, and then the outer door thudded as she left the apartment, and a framed photograph of six young women in track suits swayed on its nail and hung crookedly. He thought he could hear her after she left the apartment, walking down the gallery beyond her door, but finally he could not hear even the faint ghost of her angry footsteps, and he knew that for a while he had been listening to the sounds of the morning traffic and of his own blood in his ears.

"We could torture him," the poetic one said.

The thick one looked dubious. Tarp sat up. "Who wants to start?" he said.

The poet had a little of the fanatic's gleam, but he also had the gun, and that satisfied him. His friend, who was pragmatic and who knew that the two of them could not torture this large, muscular man, even when they had a gun, was relieved.

"We will wait for Juana," he said.

"I need to pass water," Tarp said.

The thick one got a bucket while the poet sat astraddle of the room's only chair, imagining himself Humphrey Bogart in *Key Largo*.

The man set the bucket down next to a tiny sink with one tap. "We cannot let you go to the convenience, you understand," he said with genuine apology in his voice.

"Do not be so kind to him!" the poet said.

The thick one shrugged.. "Pissing is not a political issue." He put his hands in his pants pockets. "Anyway, Juana says he may be one of us."

"If he is not DGI," the poet said. "Or KGB."

"Actually," Tarp said, "I am Chinese." He got out of bed and stood there naked, eight inches taller than either of them, his body marked with scars that were like tick marks on a map to show places of interest. In fact, he had been born in China and he had grown up there, but the two young Cubans took it as the sour joke of a cynical older man. They backed to the door and then locked him in, and Tarp knew that they were well-meaning young men who thought that shooting first was morally wrong.

His clothes were not in the room. The door was locked, and there was an angry shout from the other side when he rattled it. Tarp stalked the tiny room, first to the one window and then more carefully from corner to corner. *Well, I wanted a way to pass the time.* There was a deep ledge beyond the window glass and then a somewhat Moorish concrete grill. By opening the window and pushing his head against the grill he could look down and see that there was nothing to help him get down the three stories to the street, even if he could have gotten the grill off.

A way to pass the time, indeed. He was annoyed, most of all with himself, because he wanted to be working on the plutonium business.

He paced. The room was eleven feet long by seven and a half feet wide and was bare except for the single bed, the one chair, the tiny sink, a very small wood table that Juana used as a dressing table, and a rather large armoire that took the place of a closet. On the concrete walls were the picture of the girls' track team (Juana was one of them) and a bright-orange weaving, and on the floor was one small rug. Tarp made the bed. He hung up her dress from the ballet, which had been lying in front of the armoire like the wreckage of that pleasure. There were no scissors and no knives on the small table. There was a hand mirror that might make a weapon if the glass was broken.

The chair was very light and cheaply made and no good to him. He slid under the bed and looked up at the bottom of the box spring, which looked as if it had been made of orange crates by untrained labor. Its bottom was covered with a sleazy fabric like bandage gauze. He tore it away and looked up through tangent rings of steel wire. They might have made a weapon if he had had a tool, but as they were, they were too tough for him.

The back of the wardrobe had a twenty-inch brace, which he carefully and silently wrenched loose, giving him a club with two nails in the end. Her clothes and the handbag that lay in the bottom of the wardrobe provided nothing more than a crumpled book of matches that told him that economic self-sufficiency is national liberation.

He put the club and the matches and the gauze up inside the box spring.

Well, it helps to pass the time. He lay on the bed, thinking of the two men he had killed on the boat. It was never very good, thinking about the dead. He envied Christians, who could light candles and pray in scented, dark places. He had only his thoughts.

He heard her in the outer room a little before noon. The sunlight stood straight out from the window like a bright rectangle that had been painted on the waxed concrete floor. He heard her voice out there for several seconds, then a male voice. Then the lock on the door rattled and he backed away and went to the bed. He was still naked.

She came in and closed the door behind her very quickly as if there were an animal in the room that she was afraid would escape, a cat or a bird. She kept her right hand on the door handle. She looked around the room first, as if he were invisible, and then she looked at him. Her face was angry and her color was pale and unattractive, as if something inside her had drawn its heat back, leaving this wintry bleakness.

"I should let them kill you," she said.

"They would not know how." He was thinking that she knew something about him. Where had she been?

She looked away from him, avoiding any sign that she knew that he was naked. He shifted his weight and she looked at him angrily. "Do not do anything stupid!" she cried. Then she almost whispered. "I told them that if you did anything to me, try to make me a hostage, they are to kill me first. You understand?"

"They would not know how."

She looked at him with contempt, perhaps because she had learned somehow that he was a man who did know how. She let go of the door handle and moved to the dressing table and put her back to it so she could watch him. She put out her right hand and began to rummage in the armoire without looking.

"I have to work," she said, as if she owed him an explanation. She pulled out a flowered dress and dropped it over the back of the chair and then she began to unbutton her blouse. She was wearing nothing under it. She hesitated before she unbuttoned it all the way, and then, enraged, she tore the blouse off and threw it on the floor. She kicked off her shoes. Her nipples were engorged; she made no attempt to hide her breasts. Her slacks had an elastic top; she put her hands on the elastic, palms in, fingers out, and hesitated again—like him, she had to be thinking of her elegant and happy undressing of the night— then pushed the slacks down. She let go of them when they reached her calves and got them off the rest of the way by pushing one leg down with the other foot then walking them down over her ankles as if she were treading grapes. Then she did the same thing, but more slowly, with her panties. All the color had come back into her face. They looked at each other, and neither could hide the sexual eagerness.

As they grappled on the bed, her eyes were wide, seeming to glare at him; then they closed, and her mouth was as tight as if she had taken a vow of silence. He tried to turn her anger aside with tenderness. Twenty minutes later, they lay still; she moved her body so that she lay partly over him, both of them wedged into the angle between the bed and the cool concrete of the wall.

"Who are you?" she whispered.

"Why does it matter?"

"I have to know."

"I am Russian."

"No."

"I am a DGI agent named Ibazza."

"No. The thumbprint on the card is not yours."

Then she has access to a pretty sophisticated system, if she can find that out. She may know whom the thumbprint really belonged to. "Who am I, then?" he said.

"I think you are an American whose boat was blown up. Are you?"

But old caution was always with him. "I am Peruvian," he said.

She became angry again. "Tell me the truth!" She tangled her fingers in his hair and pounded his head against the mattress. "I swear, if you tell the truth, I will save you. But tell me who you are!"

"Who are you?" he said. He pushed a lock of black hair away from her face. "Who are you, Juana?"

She pushed his hand away. "I have to know who you are. It is all that matters now."

He moved his body, moving hers. "And this?"

"This is nothing!" She pushed herself up on her hands, away from him. "This is—personal. Therefore, it is trivial."

"It is a great deal."

She got up and yanked the dress down over her arms and head, slowly covering her wonderful body as if she were putting out a light. She pulled the panties up and then dug through the bottom of the armoire for shoes. She was very violent in putting them on. "Promise me you will not try to escape," she said.

"That would be a stupid promise."

"Promise me!"

"Where my life is concerned, I have no honor, and so my promises mean nothing. Therefore, I promise."

"It is for your own good. Those two out there are very nervous. I will come back before six. Then you must tell me who you are, or . . ."

"Or?"

"Or I will have to turn you over to people who will do terrible things to you. I do not want that to happen."

"Isn't that 'personal'?"

She looked at him, through him, then turned the door handle and went out, closing the door very quickly again as if she feared that the same cat would escape. He heard the lock turn and then her hard, quick steps.

Tarp waited for three-quarters of an hour. After that, he went to the armoire and found a pair of her stretch-fabric slacks that would at least cover his nakedness. There was a T-shirt with a colorful decoration from the Festival of Socialist Film. It looked foolish, but it clothed him.

He ripped all the gauze from the bottom of the spring, splashed her cologne over it, and put it on the windowsill with some of the plastic from the mattress cover. The old matches did not light very well, but he got the gauze smoldering and closed the window on it, leaving only a crack to make a draft to feed the fire. Still, it almost went out; then it blazed, and it began to smolder the way he wanted. He opened the window and crumbled some of the yellow foam from the mattress into it, and the smoke turned an ugly green and looked as thick as sewer water.

Tarp propped the flimsy chair under the door handle. He ran some water into the bucket with his urine and set it near the bed, where he could reach it quickly. He fed more foam and more cologne to the fire and watched the smoke drift out through the lattice over the window. He looked up at the smoke detector on the ceiling, which, he thought, symbolized as well as anything could the difference between Juana's Havana and George Raft's.

He could see flame at the bottom of the thick smoke, but he had no way of slowing it now. The paint on the bottom of the window was blistering, and as he watched, one pane of glass cracked from the heat.

A building like this one was like a village. Natural affinity and government nosiness made the people almost pathologically aware of each other. It had its own court system for minor "errors" (with Juana the judge); people were always on watch for others' transgressions. A fire would be a great event. It would offer the thrill of danger, the pleasure of somebody else's mistake, the titillation of damage to government property. There might even be revisionist or antirevolutionary meaning in it—the secret cooking of black market food or the operation of an illegal still. That the apartment where the fire started was that of the head of the CDR was even more exciting. There had to be people in the building who would be thrilled by any sign of her failure—men who had wanted her and been rejected, women who disliked her because she was a new kind of Cuban woman, political rivals.

They have to notice soon, he thought.

He heard the muffled pounding of running feet on the floor above.

He waited.

He heard a voice far away. Then another voice, perhaps in the street below.

Suddenly there was a loud voice in the room just outside and a noise like a chair or a table being pushed aside. Several voices were raised then excitedly. He heard a thump and then a strange brushing sound on the door, and he imagined one of his guards putting his back to the bedroom door to keep the nosy neighbors out.

The air in the room grew stifling. The smell of burning plastic attacked his nose, the back of his throat. He coughed. He was thinking of the poisonous gases that could be made by burning plastic. He closed his mind to that and impaled a paper label from the mattress on his improvised club, set it afire, and held it up under the smoke alarm. It screamed like a hurt rabbit.

"Fire!" Tarp shouted in Spanish. "Help me! Help. Help. Oh, Jesu, help me!" While he shouted he was opening the window and tearing down a curtain to drop it on the burning pile on the window ledge. He rubbed soot from the ledge on his hands and face.

"Comrades, for Jesu's sake! Help!"

The door handle rattled.

He picked up the pail of watery urine.

The door was pushed in an inch and stopped by the chair. Somebody was bellowing outside.

"Help me, Comrades!" he shouted into the gap.

The door crashed as two men broke the back of the fragile chair. Tarp would remember their faces after—sweating, intense, the faces of good men trying to do good—and then he looked beyond them and saw the poet.

"Fire!" Tarp bellowed, and he threw the pail of liquid over the heads of the first two men and directly at the slender intellectual.

The smoke and the smell in the room were bad, and the first two men covered their noses with one hand while they grabbed him with the other and pushed him out; one of them stayed long enough to look around so that he could make a full report of it later.

"Fire, fire!" Tarp was shouting as he came rushing out of the room, trailing wisps of plastic poison, and as he came past the poet he brought his left fist up solidly into the abdomen and felt the young man fold up like an ironing board. Tarp wrapped his arms around him and dragged the young man along. "Victim of the fire," he cried. "Make room—make room!"

He was looking for the other man, the thick one, the capable one; but he was not there. Perhaps he had called for help. There were a dozen other people in the room, however, and more looking in the doorway from the balcony. Tarp shoved through them. With his left hand, he was trying to find his gun on the young man. "Make room!" He pushed people back, but nobody seemed to care; they wanted to get past him so they could see what was going on.

He laid the young man down on the floor of the balcony, just under the big bulletin board of the Committee for the Defense of the Revolution.

"Victim of the fire," he said to half a dozen people who came out of nowhere to stand around. "Smoke inhalation."

"You were inside, Comrade?"

"The first to arrive. He was smoking in bed."

"In *la ciderista*'s bed?" They began to look wide-eyed at each other at the thought of the young man in Juana's bed.

"Open his shirt," Tarp said. The young man was still unconscious. Tarp took off his shoes. "Make him cool!" he said. He backed away down the balcony with the shoes in his hands. The crowd went on growing; when he reached the stairs, there were people coming from the floors above and below, and the sick-animal wail of a fire truck was rising from the street. Tarp crouched in a doorway and put the shoes on without tying them and then bounded down the stairs feeling the shoes pinch and trying to ignore the discomfort.

He cleaned himself at a tin wall fountain and shaved at a public restroom, where an old black attendant found a discarded razor for him in the trash.

"On the move?" the old man said.

"Waiting for my ship to load."

"A sailor. You are not from Havana, I can tell."

"From Camagücy."

"Ah." He took a cigarette butt from a plastic bag. "I was in Camagücy once. That was before Fidel." He lit the butt. "It was hard to be a black man in Cuba then. Now it is all right to be a black man." He puffed. "You were very drunk last night?"

Tarp tried to smile. "Do I look it?"

"Too much rum and just enough woman, that is how you look." He laughed, coughed on the smoke, drew the butt down to a fiery circle between his dark fingers. He wore a sweat-stained old T-shirt, and hanging around his neck was a string with a little bag that rested just in the hollow of his clavicle. *Santería*, Tarp thought. *The old religion. Magic. It must be interesting, believing in both* santería *and the revolution.* "You are happy in Havana now?" Tarp said as he wiped his hand on a paper towel.

"Very happy."

"Nowhere you want to go anymore?"

Tarp made a move to throw the towel away, but the old man took it and smoothed it over his thigh. "I was in Florida once. That was in 1937. No, there is nowhere I want to go."

"What was Florida like?"

"It was another place where it was not good to be a black man." He put the smoothed-out towel to dry with half a dozen others.

"I have no money to give," Tarp said.

"I know. You are a sailor."

"I will trade shirts with you, if you like."

They traded T-shirts. The old man studied himself in Juana's bright-colored shirt and was pleased.

Tarp made his way to the harbor and stayed on the move, not lingering in one place for long and never going back over the same route because he feared the police would notice him. Idle men stood out in Havana. At seven o'clock he had located the Angolan Memories Cafe, and he walked along opposite it. There was Repin, sitting on a bench and reading a Russian newspaper so that nobody would doubt that he was Russian. When he saw Tarp he made no sign, but he got up and walked along the promenade and then turned up a street of very old merchants' houses and went into a yard full of trucks. Tarp followed him and found him sitting in a big black car.

"Get on the floor," Repin said. Tarp got in and crouched down; Repin signaled to the driver and they headed for the center of the city. After ten minutes Repin let him get off the floor and sit back with him.

"Two things," Repin said. "First, the beautiful woman you were with at the ballet. Her name is Juana Marino."

"I know."

"She is a lieutenant in the KGB."

Tarp watched a water sprinkler playing like a fountain over a beautiful lawn. "She acted as if she were anti-Castro."

Repin shrugged. "Her father is a *niño*—Spaniard from their civil war. She is Moscow born. Moscow educated. She could have a great future." His eyes glittered at Tarp. "She has great breasts."

Tarp watched as they drove slowly past lovely old houses set back from the street, their lawns tended, their plantings brilliant with flowers. "You think she is one of Maxudov's?"

"I do not know. I do not know her father. He might be Telyegin's man, but maybe not. She is a KGB probe in an anti-Castro cell; whether she is also an agent for Maxudov remains to be found out."

"She can identify me. Fingerprints in her apartment. On my gun."

"She has your gun?"

Tarp nodded.

"You spent the night in her apartment?"

He nodded again.

Repin breathed deeply. A self-satisfied little smile appeared.

"When I was young . . . Well. You understand. We have our nights, eh?" He put his hands on his knees and sat upright, as if he wanted to make it clear that they should stick to business. "What do we need to do?" he said.

"We need to cover my tracks." Tarp looked out at the pleasant streets, the color, the sedate old houses. "You said there were two things. What's the second?"

"My agent thinks he has something. I have a message from him. He thinks he will have something tomorrow."

"About what?"

"About the plutonium, he thinks."

"Here in Cuba?"

"He would not say. He does this for the money, you understand. He is very close-mouthed."

They rode without speaking for some minutes. Tarp roused himself and said, "This is what I need. First, a gun like the one I left in her apartment—a Colt twenty-two Woodsman. Second, a team to go in and sanitize her place, wipe out every trace of me. Third, a safe house where I can interrogate her."

"Oh, that is all?"

"Are you being sarcastic?"

"Me? Sarcastic? Why should Repin be sarcastic, when all an American wants is a gun in a Socialist country, the use of a team of experts who are not supposed to exist, and permission to enter a nonexistent but secret location?" He sat back and folded his hands over his expensive waistcoat. "When?"

"Tonight. The team has to go in and plant the gun and clean the apartment while I interrogate her."

"That is not easy."

"Of course it isn't easy."

"Moscow would not be happy."

"Moscow would not be happy if it rained loaves of bread."

Repin sighed. "You are very crass sometimes. Let's have a drink."

"My place or yours?"

Repin gave him a disgusted look. "I am taking you to a place." He looked at Tarp's stained T-shirt, the woman's stretch slacks he wore. "We will perhaps find you some clothes. You look absurd. Truly absurd. Do you ever see me look like that? Of course not." Repin fingered the lapel of his coat. "London. The very best. I dress carefully, always. But you! These clothes are ridiculous. It is a wonder you were not stopped by the police and arrested as a pervert." He seemed genuinely annoyed. They drove the rest of the way in silence.

It was a scruffy little suite of rooms next to a fire station and above a hardware store that had cockfighting in the basement. Repin said it had been offered to him by a Party official who thought he might need a "discreet localization for assignations." Even Cuban bureaucrats talked that way now, it seemed. Repin sent the driver out to buy clothes for Tarp and then he busied himself behind a screen with a bottle of vodka. He had left his expensive London jacket over the back of a chair, and Tarp looked at it. It was a beautiful suit, indeed; a Bond Street tailor's label was sewn under the pocket. At the neck, however, there was another, much smaller label that read "Hire Attire. Gentleman's Preowned Suitings."

When Repin came in with two full glasses of vodka and the bottle tucked under his arm, Tarp was looking at the Hire Attire label. Repin stiffened, got red, then laughed. "Well, so you found it. So? My pension is not as generous as it ought to be."

Tarp put the jacket back over the chair. "Gentleman's preowned suitings?" he said with a little smile as he took the vodka.

"The perfect solution to anonymity, my friend. Try them! After all, what better protective coloration could an agent want than wearing some dead man's clothes?"

They drank. Tarp chose not to think about wearing a dead man's clothes as a metaphor for the way they spent their lives.

CHAPTER 9

She sat across the metal table from him, her face bare of makeup, her arms bare and strong and her hands folded on the table's edge just between her breasts.

"Do you understand, Juana?" Tarp said in Spanish.

"No, I do not understand." She had given up being angry. Now she seemed chastened. "I understand nothing."

"Are you supposed to understand, do you think?"

"Maybe not." There had been a slight tremble in her lower lip at first, but that was gone now. "I can accept orders without question."

"Good." He put cigarettes on the table next to a cheap notebook and pen. "Good." It was impossible not to play a part when he did this sort of thing, because he had watched so many interrogators and had been an interrogator so often himself. It was difficult to keep from being so detached from the role that he would stop monitoring himself. "Who am I?" he said.

"I do not know anymore."

"Who do you think I am?"

"I—" She bit her lip and colored. "I thought at first that you were the American."

"The American?"

"The one we thought had come ashore. His boat exploded off the coast. There was a circular for the *cideristas*."

He tapped his fingers together—not his own gesture, but that of a Frenchman in the old days just after Dien Bien Phu. "That was a man named Robert Plumb." The name was that of the blond young man from the Agency whom he had left on his boat.

"I never heard that name."

"Of course not. Go on."

"Then I thought that you were from Moscow."

"Yes?"

"One of us."

"Us?"

"The *sluzhba*."

"I see. And?"

"And—and that is as far as I got."

"I see. So, you thought I was KGB, but you did not identify yourself to me."

"I was not sure!"

"Nor did you try to help me."

"I did!" They were both thinking, he was sure, of her bed. "I did not let the anti-Castro people have you."

"But you did not help me."

Tarp rubbed his eyes with his fingers and then looked at her around the hand whose fingers rested on the bridge of his nose. He looked and looked; then he got up and went out of the plain room and waited for three minutes.

They were in a house on the western edge of Havana. It had once been rather elegant; now an old couple took care of it and pretended to be the only ones there, and the KGB used it when they wanted to get away from their Cuban allies.

He went back into the room and sat down again across the table from her. "Do you know what is happening in Moscow?" he said.

She seemed genuinely confused. "Politically?" she said.

"Oh, come! Surely you know better than that! Juana, we spent ten years and a great deal of money training you, and the best you can say is, 'Politically?' Come, come—in the service, Juana. Do you know what is happening in the service?"

"I do not know."

"Truly? You mean there is no gossip in Havana, Juana? Are you cut off from all communication? Have you taken a vow of silence?"

"I hear very little."

"From your father?"

"My father is a translator, nothing more. If there is some

gossip I am supposed to have heard, I would not have heard it from him.''

He got up, paced around the table as he had seen it done so often, as he had done it so often, and stood behind her. ''You were trained at Brest-Litovsk?''

She nodded.

''Many who came from that school show a devotion—a personal, almost a fanatical devotion—to Comrade Mensenyi. Our good Comrade Mensenyi, who has so many devoted followers, even in Cuba and South America. Are you a devoted follower of Mensenyi's, Juana?''

She took a deep breath. ''I am loyal to the Party.''

''That goes without saying. Do you have a personal loyalty to Mensenyi?''

''We are not supposed to have personal loyalties.'' Her voice was so soft that he could not have heard it from a few feet farther away. ''We are not supposed to have feelings.''

''Tut-tut, that is almost Stalinist. You are out of touch, Juana. 'Agents are human beings'—Directive four oh nine point seven.''

''There is no such directive. You are making fun of me.''

''Are we *not* human beings, then?''

''*I love you!*'' She twisted in her chair and shouted it at him. She caught him off guard—her naked face, her passionate voice; if he had really been a KGB officer trying to trap her, he would almost have trapped himself. Tarp took a step away. ''Are you 'personally loyal' to me, then?''

''I don't even know who you are!''

''And yet you *love* me! Wonderful!'' He moved around the table. ''I told you when this interview began, I hold the rank of colonel; I am of the service; I am in Cuba covertly. That is all you need to know. We are in a KGB safe house—you know it, I suppose; you are of the service. I have been vouched for.''

An old crony of Repin's had brought her to the house and had made a great show of authenticating Tarp's identity.

He sat down across from her again. ''Juana.'' He folded his hands under his chin. ''There is great trouble in Moscow. *Great* trouble.''

''The man you bowed to at the ballet.'' She was limp; her face was bleak. ''He is here because of it, isn't he?''

''How do you know?''

"I saw his file on a desk at Kepel's."

General Kepel was the KGB chief in Cuba. "Kepel is not your immediate officer." That was a guess, but it was an informed one.

"No." She picked at one fingernail, destroying the cuticle. She held it up. "I love you. Look what love makes me do."

"I hope it helps you to tell the truth."

"It doesn't help me do anything. It is more like being sick."

"What were you doing at General Kepel's?"

"He has me report to him once a week."

"Why?"

She glanced at him bitterly. "Because he wants to screw me, what else?"

"That would be a way to greater responsibility," Tarp said equably.

"I do not mean to get ahead on my back, thank you."

"Well, so you were at Kepel's, and you saw a file there and connected it with the man at the ballet. What has that to do with what I have been saying?"

"Kepel handed the file to an assistant and said, 'Take all this Moscow woe from wit away.' That is all." She bit her cuticle. "*Woe From Wit* is a play, you know."

"I had heard of it."

"You are making fun of me again."

"So from that one remark you immediately concluded that Moscow was sending a man to cause trouble for Kepel, and then he showed up at the ballet and you saw me bow to him, and everything fit together?"

"Yes."

"You're lying."

"I am not."

"You are! You lie constantly. Have you not lied to me since that first time? Lies, all lies—"

"I have not—I swear!"

"This excrement about love, this nonsense, these lies—"

"The truth, this is truth!"

They both began to shout. She was weeping, but he had the feeling that the tears were at least partly a device, like the word *love*; she could use tears as a kind of armor, he thought, as some people use an appearance of weakness as a strength. Oddly, he found himself admiring her. She was very tough.

He went on at her for another forty-five minutes. It was more than enough time for the sanitation team to switch guns and clean her apartment of his traces, but he kept on because he hoped that she would tell him something useful. He even hoped—laughing inwardly at himself for the hope—that she would prove to be innocent of any connection with "Maxudov," the submarine, or the plutonium.

She sat limp in her chair. Her hair was lank; there were patches of sweat under her eyes and a sheen, like the result of fever, on her cheeks.

"Have a cigarette," Tarp said. He had said nothing for several minutes and they had both sat there very quietly. Now he could see she was cold, for goose bumps were forming on her arms.

"I don't really smoke," she said, but she reached for the pack and took one. Her hands were shaking so violently that he had to light the match for her. He didn't think she was frightened so much as she was reacting to her own exercise of will for the past two hours. She had been consistent. He wished they had not been to bed together, because his objectivity was affected, although whether for or against her he was not sure.

"You would do better not to smoke at all," he said.

"May I walk around?"

"Of course."

She got up. She held her right forearm across her belly and her left forearm vertically from her hip, the cigarette in that hand. She looked thinner, less full-breasted. There was a cot against the far wall and she stood looking at it. "What do you do now," she said, "rape me?"

He hesitated. "I suppose that has been done in this room." He sounded like a pedant.

"It would be such a good way to show what you think of love." She had insisted throughout that she loved him. He believed that she believed she did, if only because such a belief was convenient to her. She blew out cigarette smoke and turned partly toward him. She was wearing a sleeveless top that was a little loose and that was far from new. She shivered.

"You use the word *love* too easily," he said. "I do not love you, Juana, no." He thought of saying *not yet* but knew it would be insincere.

She looked at him, shrugged, shivered. She dropped the cig-

arette on the floor and ground it with the ball of her flat shoe.
"Say that I am infatuated with you, then."

"You are under great stress. It is understandable that you
would think yourself infatuated."

"I know many men. None of them infatuate me."

"But you think I do."

"I know it."

"That is the result of stress."

"Why do you keep turning me off? I would think it would be
a great sign of success, to have your victim infatuated with
you."

"You are not my victim."

"Oh, yes! From the very first. I thought you were *my* victim.
And all the time you were waiting to bring me here! I'm quite a
fool, hey? Well, so what do you do? Turn me over to the DGI?
Inform on me? Send me back to Moscow?"

"Sit down, Juana." He closed the notebook and laid the pen
on top of it as if that part of the interrogation were over. She sat
in the chair rather primly. Her shoulders were rounded forward.
One brassiere strap showed beyond the edge of the sleeveless
blouse.

"When you first met me on the beach, you were suspicious
of me. You thought I might be an American spy. Only a small
suspicion, you say, so you arranged to meet me again. We went
to the ballet, we danced, we went back to your apartment. You
found my gun and my green card; then you thought I just might
be a DGI agent who was trying to penetrate the anti-Castro cell
of which you are a member for the KGB. So you checked the
card and found it was not really mine, and then you thought
again that I might be an American—except you had seen me
bow to the troublemaker from Moscow. So here we are now,
and now you know that I, too, am a troublemaker from Moscow who is trying to solve a problem inside the KGB. So you
ask me what I am going to do with you. Why should I do anything with you? You have not betrayed the service. You have
not behaved badly. In fact, I think you have done very well."

"Should I be grateful to you for that?"

He stood up. "There is a traitor in the upper echelon of the
service. We think he has corrupted part of the service here in
Cuba. Now, if you found out that one of the people you work
with had been corrupted, what would you do?"

"I would need proof."

"If you had the proof."

"Have you got proof?"

"That is not the point. This is hypothetical."

She managed to make herself look ugly. "Oh, well, hypothetically—if it were proven, I would go to Kepel, I suppose."

"Suppose Kepel could not be trusted."

"I would go over Kepel's head."

"To whom?"

"To . . ." She bit her lip. She dragged her teeth over her lower lip as if she were pulling fruit from a tough rind. "My God."

"An expression that has survived despite socialism. Yes, my God. You are far down in the levels of the service; you are insulated from Moscow by a bureaucracy that may be corrupt. You may yourself have been used by the corrupt ones without knowing it."

"*Have* I?"

"This is only hypothetical."

"Well, what is real? I don't like hypothetical; I like reality! What is real?"

He stood with his hands on the back of his own chair, looking down at her. "What is real is that atomic materials have been stolen in the Soviet Union and sent to Cuba by submarine. *Stolen*—not sent because of any authorized plan. *Stolen.*"

"*Why?*"

"I wish I knew."

"My God! If the Americans ever found atomic weapons here they would bomb us off the face of the earth! They're only waiting for the opportunity! Jesus God! What sort of lunatic would expose us to a danger like that?" She looked fiercely protective. "It isn't Fidel."

"No, I don't think so."

"It's an American trick, that's what it is. Have you looked into that? Are you sure this isn't a CIA trick?"

"That is a very interesting possibility. Yes, I intend to look into it, as a matter of fact. But—you see why I am in Cuba."

She hesitated. "If this is the truth, yes. Of course."

"You see why I have to work outside regular channels."

"If—" She put her face in her hands for a moment, then

raised her head. Her eyes were wide. "It's like being crazy! How do I know now what the truth is?"

"Isn't that always a problem?"

"No!" She stood up. "No! That is the one thing I have always had—certainty. I trust the one above me and the one below me and . . . You know how it is. If you take that away from us . . ." Her nostrils widened. "Everything becomes hypothetical."

"I want you to work for me."

"I am forgiven, then?" She said it with a sneer.

"I will try to get some authentication from Moscow, so you will feel a little less insane. It will mean your staying as you are, doing your usual work, but reporting to me through a direct line. I will give you codes, a point of contact. You will have two missions: to find out what you can about atomic materials here; and to test the service above and below you for corruption. Will you do it?"

"I can love you?" She said that with a sneer, too.

"I cannot order your feelings."

She moved away from the tables, hugging herself with her arms and protecting the bare upper arms with her long brown hands. She walked the length of the room and looked at the iron cot again and then came back, paused, and walked the two steps to him and rested her forehead on his shoulder, her arms still folded, as somebody who was too hot might have rested her forehead on a cool wall. "Come home with me," she said.

"I can't. It's too dangerous now."

"Where will you stay?"

He dodged the question. She was right: it was like insanity, when nobody could be trusted. "I have a place."

"For how long?"

"As long as I need."

"Let me come with you."

"No."

They kissed. It was a bleak sort of kiss.

He took her to the door, where Repin's KGB crony was waiting with a car to take her back.

"When will I see you?" she said.

"Tomorrow. I'll tell you where and what time. I'll use the name *mariposa*."

"A flower?" She laughed, for the first time. "My steel flower."

After she was gone, Repin came from an upper floor. "Well, how did it go?" he said in Russian.

"I think it's all right. She'll need some verification. Maybe you can go through her father—find somebody he trusts and *we* trust and have him send her the word. Can you get messages back to Moscow?"

"So far."

"Get on it, will you?"

"And who would you like me to contact? Andropov?"

"If he's the only one who qualifies."

Repin was not amused. He went to an ugly credenza and took out a bottle and glasses. "She did not report you to her KGB officer here, at any rate. She took the green card to a friend at her local police station; we traced that an hour ago. The friend did the comparison for her as a favor—she had your thumbprint on a cigarette package—so that never went any further. Still, she was seen with you at the ballet, and if her anti-Castro friends are picked up for some reason, they can identify you from her apartment. So, I think she ought to report to her case officer that she met you and went out with you once and then lost sight of you. That way she is covered if something comes back."

"It means that they'll identify me."

"Not for a while. But it is inevitable, yes."

"I suppose." Tarp accepted a glass. "It makes me an instant target, unfortunately."

CHAPTER 10

In the morning, Repin came to see him before breakfast. He was wearing a natty blazer and two-tone shoes, but he looked dyspeptic.

"What's the matter?" Tarp said as soon as he saw him.

"Matter? What could be the matter?" He put the packet of identification papers on the table and Tarp picked them up. He had brought them from the *Scipio* and Repin had had a visa and an entry stamp put into the passport.

"What's the matter?" he said again as he examined them.

"The ballet mistress snores. Nothing."

"What's the matter?"

Repin scowled. Then, after seconds of scowling, he put a hand into the side pocket of the blazer and took out a plastic bag. In it was a piece of paper that had been water-soaked and dried, and now it was thickened and crumpled. He put it on the table and Tarp could see faded writing:

Doctor Bonano
to
Schneider, BA chem
via
?

"Well?"

"You see? It is nothing. I showed it to you only because you pestered me."

"What is it?"

Repin made a face as if he had smelled something bad. "My

contact turned up dead.'' He nodded at the paper. "In his pocket.''

"Murdered?''

"He was thirty-four; what do you think, he had a heart attack? In the water. Head crushed.'' He put both hands into the blazer's pockets, the thumbs jutting forward. He was wearing a scarf in the open collar of a white shirt and he looked like a stage Englishman. "They say he was playing with somebody's wife. Maybe. But, you know, in this business . . .'' He made a face again. "Still, it was very crudely done. Not Department Five. Amateur work. Not professional *mokrie dela*.''

Tarp looked at the paper. " 'BA.' Buenos Aires.''

"I'm not a geographer.'' Repin sounded like an elitist discussing a lower class.

"Argentina is on the submarine's route. Or at least it came close.'' He waited for Repin to speak, but the old man was stubbornly looking away from him. "Since the Falklands mess, Argentina might be interested in atomic weapons.''

"The plutonium thefts started before the Falklands war.'' He sounded angry—old-man angry, petulant.

"You can't ignore this, you know.''

Repin swiveled his head slowly to look at him. "What are the possibilities? One, the paper means nothing and my contact was killed by his lover's husband—nothing means nothing. Two, the paper means something, but he was murdered by the husband—a coincidence too good to be believed; something means nothing. Three, the death is *mokrie dela*, but the assassin overlooked the piece of paper, which is unbelievable—something means nothing again. Four, the death is *mokrie dela* and the paper is a trap. Out of those four possibilities, only one suggests the paper is any use to us.'' He shook his head. "One in four is bad mathematics.''

"Five,'' Tarp said, "the paper is genuine and he was murdered because he was your agent but not because of the paper and so they didn't look for it. What do you think?''

"I think nothing.'' He looked directly at Tarp; his eyes were fierce, seemingly a darker blue than usual. "You know this work as well as I do. There are times when it is not good to think because it is too soon.''

"But now we have to think.'' Tarp touched the paper, and it

spun on the corner of a fold. "They could have killed him and missed the paper. Oversights happen."

"But you cannot count on them."

"But killing a man so you can plant a message on him is extreme. Department Five is cautious, in my experience. Crazy, but cautious. It's like the CIA and Castro; they had that insane idea to make his beard fall out, and they took months just talking about it. Crazy *and* cautious. No, if DGI or KGB killed your man, it was because he was a spy. But neither DGI nor KGB is in on the Maxudov business; the only ones who are are Maxudov's own people. So if they did it, they probably did it quickly—reflexively. *Defensively.* And then, did they have time to think out what it meant, set up a trap, and plant the paper on him? How much time did they have, anyway? When did he die?"

"Last night. About two in the morning."

"When did you see him alive?"

"Me, before you came to Havana; one of my people, yesterday."

"So they had—a few hours. In a few hours, they made up a plan and carried it through? Maybe. Yes, it could be done. If there weren't too many people involved. If they didn't have to check back with Moscow."

Repin's smile was thin and sour. He hated bureaucracy, even though he had ended up as a bureaucrat. "It isn't like shooting the pope, you know," he said heavily.

"Well, you'll admit at least that the message could be genuine."

"How did it get into the pocket?"

"He was carrying it when he was killed, what else? Whoever killed him did it on impulse—got frightened, ran away. Or killed him in such a way that the body couldn't be searched. Maybe he fell into the water from a height."

"You should write for the films."

"I'm thinking of possibilities."

"You are persuading yourself of a fantasy."

"Is the paper in his handwriting?"

"We think not."

"How did he communicate with you?"

"Code through a drop."

"This is not code."

"Obviously."

"Somebody passed him a paper with the writing already on it; he was killed before he had a chance to encode it."

Repin bounced twice on the balls of his feet. He was wearing white-and-tan shoes with lavishly fringed tongues that danced in the sunlight. "This was a good man. He would not have kept such a paper very long. Minutes. Seconds. He would read it, then destroy it."

"It was dark."

Repin nodded. "It was dark; he took the paper, put it in his pocket—he will carry it only until he reaches a light—but he is killed even before that, so very quick, within seconds—" He looked at Tarp.

"Maybe the one who gave him the paper killed him."

"Meaning that it is probably a trap. Now we are both writing films." He sounded more cheerful, however. "I knew he had a source. He had been asking about plutonium and submarines. It was down around the docks. He sent a message two days ago he thought he would have something last night. You know what that says to me? I am such an idiot!" Repin struck himself on the side of the head and his straw hat fell off. He looked at it and then kicked it.

"Well?"

"He was waiting for somebody on a ship—what do you think? I am an idiot! And he was waiting because it was probably a ship that docked yesterday. Yah! My brain is turning to dust with age."

"What would you do, question every crewmember of every ship that docked? It could be a fisherman—there are thousands in Cuba. Or it could have been somebody on a plane, Repin."

"He was killed at the docks."

"So?"

"Well." Repin stuck out his lips in that characteristic expression of disgust. "Well, there he is, then, down near the docks in the dark. He meets the contact. The contact hands over the paper, my man hands over the money to pay for it. He turns away—*ka!*" Repin raised a hand, the fingers open as if he had just let the man's life fall; his eyes followed it as it tumbled into the imagined water. "There is the body, the smashed head, the paper." He folded his arms. "Maybe."

"So the message could be genuine."

"Could be. Not the likeliest possibility. Still . . ."

"Well?"

"I am very bothered by the matter of organization. In Moscow, we know we have Maxudov. A man of intelligence, power, passion. In Cuba, maybe we have half a dozen people Maxudov has corrupted. But do they kill for him? It is very, very difficult to get a man to kill for you. Unless he is entirely yours. And it is my feeling that Maxudov does not get very close to these people. He corrupts them a little, buys them off. But there is no belief here, no ideology, no passion. Let us say, for example, that I have decided to steal art works from the Hermitage. Fine. I bribe two guards; I bribe a trucker; I bribe some border guards. And so on. Right out of the Soviet Union to, let us say, a dealer in Bonn. Now, you find out about it. One of the people I have bribed realizes that you know. What is he going to do? Kill you to protect me? Of course not. He is going to cover his own backside with both hands and hope I fall down dead."

"He might kill me to protect himself."

"He might. Not likely."

"So you don't think your man was killed by Maxudov's people?"

"I think nothing. I am *puzzled*."

Tarp took an orange from a basket and began to peel it. "Suppose your man had not been killed. Suppose you got this same message in code from him. What then?"

Repin took a step, pulling at his lower lip. "I would have taken it rather seriously."

"And so your man's getting killed actually lowers the likelihood of somebody's trying to feed us."

"Yes, yes, I see what you mean." Repin sat down. "If they want to give us false data, they would better have sent it through him."

"Yes."

Repin grunted. He picked up the piece of paper, dropped it. "I don't like any of it."

"Neither do I."

"For once, I would like the bureaucracy. To check everything."

"We have to check everything ourselves."

Repin's eyes glinted. "Buenos Aires?"

"I'd think so. If Schneider is a name there."

"It is. I already checked. There are a number of Schneiders, but only one in chemicals. Schneider Chemical, Limited."

"And Doctor Bonano?"

"Makes no sense."

"Well?"

"There is one medical doctor named Bonano in Havana. He is head of an abortion clinic."

Tarp ate part of the orange. "No, that makes no sense. Some other Doctor Bonano, then. Maybe in Buenos Aires."

"You will go?"

"Yes. On my way to Moscow."

"They are likely waiting there with one of their famous death squads."

"Maybe."

"How do you want it done?"

Tarp made a neat little pile of the orange peelings. "Get a place on a flight tomorrow to Mexico City. Order a passport in the same name from the Fourteenth Department here—my height and so on. Make some show of it. Make a separate reservation from Mexico City to Buenos Aires."

"You will take these flights?"

"Of course not."

"How will you go?"

"I don't think I'll tell you."

"I think you are wise. It is humiliating, but you are wise."

"I'll need clothes."

"Yes, yes—at once."

"I'll need a communication link."

"Very well, but only after I leave Havana. I will give you a contact in Europe. Then we will work on getting you into the Soviet Union, assuming . . ."

"Yes, assuming I get out of Argentina. Yes."

Tarp met Juana in the Plaza Marti at four o'clock, where they strolled in the sunshine with other couples, old and young—a boy going slowly on a bicycle so he could stay even with a girl, a woman in a wheelchair being pushed by an old man. Pigeons rose, swung across a quadrant of sky, settled again.

"I am going away," he said.

"When?" She sounded listless. She looked as if she had slept badly.

"Tomorrow," he lied.

"Where?"

"I can't tell you. Have you learned anything?"

She shook her head.

"Will there be any trouble because of me?"

She shook her head again.

"The man at the ballet will get a message to you. To authenticate me. Then he'll tell you how we will communicate."

She shrugged. The conversation seemed to bore her. They walked another twenty steps before she said anything, and then her voice was thin. "I want to tell you something," she said, seeming both defiant and afraid of him.

"Well?"

She folded her arms over her breasts. "I want you to understand that I am ashamed of myself. For last night. For—" She shut her mouth tight as somebody walked passed them, as if she feared to be overheard. "For saying that I loved you."

"Well, at least today you know better."

She laughed, and a flight of pigeons went up as if the sound had frightened them. "No, today I don't know better. It's *that* I am ashamed of." He saw her watch another woman who was crossing the square ahead of them; she seemed to be assessing the other woman, perhaps comparing herself. "I am not a child. I am a grown woman. I have had lovers. I have been infatuated. I was married for two years to a beautiful pig. I know what love is supposed to be like. I know what it *is* like." She took her eyes away from the other woman. "It is not like this sickness."

"What do you want me to do?" he said.

"What can you do? You are going away, that is good." She hugged herself more tightly. "You don't love me."

"No."

They walked a few steps. Her head was down now, as if she feared to stumble. "I must see you again," she said.

"I'm not likely to come back to Havana."

"Then I will come where you are. Moscow. Wherever."

"Maybe you'll get over the sickness."

"Or maybe I can give it to you." The feeble joke seemed to cheer her a little. She ran ahead of him to a handcart where a woman was selling ices, and then they went on around the plaza licking the ice out of the cold plastic cups. When he got some on his chin, she laughed at him, and she was transformed—simple, delighted, loving—and he was hurt by a realization of the price he was making her pay, the price he always made people pay, for the way he lived.

"Listen to me," he said. "I'm going to give you a way to reach me if the regular route breaks down. Memorize it; don't ever put it in writing. Don't ever use it except in an emergency." He gave her an address in Paris. "Anything that comes there addressed to Monsieur Chimère will get to me. Sign it 'Mimosa.' I'll know it's you."

"My problem would be to get it out of Cuba."

"You can manage that."

They had nothing more to talk about. She seemed angry again. He promised to see her again before he left Havana, knowing as he said it that he would not keep his promise.

CHAPTER 11

He took a bus to the airport in the twilight and bought a seat on the first outbound flight that had space. He used the Selous passport and had no trouble. He was wearing glasses and a rather silly mustache that had the odd effect of making him look both older and inconsequential.

The plane few to Jamaica. He went into the men's room there, got rid of the glasses and the mustache, and bought himself a flight bag and a sporty wind jacket in an airport shop. He booked himself on a flight to Rio; while he waited for it, he dialed a number in Mexico City.

"Five seven seven five," a masculine voice said in accented Spanish.

"I wanted Aatahualpa Curios."

"Correct."

"I'm looking for a one-armed buddha."

There was a pause, then laughter. "Is this who I think it is?" the voice said in American English.

"Probably."

"You looking for something with brass balls?"

"That's the one."

More laughter. "Hey, man, how the hell are you? Long time."

"Long, long time. Can we talk?"

"Maybe yes, maybe no. Uncle's got big ears. What can I do you for?"

"I need a piece. In Argentina."

"Argentina's a big country, m'friend."

"Name a place."

"Hold on." Silence. "I gotta think. Hold on." More silence. Then: "Fly to Santiago del Estero. Used to be able to get there from La Paz or Brasília. You'll be met. How do they recognize you?"

Tarp looked at the flight bag. "Brown shoulder bag. Cross on it in tape."

"Okay. Cash on delivery."

"Right."

"What's the purpose of this item you want?"

"Social work."

"Got you. They'll be looking for you. Hey, drop in ol' Mayhee-co sometime, you hear?"

"Will do."

"Nice to talk to you. Hey, you ever see any of the guys?"

It was not like Tarp to hesitate, but that took him a fraction of a second. "There's nobody left to see."

"I thought— When I left, there were some. Weren't there?"

"Later, there weren't."

Another silence. Then the man at the other end said, "I thought I might go look at this new memorial in D.C., you know? Look for some names."

"They wouldn't be there."

"Yeah. Well, I sort of thought that. Well. Hey, listen, drop in sometime, hey? We'll tip a few tequilas, talk over—some things. Hey?"

"Yeah."

He bought a role of plastic tape to mark the shoulder bag, then ate, read a Spanish paper and a French paper, then flew to Rio and slept until morning, when another plane flew him to Brasília for the change to Aerolineas Argentinas. At a little after noon, he came down the steps to the dry, hot field at Santiago.

A middle-aged woman had a 9mm Luger for him in an ancient shoulder holster. She led him into a baggage area, where they stood fifty feet from the clattering belt that was bringing bags past a few travelers. She handed him the gun in a paper bag.

"Cartridges?"

"There are eleven in the bag. All we had."

"Are they the right caliber?"

"My husband said so."

The gun was too big and too heavy, but there was nothing he could do about it. He gave her money. "Is it hard to get guns in Buenos Aires?" he said.

"No harder than here, maybe."

"Not so hard, then?"

She seemed very ladylike. "Nothing is hard if you have the money," she said. He thought that perhaps she and her husband had had money and had fallen on bad times. In Argentina that was not so unusual.

There was a night train to Buenos Aires. The train itself looked well intentioned but inadequate, which was perhaps a fitting symbol for a country in which so many things had started out well and gone so wrong. His sleeping car had once, perhaps, been up to the standards of a run-of-the-mill European train, but that would have been many years before. Now, layers of paint had been allowed to pile up on the inner surfaces, obscuring all detail; the sink gave only a trickle of water; the bed, when folded down, made noises as if it might collapse altogether. Through some mix-up, he had not gotten the private compartment he had paid for but was put instead into a small double with another man. When he showed his ticket, the conductor explained with some asperity that there were no private compartments on this train and it had been foolish of him to try to buy one. If he wanted a single, he would have to take the noon train tomorrow.

"This will be splendid," he said.

Tarp was uneasy about the gun. He had it in the flight bag, but he thought it might be safer worn under his arm. Any question he had about it was removed some minutes after he went into the compartment, when his companion removed his own coat, shook out a sporting newspaper, and sat by the window with a cigar. He was wearing an enormous automatic under his arm.

"Cigar?" he said amiably to Tarp.

"I don't smoke."

"Mistake. Keeps off viruses."

His cigar would have kept off anything. Tarp went into the corridor and watched the Santiago suburbs groan by. A solemn child was waving at the train. Tarp waved back, but the child's seriousness did not change. A dog watched him. Two women watched, so still they might have been frozen. He saw another child, standing under a wall with a faded message urging power to Perón, the child and the message like the national hope and the national ghost. Tarp supposed that he could have seen these things anywhere, but his ideas of Argentina were much colored by what he knew of the country's past—its seedy fascism during World War Two, its sanctification of Perón's wives. Thus, Tarp saw his preconceptions: a sad, rather baffled country where things had been done slightly wrong, not wrong enough to bring revolution, but a little wrong again and again and again, so that now it had its shaky military *junta,* its memories of Perón and Evita, and the Falklands war like a hangover.

"You *really* do not smoke?" his companion said. He had come out of their compartment to join Tarp in the corridor.

"No."

"But you used to smoke, eh?"

"A little."

"And you gave it up because of the propaganda, eh?"

"No."

"Of course you did. Where are you from, Paraguay?"

"France."

The man was instantly suspicious. Argentina had wasted a century trying to be France, an effort that made it both envious and paranoid. On the other hand, the man was certainly aware of France's help in the Falklands (here, the Malvinas) war. Thus, he was both suspicious and grateful, or about as amiable as a panhandler.

"You sound like a Paraguayan."

"France."

"What do you think of Argentina?"

Tarp had bought an American travel book to read on the plane. He knew what the correct answer to the question was. "It is the best country in South America."

The man nodded. "It is our gift for facing reality. The other countries, they are dreamers, madmen, idiots, whatever—one way or another, they do not face reality."

In Santiago, Tarp had already heard a couple of songs about the Malvinas war. They were nostalgic and patriotic. They did not, in his view, face reality.

He sat in the dining car, inevitably, with the same men and two others much like him. They were younger than Tarp, rather hearty, almost swaggerers. *Machismo* ran very deep here, and with it a suggestion of sexual uneasiness and a resulting over-playing of the sexual hand: men were too much men; women were so feminine they made the teeth ache. These men were loud and rather pleasant, except that they used the word *faggot* for everything humane and different. The British who had con-quered the Malvinas were faggots; liberals were faggots; news-paper editorial writers were faggots; Americans were faggots.

"What do you do?" his compartment mate said.

"I'm a salesman."

They all thought that was good. What did he sell?

"Computers."

Computers were fantastic, they all agreed.

When the meal was over, Tarp had not touched his huge steak.

"Not good enough?" one said. "Mine was fantastic!"

"Argentine beef is the best in the world!" said another.

"I'm a vegetarian," Tarp said.

He might as well have told them he was a faggot.

When he awoke in the morning, they were barreling through the outermost fringe of Buenos Aires. As he stepped around his sleepy companion so that he could shave and dress, he watched the landscape urbanize itself. It looked like Italy, he thought: put Mussolini's name where Perón's appeared and it could be suburban Naples thirty years ago.

"Buenos Aires is a beautiful city," the other man said with unnecessary force.

"So they say."

"See for yourself."

He gestured toward the slum beyond the window. Then, looking at the scene, he said, "Soon." Tarp smiled and took the Luger out of its paper bag and checked it over, making sure that the ammunition fit it before he put it away in the flight bag. The other man looked at him with something approaching ap-proval, as if he had made up for some of his losses of the night before.

Tarp stepped down from the train into a cool bath of morning air that smelled as sweet as a park full of flowers. He walked out of the huge old European station into streets where men in coveralls were hosing and sweeping in brilliant early sunlight. The air had just that edge of coolness that tells one it is not quite yet the warm season, or that the warm season has not quite ended. Yet the air was clean, almost pure, and it was possible to look for blocks down broad streets and see everything sharp-edged, handsome, pleasing because the air was thin. It was the kind of morning to make him smile.

Yes, it all looked very European to him. Handshakes in the street, fashionable women, nineteenth-century architecture. Like Turin or Lucerne; like parts of Paris, the later but not quite modern parts. He had coffee and wonderfully fresh, crusty croissants and watched people go by.

He found a small hotel beyond the city center and followed the desk clerk's directions to a men's shop, where he bought an Italianate sport coat and several shirts. He went to the Foreign Press Club to present his *Agence-Presse Europa* card and they told him he would have to get an authorization from the Ministry for News and Information; he followed their directions and found a room where, after being routed to three wrong offices, a man entered his name in a record and where he was given a very official piece of pasteboard that proclaimed him an "acceptable journalist."

"You are going to write about Argentina?" the official asked.

"I am working on a book."

"About Argentina?"

"About sport. Diversions. In our time, everything is play. I am writing a book about how people play." The ghost-written articles that had been published in Europe over the Selous name were all about sports.

"What will you write about in Argentina? Football? We missed the World Cup?" His native paranoia was showing.

"Trout fishing."

The man nodded. He seemed suddenly relieved. He looked at Tarp's press card, then at the "acceptable journalist" card he was about to sign, then up at Tarp. "There is no trout fishing around Buenos Aires, you know."

"I know." He did know, as a matter of fact, just as he knew where the fishing was in Switzerland and Yugoslavia and off the Bahía coast. "Lago Nahuel Huapí. Bariloche."

"Patagonia." The man seemed pleased with both of them. He held out the signed card. "If you need any help, making contacts, for example, please feel free to call on me. We want the foreign press to form the right opinions—the truth, of course—about Argentina.''

Juaquin Schneider was not a difficult man to find. He had an eighty-acre industrial park outside Buenos Aires, and his chemical plant took up most of the acreage. The name Schneider was painted in a special shade of blue on all the chemical tanks; the same blue and the same letters were on a large but tasteful sign at the entrance to the cómplex, as well as on the door and on objects in the offices—matchbooks, pens. The grounds around the plant were beautifully tailored.

Tarp drove out to look at the industrial park. It all seemed too easy. There were other Schneiders in Buenos Aires, and he hired a detective to follow up three of them, explaining that his wife was having an affair with somebody named Schneider. If the piece of paper in the dead man's pocket in Havana was genuine, then he supposed this Schneider was the obvious one, although the connection between plutonium and agricultural chemicals was not obvious at all. A day's nosing around Buenos Aires turned up nothing to change the profile of Schneider as a rich, powerful man who had made his money in fertilizers.

''Schneider?'' The speaker was one of many new acquaintances, a red-faced Englishman named Grice in the Foreign Press Club bar. Grice boasted that he had ridden out the Malvinas war better than the Argentine navy had, right here at this bar, and he knew more about what was what in the country than the government did. Or so he said. ''Of course I know Schneider. Know *of* Schneider, I mean. Very rich. Up to his oxters in agribusiness, although the real brains were his wife's. A Jewess, naturally. Dead now. Sure, I know who Schneider is. Why?''

''I am a little interested in him.'' Tarp had to remember to speak English with a slight French accent.

''Why? Let me be frank with you, my French friend, old *copain*, old ally—I don't give out information for free, you know; if it's a story, I want a share. There's actually a news service back in London that expects to hear from me once in a way.''

''I cannot give away my story.''

''Well, 'course not. No.'' The Englishman pulled at his nose with a thumb and finger as if he were popping his ears after a dive. "You ready for another?" He meant that he was ready to be bought another beer, which he downed with the gusto of a Falstaff.

"My pleasure," Tarp said.

"That's the spirit! Well, you have to understand, Frenchy, I need a little before we're done—human interest, anything of that sort—you're not into dirt, are you? Not one of the American supermarket rags, are you? 'Princess Di Pregnant by UFO,' that sort of tripe? I mean, we all have our standards, even poor old Grice. Well, this beer has bought you a swallow or two more of information, all right? On account, as it were? Dear me, I hope we're speaking the same language, you and I. Well, at any rate, about Schneider: he's second-generation Argentine, one of the fifty wealthiest sods in the country. Or was, three or four years ago. Papa came from Deutschland in the Weimar days—got out in time, I mean, before Hitler. Not a Jew, for all the present Schneider married one. But the old man—I mean, the one who emigrated from Weimar—was a nobody; it's the present Schneider who built the fortune." He drank, banged his big glass down—empty again—and stared at Tarp, his face flaming. "Not a man to mess about with."

"Mess about?"

Grice looked around, waited until the barman had moved away. He may have been doing it all for effect. "The death squads. You hear things. That he's one of the backers, you know?" His breath was warm and rich with the beer. "Squads have been lying low of late, at least around Buenos Aires. But he was in it up to the oxters, see?"

"Anything proven?"

Grice fiddled with his empty glass. Tarp ordered him another. Grice still looked unhappy. "Look, chum, we got to have an understanding, you and me. What's the split if you get a story?"

"Ten percent," Tarp said with Gallic caution.

"No, no." Grice grasped the fresh glass as if it were a lifeline. "I need stories, Frenchy, not a cut! What do I get in the story department?"

Tarp thought. "First look at my rough draft?"

Grice beamed at him. "Now you're talking, Frenchy!" He drank and left a mustache of foam on his sandy mustache. "And don't try to cross me up, love; I've got friends at Reuters

could see to it that your stories never got relayed correctly back
to Paris ever again. All right, so now we're partners, are we?
Good. Well, let me see. 'Anything proven,' you were asking.''
He chortled. He had a fat man's laugh—throaty, big, shaking
the whole torso. "Proven? *In Argentina?*" He slapped Tarp's
shoulder. "Buy me another pint, I'll tell you what the system is
down here."

When Tarp took the fat man to his apartment at two in the
morning, he had learned a lot of sometimes scandalous detail,
but little of importance that was radically different from what
he had found in newspapers and magazines. Schneider was a
widower; Schneider had a beautiful daughter; Schneider was a
rightist with ties to the military.

The only really useful thing he'd learned from Grice was that
Schneider had just returned from Cuba.

CHAPTER 12

In order to see Schneider personally, he had to go through an outer perimeter of secretaries and mindlessly smiling young men with MBAs from American universities. A day of it was enough for him, and Grice laughed at him when they met at the bar that evening. Grice rubbed his thumb and two fingers together. "Chai, *mon ami*," he said. "Chai."

Chai was the word for tea wherever tea was drunk, but it was also a word for "tea money"—bribes.

"Ah, baksheesh," he said.

"You got it, chum. How's our story coming today?"

The payments started, it appeared, at the Ministry of News and Information, so back he went next morning to the same official who had issued his journalist's card. His name was Kinsella, but he spoke only Spanish and was as Argentinian as the dry dust of Patagonia. He was a balding, slack-looking man in his thirties with a sandy mustache and the blue eyes of the Kinsella who had first come to Argentina in the nineteenth century.

Kinsella rested his head on one hand, absentmindedly pulling reddish hairs over the baldest place. He frowned at a piece of paper that lay in the circle of light on his desk. It was a dark day, and Tarp felt that he was receding into a Victorian murk, along with the city and its ideas.

Kinsella sighed. "You are requesting an interview with Juaquin Schneider." He sounded more than a little surprised, as if such a thing had never happened to him before.

"That is correct."

107

"You told me you were here because of the fishing. I remember mentioning Bariloche to you."

"I believe it was I who mentioned Bariloche."

"Why do you argue with me?" Kinsella looked annoyed. He put his face down into the circle of light as if he wanted Tarp to see its unhappy expression. "You are not a very tactful man."

"Forgive me."

"A journalist should be tactful. Especially if he has some idea of meeting a man like Juaquin Schneider." He shook his head. "You said you were going to write about fishing."

"Is that important?"

"Would I be mentioning it if it was not?"

"Is it your business to pass on everything I do?"

"Of course. What do you suppose my function is? This isn't the United States, you know. We don't want journalists running around like wild dogs, pestering people. You said you were here to write about fishing."

"I said I was writing a book about diversions. I assume Señor Schneider has diversions."

Kinsella put his hand over his forehead again and leaned on the elbow. "Señor Schneider's office is not inclined to favor your request."

"How do you know?"

"They called me twice yesterday. They said you were being a pest."

"I thought I was going through channels. I did not realize that I should go through you."

Kinsella looked at him. Kinsella already looked tired, as if his workday was ending, not beginning. "Señor Schneider is an immensely wealthy man."

"That's why I want to interview him."

"We have to clear all interviews before you file them with your home office."

"Well, all right."

Kinsella watched him with an expression that suggested he had a secret that Tarp had not yet been told. "If I recommend you, Señor Schneider will see you."

Tarp thought he understood. *Chai.* "I will be most happy to do whatever is necessary."

Kinsella smiled a little cynically. "Would you like to have dinner with me?"

The request seemed odd. "I should be gratified."

"At my home. I will telephone my wife. Tonight? Meanwhile, I will telephone the Schneider offices and recommend you. Then maybe he will see you." He took his face out of the light. He seemed genuinely pleased. "We will talk. My wife is a good cook. You like children? I have three; I will have to play with them for a few minutes, you understand. Then we will talk."

Tarp spent the day looking around Buenos Aires, poking through old files, and talking to his detective. All he learned was that he probably had the right Schneider.

Kinsella's wife turned out to be fat but pretty; the children were well behaved and went docilely off to bed with the maid when they were told to; the food was excellent. After dinner the wife disappeared and they talked about the Malvinas war and Argentina's future. Kinsella gave a virtual monologue on the failure of the United States to understand where its best interest lay in the region. Toward the end, the high cost of living was mentioned, and Tarp handed over three hundred dollars in Argentine pesos, the amount that Grice had suggested.

Walking back to his hotel, Tarp had the unpleasant sense that Kinsella knew who he really was. The talk about America had sounded like exactly the sort of thing a patriot might try to say to American leaders through an agent. Worse than that, neither Kinsella nor his wife seemed to be surprised when he ate no meat.

Schneider's offices were deep within the administration building of his chemical complex, surrounded by carpeted corridors and paneled turnings where stunning receptionists and the young men with American degrees waited. Around them was a ring of glass-fronted offices, the outermost one manned by armed guards, while around them was a modern-looking wall of steel and stone with broken glass set into the top in such a way that it could be seen only from a few high vantage points. Outside that wall were young men in paramilitary uniforms with automatic weapons. Everyone was very polite.

He was given a badge to wear on his lapel and was asked to step through a metal detector, where a sweet-faced, dark woman asked him please to leave the Luger. She tagged it and gave him a receipt and a dazzling smile.

He was led by a sleek, middle-aged man along the inner labyrinth of carpeted corridors. As he had approached the center of power, the men had gotten older and the women had disappeared. Schneider, he gathered, was not the sort who surrounded himself with young nonentities in order to build his own sense of importance; rather, he pushed the young ones to the fringe and defied comparison with his own very capable lieutenants. It was the gesture of a confident (or an arrogant) man.

Tarp was shown into a long room whose starkness contrasted with the paneled warmth he had just come through. One entire wall was window from floor to ceiling; beyond it was an enclosed Japanese garden, forty feet long, with an identical window on the other side. Some trick of technology made the far window opaque. Within the room were groupings of chairs and very plain sofas, as if to accommodate discussions of different sizes. Tarp saw no ashtrays, no wastebaskets. Two-thirds of the way down the room was a white desk, situated so that the man who sat at it had his back to the window and the simplicity of the garden.

"Señor Jean-Louis Selous. A journalist."

Light from the window made it hard to see the man at the desk. "Thank you, Perez." The voice was deep. There was no sound of footsteps in the deep carpeting, but Tarp heard a door close, and the middle-aged man was gone. "Come," the voice said.

He started down the long room. When he was fifteen feet from the desk, the silhouetted figure behind it moved. The torso moved back, turned; the figure came along the far side of the desk, still seated, the movement accompanied by a very low hum.

Schneider was in a motorized wheelchair.

Tarp saw the face as he rounded the end of the desk. He hid any surprise he felt. He had seen Schneider before—in Havana. He was the man who had been in the wheelchair at the ballet gala for the Celebration of Nuclear-Free Peace.

"What language do you prefer? I see you are French," Schneider said. He had picked up a file from the desk.

"Either Spanish or French," Tarp said.

"French, then." Perhaps Schneider wanted to show off—or perhaps he wanted to test Tarp's authenticity. Schneider spoke

French with an accent but with considerable fluency. "I have read your articles with interest." His hand was on the file. Presumably the file held the articles that Selous was supposed to have written.

"Was the viewpoint too Marxist?" Tarp said, speaking French rapidly and with the slight slurring that many French now affected. "Some people find it Marxist."

"I daresay Marx would not." Schneider laughed. "Are you a Marxist?"

"Not at all. Modern professional sport is the kind of commercial pig trough that makes one say Marxist things, however."

Schneider was slender to the point of seeming ascetic. It was hard to make out subtleties of expression against the glare, but Tarp thought he looked rather satanically amused. "Are you a Christian?" Schneider said.

"Of course." He said it with intentional glibness, as a Christian who never went to church might say it.

"Not a very good Christian, perhaps," Schneider said.

"It is a state of mind, surely—a state of culture?"

"Not to the Church." He said it as a pious layman or even a priest might have said it, austerely; Tarp made a mental note to check his ties with the Vatican. *And Doctor Bonano in Havana, the abortionist.*

"You asked only if I was a Christian, not if I was a churchgoer." Tarp smiled as Jean-Louis Selous smiled, engagingly, just a bit cynically. "I am more a Christian than a Moslem."

Schneider touched a button and the chair spun to his right. He rolled three feet in that direction, stopped, said, "I would prefer a whole Moslem to a part Christian. I do not like half men." He had meant to sound final and acidulous, but his French was not quite up to it, and *demi-homme* was too crude for what he wanted. He stopped the chair again and laughed. *"Moi, je suis demi-homme,"* he said, and he moved again and stopped opposite an armchair. "Sit," he said in Spanish.

Tarp sat. He could see Schneider plainly now, for behind him was an abstract painting in dark purples and blues, against which his face was clear. The skull was large and the dome loomed above the face, topped with dark hair flecked with silver like a fine pelt; the face itself seemed delicate, almost the face of an adolescent, large-eyed and almost feminine.

"To business," Schneider said. "You have eighteen minutes left." He sounded waspish. "You have a tape recorder, naturally?"

"Naturally." Tarp put a small recorder on the arm of the chair. He let silence settle between them, take up residence there. Schneider grew impatient. At last Tarp said, switching the machine on, "What is the purpose of wealth?"

Schneider sneered. "Wealth is its own purpose."

"But for you, I mean. Why a life of wealth—instead of a life of poverty, for example? Why not the life of intentional poverty, like Saint Francis?"

"Saint Francis *began* with wealth. He chose poverty later. It is the right direction to take. To begin with poverty and then choose poverty is to be an idiot."

"And you began with poverty and chose wealth?" *And what has this to do with plutonium?* he was wondering, but he knew only that he wanted to draw Schneider out.

"I began with the curse of curses, neither poverty nor wealth—the obscure comfort of the middle class." He snapped the words out. "And one does not choose wealth, Monsieur Selous—unless one is as big an idiot as the poor man who chooses poverty—because wealth is a by-product: what one chooses is *work*. I chose to achieve! Next to achievement, the rest is second-rate. One exists under the eye of God. One must achieve. One must demonstrate one's being."

"Because one is watched?" Tarp was thinking, *Is acquiring Russian plutonium an achievement?*

"Because it is expected!" As he grew excited, Schneider began to make gestures, as if he were tracing magical signs in the air. "When I say that we are under the eye of God, I do not mean that one is watched as in some stupid film about Big Brother. No, I mean that one is under the eye of God as, in a stadium, the athlete is under the eye of the spectators. One performs—because it is expected!"

"So, life is a form of sport."

"It is the *only* sport. The only *real* sport. What you call sport—throwing balls, running about, jumping—is only imitation. At one time, I played football. Oh, yes, I could run and jump then. But it was frivolous. Mere imitation." He sneered. "But wealth is like the gold medal. The prize after the achievement."

"So you think that wealth is a proper reward."

"Of course. God has made the athlete strong, and he accepts his medal; God has made me an achiever, and so I accept wealth."

"And the poor?"

"What poor?"

"Even in Argentina, there are poor."

"The poor do not much interest me."

"They are the losers?"

Schneider did not understand at first. "Oh, I see, yes—the ones eliminated in the early rounds. Yes. The champion hardly thinks of the duffers when he is in the finals."

"And what of the poor politically?"

Schneider smiled. "Your subject is supposed to be sport, not politics. But I will answer you. You mean, what of the poor in what is called a democracy, I suppose."

"It is a democratic age."

"It is an age of losers, yes." Schneider looked both ways, as if trying to find something in the vast room. He touched a button and the chair turned right around so that he could look at the painting that had been behind him. The chair hummed and he faced Tarp again. "You disappoint me, Monsieur Selous. The question is naive."

"I am sorry."

"So am I. You know why I granted this interview? Because in one of your articles, you wrote, 'It is the irony of sport that it is fascistic and has its greatest success in democratic nations.' I liked that. Yes, sport is fascistic, and *life* is fascistic! And you ask me about the poor, about democracy. You bore me. It is often boring, being Juaquin Schneider—surrounded by flunkies, feared by everybody. I thought you might be different. But no, you are not very intelligent and you are not bold. I can tell, you are not an achiever. You asked, What is the role of the poor in a democratic age? but you should have asked, What is the role of *government* in a democratic age?"

Tarp waited. "Am I to ask the question now?"

Schneider sneered. "I believe the moment has passed."

"Then let me ask another question. What is the role of the death squad?"

Schneider stiffened. "I take back part of what I said: you are not intelligent, but you *are* bold."

"What is the role of the death squad?"

Schneider stared at him. Their eyes met like hands meeting to lock fingers and explore each other's strength. "Or is the death squad the purpose of wealth?"

Schneider broke contact. He joined his thin hands in his lap. "Your time is almost up," he said, although he had not looked at a clock.

"For that matter," Tarp said, "what is the role of government in the *atomic* age? What is the role of the wealthy man in the atomic age? Is plutonium the purpose of wealth?" Nothing happened in Schneider's face or his hands, and Tarp said again, "What is the purpose of government? Is it the same purpose as organized sport, I wonder—and of the Church? To entertain the mass of people, while a few men of achievement run things?"

Schneider's huge eyes came up. They were implacable. The effeminate face was set. The right hand rose slowly and the index finger pointed at Tarp.

"You could die in Argentina, Monsieur Selous."

"Is the death squad the purpose of wealth?"

The finger closed back into the hand; the hand went to the arm of the shining chair, which hummed and made a sixty-degree turn. "I was mistaken about you on both counts," Schneider said. "You have boldness, and you have some intelligence. You have annoyed me, and that is very intelligent of you, because it has caused me to reveal myself." He nodded, as if he were agreeing with words spoken by somebody else. "I am giving a party tonight in my apartment. I want you to come." He looked around. "You can watch me on *my* playing field."

"I thought this was your playing field."

"This? *This?*" He spun the chair in a full circle. "*This* is not the arena, Monsieur Selous . . . this is the—the—" He laughed. "The locker room, maybe. The training field." He laughed again, apparently genuinely amused. "Will you come to my party? I want some people to look at you."

"Am I a specimen?"

"You are a possibility. Will you come?"

"I saw you in Havana."

"Did you. *Did* you! Yes, that stupid spectacle of mass sentimentality. Yet one sometimes makes a point by joining with such idiots. It is very important that we keep nuclear weapons out of countries like Cuba, don't you think? But that is another matter. Will you come to my party?"

"Thank you, of course."

"You must dress. Black tie. We are rather out-of-date. Do you like women? There will be some very decorative women. Are decorative women the purpose of wealth?" He laughed. "Hardly! Come, I will show you my factory."

"My time is up."

"I told you, I want to look you over. Your time will be up when I tell you. *My* clock keeps the time here."

"Why am I being looked over?"

"Maybe it amuses me. Maybe I think you would make a good playmate for my cat. Maybe I want to employ you. Who knows?"

They spent two hours going from building to building, and Tarp felt that there was little of the complex that he did not see. The wheelchair moved fast; between buildings they moved much faster in electric wagons that were always waiting for them. Schneider was careful always to tell him exactly where they were, as if he wanted to make sure that Tarp understood everything. In two buildings they had to wear protective clothing and masks. They passed through greenhouses where the smell of humus was almost threatening, like a cemetery in the rain. They went through a computerized warehouse worked by robot machines on monorails. Under a watery sun they drove along the edge of test fields where green shoots were poking through chemically treated soil far out of place in their seasonal cycle.

"The goal is to grow foods in less space, at lower cost, than ever before." Schneider seemed rather bored. They had already visited a laboratory where figures in space suits worked with electron microscopes. Through genetic engineering, Schneider said, they hoped to produce disease-free crops with greater climatic tolerance.

"A great boon to the world's poor," Tarp said.

"Yes, I have thought of that. I suppose I should be developing something to kill them at the same time, so we won't be overrun." He grinned at Tarp. "Come, monsieur, you don't find that humorous? You are less intelligent than I thought, then."

"I was thinking that what you said is at odds with the Celebration of Nuclear-Free Peace."

"Not entirely. What I said was, you will remember, I want to keep nuclear weapons out of countries like *Cuba.*"

They had lunch in a small dining room near the windowed office. There were four other men there; Tarp could not escape the sense that he was being watched and the conversation, which was all about politics and American failures and hemispheric power struggles, was staged for him. Yet something seemed wrong to him, and what seemed wrong was his own belief that Schneider was connected directly with Maxudov. *If they know who I am, why the examination?* he wondered as he ate a clear soup. *Or are these five the patrons of a death squad, looking over a victim?* But they seemed very leisurely about it. It was very easy to believe that Schneider and his companions could be willing to buy plutonium for the greater glory of Argentina and fascism, but their behavior was utterly at odds with any idea of conspiracy. Unless, of course, they liked elaborate jokes.

He sought out Grice at the Press Club bar late that afternoon after spending several hours with two other journalists who were supposed to know what really went on in Argentina. Grice was impressed that he had been shown the Schneider complex and had actually been asked for lunch.

"What'd he serve you, carrot juice and a slice of beetroot? He's a lunatic about food, they say."

"It was very good. Yes, lots of vegetables. Fruit."

"The man's demented about his health, of course. But I am impressed, Selous—lunch in the great man's private room! That's light-years farther than the rest of us have ever got. Whatever did you talk about?"

Tarp was thinking that Grice had not survived the Malvinas war in Buenos Aires by being an entirely loyal British subject. He must have had some way of paying off Argentine authority—like reporting to somebody about what people like Tarp said. "Oh—achievement," Tarp said vaguely. "Things like that."

"Achievement!" Grice guffawed. "What the hell does that mean to a man like Schneider?"

"He wants to develop disease-free vegetables."

"Oh, Christ, that's all his wife's work, not his! She was the scientific brains. Always. He's a money man, a businessman. Is that what he calls achievement? Turning her scientific genius into cash?" Grice laughed too loudly. He seemed angry. "Christ! The cheek of these bloody millionaires. Well, there's a story in it, anyhow. Right? Eh? We *are* going to get our story, aren't we?"

"I'm going to a party at his place tonight."

Grice stared at him. "At his *home*?"

"Yes."

"What—the apartment?"

"Yes. Is that so unusual?"

Grice put down his empty beer glass. "That's too much. That's just too much. God, I can't take that on beer." He rose halfway from his stool. "Here, bartender! A double whiskey here—*pronto*!"

CHAPTER 13

Schneider's apartment took up an entire floor of a new building near the Congressional Palace. A uniformed doorman saluted and showed his teeth and fiercely directed two boys who parked cars with what seemed to be enormous glee. The elevators were open glass boxes that seemed to rise quickly into the night itself, to glide smoothly to a perch at Schneider's door.

A butler took his coat. The man pretended not to notice the gun, which was heavy in one pocket; perhaps he had been handling gun-heavy coats all night. Tarp had considered leaving the weapon behind, but he was very uneasy. However, there was no way he could carry the gun in the tight-fitting dinner jacket he had picked for himself that afternoon. He might as well have carried it in his hand.

There was another butler at an inner door. He pointed, said something about drinks, and looked away. He had a hard, dark face, and Tarp wondered if he was Indian. In the large room beyond the doorway, there were two more such men, as if, having seen a film that had an English butler in it, Schneider had decided to have a corps of them. These men looked to Tarp like bodyguards, however, and he supposed they were doing double duty. He took a glass of champagne and wondered if they were Schneider's death squad. It would be handy for a millionaire, probably, to have one always on call.

He moved slowly around the room. He acknowledged Schneider's nod from the center of a cluster of pink-faced men, where a beautiful female back seemed to share attention with the industrialist himself. Schneider had said there would be

118

women; as Tarp looked around he had to admit that Schneider had been right. Many of the women were stunning, and most of them were years younger than the men they were with.

"Rather handsome lot, ain't they?" a voice said next to him. It was a pleasant, rather hearty voice, with a British gusto that sounded somehow out-of-date. "Lot of raving damned beauties, in fact!"

"Monsieur?" Tarp said. The man was several inches shorter than he, ruddy-faced and white-haired, almost Dickensian in the good cheer of his smile and his eyes, which were looking at him from a network of wrinkles and folds created by a lifetime—or so it seemed—of laughter. Tarp's one word of French had thrown him into confusion, however, for he looked bereft and began to stammer in an atrocious French accent, "Oh, uh, ah—hmm . . . Oh, *j'ai dit*—oh, damn—*monsieur* . . . *j'ai dit que* . . . *les femmes—filles* . . . Oh, dammit, this is no good. Um, *beauté* . . . *beauté*? Isn't that a word, *beauté*?"

"Would you prefer that we speak English, monsieur?"

The old man's smile returned instantly. "Jolly good!" He chuckled. "Ain't I a dreadful linguist, though. Ah? Ain't I?" He chuckled. He crowed with delight at his own shortcomings. "What a horror! Yes, yes." He shifted his champagne glass from his right hand to his left and held the right one out. "Pope-Ginna."

"Jean-Louis Selous." Tarp was thinking that he had seen the old man before. There was nothing much to the memory, something fleeting and inconsequential. He gave it up and squeezed the hand, thinking, *What a lucky accident to meet such a pleasant man. Except that there are no accidents.*

"You're the journalist," the old man said. "Ha-ha! See? I don't miss much. How old d'you think I am? Never mind; you'd be off by years, everybody always is. What I say is, don't guess, because if you're wrong you'll be embarrassed, and if you're right, I'll be humiliated. Ha-ha! I'm seventy-nine."

"That is amazing, monsieur."

"Well, it's gratifying, anyway. Still able to guzzle the bubbly and cast a weary eye over the young ones. Eh? Eh? Ha-ha!" He patted Tarp's arm. "Jock said he was going to have a journalist here. Didn't say you'd be French, though. Damned unusual. Not being French, I mean—him having a journalist.

Normally, for Jock, that isn't on. I mean, it just isn't *on.*" He
leaned closer and dropped his voice. "Between you and me and
the gatepost, m'syer, he ought to do it more often. Open himself up to the world. Eh? Eh? Of course he should." He leaned
away and looked over toward Schneider. "A raving, absolute
beauté!" He was looking at a woman with Schneider. "What
sort of journalist are you?"

"Of sport and entertainment."

"Hmm." The old man looked him up and down uneasily.

"I mean, I do not engage in personalities, monsieur."

"Ah, aha. Hmm. Good thing, too. Lot of nasty stuff about
these days, what? Frightful stuff gets published—prowler in the
queen's bedroom, all that. Some things better kept under one's
hat, eh?"

"Or under the Crown."

"What? Oh, I see. Yes. Under the Crown—ha-ha, damned
good."

The old Englishman began to point out a few people in the
room, describing them and their importance. He seemed very
impressed by wealth and seemed able to give the size of other
men's wealth in dollar amounts. He lingered by Tarp; it might
have been politeness, but Tarp felt it was something more. He
introduced him to three men, waving them over in order to do
so. It was as if he had been put there as an official greeter. Tarp
glanced at Schneider to see if there was any coaching coming
from that direction, but Schneider seemed busy with one of his
"butlers."

"Millions in this room," Pope-Ginna was saying. "Millions. Interesting, when you think about it. Do you ever write
about money, m'syer?"

"Only insofar as people who take part in sport have money."

"Mmm. Never found sport very interesting, myself." Pope-
Ginna was sipping another champagne and seemed even more
red-faced than before. He was watching Schneider now.

"You are close to Monsieur Schneider?" Tarp said carefully.

Pope-Ginna guiltily looked away. "Close? No, not as you'd
say *close*. Know him to talk to. Share a bit of business wisdom
with him now and again. We sit on a board or two together."

Tarp looked at Schneider. Two of the "butlers" were standing near him at that moment, and perhaps it was that juxtaposi-

tion that caused him to remember where he had seen Pope-Ginna. He had had medals on his chest, and he had been with Schneider in Havana. He looked at Pope-Ginna again. "You are English, monsieur?" he said.

" 'Course I am, and damned proud of it. Now you're going to ask me about the Malvinas thing, I suppose, but please *don't*." The old eyes, their look of jealousy gone now, darted toward him, then almost disappeared into their frame of laugh lines. "I've dealt with journalists before, you see, ha-ha, ha-ha."

"But you are an Argentine resident."

"Oh, absolutely."

"There are many English residents in Argentina?"

"A colony of us, yes, a colony of us. It's such a lovely country. The best country in South America!"

"So everyone says."

"It has its faults, but what country hasn't? I mean, a man can't live in England anymore. What? I mean, the taxes!"

"Are there many Russians here, monsieur?"

"What? Russians? Certainly not."

"I thought that certain overtures were made during the Malvinas war. . . ."

"We have some trade connections, naturally. Argentina is more or less a nonaligned country. Yes, we have some connections. Trade connections."

"One hears rumors of Russian weapons here since the Malvinas war. Would they be credible, do you believe, monsieur? Even atomic weapons, it is said—from Russia. . . ."

"Poppycock!" Pope-Ginna was very red in the face. "You said you aren't that kind of journalist, there you are spouting rubbish. Pardon me, m'syer, but I have to say it. It's rubbish."

"Argentina has no interest in atomic weapons?"

Pope-Ginna's eyes seemed to swell, as if they were going to burst. "Jock's absolutely right not to invite journalists to this place. Especially when they spout damned rubbish!" And he spun around and toddled off, moving a little from side to side like a penguin.

Well, tit for tat, Tarp thought. He believed that Pope-Ginna had sought him out, perhaps knowing who he really was. Or perhaps he was one of those people who, Schneider had said, would be "looking him over." At any rate, if Tarp had wanted to get a response from him, he had certainly succeeded.

Tarp talked with other people. A number of sober, rather dour men introduced themselves, each saying he was "a business associate of Señor Schneider's," as if it were a formula that had been taught to them. Tarp felt now that he very certainly was being looked over, as if he were a prospective groom meeting the bride's family for the first time. The dour men introduced him to young women whose names they pronounced with great precision, as if to make it clear that *Señorita* So-and-so was not married. Tarp danced with them and quickly concluded that they were there as part of the entertainment.

At eleven, Schneider came to his side.

"People tell me you are a very serious man, monsieur," he said.

"I thought I had been quite congenial."

"You have been described to me as a man who lets other people put their feet in their mouths."

"Did Señor Pope-Ginna say that?"

"Señor . . . ? Ah, *Admiral* Pope-Ginna."

"Admiral! Yes, I thought I saw him with military decorations. In Havana."

He thought that Schneider's forehead wrinkled just a little at that, but at that moment one of the "butlers" came near and bent to offer Schneider a tray of hors d'oeuvres. Some look passed between the two men, and Schneider's mood seemed to change. Tarp glanced at the servant, who looked to him like a probable veteran of at least one African war. *A merc, I swear he's a merc. Nice people Schneider hires.*

When the servant was gone, Schneider said softly, "Would you be interested in undertaking a task for me?"

Tarp's mental alarm went off, yet he was able to say lightly, "In what capacity? My intelligence, or my boldness?"

"Are you interested?"

"I am always interested in stimulating work."

"Come to see me tomorrow morning, then. At the factory. About ten." Schneider seemed about to say something else, but he thought better of it. The wheelchair hummed, and he moved off. Ahead of him the crowd of people opened and then parted like a sea and closed again behind him.

Now what is that all about? Tarp thought, and, as if it were toward that point that the whole evening had built, he found himself left increasingly alone. He had met the people who mattered, the party seemed to say to him now, and he had been introduced to the women with whom he might lawfully flirt, and now he was on his own.

Given that head, Tarp decided to go home.

At the door he bumped into old Pope-Ginna, who was almost certainly waiting there for him, for he smiled hugely and put himself where Tarp could not possibly avoid him. "Going so soon, are you?" he said. He laughed. "Awfully early for a young chap like you to be slippin' away, what with so many of the *beautés* here. Eh?" He held Tarp's arm. "Owe you an apology. Made a frightful ass of myself earlier; rather got a tongue-lashing from mine host about it. Most abjects, etcetera. Do say that you forgive and forget, that's a good fellow."

"Of course. My pleasure, Admiral."

The title did not seem strange to the old man. "You're a decent fellow," he said. He seemed to have been drinking a little too much, and his speech was faintly slurred.

"I spoke much too strongly, Admiral. It is I who owe you an apology."

"Oh? Not at all. Damned decent of you to say. Damned decent. Look here. Why not have lunch with me at the Hurlingham Club one day. Tomorrow, for the matter of that. Eh? If you'd give an old fellow like me the pleasure of your etcetera for a few hours."

Two in one evening. Not bad. He felt more than ever like a hapless bridegroom.

"Saw you chatting with Jock. Got along with our resident King Midas, did you?"

"I try to get along with everybody, Admiral."

Pope-Ginna stared at him with slightly reddened eyes and then burst into loud and somehow inappropriate laughter. Something that Tarp had said had amused him hugely. He slapped Tarp's shoulder and moved away, still laughing; then he seemed to see somebody he knew, and he said a hasty good night and was gone. When Tarp looked into the far room where most of the party was, he saw Pope-Ginna with one of the "butlers," lifting another glass from a tray of champagne.

An odd party, Tarp thought. *As if it had been put together for my benefit. But maybe that's egoism. Except that there are no accidents.*

Tarp retrieved his coat. The weight of the Luger dragged one side down, made it difficult to carry over his arm. He turned from the apartment doorway and looked back into the room where there was dancing.

He plummeted in the high-speed elevator. There were several other guests from the party, and he left it with them and stepped from the bright world of the apartment house into the soft darkness of the streets. The lights were slightly hazed; more distant ones looked less like jewels from down here. The pavements were wet but there was no rain, and, not seeing a taxi, he set out along a broad sidewalk. Two big American cars had been pulled up for the others. They sailed past him like boats setting out on placid water. Far away down the boulevard before him, another car came toward him, then turned off. The night became quiet. Music, almost ghostly now, came from somewhere above him and to his right, and he thought he recognized one of the tunes about the Malvinas that he had heard in Santiago.

It was about then that he realized he was being followed. He put his hand on the Luger in the overcoat pocket. He could hear only one person behind him. Still, it was definitely somebody following. He eased the safety off and waited.

He heard a car coming along the cross street before he saw it. The tires hissed on the wetness. The engine changed voice as the driver shifted down for the corner, then took it at speed, letting the tires squeal as he gunned down the boulevard toward Tarp. The house fronts came to the street here and there was nowhere for him to run except along the sidewalk itself. His strides lengthened; his eyes began to search the dark buildings for a hiding place or a handhold, for anywhere to make a stand.

The car passed him, but it was braking. Doors popped open. Two men were out of the car before it stopped and another was pulling himself awkwardly from the rear seat.

Is the death squad the purpose of wealth? he had asked Schneider. It seemed squalid now. Violent death always seemed squalid to him—bodies left along highways; shallow graves with silent, frightened peasants watching. Stupid men like these, spilling from cars on sidewalks to commit murder— was this what it was all about?

Tarp pointed the Luger at the first man and pulled the trigger. The pistol was not loaded.

At the party. They unloaded it at the party.

He had dropped the overcoat into his left hand and he swung it forward and up to make a swirling wall between them; in its cover, he moved to his right and back-kicked and felt his foot meet the man's chest.

There were no shots. They carried guns, but they had not used them.

In the country. First, a talk; then the shots. The body by the road. The hands or the head cut off.

He wanted one of their guns. That was all he was thinking, to get the gun of the man he had kicked. There were three of them, one or two more in the car; he had little chance, perhaps no chance, but his body was doing its own thinking.

He let go of the coat, which settled over the man as he dropped toward the sidewalk. He was trying to see where his gun was going to fall when an automatic weapon started to fire. The shots came out like angry words, like those terrible, short, uncontrollable bits of hatred that are said when we mean things most.

The other two men fell to the pavement, one shrieking in Spanish. The machine pistol continued to chatter. Windows blew apart in the car. There was a change in the sound as another automatic weapon joined in.

A car came around the corner to his right and blocked the car at the curb. Men erupted from it. They knelt on the street and the sidewalk, using the doors as shields, and poured fire into the first car.

Tarp bent over the man he had kicked. He was stretching to grasp the man's pistol when he was struck on the back of the head and he stopped seeing. He fell forward on his knees. He was still conscious; he felt his knees hit the stone. Blackness, then a slow brightening, the return of vision—stones, the sickly glare of the streetlight, the shadow of a tree—and pain in his head and his knees.

And then a sharp burning in his left shoulder. Hot. Spreading. Ice, fire, knife. *An injection.* It took all his strength to raise his head. He saw two men coming toward him, moving slowly and raising their knees as if they were walking in snow. He saw two bodies on the sidewalk. He saw that the first car had no glass in the windows anymore. He saw the driver with his head thrown back over the seat. He saw that the rear door on his side was open and the soles of two shoes were pointing at him through the opening.

He twisted his head to the left and heard himself groan when he did it. He used his last strength to twist his head farther. He was dropping forward on his hands and then his elbows. He put his right cheek down on the cool stones. He looked up—up legs, up thick waist, up black nylon jacket. Up. The throat. The jaw. The face.

It was Kinsella, the bureaucrat who had signed his journalist's card.

But . . . He tried to think, but he was unconscious.

CHAPTER 14

He was in a moving car. He had been unconscious; now he was coming to. It was still night. Lights passed over his face, coming and going with the regularity of heartbeat. The lights stopped coming, and they drove into darkness. Cold air blew over him and he slept again.

He awoke to find no movement. He smelled oil, machinery. There was a naked light to his left, far away.

Then he was being lifted. He felt hands on his ankles and under his arms; there was a voice cursing in Spanish.

Bright light. He winced. The light searched out his eyes and one eye was forced open. He tried to speak, but his tongue was too slow and too thick. The light left his face and moved to his left arm. There was more muttering, more cursing in Spanish, the sound of ripping fabric. He felt another injection.

A face came close to his.

"Do not come back to Argentina," a voice said. The face and the voice were connected.

The lights went off and he dropped into unconsciousness. His dreams were ugly. He came up toward waking sometimes, enough to feel cold and to resent the constant yammer of jet engines, but he would sink away again. Outside time, outside thought. He felt pain and nausea—and fear. Not fear of anything specific. Simply fear. He told himself that the drug was doing that to him, but knowing it did no good. He was still afraid.

When the floor tilted under him and he could feel the world dropping, he was more fully awake, and he knew that he was in an aircraft that was on a final approach. The fear started to focus on crashing, but he talked himself away from it; he talked himself and the aircraft down, through the final turns, down to the runway. The tires screeched and he told himself that he was on the ground and safe, but he was still afraid.

There was a sound of small motors and of moving metal. Warmer air bathed over him as the plane slowed. He smelled something rank, organic. The plane stopped altogether and then rolled forward again, turning in a tight arc, rolling off a hard surface and then stopping again.

"Quickly," a voice said in Spanish.

Hands pushed on his left shoulder and left hip. He began to roll over, paused, rolled, and dropped heavily.

The drop had only been about four feet. He landed on his right hip and his shoulder and his face and he had the breath knocked out of him. Engines deafened him. He tried to turn his head. There was a dark rectangle above him with many small lights in it. As he looked, the lights began to move and the rectangle got narrower.

Bomb bay.

He was lying on sand and scrub grass. The plane passed over him and went away, out of his field of vision, leaving him in the marshy night. He managed to roll on his back and look up at the sky. After a while, he believed that these were not the stars of Argentina.

Other aircraft landed and took off next to him. He would hear them coming behind him and then their great wings would pass over him.

Pass me by, angel of death. Pass me by.

What time is it?

When he was able to lift his arms, he tried to look at his watch, but it had been smashed. He felt the back of his head, which had a lump, and then he felt his pockets, which still held his papers and his money and a key to a Buenos Aires hotel room. Half an hour after that, he was able to roll to his left side, then to his belly, and slowly to draw his legs up so that he was on his face and his knees. He threw up. He rolled back on his haunches and lay like that for a while. Only two planes came by, and they seemed not to see him in the ruin of his tight black evening suit.

After he had sat there for a while, he crawled away from the runway like a crab. The sand hurt his palms and his knees. He thought he was crawling in a straight line, but he was not. He threw up again and then lay in the sand for a while.

Eventually he reached a chain-link fence. He could have slept by then, he was sure, but he thought that if he could get over the fence, he could get away from whatever he was afraid of, which had become a blond angel in an airplane, at least some of the time. Being inside the fence with it had to be worse than being outside the fence. Although inside and outside were only relative terms.

Getting over the fence was very difficult. There were green plastic ribbons woven through the diagonal openings, and his fingers kept tangling in them and the wire. It was not a very serious fence, for it had no barbed wire on the top, but it was very difficult for him to climb nonetheless. Falling off the top on the other side was easy by comparison. He lay next to the fence, looking at the stars again. The aircraft were taking off some distance away from him now, and he wondered how they had moved the runway.

There was a swamp a few feet from the fence. He knew the smell and the sound of it. He knew the tree silhouettes that were beginning to show as the sky brightened with dawn.

"Onward and upward," he said. Or thought he said.

He staggered along the fence, using it as a support. The fence came to a road; the road headed straight for the dawn.

"Big night?" somebody said. The voice was too cheerful to be his own. With difficulty, he turned his head. There was a pickup truck and a young man with a neck like a ham and a head with a baseball cap on it. Tarp tried to say something but failed.

"Man, you really been *on* one! Git in here, 'fore you *die!*" The young man laughed. Tarp crawled to the door of the pickup, tried to stand up, missed the door, and crashed into the door frame so that he fell facedown on the slippery seat. The boy laughed again and then said, "Aw, shit" with disgust. "Hey, man, you okay?"

Tarp looked up. He formed a word very carefully. "Yeah," he said after several seconds.

"Well, git *in!*"

Tarp put his hands on the seat directly under his shoulders and pushed, then pulled a foot up and braced it in the door frame, then pushed and pulled and got his body in. The boy reached across and slammed the door. "Hey, man, that musta been a party. I mean, some kinda party! Jeez! Holy shit, a tuxedo and ever'thin', no shit! Where you been at, man?"

Tarp got his mouth ready and said, "Buenosh Airesh." The boy howled and hit the steering wheel with his fist. They were tearing down a narrow road and Tarp was trying not to be frightened. He shut his eyes. "Huh?" he said when he realized the boy had been talking to him.

"I said, you wanna go into Orlando or don't you?"

"Huh?"

"Orlando, man, you wanna go t'Orlando or not?"

He thought he knew what Orlando was. A city. A city would have death squads and angels. "No," he said.

"Okay, but you don't look so good to be trompin' 'round the roads, 'f you don't mind me saying. I mean, you look like twenty-four hours in the sack would be *mucho* help, you know what I mean?"

Tarp tried to make a smile. After a while, the boy stopped the truck and let him out. He leaned against a palmetto and threw up again, and then he sat for a while and watched a lizard. He took off the dinner jacket and emptied the pockets and tossed the jacket away, then ripped the sleeves from the white shirt and threw them away. He had a French passport, a Jockey Club card, some other papers, a penknife, and a lot of Argentine pesos.

A black child came down the road. When she got opposite him, she stopped and looked. After a long time, she said, "You sick?"

"Feels like it." He was able to talk more clearly.

"Look like it, too." She went away.

Tarp got on his feet and started walking in the hot sunshine. He thought he was heading north. If the boy had been talking about Orlando, Florida, then he wanted to go north. He was thinking somewhat clearly now. His boat ought to be back in the slip at the marina, but there was no point in going there because the Agency people would have impounded it or staked it out or done something equally troublesome. He needed to go to Washington. That was about as much sense as he could make just then.

He passed through a small black community where people

looked at him with a mixture of hostility and contempt, and they made no move to stop their dogs when the dogs barked and snarled. He didn't blame them. He was not frightened anymore, so he thought the effects of the drug were passing. He had a cruel headache and he felt weak.

He washed himself in a creek and drank a lot of water from a hose at a gas station. He asked a fat black man what day it was and found that he had lost an entire day and night.

I missed my appointment with Schneider.

He traded the fat man the penknife for two candy bars and ate them sitting by a highway, waiting for a ride. *Who laid on a death squad for me? Schneider? The funny old Englishman?* He thought of all the people at the party.

By noon he had gotten a short ride with a half-drunk real estate salesman who drove as if he were going to kill himself before the day was over; by three o'clock he was near Jacksonville with a sailor; by nine that night he was passing through South Carolina. At a truck stop he found a six-wheeler that was headed for D.C. At seven the next morning he was in the District.

"Where you goin' at?" the driver asked him.

"The White House would be fine."

"Oh, yeah." The man laughed. They had been talking about football, women, war, hunting, unemployment, and the promise of space. Tarp had not slept. "Oh, yeah."

"Drop me anywhere, then."

"Shit, I can put you out on Pennsylvania Av. if that's what you want."

"That's fine."

"You got it."

He got down six blocks from the White House and walked from there, turning off the avenue opposite the mansion and walking half a block to an unassuming stone entrance in a block of handsome old buildings. The only indication of the building's identity was a very small brass plaque that read New Monroe Hotel in letters so small they were unreadable from the street. There were three steps up from the sidewalk; a man in a dark suit stood on the top step. He looked Tarp up and down—the torn sleeves, the grimy dress trousers, the ruined evening shoes.

The man touched his cap.

"Good morning, sir."

"Hello, Frederick. I'm not expected."

"I'm sure that's all right, sir. Go on in." Frederick led him to a reception desk that was little more than an alcove in a beautifully paneled little foyer. There were fresh flowers on a table and a strong smell in the air of furniture polish and wax. "Mr. Tarp will be needing a room," the man named Frederick said.

A gray-haired man with a very large mustache leaned over the reception counter. "Of course," he said. He had red cheeks of the sort that are supposed to be associated with jollity and convivial drinking; in fact, he was a recovered alcoholic who had once held a fairly high post in the State Department. Frederick disappeared and the man held out a pen. "Good to see you again."

"Thank you." Tarp signed the old-fashioned book. "No luggage and no money this trip."

"No problem, Mr. Tarp. Clothes?"

"Please."

Only minutes after he was shown to a small bedroom on the fourth floor, another man in a dark suit appeared with a garment bag. In it were a tweed jacket and corduroy trousers that Tarp had left there some years before, along with a turtleneck shirt and a pair of old but still serviceable Cordovan shoes. A discreet cardboard box held new underwear, toothbrush, and shaving kit. In the lining of the jacket was a hundred-dollar bill and the key to a safe-deposit box in a nearby bank.

"All I've got is Argentine pesos," Tarp said.

"Fifty thousand a hundred and five to one, sir."

"Street price?"

The man laughed. "On Argentine pesos, there isn't a street price." Tarp gave him a quarter million.

He put the clothes away, dropped on the bed, and was instantly asleep. Hours later he awoke as suddenly. He lay still, taking inventory. He remembered it all—the attack, the injections, the airfield. The fear. He had a lump on his head and a brutal headache.

He lay in hot water up to his chin and tried to smooth over the torn places in his mind. He was badly hurt there, not in the way the body is hurt, but with guilt and the knowledge that he had almost been killed because he had been careless. It was humiliating. He lay in the tub until the water was cold, trying to come to terms with it. The best he could do was that he had blundered but that it was still recoverable. Whatever he had gone to Argentina to do, he had botched it, and he was lucky to be alive—and he was alive only because a completely unexpected force had intervened.

Kinsella. He had not told Kinsella that he was going to Schneider's, but he had told Grice, the fat English newsman. *Grice worked for Kinsella; that makes sense.* Kinsella had saved his backside, then had turned him over to somebody who had told him to stay out of Argentina and who had then shipped him home. *That says Argentine air force. Permission to land at Orlando; some sort of routine mission, with U.S. knowledge. Returning damaged goods.* They had dumped him without hurting him, meaning that they had known he was American and had assumed he was working for the U.S. Meaning that they did not know about Repin and Havana, perhaps did not know about Maxudov and the plutonium. *Good guys or bad guys?*

Tarp surged out of the cold water and stalked to the telephone. Water turned to dark stains on the New Monroe's carpeting. He ignored it, ignored his own shivering, dialed a number in Virginia.

"Three nine seven five," a male voice said.

"This is Mr. Black. Tell Mr. Green I want to see him."

"Yes, sir."

"As soon as possible. Call me at the service number and have them relay."

"Yes, sir."

He toweled himself dry with a towel as thick as the carpet and rubbed his skin to a bright pink. It was getting dark outside now. He saw himself in the window, draped in the towel as in a toga: straight ahead were the stark branches of the trees, silhouetted against a cold sky; below, as if part of another world, was the White House, lighted, its windows cheerful and bright and probably ready for an evening reception.

There was a robe in the closet, courtesy of the hotel. He put it on, went again to the telephone.

"Front."

"It's Mr. Tarp. Can I get some food?"

"Of course, sir. You're a vegetarian, I believe."

"Right."

"Let me have a word with the kitchen."

They sent up two poached eggs on a bed of lightly cooked spinach, a cold smoked trout, a huge dish of fresh fruits, and a plate of cheeses. He limited himself to a single glass of clean-tasting white wine—one of four that were sent along—and ate his way through the eggs, the trout, a salad, three fruits, and two cheeses. Then he sipped French coffee and waited.

At seven the telephone rang.

"Yes."

"Unarmed services here."

"Yes."

"Mr. Green will be at Mr. White's and will meet you in the square at plus three."

"Thank you."

He put on the comfortable old clothes and went downstairs. As he passed through the small lobby, he recognized a heavy-set, tall man by the desk. Not too long before, he had been the president of the United States. Their eyes met and politely disengaged. At the New Monroe, most people wanted to be unrecognized.

The duty man at the front door held out an umbrella. "Started to rain, sir."

"Thanks, Jack." He paused, one hand on the umbrella shaft, ready to open it. "I'm not here, if anybody asks."

"Okay, glad you told me. A nightcap when you come in?"

"That would be nice. Yes, thanks."

He walked to a bench in Lafayette Square and stood behind it next to the thick bole of a tree, where the glow of the streetlight did not fall on him. It was raining but rather warm. Cars hissed by on the shining pavement, but the little park was deserted. Tarp waited silently, motionless, trying not to think of the shame that troubled him like an ache.

At two minutes before eight, a squat figure appeared from Pennsylvania Avenue and walked slowly along one of the sidewalks. The man was wearing a dark overcoat and a hat and carried a folded and now sodden newspaper under his arm. He looked as if he carried some terrible sadness, perhaps because he was wearing thin-soled evening shoes that were useless in the inescapable puddles. When he passed near a light, the white shirtfront and black bow tie of evening dress appeared.

"Hello, Hacker," Tarp said when the man came near.

The man raised his head to look at him under the brim of the hat. He had bags and jowls, and his little eyes looked angry. "You bastard," he said.

"Let's walk."

"Do you know who I was having dinner with? Do you know what it's like to have to excuse yourself between the drinks and the first course to the president of the United States?" He had a Georgia accent that got thicker when he was angry.

"He probably thought you were coming out to meet your Moscow contact."

"You bastard."

"The president knows all about you, Hacker. Come on, let's walk."

"What the hell you get me out here on a night like this for?" Hacker turned up his coat collar.

"Two Agency men tried to interfere in my business. That sounds like your work."

"I don't know a thing about that stuff."

"Two Agency men leased a boat in Florida and followed me around the Gulf. Why?" When Hacker said nothing, Tarp prodded him with his left elbow. "Answer me, Hacker."

"I don't know nothin' about it, you hear?"

"Hacker." Tarp stopped. He held the umbrella high enough so that he could look into the other man's eyes. Rain cascaded off it onto the other's hat, then off the hat brim onto his shoulders and his nose and his shoes. "Hacker, when you decided to take Moscow's money so your wife could live in that big house in Potomac, you gave up your claim to being treated like a human being. When I turned you and made you a triple agent, you at least got yourself back on the side of the angels. I can still blow your situation any time you stop cooperating. Now, why did you put your people on me, Hacker?"

Hacker hunkered down into his raincoat. "You don't need to talk so high and mighty about Moscow money. I guess you know what Moscow money is, all right, all right. We got word you was havin' a ron-day-voo out in the Gulf with a certain representative of a certain security service that happens to have its headquarters in Moscow, U.S.S.R."

"What rendezvous?"

"That bigwig you met up with."

"Who said?"

"You know I can't tell you that." Hacker seemed pleased.

"You know you'd better. *Who said?*"

They started walking again. Hacker moved closer and put one hand on the umbrella handle. "Moscow," he whispered.

"Who in Moscow?"

"Aw, shit." The plump man looked around as if they were in a crowd. "The usual." His voice was almost inaudible.

"Your usual officer?"

"Well, yeah."

"Who's at the top of your pipeline?"

"How the hell should I know?"

Tarp looked down at him, seeing only wet hat brim. "What rank are you now in the KGB, Hacker—a captain?"

"Like hell! I'm a lieutenant-colonel!"

"And you don't know who's at the top of your pipeline? Tell me another."

"Aw, shit. It's Galusha."

A lieutenant-colonel in the KGB and a section head at the Agency, Tarp thought. *Not bad for a Georgia boy.* "All right," he said aloud, "I want the word to go back to Galusha that there was no rendezvous so far as your people could find out. Got it?"

"Shit."

"And I want my boat back."

"You're a complete prick, you know that?"

"Yes." They crossed a street and headed back toward the square. "I want my boat back. No strings. Same condition I left it in. Any damage, I'll come to you personally."

Hacker sighed deeply again. "Okay. Christ, you shot one of my ___ men."

___ him, Tarp said, "Next, I want the digest of atomic ___ he Southern Hemisphere for the last twenty-four ___ you a code; you can pipe it into my data

___ rage of atomic installations in the ___ me period."

___ 're a traitor. Traitors are ___ you must be, work-

Hacker said nothing while they took several steps. He was breathing heavily, and he stopped and looked down into a puddle that was too wide to step across. "I live for the day when I will have your ass," he said in a strangled voice.

Tarp walked away, leaving the useful traitor in the rain.

There were fresh flowers in his room at the New Monroe and a little fire was burning in the fireplace, above which an Adam mantel gave grace and dignity to the little space. The New Monroe was not an inexpensive hotel. Far from it. It offered rare amenities, however. For people who spent part of their lives in very uncomfortable pursuits, it was a respite, and it had the unique virtue among hotels of offering an absolute guarantee against bugs of any kind.

There was a short bookshelf with a wide range of reading material. Tarp was trying to decide between *Little Dorrit* and the latest *Jane's Fighting Ships* when there was a knock at his door. He opened it to see a tray with a bottle of Laphroaig and two glasses, and, behind it, the man he had seen earlier in the lobby.

"You ordered a nightcap, I think."

It was not often that room service was performed by a former president, even at the New Monroe. Tarp stepped back; the man came in, moving with a westerner's rolling stride and the sort of boyish grin and haircut that Europeans thought of as typically American. "Mind if I join you?" he said, looking around for a place to set the tray down.

CHAPTER 15

Tarp was wary. "My pleasure, sir," he said, not very pleasantly.

The former president put the tray down and touched the top of the bottle. "Your brand, isn't it?"

"It is, indeed."

"They said at the desk it was." He was wearing a cardigan sweater and leather slippers, and he stood in front of the fire looking relaxed and taking up a lot of space. "My name is Smith." Being called Smith amused him a lot, the joke being that his name was something else, that both his name and his face were so famous that calling him Smith had a profound silliness to it.

"Mine is Tarp."

"I know." He looked behind him so he could lower himself into an armchair, and when he was comfortable he said, "You pour," like a man accustomed to giving orders. He watched Tarp open the bottle. "I've been across the street," he said. "Visiting the present occupant." That seemed to amuse him, too.

"There is a formal dinner, I think," Tarp said.

"Well, I was the hors d'oeuvre. I didn't stay for the meal." He accepted a glass, sniffed it, made a face that suggested that Laphroaig's smoky glory was a little stronger than he was accustomed to. Tarp sat down on the other side of the fire.

They took a sip in silence. "Mr. Smith" put his slippers toward the fire. "Fire feels good." He sipped again, seemingly absorbed in reverie. Abruptly, however, he said, "We're

138

worried. Damned worried. I guess you know who we are." He jerked his head. "The present occupant and me. And some others. We're worried about you."

"Me?"

"Yeah. Now look, Tarp . . ." A sudden toughness showed behind the aged boyishness. He had been a good politician, meaning that he had been cruel and opportunistic and perhaps unfair at times; the potential for that showed now. "They want me to talk to you."

"Is this official?"

"Of course not. Some things can't be said officially. But they can be said by somebody like me. Okay?"

"Yes, sir."

"Okay. Now, look: We think you're in a pretty big business. We—they—think it's *very* big."

"What business is that, sir?"

The former president held the whiskey glass between his hands and rolled it back and forth a little before giving Tarp a long look that was meant to seem straightforward. "Cards on the table, okay? We know that KGB Central is in an uproar. We knew it before you got involved. It looks like the cow-flop's going to hit the fan unless somebody pulls it out for them—and somebody is you. Right? Well, am I right?"

"That seems to be the idea."

"Okay. Now." He bent forward. "*It's okay with us.* Understand? I was told to bring that message across the street. *It's okay with us.* Let me tell you why." He swirled his glass. "How about a splash more of that stuff. It kind of grows on you." As Tarp was busy with the bottle, "Mr. Smith" settled back and said almost dreamily, "It'd be tempting to let the Soviets kill each other off. Most of all the KGB. That's what the British are going to do, in fact. But it's a very tricky time. Hell of a tricky time, with the arms negotiations, and a new ball game with Andropov in the driver's seat. There's this feeling that we could do a lot worse than Andropov—you follow? I mean, we may be able to deal with Andropov."

Tarp finished pouring and handed over the glass. "Don't count on it."

"So we don't want him to feel threatened. And we don't want him to spend all his time putting fingers in the dike. We don't want a potentially embarrassing KGB problem to blow up in his face. So we're willing that they put their own house in order as quickly as possible.''

"With my help."

"If need be, yes." He cleared his throat. "The only trouble is, uh . . .''

"The only trouble is, what if Andropov himself is the rotten apple in the KGB barrel."

"That's about it. That's just the question we're asking. What if it's Andropov himself?''

"Well?"

"Well, then . . .'' The former president sipped his Scotch, looked into the glass, smiled, looked at the fire. "Then you'll have to promise to do nothing."

"Swallow it?"

"Not get him into trouble. Uh, that doesn't mean you wouldn't report it over here. In the right quarters."

So you could blackmail him. Nice. "And if it isn't Andropov?''

"Well, of course it won't be. I mean, we don't believe it will be. But just in case, you know what to do.''

"And if it isn't Andropov?"

"Well, then use your own judgment. We'd like to ask a favor, however.''

"Sir?"

"We want you to give us the name before you tell the Russians.''

A gust of wind rattled the window, like a reminder of the cold darkness outside. The former president was sincere, Tarp believed—a decent man, as that expression was used nowadays. Tarp was not much taken with decent thoughts that night, however; instead, he was thinking of the indecencies of the agent. *They have somebody in the KGB top brass, and they want to cover his backside.* Tarp studied the friendly, decent face opposite him. *They're afraid I'll turn up their man, of course. Because he could be their man and a bad apple at the same time.* He thought of Hacker, and what a slimy specimen Hacker was; he imagined Washington's KGB probe as the same type, motivated not at all by belief, but by greed. "What if I find out it's the wrong man?" he said.

"I don't follow you."

"Don't you, sir? What if I find the bad guy and he's somebody your people don't want blown to Moscow?"

"Kind of fishing, aren't you?"

"I think it would be a little dangerous, Mr. Smith, if I found that the man Moscow is looking for is Washington's man in place." Tarp nudged a fallen log with his toe. "There I'd be, you see, a man with information that neither side would like him to have." He looked calmly at the other man. "I wouldn't like to be the victim of an unfortunate accident or an unexpected heart attack, Mr. Smith."

"We don't do things like that," the other man growled.

"Yes we do."

"Now, look here—"

"Pardon me, Mr. Smith, but I know the business. I know how things are done." Tarp stood up and went to the window, to stand there with his hands shoved into his pockets and his forehead pressed against the cold glass. Something reminded him of Juana; he could not see the connection. "Tell them that whatever I find will be put where it will be made public if anything happens to me. Tell them I keep my bargains, and I've made a contract with a Soviet. I'll keep it, or I'll give the job up. Tell them that I won't protect Andropov or anybody else, because that wasn't in my deal."

"I'm asking you to think of the contract you have here."

"I don't have a contract here, Mr. Smith."

"You're an American."

"Yes, sir." Tarp leaned away from the window. Idly, he drew a finger through the circle of steam that his breath had left on the window. "You want me to say that I have an implied contract here because of loyalty and because of birth. Do you know why I left the Agency, sir?"

The other man cleared his throat as if to say something and then seemed to changed his mind. "No," he said simply.

"I was fired. I was fired because I was 'uncontrollable.' What I couldn't control was my conviction that we should win a war if we were in one." Tarp mad more marks in the steam, which he had turned into the Chinese character for hope. The circle shrank and the character disappeared. "I don't make contracts with the people who fired me anymore. You can tell them that, if you like." He made it sound kind and gentle.

The former president changed his position, drummed his fingers on his glass, sighed noisily. "Can I tell them you won't do anything to actively help the Soviets, other than this one thing?"

"Of course."

"Some people think you're going over."

"Some people always think that."

"Well . . . Well. Well, sit down, will you? You make me nervous, standing where I can't see you like that." The man was angry, and he was laughing to cover the anger, which showed in his eyes and the redness of his cheeks when Tarp looked at him. "Mr. Smith" shook his head. "They told me what you'd be like. One of the staff people laughed at me when I told him I was coming to see you. You know what he said? He said, 'Get yourself a rock, Mr. President, and practice squeezing milk out of it, because that's what it'll be like.' " He shook his head. He was still angry. "You wouldn't have lasted five minutes with me."

"No, sir. I was never good at team sports."

"Okay. O-*kay!* At least we know where we stand. Now, a couple more things." He was a good manager: finding that his anger was wasted, he put it behind him and went on.

"The administration wants some distance between itself and, uh, this business, but at one and the same time they want to keep some contact, so . . . The people across the street hoped you and I could stay in touch."

"What our Russian friends call a *bomsha.*"

"What's that?"

"Sort of a nurse."

"More like a communications link."

Tarp looked at him. "What can I expect from you? Support?"

The former president shook his head. "Case by case. Nothing out of Operations Division, I was told to say."

Tarp nodded. "Information? Analysis?"

"On a case-by-case basis."

They talked for a few more minutes about ways and means of communicating—contacts, fallbacks, ways of working. "Mr. Smith" could not conceal a delight in the mechanics of it all. He had administered a country and he had made great decisions, but he had never been down in the dirt of intelligence work. Now, like the well-bred boy who has finally been allowed to go out and play in the mud with the roughnecks, he was having the time of his life. *Just like the movies,* Tarp thought. *Well, maybe they'll let me play at being president someday.*

"Mr. Smith" had another Scotch and, only a little tight, went off to his own room at midnight. Tarp was asleep within minutes.

He went down early the next morning to the New Monroe's almost hidden dining room and sat alone so that he could mull over what had been said. The Buenos Aires failure still weighed on him like one of those dull, relentless pains of the ear or the neck that seem not quite bad enough to require a doctor but are always too bad to be ignored. Behind that dull ache was a lesser but more threatening one: a feeling of malaise whose source was the suspicion that the basic problem Repin had given him was unsolvable—or that, even if it was solvable, it was too involved and too profoundly soiled for anybody to get out of it clean.

After breakfast, Tarp went to his bank and sequestered himself with his safe-deposit box. There were three passports in it and three credit cards in the same names; nineteen hundred dollars in several currencies; a thousand in gold; a Browning .38; and a flat object that was in part a cigarette lighter. He took a Canadian passport and its credit card, three hundred American dollars, and the lighter and closed the box up. In a nearby store he bought a down jacket, a pair of winter hiking boots, a sweater, another turtleneck, and a silk undershirt, all with the credit card; and back at the hotel he put a hundred-dollar bill into the lining of the tweed jacket and gave it to the housekeeper to sew up. He changed into the new clothes, and, when she returned, he handed her the garment bag with the other things.

"Into storage, please, Mrs. Mims."

"Like usual, I assume."

"Please."

He could go away for a year or twenty. When he came back, the clothes and the money would be waiting. Or he could come back tomorrow.

One end of the lighter produced a thin jet of propane-fed flame that could be adjusted to a needlepoint that would melt silver solder. A pull at the other end raised a solid block machined to a block below it, in which were two .22 holes and a firing mechanism. Two inches below the holes a small decorative logo pushed forward as the block was pulled up and served as a trigger. Tarp checked it over, tested the flame, looked into the .22 chambers. They were empty. The desk was able to supply him with two .22 shorts, which he inserted before he closed the little weapon up so that it looked like a stainless-steel lighter again.

"Leaving us?" the clerk said when he went down.

"For a while."

"Everything satisfactory, I hope."

"Very." He put down the Canadian credit card, which had a quite different name on it, but the other man's beautiful mustache did not so much as twitch.

"Did you have one egg or two at breakfast?"

"One."

"Ah." The ends of his mustache climbed his cheeks as he smiled. "I would have overcharged you. Glad I asked."

The bill was over a thousand dollars. Eggs were about eighty-nine cents a dozen in the supermarkets.

CHAPTER 16

He flew to Boston and then to Bangor, and there he walked down along the cargo hangars and beyond them to a shed that had pontoon aircraft parked around it, their wings covered with. snow. It was hot inside the tiny office and there was a smell of coffee and cigarettes.

"Billy," he said to a skinny man in a plaid shirt.

"Well, well—Mr. Tarp." He pronounced it a little like *tahp* and a little like *tap*. "Kinda early in the year for you."

"Ice out, Billy?"

"No sirree. Plenty of ice still on Moosehead. Could put a twin engine down on Moosehead. Don't know 'bout your pond."

"Want to try it?"

"Well, now . . ." He stretched his skinny neck out of the flannel collar and made a face. "I'd rather take the helicopter."

"That's okay with me."

"Cost you more."

"That's fine."

"Be half an hour or so."

The little helicopter zoomed in over his woods, and he watched a startled moose begin its awkward, crazy gallop down a hillside. The leafless trees looked like dark lines scratched on the white veneer of snow. Blow-downs made crosshatching, like the shadows in an engraving. Billy put the chopper down in the cleared area below his cabin. When Tarp stepped out, the snow was up to his knees.

"Want me to come back for you?" Billy shouted.

"I'll call you if I need you."

Tarp ducked under the rotors and ran. The engine blasted and the little machine danced off the snow and swung away over his trees; then it was gone, leaving its smell and the terrible hush of the silenced woods.

Tarp looked around. He acknowledged a sentimental pleasure. This was home—as much as he had a home. To his left, his pond was a flat snowscape with a dark tracing of deer prints. His log dock appeared to have dragged itself to the pond's edge and put its head in, for the far end was buried under the snow. His canoes were stored under a mound of snow and logs nearby; to his right, a line of woods curved from behind the cabin around the clearing to join the woods that ringed the pond in a sweep to the river, three hundred yards away. Across the river was Canada.

Tarp went up the slope to the cabin. The big window had been shuttered for the winter. The log porch was stacked with firewood. Tarp circled the cabin, but nobody had troubled it; after his first year here, not even meddlers on snowmobiles had come near. He had bought his privacy with two fights, a lawsuit, a large gift to the police retirement fund, and some rifle shots. He bothered nobody; nobody bothered him.

It was dark inside and cold as a mausoleum. He laid a fire in the wood stove, opened the shutters, and turned on two lights, then went to the roof and swept snow off the solar panels that backed the power company's line. In half an hour the stove was beginning to give up its slow heat; there was hot coffee on the gas stove; and his computer screen was glowing. Tarp checked the locker where the long guns were, then the wall panel where another .22 pistol was hidden.

The daylight was fading. He stepped outside to see the last of it on the treetops across the clearing. The surface of the ponds was velvety blue. Nothing stirred. In its lair beyond the edge of the woods, the badger would sleep another two weeks; high in the trees, the squirrels would nestle in the beds of leaves, warming each other.

He sniffed the air. "Snow coming," he said aloud. His breath came out like smoke. The cold of night was coming down.

He awoke before sunrise and enjoyed those moments that first waking in a cold room allows, the luxury of lying in a down-filled bag while just beyond that shell the cold waits. The room was dark. The cabin creaked in a wind, which snuffled at the corners like an animal. The cabin was as tight as logs and six inches of insulation could make it, but when the "Montreal Express" blew, a damped-down stove would not keep it warm all night. He put his head out and felt the fresh shock of cold air on his cheek. He smiled. He was beginning to feel better.

He slipped out of the bag and stood naked in the dark, feeling the cold like a fluid poured over his body. He pushed three chunks of wood into the stove and opened the damper, and for a few seconds he held his hands over the brightness of the coals before he closed the door.

By the time the sun was up he was padding around the now warm cabin in stockinged feet, wearing wool-lined khaki pants and a thick sweater. He opened the interior shutters to the light. Pale pink and yellow, the sunlight turned the snow shadows blue and lavender; the rising sun hung in the black trees like a ball of ice. There was cloud between him and the sun. By nine o'clock the first snow would begin to fall.

He made biscuits in a stovetop oven and ate them with strawberry jam that had been frozen all winter, and Danish butter from a can, and coffee like liqueur. Then he sat at the computer, wiping his fingertips on his pant legs.

QUERY MODE, he typed.

ACCESS: BLACK SUN.

VISUAL PRESENTATION: SOVIET SUBMARINES CARIBBEAN AND SOUTH ATLANTIC/ END.

It gave him a map, white on green, with a column of more or less parallel lines running down to Cuba, then out around the bulge of Brazil and south to a common point east of the Falklands. From there the routes diverged, one cutting east toward the tip of Africa, the other cutting between the Falklands and South Georgia to head close to Tierra del Fuego and the southern islands of Argentina and Chile, and from there into the Pacific.

DELETE NUCLEAR-POWERED, he typed.

One line disappeared, but the patterns were the same.

DELETE DISPLAY/ VISUAL PRESENTATION: SOVIET SUB SUPPLY STATIONS.

Four areas were lighted—one in the Atlantic well east and

north of Florida; one in Cuba itself; one east of the Falkland Islands; one in the Pacific far west of Chile.

The computer gave him data on number of missions, on submarines actually sighted and identified over the past five years, on routes taken leaving Russia by conventional subs—out of Murmansk and Archangel, some down the White Sea Canal and into the Baltic; some out of Tallinn into the Baltic directly.

He called up a map of the tip of Argentina that stretched from the Soviet supply point on the northeast to a point equally far west of Tierra del Fuego, which stood at the center. Below the Argentine tip was only open ocean; far toward the upper-right corner were the Falklands; and beyond them was the area worked intermittently by the Soviet submarine supply.

Where the hell is Antarctica? he thought.

OPEN VISUAL TIMES TWO.

The scale halved. Now a curving finger of land beckoned from the bottom of the screen.

IDENT. He moved a stylus of light toward the finger.

IDENT FOLLOWS: ANTARCTIC PENINSULA AKA GRAHAM LAND/PALMER LAND/ PRINCIPAL ISLANDS: ELEPHANT/KING GEORGE/SOUTH SHETLAND/BISCOE.

Tarp rubbed a finger down his jaw. QUERY: LOCATION ICE, he typed.

SEASONAL OR PERMANENT?

BOTH: SEGREGATE AND IDENT.

A thread of light ran around the finger of land. PERMANENT. A series of dots marked another line farther out. SEASONAL.

QUERY: SEASONAL ICE?

DEFINED AS DRIFT ICE/ FORMS ANTARCTIC WINTER/ WIDEST EXTENT SEPTEMBER–OCTOBER/ SHRINKS TOWARD PERMANENT OR PACK ICE SUMMER.

QUERY: NAVIGABLE?

NO NAVIGATION PACK ICE CONVENTIONAL VESSELS/ DRIFT ICE NAVIGABLE BUT UNPREDICTABLE/ EXAMPLES: N B PALMER YEAR 1820 EXPLORER/ SAILING SHIP/ REACHED PENINSULA FROM FALKLAND ISLANDS/ SCOTT 1910 EXPLORER REACHED

MCMURDO SOUND FROM NEW ZEALAND/ AMUND-
SEN 1911 EXPLORER REACHED KAINAN BAY FROM
ENOUGH, Tarp told it sharply. He was thinking.
QUERY: DEPTH OF DRIFT ICE?
INSUFFICIENT DATA.
QUERY: IS DRIFT ICE AREA NAVIGABLE BY SUB-
MARINE?
INSUFFICIENT DATA.
He looked at that unpromising message for a while, and then
he looked at a map of Argentina.
QUERY: SUBMARINE FLEET/ ARGENTINA?
The answer was not interesting to him until the following
message spread across the screen:
SUBMARINE VESSEL ADMIRAL JORGE CANOSSA
COMMISSIONED 1978/ LAUNCHED MURMANSK, USSR,
1963 AS WHISKEY CLASS SOVIET VESSEL SVETAN-
LAYOSK/ PURCHASED BY ARGENTINA 1977/ REFIT-
TED MURMANSK 1977–78 FOR MARINE RESEARCH.
He waited, but nothing more came.
QUERY: DETAILS ADMIRAL JORGE CANOSSA?
NO FURTHER DATA.
He played with the Argentine submarine fleet for a few min-
utes, but nothing more of interest appeared. The Argentines
had a small, conventional undersea navy and had used part of it
to try to resupply their troops during the Falklands war. Their
subs were a conglomerate of other nations' secondary vessels—
conventional boats from the United States, France, Israel, and
the U.S.S.R. There was no indication that Argentine submarines ever made contact with the Soviet subs that plied the area.
Still, he found the coincidence of the Argentine marine-re-
search submarine provocative. There was at least an Argentine-
Soviet connection there. Could it lead to ''Maxudov''?
What did the Argentinians want a submarine to do marine research for? he wondered.
QUERY: ARGENTINE SUBMARINE PENETRATION
DRIFT ICE/PACK ICE?
NO DATA.
The ice fascinated him. It suggested another world, one
unexplored and so full of possibilities. Its closeness to Argen-
tina was inescapable. The Argentinians had fought a war over
the little duster of rock that they called the Malvinas. Would

they extend their ambitions to include Antarctica? And might they, if they did, want nuclear weapons to back a claim? If they did, they would again find themselves in a confrontation with Great Britain, and Tarp wondered how much the British refusal to cooperate in unmasking "Maxudov" might have to do with their apprehensions about Argentina.

If the Soviets decided to help the Argentinians, he speculated, *beginning with some sort of venture in Antarctica . . .*

QUERY: SOVIET ACTIVITY ANTARCTICA?

The screen came alive with a map of the Antarctic. Many lines flowed into it from the perimeter, most of them headed for the Soviet base at Mirnyy. Laboriously, Tarp queried one after the other, got nothing.

There was one rather short penetration of the drift ice, however, that was well away from the usual Soviet activity and closer to South America. He touched it with the stylus.

QUERY?

SOVIET U.S. JOINT SCIENTIFIC EXPEDITION/ SOVIET ICEBREAKER MIKHAIL SOMOV/OCTOBER 1981/ PURPOSE: INVESTIGATION OF POLYNYA.

QUERY: POLYNYA?

POLYNYA: RUSSIAN NOUN/ MEANING: OPEN WATER SURROUNDED BY ICE/ CAUSE UNKNOWN/ HYPOTHESIS: WARM WATER SUB SURFACE.

QUERY: RESULTS OF SOVIET-U.S. MISSION?

ENDED NOVEMBER 1981/ ICE/ NO POLYNYA.

QUERY: LOCATIONS ANTARCTIC POLYNYA?

POLYNYA SIGHTED 1974, 1975, 1976 LONG DEGREES: ZERO/ LAT DEGREES: SIX TWO/ ESTIMATED SIZE: TWO HUNDRED FIFTY MILES DIAMETER PAREN HIGHLY VARIABLE PAREN/ SUMMER PHENOMENON.

Tarp called up the map of the tip of South America and the Antarctic finger. The *polynya* lay seven hundred miles east.

Tarp got up and stretched and made himself a curious lunch from the foods that had stood in the cabin all winter. He moved around the cabin, eating, looking out the window, looking at his feet, occasionally returning to the computer terminal and asking questions that produced fruitless answers. What he wanted to ask it was its opinion of an idea, but the computer did not give opinions. What he wanted then was Repin or Juana to talk to; and then when he had thought about them for a little, it was Juana that he wanted.

Tarp shook himself like a dog who has just climbed out of the water. *That won't do. That won't do at all.*

He went to the computer for facts again and ran Schneider's name, but got no more than he had learned in Buenos Aires.

QUERY: KINSELLA, JAIME.

ALL NEW DATA: BORN JUNE 1947/ MARRIED THREE CHILDREN/ RES BUENOS AIRES ARGENTINA/ ASSISTANT DEPUTY DIRECTOR FOR FOREIGN JOUR-NALISTS, BUREAU OF NEWS AND INFORMATION/ HOLDS CURRENT RANK CAPTAIN ARGENTINE AIR FORCE SPECIALIST INTELLIGENCE/ ACTIVE DUTY 1968–77 INCLUDING AIR INTELLIGENCE SCHOOL, WASHINGTON D.C./ NO KNOWN CONNECTIONS PO-LITICAL GROUPS ARGENTINA BUT INVESTIGATING/ SOURCE: MR. SMITH

Tarp wondered how deep the split between the Argentine navy and air force had become since the Falklands war. Was it deep enough for the two services to be shooting at each other?

QUERY: POPE-GINNA, ADMIRAL, he asked it.

The machine began to give him information at a remarkable rate. He turned on the printer and let it give him the data that way, so that he could have time to absorb it. The printer chattered like a self-absorbed animal, and a tongue of paper was extruded, to fold over on itself and wait obediently for his hand.

POPE-GINNA, ANTHONY MARCUS AURELIUS, it said.

BORN PORTSMOUTH ENGLAND AUGUST 1904/ COMMISSIONED ROYAL NAVY 1923/ FIRST POSTING AS

Tarp's eyes skimmed the paper, passing over a remarkably detailed summary of a naval career. A fact buried in the middle of it caused him to stop, then to backtrack.

COMMANDING OFFICER LIGHT CRUISER HMS LOYAL 1943–44 AND BLUE ATTACK SQUADRON SOUTH ATLANTIC HQ FALKLAND ISLANDS PAREN 4 DESTROYERS, 1 LIGHT CRUISER, SUPPORT VESSELS PAREN/ PURSUED AND SANK GERMAN CRUISER PRINZ VON HOMBURG WATERS SOUTH-SOUTHWEST

GEORGIA ISLANDS 1944/ PERSONAL CITATION/ UNIT CITATION/

Then there were more details, and:

TO ADMIRALTY OFFICE FOR PLANNING AND PREPARATION 1945/ TO SUBSURFACE TRAINING CENTER BRISTOL HAVEN BY OWN REQUEST 1946/ COMPLETED 1947/ STAFF EXEC ATLANTIC UNDERSEA COMMAND 1947–49/ TO ADMIRALTY OFFICE FOR UNDERSEA RESEARCH 1949–51/ REQUESTED RETIREMENT 1952/

Tarp skipped a summary of Pope-Ginna's London life that included his clubs and his wife's gardening society and jumped to:

ARGENTINE RESIDENT 1955 TO PRESENT/ ADVISER ARGENTINE GOVT MARINE RESEARCH AND FISHERIES/ MEMBERSHIP BOARDS OF BANCO FIDUCIA BUENOS AIRES/ SCHNEIDER AGRI-CHEM INC/ SCHNEIDER AGRO-INDUSTRIA/ CORTILE DEL DEVELOPMENTE MERIDIONALE/ ANGLO-ARGENTINE EXPLORATION COMPANY/ NAVOLINEAS ARGENTINAS/ INTELL REPORT MAKES HIM ACTIVE MEDIATOR GB-ARGENTINE FALKLANDS DISPUTE/

Tarp stared at the sheets, over which the letters marched like neat bird tracks.

He called up the map of the tip of South America and the Antarctic Peninsula again.

LOCATE: SINKING OF GERMAN CRUISER PRINZ VON HOMBURG.

A light pulsed on the screen, just at the edge of the drift ice. At the top of the screen the words ESTIMATED LOCATION ONLY appeared.

LOCATE: POLYNYA.

A dotted circle appeared within the line of drift ice. The estimated location of the sunken German cruiser was about two hundred miles outside the circle, north and west.

QUERY: WAS THERE A POLYNYA IN 1944?
NO DATA.
QUERY: EXACT LOCATION PRINZ VON HOMBURG?
NO DATA.

Tarp wanted to argue with the machine.

QUERY: SOURCE FOR ESTIMATED LOCATION PRINZ
VON HOMBURG?
ROYAL NAVY HISTORY OF WORLD WAR TWO.

That made no sense. The Royal Navy did not deal in estimated locations. The war had been over for a generation, so
there seemed no reason to classify the matter. Surely, he
thought, they knew where their ship was when it sank a major
German ship?

Of more interest, however, was just what the German ship
had been doing at the edge of the Antarctic drift ice—and so
close to an area that might now interest Soviet and Argentine
submarines.

I believe I ought to visit London.

Tarp took out a pack frame and put a change of clothes and
food for three days into it. He put both the French and the Canadian identifications in, and the little cigarette lighter with the
two .22 rounds. He put in survival gear—matches and fire
starter; two reflective, ultralight plastic blankets; a light tent; a
subzero down sleeping bag. He propped the pack frame next to
the door with a pair of snowshoes.

That night he sat up with the computer and a glass of Laphroaig, but nothing more could be coaxed from either the machine
or his brain. Yet he felt better. Buenos Aires had become a puzzle rather than a pain. He went to bed with the wind sighing
against the cabin wall behind his head and snow grating against
the window shutters like sand.

When he awoke in the dark of the morning, it was quiet.

Snow's over.

He fried the rest of the biscuits in canned butter and ate them
greedily with the rest of the jam, washed his few dishes, and
propped them in the steel sink as if he would be back for lunch.
He poured antifreeze into the drains again and turned off the
computer. Electric heating units would keep its vital systems
ready to start again.

The sun was hanging in the black trees again when he went
out, but it was not obscured by clouds now, and above it the sky
was a thin yellow and, overhead, cold blue. The day would be
bright, bitter cold, and windless. He put his feet in the snow-
shoe harnesses and put the pack frame on his back and
went down across his clearing and through his woods, down the

river bank to the frozen water, to pick his way among boulders that in the summer made the river a peril to canoes.

He climbed the other bank and headed into the woods, in Canada now. He knew the land here. That night he camped in the hollow under a canopy of trees, and the next night he spent in a motel outside Fredericton, having come the last twenty-three miles in an oil truck. He sent all his gear back to a Canadian border town marked Hold Until Spring. They understood that sort of thing there.

That afternoon he caught a plane to Montreal, and from there he flew to London.

CHAPTER 17

There were hotels above the British Museum where nobody knew him and nobody was likely to look for him. They accepted Mr. Roger Murdock and his Canadian passport without question, and, if the hotel was different from the New Monroe, it was discreet and comfortable enough.

He walked down toward the museum, found a coin telephone box, and called a number at Whitehall. The voice at the other end was very young, very tight, and very officious—the voice of an ambitious boy whose job was to protect his master.

"Seven nine five, Kennington speaking."

"Mr. John Carrington, please."

"Who shall I say is calling, please?"

"An American friend."

"I'm afraid I really can't consider any request to speak to Mr. Carrington without knowing who is calling, sir."

"My name is Friend. Mr. American Friend."

The boy never missed a beat but said in a voice as smooth as butter sliding down a warm skillet, "Mr. Carrington is in conference at the moment, I'm afraid."

"Please tell him that Mr. Friend called, then."

"Certainly."

"Thank you."

"Thank *you.*"

"Good-bye."

"Good-bye to *you.*"

Tarp could picture him—twenty-two or -three, terribly

proper, got up in a diplomat's costume. He could be prime minister one day, if he proved both ruthless and lucky.

Tarp pulled at his lower lip, trying to remember a telephone number. When he could not get it he swung up the directory and began to leaf through the Bs. He stabbed with a finger. "Bentham!" It had been eleven years, but he still disliked forgetting such details. He dialed and put in another coin and held more ready.

"Yes?" cried a shrill but proper female voice. "Yes?"

"Mrs. Muriel Bentham, please."

"This is she!" Mrs. Bentham sounded a little like Margaret Thatcher and a little like an Alpine guide coaxing an echo from a peak.

"I'm looking for the Muriel Bentham who does research."

"Oh, yes." Mrs. Bentham seemed to be hunting for the *mot juste,* but she settled for, "Yes, this is she."

"Yes, Mrs. Bentham, my name is Rider; you did some work for me a few years ago, it had to do with some historical research."

"Oh, yes, Mr. Rider!" He was sure she didn't remember at all, but she said, with that same high-pitched, remarkably loud voice, "The Canadian gentleman who was writing the book about weather."

It turned out that he was the one who had forgotten. He wouldn't have remembered what book he was pretending to write. "Yes, very good," he said.

"How did the book turn out?" she demanded.

"Very well. Thank you."

"I never saw it in the stores."

"It wasn't sold in the stores."

"Oh. How very odd."

"I'd like you to do something more for me."

"Oh, yes, I'd be delighted." Her powerful voice took on a sharpness. "My rates have gone up. Because of the economy."

"Of course."

"Is this about weather?"

"Military history."

"Ah. Very much the same thing."

He supposed that that remark meant something to her. It certainly meant nothing to him. "Naval history, to be precise."

"That's nice. I respect the navy."

"Yes." He wondered if Mrs. Bentham had gone funny in eleven years. She had been, he thought, in her fifties back then, already widowed, the sharpest researcher he had ever encountered. She had been a librarian who had grown impatient with poor pay. "It's about a ship in the Second World War. Can I give you the details now?"

"I was dusting."

"I beg your pardon?"

"I don't have a pencil in my hand. I have a duster."

"Ah."

"I shall need to write it down. Shall I get a pen?"

"Please."

She was back within seconds. "Yes?" she bellowed.

"HMS *Loyal*," he said.

"Yes?"

"I want to know everything about its encounter with a German cruiser called the *Prinz von Homburg* in 1944."

"Surely not everything!" she cried. "Everything would fill volumes."

"Very well, not everything. Salient details."

"Ah, what a nice word *salient* is! You even talk like a writer, Mr. Rudge."

"Rider."

"What?"

"My name is Rider."

"Of course it is." She began to tell him how she would proceed. Her grasp of that seemed very sharp; he decided he would trust to his first experience with her and hope for the best. He said he would call her each evening at the same number, then rang off.

He had several hours until Johnnie Carrington's young man would give him the message or, failing that, until he could get Carrington at home. He had brought no clothes; he would need some. He started to leave the telephone box to hunt out a store, and then, with a smile, he thought of the label in Repin's coat, back in Havana. Hire Attire. He found it in the telephone book, and, still smiling, he headed for the underground.

It was in an area of shops and small restaurants above Knightsbridge. Here, in a back street that was almost an alley, a black sign no larger than the New Monroe's advertised Hire Attire in chipped gold letters. In the window were several dusty bolts of cloth and a faded picture, circa 1965, of a man in evening dress. Inside was the odor of clothespressing, a mixture of steam and burned fiber. There was a counter that divided the shop, shelves stacked with boxes and two clothes racks behind it, and, beyond that, a doorway through which he could see an old man bent over a tailor's bench. The long walls were lined with ranks of closed cupboards, from floor to ceiling.

"I think I need some clothes," Tarp said.

"Oh, yes." The man behind the counter was tall, old, bald, and beaked, but unbent. He looked as if he had been a gentleman or a butler or an actor.

"I'd like a decent suit."

"Of course." The huge nose dominated the face; on each side of it small eyes darted back and forth as if trying to find a way around. The old head was thrown back—it was this gesture that made him seem an actor—and he looked Tarp up and down and all around. "Six feet one, sir?"

"And a quarter."

"Chest forty-four," the man murmured to himself. He raised his eyebrows almost disapprovingly. "Your hips are a problem." He inhaled, ending in a sniff. "So *very* narrow." He turned his head halfway toward the rear doorway. "Mr. Goldberg!"

The other old man got down from his tailor's bench as if every joint in his body hated him for it and came slowly forward, pushing aside a drape that had already been pushed aside, perhaps years before. He had the remains of a once abundant crop of curly hair plastered against his skull with sweat or oil; on the back of his head was a plain black yarmulke. He wore a shirt but no tie, a vest open all the way down, and pants that sagged under a round belly.

"Yes, Mr. McCann?" he said in a sepulchral voice.

"This gentleman wants suitings, Mr. Goldberg, but you see the matter of the hips. Would you prefer that I go small so that you may enlarge, or large so that you can make small?"

Goldberg whipped a worn measuring tape from around his neck and passed it about Tarp's waist as if he were about to do a magic trick. He joined the tape again in front and held it with one hand. "That is some waist you got," he said. "What are you, an ath-a-lete?"

"I'm a farmer," Tarp said softly.

Mr. Goldberg looked up at his eyes, then down at his shoes. "Nice clean farm you got," he said. "Fit his chest and height and I make good the rest, Mr. McCann."

"Thank you, Mr. Goldberg."

"That lot come up from Surrey last month, Mr. McCann. Like it was made for him, except the waist."

"My very thought, Mr. Goldberg."

Goldberg padded back to the workroom, and McCann pulled a wheeled ladder from the back of the store and rolled it along the ranks of cupboards, then stopped partway along and went elegantly up the ladder as if he were rehearsing for an ascent into Heaven. He opened a cupboard up toward the ceiling and took down several garment bags, which he brought down and on an aged circular rack. "The very finest quality, sir," he said. "The *very* finest. The owner was from one of our best families. I cannot mention the name—it is our policy, Mr. Goldberg's and my own, never to mention names—but one of the very best. These are from his estate. I am able to say that such quality can hardly be found anywhere in the world anymore. You know what times we live in." He flipped back a lapel. "Hand stitching, of course—*look* at it." He lowered his voice. "Mr. Goldberg says it is *almost as good as his own*!" He took four suits out of the bags, one a dinner jacket.

"I don't need them all."

"No." McCann sounded sad.

"I need a suit today."

"That is possible, sir."

"I think a friend of mine is one of your customers."

"We are pleased to hear it, sir."

"A Russian."

"I believe we have a Russian client, sir."

McCann's discretion was remarkable. Tarp warmed to him. He tried on the suits. They fit beautifully in the chest and shoulders but were large in the waist, as had been predicted.

"I could make a discount for all four," McCann suggested.

"I could take two of them."

"We'll never find another pair of shoulders like yours. Not to go into those suitings. It's a crime not to take all four."

"Well . . ." He was wearing the dinner suit, which must have been made when its owner was slimmer, for it fit the best of the three. Its style was so out of fashion that it was in fashion again. "I'd take all four if I could store them here indefinitely. And have them always available."

"How long is indefinitely, sir?"

"*Indefinitely.*"

McCann coughed delicately into his right hand and withdrew to confer with Goldberg. He came back smiling. "Since, if you bought all four, sir, you would be a valued customer; and since we do what we can to oblige our valued customers . . . indefinitely is on, sir."

"I'll take the four."

"We'll put a bag in that upper cupboard with your name on it, then, Mr. . . . ."

"Black."

"Yes, I see. Mr. Black." He coughed discreetly again. "Then your suitings will always be there. *Always*, you understand, being a relative term, given my age and Mr. Goldberg's."

"Given the world, *always* is a relative term for everybody."

While the suits were being altered, Tarp found another phone booth and tried to call Johnnie Carrington again, and again he was intercepted by the young man. He bought shoes and shirts and other things and went back to the half-hidden shop.

"That suit is *perfect*," Mr. Goldberg said. "That's a perfect suit you got on. That's a suit has been looking for your body since the day it was made—right, Mr. McCann?"

McCann beamed. "Quite right, Mr. Goldberg."

Tarp wore the suit, which was dark and "correct," and carried the dinner jacket. He stopped his taxi by a telephone and called Whitehall once more, and this time the boy at the other end was almost pleasant.

"Mr. Carrington *will* talk to you, sir." He seemed quite astonished.

The telephone made curious noises, like a stomach.

"John Carrington here."

"Johnnie—it's your friend from Maine."

"It *is* you. How delightful! You *are* the one for dropping in from outer space, aren't you. Are we going to see you?"

"That's why I called."

"Well, sad to say, I can't make dinner, because we dine out it seems every night; if it isn't my career, it's Gillian's charities. We've become terribly social. Terribly."

Laughter came through the voice. It was just a little ragged, as befitted a man in his early thirties who was on the verge of success and power. He was the rising star of MT-5, the son of an agent, fiercely dedicated, ambitious, wealthy through marriage. That he owed his success in part to Tarp was a fact that he never tried to disguise. He had that oddest of qualities in an ambitious man, gratitude.

"How is Gillian?" Tarp said.

"Oh, divine, as always. You know." Indeed, Tarp did know. He had had a brief, splendid affair with her before Johnnie had ever thought of marrying her. Tarp wondered if Johnnie knew and hoped he did not.

"I need to talk to you privately," Tarp said.

"I see. Well, not on this line. Hmm. I've got a dinner I can leave a little early, if needs must be. Why not meet me at home? I'll tell the staff to expect you. Would that do?"

"It would be fine."

"Good, then. About nine-thirty, I think." He gave the address, a very posh one near St. James's, and Tarp rang off and stared briefly at an obscene scribble on the phone booth wall, hoping that he was not going to find an obstacle put between him and Johnnie Carrington by the British decision about the "Maxudov" problem.

He wore the dinner jacket that evening, for no better reason than that he owned it and he knew he looked good in it. In the hotel lobby, the owner, in a sweater and old corduroys, was doing his books behind the rather makeshift counter. He looked over his glasses as Tarp came by. "We don't see many of those in here!" he said.

"I'm an actor," Tarp said. The man laughed and then looked uncertain, and Tarp went out. It was unseasonably warm, and he strolled down Gower Street as the light faded, thinking idly about submarines and the Antarctic and the *polynya*. As he passed a newsstand, some word or phrase in a headline caught his attention, as now and then a word will seem to spring from a page even though the eye has not been seeking it. He had to stop and look over a table spread with newspapers before he could find it again. It turned out to be not even a major headline, but a smaller one partway down a front page.

SOVIET AIRLINE CRASH TOLL SET AT

it said; the rest was over the fold. Tarp dropped a coin among those scattered over the papers and picked it up.

SOVIET AIRLINE CRASH TOLL SET AT 72 IN LUXEMBOURG

He read as he walked. His face betrayed no emotion. His pace did not change. When he finished he folded the newspaper and dropped it into a trash bin and rubbed his fingers to rid them of the dark stain of newsprint.

He went on toward the evening as if he had not just learned that the entire Soviet dance company, including Repin and his mistress, had been killed while returning from Cuba.

CHAPTER 18

An elderly maid showed him into a study in the back of the Carringtons' second story. She told him that Johnnie had telephoned and would be on his way shortly. An Asian butler offered him a drink and then a cigar, and a few minutes later an East Indian maid passed the open door on her way somewhere. It seemed a house of international servitude, in the midst of which Tarp sat very still, hearing little, thinking about Repin's death and wondering if it was time to pack it in. Then he heard voices downstairs in English and a determined step across the foyer, and he knew that Johnnie Carrington had come home.

The first time he had ever seen him, Johnnie had seemed merely a silly young Briton of a certain type—rather chinless and self-consciously foolish, with wonderful manners and a laugh like a horse's whinny. He had turned out to be a courageous man, however, and the foolishness had been self-conscious because it arose from such a deep self-awareness. Now, he was still a little chinless, but he was wearing enormous pale-rimmed glasses that made him seem both older and more serious, and his horsey laugh had been tinged with that raggedness that Tarp had detected on the telephone. There were new lines around his mouth and his eyes, and as he stood there pumping Tarp's hand, he seemed to Tarp somehow older than he was himself.

"How long, how long has it been!" Johnnie exclaimed in that nervous way people use when they do not quite know what to say. It was Tarp's first clue that Carrington was ill at ease with him. *Her Majesty's policies put us at odds. That's bad.*

"Is it two years?" Johnnie was saying. "Not quite. By God, you look amazingly fit, though! Wherever do you get your clothes? I can't get clothes like that! Will you drink with me?"

Carrington was in that heightened state of restlessness that comes from pouring alcohol over fatigue—not drunk by any means, but about one glass beyond what his body wanted.

"What are you drinking?"

Carrington stared quizzically at an array of bottles. "They seem to have put out mostly things I'd eat over pudding. Our staff is a bit polyglot, to say the least, and they don't seem to comprehend what the word *brandy* means. As a result, when one asks that a drinks tray be left out, they supply this sugary pot luck. There's a decent Armagnac here, but so far as I can see, the rest is unspeakable."

"Armagnac is fine, if you're having some."

"Indeed I am." Johnnie poured. Like Tarp, he was in evening clothes. He held out a small glass. " 'Your honor was the last man in our mouths,' as Shylock says." He smiled disarmingly, too disarmingly. "I've been hearing your name a good deal, Tarp."

"Oh?" Tarp set the glass down next to him, untasted.

"Oh, indeed." There was a sharpness in Carrington's voice. He had remained standing; his left hand clenched and unclenched, probably unconsciously. "I had a little speech prepared, you see, but . . . Oh, damn it." He drank off the Armagnac at a gulp. "What's going on?" he said hoarsely. His face flushed, and he suddenly looked middle-aged and burned out.

"I don't understand the question," Tarp said easily.

Johnnie was pouring himself another. "Come off it, Tarp. All hell's breaking loose in Moscow, and your name's in it." He dropped the stopper back into the decanter with clink. "I've been deputed to ask you the question: Have you been recruited to the other side?"

"Who wants to know?"

"Answer the question, please do. Because we're friends. Did Repin recruit you?"

"Repin's dead, they say."

"Please answer me."

"You wouldn't have used that tone of voice two years ago, Johnnie. Maybe authority doesn't sit well on you."

Carrington sagged. He pushed his glasses up his nose, and then the hand continued up his forehead to smooth his dark hair back. "Please forgive me," he said simply. "This is damned difficult for me. I owe you—almost everything. But one of the things I owe you is the lesson that nobody can be trusted all the time."

"Meaning, you don't trust me now?"

"Meaning, have you been recruited?"

"What makes you think so?"

"A hundred and twenty-five thousand dollars in gold showed up in your bank vault Thursday last."

"Bank transactions are supposed to be confidential."

"Oh, come!" Carrington drank off half of the second Armagnac. "I used to work in economics branch; I know the banks damned well. *Confidentiality* is a relative term."

"Where did my gold come from?"

"It came from a KGB front called Bjornson-Bors Holding Company, Limited."

"Are you sure it's KGB?"

"Oh, come."

"Oh, come, yourself. How do you know I did something for the gold?"

Carrington started to speak, then checked himself. "Oh, I see—you think somebody's priming us." He reached for the decanter again, and Tarp said coldly:

"Don't drink any more."

"*What?*"

"If you're going to accuse me of things, I'd prefer you were fairly sober."

"*Damn* you!"

Tarp looked at him, quite unmoved. "There are three things that ruin a career like yours, Johnnie—laziness, selfishness, and alcohol. You're not lazy and you're too decent to serve yourself and let the rest go hang. But you'd better watch out for the third."

Carrington stared at him and then put the little glass down on the tray, empty. He pulled a chair into the circle of lamplight near Tarp and sat down, his hands clasped between his knees and his shoulders rounded. "It's been a terrible few months," he said. The raggedness was gone. He sounded desolate. "We've got a leak and we can't plug it. Everybody's on tenterhooks. HM's government have taken the tack that Moscow can be hoisted on its own petard with their current mess, so when I saw the message traffic implicating you, it was the last straw." He raised his head and smiled apologetically. "You're rather a hero to me."

"Why did you believe I'd been recruited?"

"A report had you in Cuba at the same time as Repin."

"That's very interesting. There seem to be leaks in both directions. But I haven't gone over. Johnnie, come on! I haven't gone over."

Carrington's face was haggard. Tarp knew that the man was fighting the self-knowledge that he wanted to believe Tarp; he had to be forcing himself, therefore, to be especially skeptical.

"How high up are you now?" Tarp asked.

"Five. Number five."

"Who made the decision about your government's tilt in the Moscow mess?"

"There are three committees. It came out of the Foreign Office Policy Advisory Sub-Committee, I suppose. One's never quite sure."

"You weren't involved?"

"I drafted some papers. I never sit on committee."

"I've agreed to do a job for the Soviets for money, Johnnie. Now you tell me that it's a job that your government disapproves of. Do you want me to leave?"

Carrington gave him a half grin. "I wouldn't be very good at my job if I sent away everybody my government disapproved of."

"Somebody killed Repin, Johnnie. That somebody is in Moscow. Somebody tried to kill me in Havana and somebody tried in Buenos Aires. I think that's connected to Moscow, too. I haven't gone over. Part of Moscow is trying to kill me. The other part—may be tolerant of me, nothing more."

"But you took KGB money."

"Yes."

"To help the KGB?"

"How much do you know?"

"We know they're in hot water—and we love it."

"You wouldn't love it if they panicked and decided to start a war."

"That's a bit extreme, isn't it?"

"I didn't think so when I took the job. I don't think so now. It's a choice of evils, I admit. Nothing's easier and more noble than backing away from a choice of evils, I know—I don't touch such filth, one says; let them stew in their own juice. I'm not backing away."

Carrington hunched his shoulders more and squeezed his hands between his thighs. "What is it you want?" he said abjectly. "You want something from me, I know. What?"

"Information."

"What sort?"

Tarp shook his head. "First I have to have your word that you'll say nothing to anybody. *Nothing*. Absolute confidentiality."

"I can't."

"You say you've got leaks, Johnnie! I've got a problem that's as tangled as a head of dirty hair; I can't afford to let anything go. No, I've got to have your word: absolute confidentiality."

Carrington thought a long time. He took his hands from between his thighs and put them on his knees and then he gave Tarp a halfhearted smile. "I'll keep confidential the subjects of the information you want. Then I'll think it over. I may then refuse to give you any information."

"Will you keep quiet even if you do?"

Carrington made a face. "All right."

"I want what you've got on Argentine nuclear armament."

"That's no good. They haven't got anything."

"They're not supposed to have anything, I know. But your people must have such a thing as a contingency. You must have people down there looking into it. I want to know what you have, that's all. If your reports show they haven't anything, then I'll be satisfied."

"This is part of the Moscow business?"

"I think it is."

"Well, I'll think about it. I'd be a dreadful servant of the crown if I gave you such information for free."

"I'll make it a trade, of course. What I learn when it's all over for what you've got now."

"You think it really involves Argentina?"

"It may."

"That's an awfully sore spot for us, you know. The Franks

Report didn't deal too kindly with us. There's an Argentine Committee now. I suppose I oughtn't tell you that.''

"Are you on it?"

"As a matter of fact, I'm not. I'm more European."

"There seem to be lots of committees you're not on."

"Well, it's a question of rank. The Argentine is very important now."

"Who's on the Argentine Committee? Matthiessen?"

Carrington flushed and gave his old horsey laugh of embarrassment. "As a matter of fact, yes. You never liked Matthiessen, I know. But he's awfully good. Awfully good."

"Awfully priggish."

"He's careful, yes."

"Priggish."

Carrington blushed again. "He's my superior. I'd really rather that you didn't . . . It's difficult for me—"

"Sorry. Well. Let's change the subject."

Carrington had flung himself back in the chair. He looked exhausted now, one hand shading his eyes, the other hanging down limply almost to the carpet. "Was Repin your control?" he said.

"I don't have a control. It's not that kind of arrangement."

"You're on your own? Good God, you have got nerve, haven't you! How will you manage with Repin gone?"

Tarp grunted. "I've been wondering that myself."

"Well, it isn't as if you were friends. Is it? I mean, you and Repin didn't owe each other anything."

Tarp kept silent. He was thinking of Southeast Asia, when Repin had been running the Soviet stations and he had been an agent moving back and forth across the Chinese border. Repin's people had almost killed him four different times. "It isn't a question of owing," he said. He was tempted to tell Carrington about the plutonium and Maxudov then, but he did not. "It's simply a question of having made a contract."

Carrington continued to study him from the shadow of his hand. "I wish sometimes I'd done more fieldwork," he said. "You people have that very odd ethos. It gives you and Repin more in common with each other than you have with me." His mouth turned wry. "Most of my life is managing piles of paper, and after a while that's all the reality a civil servant knows—paper. It all becomes paper. It might be good for us to get out in the field and smell the brimstone now and again.''

A few minutes after he said that, his wife came in, and the talk became social and, to Tarp, trivial. Gillian was as lovely as ever, just beginning to show the first signs of maturity. She had stayed behind at the dinner because she was relentlessly social and because, she told Tarp, she believed in her husband's "enormous promise." The implication was that she could help him realize that promise by going to dinner parties. She was probably quite correct, although the promise realized in that fashion would lead him inevitably to more and more paper and less and less "brimstone." She and Tarp exchanged brief looks; he thought there was a hint of challenge, perhaps of flirtatiousness, and he wondered if she was entirely faithful. It was not a curiosity he thought worth satisfying, and after a few minutes he got up to go. She would have gone on, he knew, but her husband was visibly sleepy.

"See here," Johnnie managed to say as he saw him to the door, "I'll let you know tomorrow. About—the matter we discussed."

"I'll call you."

"No. Meet me someplace. I'll have made a decision; one can't shilly-shally. Do you know Prong's?"

Prong's was a club, one of the oldest and least accessible in London.

"I know where it is."

"Meet me there at half five. I'll tell the porter to show you in. I'll have an answer then, I promise."

Tarp refused Carrington's offer of a car and driver and walked. He headed for the theater district, knowing there would be crowds and light there. He supposed that he was being followed: Carrington would have posted somebody in order to keep track of him.

Tarp crossed a busy street and got into a queue waiting for a bus. He watched the people who crossed after him and thought he could identify a thin, tired-looking man as his tracker. The man did not get in the bus line but went up the street and seemed to become interested in a store window offering cheap tours to the Kenya coast.

Several bus routes were served by this one stop, and the queue sorted itself out as buses came roaring in. Tarp lingered where two groups overlapped; he could see the tracker, turned partway toward him, waiting to see which bus he would board. Then a passerby bumped into the man and he lost his balance, put out a hand toward the window and almost fell, and in that moment Tarp pushed past the bus line and cut up a narrow street toward Soho. After half a block he went into a Chinese restaurant whose windows were steamed to translucency by great pots of noodles that were cooking in the front. He picked a table not far from the door and sat where he could watch it, opening the menu but not reading it.

Two people came in, neither of them the tracker. One was a young Chinese who went directly to a flight of stairs and on up; the other was a short, stout man with apple cheeks and a bristle mustache and silver hair that to Tarp looked artificial. Tarp merely glanced at him before turning back to the door; still, he was aware of the man's movements as he came toward the back.

Tarp looked up.

The man pulled out a chair and sat down opposite him, rested his umbrella against the table and began to pull off his gray gloves. Tarp now saw that the redness of the cheeks, the hair, the mustache, were all false.

"Repin!"

The wily old Russian removed his hat with great care so as not to disarrange his wig. His round face was split with a smile. "Is not so easy to kill Repin as Maxudov thinks!"

CHAPTER 19

"How the hell did you find me?"

Repin tapped the wig, meaning to tap the skull under it. "Is not an idiot, this Repin."

"That's a Russian gesture, not an English one. You're too flamboyant for a Brit."

Repin showed his false teeth in a pleased grin. He liked being called flamboyant. "Repin thought he looked the picture of British civil servant."

"How did you find me?"

"Hire Attire. Repin remembers telling you. Repin says to himself, This Tarp, he will look for this place because he likes oddities and he likes hiding places. Yes?"

"I thought they were supposed to be discreet."

"Oh, very discreet. I tell them my tall friend is coming to buy clothes, will they please to give him special treatment. They tell me my tall friend is here already. Aha, I tell myself, he goes next to his old friend Carrington. So. I wait outside Carrington's house. In truth, I never thought I find you that way; tomorrow, I try dead drop in Geneva, which takes a week to reach you."

"You're on the run?"

"*Da*—very fast."

A waiter appeared and proved immediately that he did not know enough English to matter, and they both started to speak to him in Chinese, then stopped, aware that it was a mistake. Tarp stumbled through an order in English for noodles with garlic fish for two. When the waiter had ambled off, looking

171

cocky and careless, Tarp said, "Are you supposed to be dead?"

"Oh, yes. Was very bad, that plane crash. Many bodies still unidentified."

"Were you warned?"

Repin shook his head. His small eyes were angry, his face impassive with a control that came from rage. "The KGB flunky I show you in Havana, at the ballet, you remember? At Luxembourg, I see him leaving plane. Very peculiar. I see him meet with man in mechanic's overalls. They go away. So, I tell Svetlana Mikhailovna, do nothing, act natural, I must leave. Young woman of air crew, she tries to stop me; she tells me pilot has very strict schedule. I tell her I am KGB, which she really knows anyway, and I do what I want. I leave airplane, sniff around, follow young KGB fellow. You know where I find him? In a trash container, dead. By then my aircraft is in flight. Then it is over—within sight of the airport." He raised his hands quickly: an explosion. Tarp thought of the dancers who had been so lithe and so young.

"Who knows you're in London?"

"Nobody." Repin looked unhappily into his teacup. "I had extra set of papers, you understand. Insurance. You understand insurance."

"Yes."

Repin sipped the tea. "Has not been easy, however. Repin is not used to being renegade. Yes, renegades—is what we are now." His thought had kept pace with Tarp's. "A place like this—is our home, eh? Our China. Is for you and me like rendezvous on moon." The angry calm came down over his face again. "Repin did not think this Maxudov would try to kill him. Repin did not think he would kill Svetlana Mikhailovna. Such legs! Even, forgive me, for a woman of her age—forty—a body of great character. And dead now. Is very clumsy kind of assassination, this. Like murder of my man at Havana, yes? Is not *mokrie dela* either one, not like Department Five. Is clumsy, desperate. Is . . ." He searched for the word. "*Wasteful.* You know how I know is bad work? When I see the little KGB fellow leave the aircraft, then I begin to know. Why? Because, if Repin decides to send flunky with aircraft to be blown up, he does not tell flunky about it—flunky gets blown up, too. This is because Maxudov has not enough people. No organization. No bureaucracy, eh? Must make do with few people." He looked away from Tarp, his face grim. "Still, is very, very bad, this. Is very deep business."

"Is there anybody you can call on for help?"

"Nobody I trust." He laughed. "Except you!"

Tarp did not laugh. " 'When the hunter comes, the tiger runs with the deer.' Where are you staying?"

"Last night, Hyde Park. A little cold, but not bad."

The noodles came, clean and shiny on thick white plates, with chunks of browned onion and garlic and pungent fish lying among them like flowers. Fragrant steam filled the space between them. Repin bent his face into the steam and inhaled luxuriously. He was very hungry, Tarp saw.

"Shall we give it up?" Tarp said.

"No."

"The British aren't going to help me. We're very isolated."

"No."

"You were going to be my contact in Russia; now you can't even get back there yourself. The top echelon is supposed to have guaranteed your safety; they couldn't even keep you safe on an Aeroflot flight. If you stay outside the Soviet Union, you're neutralized; if you go back . . ."

"What do you suggest?" Repin said through a mouthful of noodles.

"I have no suggestions. You know that you could go over to the West. You have money here, I'm sure. Files. Johnnie Carrington would be delighted to protect you, I'm sure."

Repin chewed. His eyes, hooded now, seemed fixed on Tarp's nose. Repin swallowed, drank tea, never looked away. "I am Soviet citizen. Bad or good, I am Soviet citizen. You understand?"

"Yes."

"You read Pasternak?"

"Yes."

"Do not ask me again if I defect. Nor do I give up this Maxudov thing. Especially after this madness with the aircraft." He laid his left forearm on the table so that it enclosed the plate of noodles and bent over it, shoveling food in again. After he had swallowed again he said, "I have message from your woman. From Mimosa."

"Yes?"

"She is sending a messenger to the place you told her. Noon each day."

Tarp frowned. He had given her the address of a place called Ivan's in Paris. "Was that the whole message?"

"Yes. No sweet nothings, I am afraid."

"How was she?"

"Much too good. Too cheerful. She is new at all this, I think. Plus also, she thinks she is 'in love.' Ha-ha. When you meet messenger, you carry a Havana newspaper; the messenger carries a rose. Sweet, yes?"

"A rose?"

"A rose. Yes. Is infantile."

Tarp thought about that. "It's all infantile," he said vaguely. He watched Repin eat. "You need a place to stay."

Repin shrugged. "Another night in the park is possible." He smiled sarcastically. "I have your gun for protection."

"My gun!"

"Yes. I bring it from Havana."

"I really wouldn't like it if you shot somebody in London with my gun."

"Well, if the choice is shooting somebody with your gun and shooting somebody with no gun at all, and I need to shoot somebody, I think your gun will be my choice."

"I'll find you a place to stay. What sort of passport have you got?"

"Belgian. Is very good passport. Very expensive."

"I'll call somebody."

"Who is somebody?"

"One of those people who are useful for money. You know those people, right?"

"Very useful people." Repin's plate was empty and his eyes strayed to Tarp's plate. Tarp pushed it across and Repin began to eat. "I'll be back," Tarp said. He moved toward a telephone on the wall, and on the way he stopped the waiter and ordered stuffed dumplings for Repin. He dialed a number in the East End and waited while it rang and rang. When at last the telephone was answered he heard a pounding din and loud voices, and then somebody shouted, "Other Cheek, hello!"

"Jenny Barnwell!"

"Can't hear you, it's a madhouse here."

"Jenny Barnwell!"

"Not here."

"Of course he is."

"Not here."

"It's a hundred pounds for him and ten for you."

The racket at the other end seemed to increase, underscored by the hard pounding of a rock band's bass. The voice he had been talking to seemed to have gone away. As suddenly, it was back. "Gimme a number," it said. Tarp read him the telephone number from the wall telephone. "Five minutes," the voice said and hung up.

Tarp waited by the telephone. He watched Repin welcome the arrival of the dumplings and begin on them. He cleared a quarter-sized place on the window of steam and looked out, checking for Carrington's—or anybody else's—tracker. When the telephone rang, he picked it up on the first jangle.

"Well?"

"This is Jenny, who's this?"

"Jenny, it's the Chinaman."

"Oh, Christ, I should have known." Jenny was male and well past thirty and even when he was happy he sounded dyspeptic. "I was led on with talk of a hundred pounds." Behind him the Other Cheek's music pounded unmercifully.

"The hundred pounds is real, Jenny."

"For what?" Barnwell said suspiciously.

"I've got a friend needs a bed."

"What is he, an ax murderer? I know your friends."

"He's a man with a hundred pounds a night."

"In advance?"

"In advance. But he's got to be secure, Jenny. You know what would happen if he wasn't."

"Christ, yes, I know you. What is he, a Chink?"

"Belgian."

"Oh, come on! Belgian, my ass! Well, all right. When?"

"Now."

"Now? Christ, I was just meeting somebody nice!"

"Meet me."

"Oh, Christ, just when I was settling in." His voice had an adolescent tone of abused righteousness. "Where?"

"Have you got wheels?"

"A borrowed cycle is it."

"Camberwell New Road in half an hour. Pick a place."

"Oh, all right. Christ, I hate you. All right, there's a BP petrol stand halfway along; go another street and you'll see a lighted sign on the left. It says 'Rose.' That's all, just Rose. I'll be there. It's dark and nothing ever going down."

"Half an hour."

"All right, all right!"

When Tarp got back to the table, Repin was sitting with his hands hanging down beside him, smiling contentedly at nothing. He belched discreetly and said, "My first food in thirty-six hours."

"I've got a place for you. A hundred pounds a night."

"Where is this, please, Buckingham Palace?"

"With an acquaintance."

"He is what, financier?"

"Actually he's a leather queen, but he's safer than the Bank of England. Come on."

He hustled them into a taxi. There was, indeed, a small neon sign that read only Rose on the left side of Camberwell New Road, shocking pink against a particularly black stretch of ugly building. It seemed to mark no doorway, no shop or restaurant.

Barnwell had pulled the cycle into the shadow of a building, and he was lurking sullenly with his haunches up on the rear fender.

"Hello, Jenny."

Barnwell sighed. A slight odor of alcohol drifted between them. Barnwell was wearing a black leather jacket and leather pants and sunglasses. "Where's your friend?" he said.

"Don't be a smart-ass, Jenny. Nobody loves a smart-ass."

"Nobody loves a hard case, either. Christ, what am I doing, messing about with you again? I swore I'd never do it."

"I pay well."

"Bloody hands, that's what you've got—fucking bloody hands. Bloody well better pay well, the hands you got."

Tarp gave him a hundred-pound note. Barnwell sighed again. "Nobody'll crack a note like this where I come from," he whined.

"Life is hard, Jenny. Want to do a job for me?"

"Wot, another?"

"Yes."

"Oh, Christ! Well, all right, if it pays. You're fucking Mephistopheles, you know, seducing my innocence?"

"Give me a number where you can pick up a message. I'll leave a time. Add three hours to that time and call me here." Tarp gave him a slip of paper with the number of a phone booth near Russell Square.

"Wot's this, then, cops and robbers?"

"Spies and hard cases. It's the new fad." He signaled to Repin, who got slowly out of the cab and lumbered toward them. "Don't cross him," Tarp murmured. "He's very tough."

"Christ, if he's a friend of yours, I wouldn't dare say Ta to him. Wot you take me for?"

Tarp introduced them in the most cursory sort of way, using no names. They appraised each other and were, it seems, about equally appalled.

"Mind your manners with each other," Tarp said. "Jenny, I'll call you. Remember what I said."

"Yes, Mum. I'll be a good boy."

He touched Repin's shoulder. *"Dormez bien, monsieur."*

Barnwell kicked the big cycle into a roar and, without a word to Repin or Tarp, took it down over the curb and into the street. Tarp saw Repin's arms go around the leather-clad waist, and then they were up the road, and he could hear them long after the taillight had disappeared.

Tarp went back to his Bloomsbury hotel. As he slipped into sleep his last thought was of Maxudov, the faceless power who seemed able to check him now at every move.

CHAPTER 20

He awoke from a dream of anger and lay in the strange bed keeping it alive. A man who had tried to teach him martial arts long, long before had been in it; and Juana had been in it. The dream had been erotic; he had the evidence of his body for that. They had been coupled, he and Juana; there had been some fear of interruption. "Your lesson, your lesson," she had said. Then—or had it been earlier? Or had he dreamed it several times, so that each preceded and followed each—that awesome battler from his past had tried to teach him self-protection.

I was always afraid of him. Tarp scowled into the dark room. *I was always on the defensive.*

The teacher had been Maxudov, he realized. Yes, he was certain of it now. Somehow, in the cocoon of the mind, the unknown Maxudov had metamorphosed into the long forgotten teacher. *And put me on the defensive.*

There was the source of the anger. Tarp stood up, naked. *Because I've been two moves behind him ever since I got to Cuba. I haven't been able to make a move. I've done nothing but react.*

He left the little hotel before the front door was unlocked, letting himself out into a silent street where the day was only a gray wash by which the eye could distinguish a tree from a car, an iron paling from a building half a block behind it. The dream stayed with him like vapor trailing from an engine. *On the defensive.* He could not stop being angry.

He found himself resenting Juana's messenger and this trip to Paris. He ought to be doing something different. He ought to be making his own move; he ought to be on his way to Moscow. Now Maxudov had made that more difficult by negating Repin.

A taxi put him down near the Opéra before ten. He had not been in Paris for a year, but it was not a city he greatly cared for. Still, it had been the center of the world for him at one time, and so he returned to it with a certain curiosity, as if he might find himself walking down one of its side streets, a slight, perhaps not remarkable adolescent. It was hard for him not to look at Paris as if it, too, partook of his dream, so firm was the grip of the night on him. He began to walk. He passed a building where a trading company had in other days had an office, actually a front for French intelligence. He walked down toward the Quai d'Orsay, then turned away from it. He had been in and out of Paris a lot just after Dien Bien Phu, putting a network together from the shreds the French had left behind. Now he was gone from Southeast Asia and other people had patched his nets and put something new together. He saw Paris mostly in that context, as a place where he had begun something that had failed. Perhaps surprisingly, he was not made sad by the place and its reminder of failure; far less was he made bitter by it. He had learned that from his French mentors, who had known so much failure that they accepted eventual failure as part of the learning process that is history.

In the dream he had had only one eye. No wonder he had been on the defensive.

Dreams were a form of thought, perhaps a form of learning. They spoke in puns and seeming riddles, as oracles used to speak to the antic half of the brain. He thought of all the sayings about eyes: to see with half an eye; he closed one eye to; in the kingdom of the blind, the one-eyed man; to have eyes to see. *I-eye. With only half of I.*

He was passing Palais Royal, but his inner vision was so startling that he stopped where he was and almost collided with a woman coming behind him. *A dark circle of water like an iris in an ocean of white—the* polynya *like a dark eye in the ice.* Had he read that? Or was it simply the ability to see in metaphor?

He turned left around Palais Royal and made his way toward the Pont Neuf; on the bridge itself he began to overtake clusters of people moving toward the Left Bank. Many of them were young, but some were middle-aged and older; he thought he recognized Scandinavians and Germans, a few East Indians, and here and there an African in a bright-colored printed cloth over warmer European clothes. He heard English spoken, recognized the nasality and the hard r's of American. There were many French. An unusual sense of community prevailed, and he looked more closely at the signs on the lampposts and on the placards that some of the people were carrying. *Givrage mondiale. Journée de paix atomique.* A young woman with pretty breasts was wearing a shirt that read *Veux-tu qu'on les bruler?* Some of the signs had been tied to the posts with string and hung down slackly, like masks pulled down around their wearers' necks. *Journée de témoignage contre la guerre atomique,* with an arrow pointing ahead—Day of witness against atomic war.

A girl pinned a button on his coat. It was white. In blue letters in a circle was the single word *Givrage*: Freeze. She smiled up at him, then kissed him with an impulsiveness that was easy and erotic. Some image from the dream flashed: Juana, a kiss, her beautiful face.

The crowd turned left at the end of the bridge and he turned right, then left again into the little streets of St.-Germain. He had lived here during one winter. He did not envy these young ones now. He touched the button on his lapel, thinking of the futility of such gestures. Still, he left it where she had put it.

Ivan's was a cafe not far from the church of St.-Germain-des-Près, as French as a tourist poster but recognizably Jewish to those who loved the food. In the mornings the pastries looked like relatives of New York's Danish; at lunch and dinner Eastern Europe and Second Avenue were not too far away. Ivan's had always been there for Tarp; it went back before the war, it was said, although Ivan, whoever he was, had disappeared with others of the Resistance. Today, its outdoor chairs were tipped against the tables and no waiters leaned in the doorway, watching for sidewalk customers. Inside, however, the brass and mahogany shone, and the warm smell of coffee mingled with that of pastry and something slightly sour that was being readied for lunch.

Tarp sat against a wall between two long windows. There were at least thirty people in the place, although it was early for lunch, late for breakfast. He ordered coffee and spread the Havana paper on the table so that the masthead was visible. Now that he was there, he could try to cleanse his mind of his anger and the dream. He sat quietly. He looked at a neutral piece of wall, which long before had been painted to imitate marble and then varnished so many times that it had become simply a varnish-colored space.

The Maxudov of the dream reappeared, with the face of the man he had not thought about in years. Is that what Maxudov was—one man in another? Or was it rather that Maxudov's identity was less important than something else? Was it, instead, that Maxudov existed in relation to something else? *A bargain has two hands,* was the saying. So that it was not simply Maxudov . . . His attention flickered. *Not simply Maxudov . . .*

He had seen the rose. That was the signal, and it brought him back to the world of Ivan's and the gleaming white button on his jacket, back to *Givrage Atomique* and the message from Havana. The rose was red, and its stem and and all but one leaf of the flower were wrapped in white paper. It was carried in the hand of a tall woman with a stunning figure who had come in and who was standing with her back to him so he could not see her face, one of those women who give Paris its reputation for style despite the silly clothes its designers force on other women. She was wearing blue jeans so tight they outlined the cleft of her buttocks; a wide leather belt of the sort that American bikers used to wear; high, shiny, cruel-looking boots with soft insteps; and a tan nylon jacket with a boyish, stand-up collar, the jacket so short it showed off most of the studded belt. She was wearing enormous sunglasses, but what he noticed was her hair, which was cut like a punk rocker's, with a high comb of black, feathery strands along the top of her skull and short strands over her ears and around the back.

She strode to a table across the restaurant, turning toward him as she bent to sit. She was wearing a black T-shirt under the jacket, with a luridly fluorescent picture of a mushroom cloud and a fireball on it. Her face turned to him, as stark and beautiful as a piece of sculpture within the clasp of the demonic hair.

It was Juana.

He supposed he had been expecting her all along. It was a very different-looking Juana, to be sure. She looked slimmer. She did not look as if she came from a people's republic of anything; her makeup was lavish and deliberate. She looked—there was no other way to put it—*rich.*

She saw him but she gave no sign of recognition. Tarp glanced around the restaurant; several men were looking at her. He was aware of motion near the door, but when he looked there, whoever had moved was gone. The dream, the idea about Maxudov, vanished at once; an internal alarm began to sound.

She stood up. She held the rose. *Follow me,* she and the rose were saying.

Tarp got up. *Danger,* his internal sense told him.

She had gone into a short corridor that led to the toilet. He started after her. His eyes continued to search the room for the source of danger—somebody watching her too closely, somebody watching him, somebody with a weapon.

He entered the corridor, the dining room now behind him. She was standing by a door at the far end, a dozen feet away. He stopped to look behind him.

Wrong, said the familiar voice inside his head. *It's wrong.* He was turning back to look at her, turning to see if she had a weapon, turning to see if it was she who was betraying him, turning to see how Maxudov had put him on the defensive again—to see she had no weapon, but welcomed him, smiled, waited—and he knew as he turned that whatever was wrong was behind him: he had seen it in the flash of a car door out the restaurant window, seen it in movement in the street: a human head, a hand, the hand reaching up to the black wool cap above the face, pulling the front down, making a mask of a rolled-up ski cap.

He threw himself at her. She had no sense of danger. Her smile was real and loving. She was raising her hands to embrace him, the rose in the left. He threw himself at her and wrapped her up in his long arms and crashed through the door of the restroom.

Somebody screamed behind him. The scream was obliterated instantly by the obscene clatter of an automatic weapon. *Oh, God, no,* Tarp thought, *not here. They've been through enough here,* but the weapon went on in outrageous spurts. Many people were screaming; somebody was shouting in rage. The smell of spent ammunition reached him, hot oil and nitrite, then a smell of plaster. Glass was breaking. Another weapon began firing, then the two together.

Tarp let her go as he smashed through the door with his shoulder; he swung her into the room and pulled his hands free, tearing at the little metal cigarette lighter in his pocket. There was no way to get out of the restaurant from here, but there was a back door down another corridor. But that was where the first weapon seemed to come from, and he knew that somebody had come in the back and had started shooting at thirty people, most of them French Jews, who were drinking coffee and eating pastry on this slightly gray Parisian day of witness for atomic peace.

He popped open the derringer barrels as he was swinging back into the corridor. Behind him he heard her shout, *"No!"* but he drove on, moving fast now, a large man with great quickness and a huge anger. He was a stride from the main room when a man wearing a ski mask moved into the opening ahead of him, his left side to Tarp, his eyes on the restaurant. Tarp could see smoke and dust beyond him; he could see an overturned table and a trickle of coffee on the floor, and an old man who had been hit in the chest and stomach by automatic weapons fire, lying against a table with blood gushing from his heart.

Tarp raised the little gun.

The man in the ski mask was changing clips. He turned. Tarp saw the eyes. They looked young and surprised and therefore innocent. Tarp put his fist against the mask and pulled the trigger and shot one of the eyes, and the man screamed and tottered backward.

Tarp lunged for him, wanting his weapon. He saw the other figure silhouetted against the silver light of the door. He wanted the assault rifle to turn on that other one.

Juana was clawing at his left shoulder. He tried to push her away. She was screaming. She was weeping—the tears astonished him, as if tears were out of place in such atrocity. He put his hand on her face and tried to shove her back. She caught his arm and he slipped; off-balance, he dropped to his left knee, just inside the corridor. She was standing over him.

A grenade exploded on the far side of the restaurant. He was looking up at her. One moment she was weeping, trying to pull at him, and the next she was lying on the worn carpet of the corridor, blood where her tears had been and her hands scrabbling at the carpet in confusion and pain.

The concussion stunned him. Deafened, he lost contact with his world: Juana's mouth was open, working, but he could not hear her. The screams and the firing seemed to have stopped. For him they were ended.

The air was thick with plaster dust. He bent over her. Her fashionable jacket and the T-shirt had been slashed from under the left arm across the shoulder and the neck. The left side of her face looked like red lace. He could not see her left eye.

He was thinking only of getting out. The two attackers had been after him, he was sure: the movement he had seen just after she had come in had been somebody following her, looking for him. And when they had started to fire, they had aimed at the place where he had been sitting. He wanted to get out before the police came and made their gory, helpless sense out of the scene, before they took down names and identified the dead. He wanted to get out while there would still be a few hours when his pursuers thought he was one of those in the other room.

He picked her up. The fluorescent picture on her shirt was obscured by blood. Her rose was gone.

CHAPTER 21

He carried her out the back door of Ivan's the way he had carried the poet out of her apartment in Havana. This time the danger was real and his heart was pounding and he was urging himself on because he wanted to save her. There was the abrasive noise of sirens now, as there had been in Havana; there were muffled screams, shouts. The grenade had blown out all the windows of the restaurant and then the second attacker had disappeared; Tarp had brought her out in the seconds between the explosion and the noise of the first siren.

He put her down by the rear entrance and went outside alone, waiting for the bullet, almost eager for it; when he knew it was safe, he picked her up and ran along the curving, alleylike street. A dumply woman in black with rolled-down black stockings came clumping toward him with two long loaves of bread under her arm, and as he ran past she saw Juana's face and bloody shoulder and she backed against a wall on the other side. He was already past her then, and he ran on, coming out on the rue Jacob, pushing himself past concern for breathing or fatigue. There had been a *pharmacie* along here years before, and he ran toward the location. In the next streets, ambulances and police cars made inhuman noises.

He carried her into the narrow shop. The astringent smell seemed not to have changed in thirty years.

"Aidez-moi!" he gasped. *"Secours!"* Two middle-aged women looked up from a display of hot-water bottles. Somebody appeared at the back of the shop, a younger woman with a suspicious face.

"A woman is hurt!" he shouted at her in French. He put Juana down in the single aisle between the ceiling-high shelves and pushed the women out of the way as he grabbed at bottles of disinfectant and paper packages of gauze.

"What is it? What is it?" one of the women said excitedly. Her voice seemed to come to him from the vaults of a church because his ears were still affected. "Was it a bus?" she said.

"Terrorists."

The woman sucked in her breath. "Eh, terrorists," said the other one, as if that explained everything. She looked down at Juana's bloody face and winced and pulled the other woman away.

The younger woman came very deliberately from the back of the shop. He had ripped the tan jacket from the shoulder by then and was ripping apart what was left of the black T-shirt, rending it down the side below the arm so that Juana's torso was bared.

"This is a matter for the police," the younger woman said. She was wearing a white shop coat over a dress.

Tarp was spilling disinfectant over the wounds. "There are people dead," he said. "The police are already there." He was shoving a whole pack of wadded gauze into a hole in Juana's shoulder, trying to stop the blood.

"She is dying," the female pharmacist said.

"Check her legs for injuries." He could see the gash along the pectoral and the shoulder; it was deepest close to the arm, where blood was welling through the scarlet bandage.

He wiped the side of the beautiful face. There were a bruise and a gash under the ridiculously short hair, and three deep cuts high up on the cheek, as well as a pulpy abrasion on the temple. He could not see the left eye at all.

"Nothing," the woman was saying as she knelt over Juana's legs. She ran her hands over the thighs, then over the pelvis and abdomen. "Nothing. Nothing. Nothing, nothing."

One of the middle-aged women had pulled an invalid's cushion from somewhere and put it near, but not under, Juana's head, and the other was in the back of the store, running water. "Poor thing," the first woman muttered.

"We've got to stop the bleeding," Tarp said.

"We can't." It was the pharmacist.

"We've got to stop the bleeding!" He was shouting at her, furious. "Stop the bleeding!"

"Poor, poor thing. So pretty."

"You've got to stop the bleeding." Tarp pushed rolls of bandage into the pharmacist's hands and ran to the back of the shop. To his surprise, he was limping. He found a telephone on the counter and dialed without even thinking. The telephone was picked up before it had rung twice.

"Central."

"This is Chimère. I must talk to Laforet."

"You have the wrong line."

"No, I haven't! This is an emergency!"

"I know no Laforet. Please free this line."

"Put me through to Laforet! It's Chimère!"

But the man had rung off. Tarp looked down the shop. The three women were looking down at the floor. They looked dumbstruck. One of them was holding a rubber hot-water bottle that she had filled with water. She held it with both hands, numbly. The pharmacist knelt, and when she stood up she held a ball of dark-red, dripping gauze.

Tarp scrabbled through the pages of the telephone directory. At last he found the number and dialed, hearing background traffic and pops and fizzing sounds.

"The Office of the Sub-Minister for External Affairs."

"Monsieur Laforet, please. It's an emergency. Tell him it's Chimère."

"On the part of whom, monsieur?"

He looked down the shop. Two people came to the door and peered in. One was a woman who had been crying. There was a smear of blood on her skirt.

"Chimère."

The woman came into the shop. She was gesturing behind her, but she had seen Juana on the floor, and she seemed unable to speak.

"Laforet here."

"Jules, thank— I've got an emergency."

"Are you in Paris?"

"Yes. It's medical. I need a doctor and blood. And protection."

"You understand the rules—"

"Fuck the rules! I'll explain later."

"Where are you?"

"A pharmacy, rue Jacob just east of rue Napoleon."

"The identification will be 'Marc Antoine.' "

He started back down the aisle. His right leg did not seem to want to move very well. The pharmacist was piling bandages into the arms of one of the women; the newcomer with blood on her dress was weeping and in shock and unable to take her eyes from Juana.

He knelt again by the injured head. A puddle of blood had formed under her. Someone had laid white bandage over her bare breast.

He could not find a pressure point with which to control the bleeding, but the blood was dark and steadily flowing and so he thought at least that it was not arterial. He put another fist-sized wad of gauze into the wound and pressed down, and he was still kneeling there, trying to control the bleeding, when a voice above him said, "I am looking for Marc Antoine."

"Here!" he said. A dumpy-looking man in a raincoat knelt next to him. "Her?"

"Yes."

The man stood up quickly and shouted, "In here!" to somebody outside, and two men in hats and coats came in quickly, picked Juana up, and went out again. They looked like gangsters. They might have been gangsters, for all he knew; they showed no interest in her. Their care was for speed, that was all. Tarp was pushed into the back of a van with her and the dumpy man, and he was hardly in before one of the men was slamming the door and pounding the side of the van as he ran forward, shouting, "Go, go!"

Tarp had seen the logo of a delivery service on the van. Inside, however, there was a stretcher clamped to the floor and an IV bottle. The dumpy man was holding on to a cleat and swaying above her. "That cut's a bitch," he said. "Not a knife."

"Grenade."

"Shit." He bent close, then straightened. "In that restaurant?"

"In a restaurant, yes. Are you a doctor?"

"We're going to the doctor. We heard about the restaurant as we came out. After the Jews again, were they?"

"It's a Jewish restaurant," Tarp said heavily. He was thinking of the old man whose blood had been gushing from his chest.

The van darkened as they passed under an arch, and a heavy door closed behind them. They drove for another eight feet, coming out into light again. There were walls close in on both sides. They made two turns, then backed for several yards.

"Where are we?" Tarp said.

"Safe house." The dumpy man gave a rubbery smile. There was a smear of blood on his right cheek; when he gestured, Tarp saw that he was wearing bloody surgical gloves. "The best in Paris. You must be a big cheese." He kicked the door open and held it with his foot while Tarp got painfully out; by then two men were there with a stretcher, and a nurse was standing by the van looking up at the smoke-darkened stone walls that rose five stories above them. Tarp could not hide the limp as he went went through a neoclassical doorway after the stretcher and then along a tiled floor into an elevator almost too small for the stretcher. They went up three slow floors and came out in a bright corridor with ceiling-high windows with curved tops. Tarp could see the Seine and the bridge he had crossed ninety minutes before. *For my day of witness.*

The doctor was a young man who looked as if he disapproved of everything that was happening. He had been called from somewhere else, clearly, and he was still struggling into a gray surgical gown. He noticed Tarp's leg, then looked at Juana as they wheeled her past him, and he said, "The woman first," and disappeared through a big oak door.

"Are we on the Ile de la Cité?" Tarp said to the dumpy man, who was fanning himself with one of the sleeves of his raincoat. It was cold in the anteroom, but he was not used to hurrying.

"Mm," he said. He raised himself from his chair to look out the window. "Notre Dame is the other way."

Another man appeared with a telephone and plugged it in near Tarp. *"Le chef,"* he said. He looked meaningfully at the dumpy man. *"Privé."* The dumpy man got up and moved away to the far end of the room.

"Chimère here."

"Tarp, I just heard about the bombing. How are you?"

"I'm good, Jules. A woman with me is hurt."

"Yes, I've been told. I shall want you to be debriefed."

"Of course."

"Were they after you?"

"Why would they be after me?"

"I am not pleased that you have brought this sort of trouble."

"I didn't know it would be like this."

"You are not an innocent, I think."

"No."

"I am not grateful at all. We have enough violence here."

"Jules, I'm sorry. Truly sorry."

Laforet was quiet. "We are always truly sorry. Afterward."

Tarp sighed. "Yes." He was looking at his right leg. The trouser was torn from the knee to the ankle, and the calf was dark with caked blood.

"I may hold you for a while, Tarp."

"Why?"

"Come, you know why."

"Not too long, Jules."

"That depends."

"On what?"

"You know 'on what.' "

On my telling him what I am doing, yes.

"All right."

"I'll send an interrogator to you. It's routine, you know. Be honest, please, and be consistent. Nobody expects you to be entirely truthful, of course. I shall have to file a report. I want to talk to you myself, too. Tonight?"

He thought of Repin. "Sooner?"

"All right. Wait." Laforet left the telephone, probably to talk to an appointments secretary. When he came back he said, "I can spend half an hour before lunch. Will you be frank with me?"

"Yes. Jules, it's important that I get back to London."

A pause. "We shall see." Another pause. "Who is the woman? Come, come, my friend; if I can start things now, you will leave that much sooner. Well?"

"Her name if Juana Marino. She's Cuban. Born in Moscow."

"Ah. Would I have a file on her?"

"You might."

"Ah. Well, we shall have things to talk about. Until lunch, then."

"Thank you, Jules."

He handed the telephone to the other man. He turned and stared out at the Seine, thinking of Juana and the old man dying on the restaurant floor. Unthinkingly, he put his hand up to touch the shiny button the girl had pinned on him, but it was gone.

CHAPTER 22

Jules Laforet was nearing sixty, but he was still austerely handsome. Once, he had been romantically handsome, like the men on the covers of cheap editions of Malraux—a weapon in one hand, the face turned to look at some ideal that was just out of view—but age had refined and tempered him. He had begun as a Socialist but he had become an aristocrat, proving, perhaps, that it is easier to keep one's looks than one's ideals. Thin, silver-haired, beautifully dressed in the slightly flamboyant style of French tailoring, he looked like a very rich poet. He shook Tarp's hand, holding it a little longer than was necessary because they were old friends, and then he sat in a fragile chair with his back to a view of the river.

"I have the interrogation report. They were very cursory, as I instructed."

"Very."

"And your leg?"

"Not bad."

"Nine stitches is not bad, no. You look a little as if you may be still in shock. The woman, on the other hand . . ."

"Yes, they told me."

"She is more serious."

"Yes."

Laforet took out a thin silver cigarette case and opened it one-handed. The action seemed dated, of the thirties, though he was not so old as that. "A very evil business," Laforet said. "Six dead, seven injured. Two of them children." He selected a cigarette and then lit it with Tarp's lighter-derringer, which he pro-

192

duced from his own pocket. Tarp had been searched earlier. "One of the attackers was killed," Laforet said. "A Palestinian. A stray bullet or a piece of one, the police think just now." He held up the lighter. "You?"

"Yes."

Laforet pulled up the end so that the .22 chambers showed. "Not at any distance, I should think."

"About an inch."

"That would seem about right." Laforet exhaled. He crossed his long legs, down which the trouser crease ran like a wire. He moved a finger and thumb along it as if to make it even sharper. "What is going on?"

"Dzerzhinsky Square. Repin asked me to look into a problem there."

"Why you?"

" 'We love the enemies of our enemies.' "

"I thought Repin was out of favor."

"That's why they picked him."

Laforet drew lightly on the cigarette. "I suppose, to a modern Russian, an old Stalinist seems rather quaint." He tapped ash with a practiced movement. "How bad is this business?"

"Bad." He told about the attacks in Cuba and Argentina, the crash of the Soviet aircraft. "And now this. It's a bloodbath."

"Buenos Aires," Laforet said musingly. "Why Buenos Aires?"

"I can't say yet."

"Yes you can."

"Jules—"

"My friend, you are in no position to bargain. You are in France on an illegal passport; you have an illegal weapon; you were meeting a Cuban agent at the time of a terrorist attack! If we chose to put you on trial, we could send you to prison for life."

"That would be embarrassing for you." Tarp knew a lot about French intelligence.

"Of course it would. But your positon is a weak one."

"Let's make a deal."

"What?"

"Information for a protected base."

"What information?" Laforet put the cigarette out carefully in a brass ashtray.

"A full report when it's over. An outline now."

"What sort of protected base did you have in mind?"

"A safe house where the woman can recuperate and where I can come and go. Some basic communications."

"Sanctuary?"

"Yes."

"That would implicate my government."

"Not if you keep your distance."

"Now, would you tell me, could a sub-minister of my experience and reliability 'keep his distance,' might I ask?"

"A cover story." They held each other's eyes for some seconds. "You are like a stone," Laforet said. "Unmovable." He laughed softly, like a man who has spent his life in places where loud laughter was improper. "And outrageous, as well. What is France getting in return?"

Tarp rubbed his eyes. He was worried about Juana now, and his thoughts kept snapping back to her. He had to focus to talk to Laforet, shutting her out. "I think that Soviet plutonium is getting to Argentina," he said. "I don't think your government will want it to show up as the atomic warhead on a French-made missile."

Laforet grew even quieter. "Are you sure?"

"No."

"This is part of the Dzerzhinsky Square business?"

"Yes."

Laforet smoothed his trouser leg some more. "What would be the cover story if we give you a base and protection?"

"I'm working on something in England."

"Aha." Laforet raised one slender finger in the gesture of a medieval saint. "We pretend that the Moscow business is the cover!" He shook his head. "It is so outrageous I am tempted to do it simply for the amusement."

"It's workable."

Laforet looked out the window. A barge was coming up the river, and, behind it, one of the glass-topped tourist boats was overtaking it. The sun was breaking through, making the water dance with light. "Anything is workable if it is made to work," Laforet said. "What is it you would be doing in England?"

"Plugging a leak."

"Do they have one?"

"Don't they always?"

Laforet looked at his wristwatch and then stood. The watch was gold and matched his gold cuff links; Tarp remembered that Laforet had married the daughter of a millionaire. "I have to leave in four minutes," Laforet said. "What you have told me about the plutonium is very disturbing. Very disturbing. I think . . . I believe we will want to support you. For now, you are free to go, and we will keep the woman under guard. What sort of safe house did you want?"

"Something handy to the Channel ports. Normandy, Brittany. With a car. I'd expect you to keep trackers and watchers; I'd want a trustworthy caretaker. Plus whatever medical help the woman will need."

"I shall have some paperwork drawn up."

There were footsteps in the corridor as somebody approached to tell Laforet he was due for his next appointment. Tarp stood up and touched Laforet's arm. "This is a bad business, Jules. I can't seem to catch up with it. Whoever it is who's on the other side—he doesn't care about blood. He doesn't care about anything."

There was a knock at the door. "One minute!" Laforet called. He tried to make a joke of it. "From what you have told me, it sounds like not one man but a dozen. A dozen very bloody men." He adjusted his cuffs with long fingers. "I must go." He put out his hand. "Where will you be?"

"London."

"Ever the fast mover."

"I'm on the run. The trouble is, I don't where my hiding place is."

"My assistant will give you a communications route. I should like to talk again within forty-eight hours. In the meantime, we shall do everything we can for the woman."

"Of course."

Laforet went out. The sun broke through again to sparkle on the polished floor and on Tarp's steel lighter, which Laforet had left for him.

He rented a car at Heathrow and drove slowly toward London. Something that Laforet had said had stuck with him. *It sounds not like one man but a dozen.* The idea was mixed up with the dream of the night before, that anger and that sense of helplessness. *Not one man but a dozen.* Not a dozen men in

Moscow, but perhaps several men in several places. Even, perhaps, several unconnected men. Except that that made no sense, for they were connected at least by their bloodiness and their desire to stop what he and Repin were doing.

A few minutes later he remembered that Juana had never delivered her message to him. He found that he was angry with her.

It was almost time for him to meet with Johnnie Carrington at his club, but he pulled the car over in Kensington and found a telephone. First he called the number that Jenny Barnwell had given him and said, "Tell Jenny to call the Chinaman at seven," meaning that Barnwell was to call the phone booth near Russell Square at ten. Then he readied another coin and dialed Mrs. Bentham's number, which he had by this time memorized.

"Yes?" her imperious, high-pitched voice shouted.

"Mrs. Bentham, it's Mr. Rider."

"Yes?"

"I asked you to do some research for me."

"Oh, yes?"

He did not seem to be getting anywhere. "I wondered if you'd had any success as yet."

"Oh, yes."

"Ah, I wonder if you could tell me something about it."

"I shall put my report in the mail, Mr. Rider. Actually, you gave me no address. I must say, I thought it a little odd, your not giving me an address. I don't work on speculation, you know, Mr. Rider."

"Of course not."

"And I don't undertake anything of a questionable nature."

"This isn't of a questionable nature, Mrs. Bentham."

"You have no address."

"Of course I have. I simply didn't give it to you."

She sniffed. "The effect is the same."

Tarp was trying to think it through. She lived in Croyden, he remembered. "Mrs. Bentham, would it be better for you if I paid you personally and picked up what you've done so far?"

"Visit my *home*?" she said icily.

"Ah, no, I can see that that wouldn't do. What if you were to bring your materials up to town, and of course I'd pay for your getting here and back. And your time, of course.''

"Tomorrow?" She seemed a little softened.

"Tonight, actually."

"I never go out at night." She sniffed. "Except when I am fortunate enough to go the the theater, which is pitifully seldom these days. It has become so very expensive!"

Tarp smiled into the mouthpiece. "Mrs. Bentham, it would be my pleasure to let you be my guest at any theater you care to name. Then, let's say, I could meet you in the interval. In the bar, how would that be?" A theater bar would be good for both of them, crowded, public, utterly without intimacy. "I couldn't stay, of course, but we'd have time to talk briefly and you could show me what you've got so far."

"You're a very impatient man," she said, but the words were not spoken harshly.

"I'd want to pay for a taxi to take you home, naturally. Because of the hour."

She named a play that she had been longing to see. "May I make a reservation for you?" he said.

"Well . . ."

"The stalls?"

Her voice became little-girl small. "The stalls would be quite acceptable," she said.

"Then I'll meet you in the stalls bar between the first and second acts. If there's a problem with the ticket, I'll call back; if you don't hear from me, we'll meet there. All right?"

"It *seems* all right," she said. Some of her grander manner had been recovered.

Tarp called the theater and reserved her ticket on his Canadian credit card, and then he drove toward Carrington's club.

Prong's had occupied the same building for a hundred and thirty years. It had survived a German bomb and had stood from 1942 to 1946 with two wooden props holding up its eastern wall, a situation that had led to a newspaper cartoon that showed England, as Prong's, supported by Humour and Determination. Prong's was an upper-civil-servants' club, and it had had its share of prime ministers.

"Sir?" the fat porter said when he opened the door.

"I'm meeting Mr. Carrington." Noise, smell, and heat met him in the open doorway.

"Is it Mr. Tarp, sir?"

"Yes."

"Go right on up, sir. Third floor. Mind the stairs, they're ever so steep."

He had a glimpse of a former kitchen on his left, where a government figure whom he recognized was howling with laughter as he leaned against an old wall oven. Tarp could see part of a bench and the leg of a chair and several pairs of feet. The place was packed, hot, and noisy. Glasses of whiskey were much in evidence; the cigar smoke was thick.

He went up a flight of dangerous stairs and ducked his head under a black beam at the top. Prong's was, in fact, little more than an eighteenth-century cottage. Elegance was not its attraction—the floors sloped; the ceilings were too low.

There were three doors on the third-floor landing, one to a lavatory from which a red-faced man was just stepping; one to a tiny library that was packed with grinning, shouting men; and one that was closed. He knocked lightly, then opened the door far enough to peer in.

"Aha!"

It was a billiards room hardly big enough for the billiard table. Two lights hung on cords above the green felt. Just at the edge of their brightness, a man was standing, his body in the light up to his chin and his face obscured.

"Come in, Mr. Tarp, come in."

Tarp stepped in and closed the door. "I was looking for John Carrington."

"We've met before. You don't remember, I'm sure."

"Of course I remember. It's Matthiessen, isn't it?" *And the last words I said to you were, You go to hell.* Tarp shook the man's hand.

He was several inches shorter than Tarp and just slightly plump; he had slicked-back black hair that was growing thin. He was over fifty now, and since Tarp had seen him two years before the blotchy purple places under his eyes had gotten darker and the skin on this cheeks had gone from pink to maroon. *Still drinking too much.*

"Ramsey Matthiessen," the man said.

"Number three at MI-Five."

"Ah, you do remember! I consider myself highly flattered! Whatever do I do to earn such attention?" Matthiessen grinned

He considered himself a wit, one who made his subordinates laugh spontaneously and his superiors admiringly. "Been well, Mr. Tarp?"

"Pretty well."

"You look very fit—very healthy, very brown. Is that from the sun of Florida, I wonder, or of Cuba?" He seemed to wait for an answer. He produced two cigars. "Cigar?"

"I don't smoke."

"Ah, yes, that American passion for good health. You don't mind if I smoke, I hope."

"I do mind."

Matthiessen bared his teeth; it could hardly have been called a smile. "You say what you think, yes, I remember." His cheeks turned to red apples as he made it a wide, false grin. "Very refreshing. I often say to the sad creatures who are forced by circumstance to work for me, Pray, don't deceive yourselves and me with false modesty; say what you *think*!" He laughed. "Then if they do, of course, I have them removed. Honesty in a civil servant is the first sign of lunacy. 'Madness in great ones must not unwatched go,' hmm?"

"What do you want?"

"More matter, less art?"

"I have to meet Carrington." Tarp turned to go.

"The substance of your meeting is here with me, Mr. Tarp. Not that young Carrington won't appear. I wouldn't deny two old friends the pleasure of each other's company." He smiled a perfunctory, professional smile that vanished at once. "This room is secure. The sweepers check it every day. We can talk."

"Yes?"

Matthiessen pulled himself up straight and put a hand in the small of his back, pushing the pelvis forward as if he might be suffering from some sort of backache. "We understand you've gone on the Moscow rolls," he said, lavishing a care on the vowels and the *l* sounds of *rolls* that made the words acutely sarcastic. "We understand you have sold your—shall I say, your *services,* and not use a more theological term—to Mr. Andropov."

"Yes?"

Matthiessen made a clicking sound with his tongue. "How very reticent you are! Dear, dear, it's rather like having discourse with a stone. And a rather tongue-tied stone, at that. People have pet stones in America, I understand. Come, come, do exercise the gift of speech, if only to prove that you are a sentient being, Mr. Tarp. I am only a minor figure in the great scheme of things, I realize, but Her Majesty's government do entrust me with a certain, shall I say, responsibility, and *here I am*! I have come here to talk with you. Expressly for the purpose. This is not idle chat.''

"Are you asking me a question?"

"Let us say that I am laying the groundwork."

"For what?"

"For, let us say, something in the way of an official statement.''

"Make it."

"I should like some indication that at the very least I am being heard."

"I hear you." Not entirely perfectly, because his ears were still humming with the noise of the explosion, but he could hear well enough for Matthiessen's purpose. Matthiessen inhaled very deeply, the breath an expression of long-suffering, aristocratic patience. He walked in a very small circle, all that could be managed with the billiard table taking up so much of the room, still with his hand thrust into the small of his back. "How very annoying you are being," he murmured when they had come face-to-face again. "No matter. Well!" He pushed his buttocks back against the billiard table and folded his arms. "Her Majesty's government wish you to know that as you have chosen to accept a professional liaison with the government of the Soviet Union, you are not welcome in Great Britain." He cocked an eyebrow at Tarp. "H.M.'s gov have found it necessary to formulate a policy independent of other nations. Since the unfortunate adventure by Argentina in the Falklands matter, when we didn't receive the sort of support from traditional allies that we might have expected, we have found it advisable to, in the words of a rougher and more direct speaker than I, 'go it alone.' In brief, Mr. Tarp, we do not condone helping the Soviets with their internal security apparatus, which is notorious both for its inhumanity and its antipathy to English—and, I should have said, American—ideas of decency and freedom. We do not believe that the Devil will be easier to deal with if the kink is taken from his tail. Do I make myself clear?''

"Are you going to throw me out of the country?"

"Dear me, no. Not if you behave yourself." Matthiessen was enjoying himself. "But I want to be very clear when I say that you will receive no help here. Was I very clear?"

"Why don't you explain."

"Oh, very well. No weapons, no identity papers, no information, no shoulder to weep upon. You will be kept always under surveillance. You will be made uncomfortable. You will be encouraged to take your enterprises elsewhere. You will not be allowed, for example, to travel about using a forged passport."

"Is that what I'm doing?"

"Let me see your passport." He held out a hand.

"Why don't you try to take it?"

"Oh, shame. Oh, the bully-boy! Really, Tarp, that's too vulgar, even from you." Matthiessen was delighted with himself. He bit his lower lip and his eyes flicked happily over Tarp's face. "Have I made myself clear, then?"

"I think so. It seems fair enough."

"Oh. You disappointed me. I'd so hoped you'd want to bargain, so that I could say no. Alas." He flashed his teeth. "Another time, perhaps."

There was a noise behind Tarp; the door opened and the cacophony of the house swelled in. "Aha!" Matthiessen cried in a different voice. "Her Majesty's messenger riding comes. What news of the Rialto, Carrington?"

"Am I interrupting, sir?"

"Not at all, not-at-all, my boy!" Matthiessen clapped Tarp on the shoulder. "We just had our little chat. Mr. Tarp has an excellent grasp of the situation now—am I right, sir?"

"I believe so."

"There, you see. How perfectly splendid. Well, this was a pleasant meeting! Carrington, I leave our guest in the capable hands of youth; I'm off to dinner with some perfectly dreadful people from the Exchequer. Love to stay and jabber, but I daren't." He smiled at Tarp. "Do try the Dover sole if you dine here; they don't do much well here, but the Dover sole is not inedible." With that, he saw, or pretended to see, somebody he knew outside the open door. "Aha, Jepney, there you are! Hold on, Jepney!"

Johnnie Carrington looked shamefacedly at Tarp. "I'm sorry."

"Don't apologize. I can't think of anybody I'd rather have order me out of the country."

"He's under a strain. His wife's been ill."

"That must be convenient for him. He enjoys being a bastard so much."

Carrington blushed. "I am sorry. I can't help you with any of the things you asked about last night." He spread his hands, then plunged them into his coat pockets. "Orders."

"It's all right. It's perfectly all right."

But it wasn't all right at all.

CHAPTER 23

They stood just inside the door of Prong's, making that meaningless final chatter that ends a stiff evening. Johnnie Carrington was still embarrassed and probably angry about Matthiessen; Tarp had shrugged it off and was thinking how best to cut his losses.

"Am I to be followed?" he said.

Carrington grimaced. "That's a bit low, isn't it?"

"Am I?"

"Yes."

"How many?"

"Really, I can't—"

"I've been attracting violence, Johnnie. I don't want to lead your people into a mess that's not of their making."

"Whyever should you do that?"

"I've been thinking that if somebody wanted to set me up, what a good way this would be to do it." He decided to be honest with Carrington, although he was suddenly wary of him because of the meeting with Matthiessen. "I was in a mess in Paris this morning. Very bad."

Carrington looked grim. "Let me get you some protection."

"Not necessary."

Carrington stiffened. "I'm sorry, but it is. While you're on British soil, you're our responsibility—both to neutralize and to protect. Give me three minutes."

Tarp did not wait the three minutes but strode up the short street and turned into the thoroughfare. It was about forty-five minutes before he was to meet Mrs. Bentham. He headed northeast, rather away from the Shaftesbury Avenue theaters, into streets that were at first packed with people and then, after he crossed Oxford Street, much quieter and darker. A car passed him, going slowly; he saw a man and a woman and wondered if they were part of the protection that Johnnie had laid on.

He had not seen his trackers yet. He would have to lose them before heading back toward the theater. He came to a passage that was lined with shops and whose ends had been closed to cars with concrete posts. He turned into it. It was a city block long; the shops were all locked now, the only lights those high up on the buildings. He walked slowly, his long strides easy, his footsteps falling dully on the concrete. A third of the way along, he stepped into the deep shadow under an overhang. The night sounds of nearby streets came clearly.

He moved into a shop doorway. In the angled window next to him, he could see the reflection of that part of the passage he had just walked; through the window and the front window of the shop, he could see the passage's other end. As he looked, two figures turned into the passage behind him. Seconds later a car pulled across the other end. It was not the car he had seen before.

He turned up the collar of his jacket and folded it across his white shirtfront. He took the cigarette lighter from his pocket. The situation was rather like the attack in Buenos Aires, and he was reminded of the empty gun he had carried then. He had fired one round from the .22 that morning: had Laforet's people removed the other? Very deliberately, he pulled up the end of the lighter so that it made no noise. One copper-colored casing showed in the dim light from overhead.

One is better than nothing, although with this thing, it's not much better.

Now there was some question as to whether the two men in the passage were Carrington's "protection" or something more dangerous.

The two came up the passage slowly, walking about ten feet apart. The one closer to Tarp was a half step ahead. They both looked like quite ordinary men, upon whose cheap overcoats and tired faces the light fell cruelly. Tarp noticed a plastered-down lock of hair, a pug nose, a habit in the lead man—perhaps born of tension—of carrying his head very high, as if he were constantly looking overhead.

Tarp wondered if they would use guns. Guns were still somewhat a rarity in London, and it was not like Moscow to shoot people down here as if it were Chicago in the twenties. On the other hand, if they had hired local talent—Irish or splinter Maoists—anything might happen.

In Buenos Aires, they wanted me alive. Maybe here, too. He thought of what Laforet had said. *Twelve men, not one.* Maybe there would be a difference in style, then.

He moved to his right and pressed hard against the wall. There was no window on that side. The wall was cut stone, with a deep crevice every fourteen inches and a rounded nosing at the corner. He pressed the bottom of his right fist into a crevice and pushed it forward against the rounded corner. Even braced that way, the little gun would be laughable.

Tarp listened to their slow footsteps.

Staying alive is knowing when to shoot first.

At the far end of the passage, the doors of the car were open as if to receive anything that was driven up that way.

Tarp braced himself to shoot. *Three steps,* he told himself.

"Excuse me!" The voice was rather high and very polite in the tone that well-bred Englishmen use when they are giving a definite command but are not yet angry. "Excuse me, please— you men there." Tarp recognized it as Johnnie Carrington's voice.

The footsteps coming up the passage stopped. A shoe scuffed.

He could see their dark reflections in the slanted window. The angle was wrong for him to be able to see Carrington, who must have been back at the entrance.

"That bitches it," a male voice said very low.

The two men began to run. At the other end, a car door slammed. Tarp fired the .22 as the men lumbered past him. He had aimed low; neither man paused, but two steps beyond him one of them gave an odd bouncing step, almost a hop, and then limped as he ran. As he did, the man farther away drew a gun from his overcoat pocket. It looked enormous. It was a big revolver, probably a .44 with a four-inch barrel, he thought.

The man was trying to fire while he ran, aiming behind him and trying not to hit his companion. He fired one shot, seem-

ingly for the hell of it. Tarp was crouching in the doorway by
then and he ducked under his own arms as glass shattered above
him. The noise of the gun in the enclosed passage was hideous.

"Stop!" Johnnie shouted in his polite tenor. Then he said in
an almost conversational tone, apparently to somebody with
him, "One of them has a gun."

From the other end of the passage came a squeal and a very
loud thud. In seconds the situation had turned upside down;
now it seemed to be the two gunmen who were on the run, with
their way out blocked now by the arrival of the MI-5 car that
Tarp had seen earlier.

Tarp shook glass from his back and peeped out under his
arm. Johnnie Carrington was walking up the very middle of the
passage, carrying a walkie-talkie. A man in a belted raincoat
was walking up the far side, keeping pace with him. "No
shooting," he heard Carrington say into the device.

With that, there was another deafening shot from Tarp's left,
then another, and the man coming up the passage with Carrington gave an involuntary squeal, as if he had grabbed a hot pan
handle. Tarp saw Carrington hesitate, and then his attention
was taken by noise on his left as the two gunmen began to come
back down the passage, one of them limping badly. He had a
gun now, too, however.

They fired almost deliberately as they came. Somebody
shouted. Glass erupted from a window across the way. Tarp put
his back against the shop entry wall and kicked at a big piece of
jagged plate glass that still stuck out of the frame like a tooth;
then he put his foot on the chipped stone ledge and vaulted inward, knocking a display of extraillustrated books into a pile of
debris, striking a pasteboard wall that separated the window
display from the shop within and taking it all with him as he
went crashing through.

He crouched in the lee of the window, hearing glass explode
and the big guns boom. The footsteps pounded past; there were
more shots and a cry, and then silence.

Tarp raised his head.

"Mr. Carrington?" a small, tinny voice said. "Mr. Carrington, are you there?" It was the walkie-talkie.

Tarp got cautiously to his feet. He shook himself like a dog.
He stepped up on the window ledge, hearing glass crunch under

his weight; he shuffled into the display area of the window. The air felt cold as it blew through the glassless frames.

A car swung into the far end of the passage and shone its lights between the concrete posts. Somebody stood just at the edge of the dazzling beams and called, "Mr. Carrington? Mr. Carrington, are you there?"

"Down here!"

Tarp looked to his right.

The tracker who had come with Carrington lay almost in the center of the passage. Even in the watered glare of the headlights, it could be seen that he was lying in his own blood. Farther along, Johnnie Carrington was just sitting up. His left arm seemed to be of no use to him. He looked to be in shock, but he said, "Down here. Billups needs help, I think."

The two gunmen were gone.

Tarp got out of the window and went to Johnnie. "Billups doesn't need help," he said.

"Oh, yes, he's hurt."

"He's dead."

Carrington looked up at him numbly. He tried to stand. Tarp reached for him and then saw what he had missed in the tricky light. Blood was spurting from Carrington's sleeve.

"I was hit, you see. . . ." he said.

Tarp grabbed for the arm, feeling for a pressure point and realizing sickeningly that where the bullet had hit there was no arm anymore. It had been almost severed, the bone and muscle blown through. *Magnum. Softnose,* he thought. Tarp jammed his own hand into the armpit, feeling for the pressure point, knowing that Carrington's strong heart would pump his body empty of blood. He paid no attention to Carrington's attempt to get up, gave no thought to being gentle with him; instead, he was thinking of the morning and his feeling of helplessness as he had tried to stop Juana's bleeding. Now, he manhandled Johnnie Carrington, ripping back his silk-lined black overcoat and his dinner jacket and reaching into the sodden mass above the elbow to shut off the blood with a grip that in other circumstances could have killed.

"It's Billups who needs—"

"Shut up." Tarp turned to look into the headlights. "Down here!" he bellowed. "For Christ's sake, get an ambulance down here!"

"I really must insist that you see to Billups," Carrington said.

One moment they were alone in the peculiar light; the next, people swarmed around them. One was a woman. They all seemed confused. The death of Billups had unstrung them. One man was being sick by a shopfront. They looked like actors getting ready for a scene they had never rehearsed, carrying walkie-talkies and big flashlights like props they had never seen before.

"The chief's hit."

"It's only his arm."

"Poor Billups."

"I can't look. Poor Billups. Poor Harriet. Who'll tell her? God, telling Harriet will be awful."

The woman bent over Carrington. "We've called an ambulance, sir. Just in case."

Just in case you don't bleed to death in the next thirty seconds. Tarp kept the grip on the arm. The blood had slowed to a steady trickle.

"I should like to stand up," Carrington said.

"Stay where you are," Tarp growled. "Shut up."

Lights flashed where the gunmen had got away, and somebody said disconsolately, "They got away." He seemed surprised.

"How did that happen? I thought we had them."

"The chief said no shooting. Then they started shooting."

"Billups was armed."

"Was he?"

"Wasn't he?"

"He didn't defend himself."

"The chief said no shooting."

"What about that car?"

"They rammed our vehicle and got clean off."

"I thought Gregson was following."

"He was, he was, but he lost them."

"Oh, Christ."

"What was all this about, anyway?"

People with a dolly came running. They alone seemed to know what to do, and they pushed the MI-5 folk out of the way like professionals moving among rank amateurs. They plunged a needle into Carrington's good arm while another medic was tightening off the closure on the shattered one. One of them tried to peel Tarp's fingers away.

"You can let go now," he said, having been no more successful than if he had been a child trying to loosen the hold of an adult.

"You sure?"

"Yes, please. Let him go now, would you? We want to get him to hospital."

"What hospital?"

"Grimes."

Tarp took his hand away. The wheeled stretcher began to roll.

"What's the procedure here?" one of the MI-5 men was saying. "Don't Metropolitan Police have to be called?"

"Don's looking it up."

"Well, doesn't he *know*? Christ, I was just assigned to this group; I've been in bloody Taiwan for three years. I'm an escape specialist. Come on, people, has anybody noticed that we have a dead man here?"

Tarp walked away. When he was near the end of the passage, he heard quick footsteps.

"Where are you going? Sir?" It was the woman.

"Home."

"Do not move another step!"

Tarp looked at her. "Shoot me. It would cap the evening for all of you." He turned into the darkness and was gone.

He went into an Indian restaurant on the Queensway and washed the blood away. The tweed jacket was a mess, soaked in blood to the elbow. He soaked it again and again. It was Johnnie Carrington's life, running down into the sewers.

Who'll tell Harriet? He thought of Johnnie's beautiful, flirtatious wife. *Who'll tell Gillian?*

He had never seen such bungling before. Even for an operation put together too quickly, it had been mismanaged. It was a nightmare example of bad work, and MI-5 would be very lucky if some sort of question were not raised in the House of Commons.

And who'll tell Gillian?

He walked to the Bloomsbury hotel, where he still kept a room. He changed his clothes and put antiseptic on several cuts. He looked bad—pale, perhaps sick. *I am sick. This is sick-*

ening. What I've done is sickening. On the way out, a woman in the lobby looked at him and looked away with that intensity that comes of wanting not to have seen something.

CHAPTER 24

He reached the theater bar ahead of Mrs. Bentham and ordered a whiskey from a pretty woman before the act quite ended and the crowd poured in. His hand was shaking as he took it from her; he looked in a mirror and saw a man he hardly recognized.

He recognized Mrs. Bentham, however. She seemed not to have changed in eleven years. She was a quintessential Englishwoman of her class, conservative, assured, often rude in her insistence on politeness; red-cheeked with broken veins, too tight in her hairstyle, years behind in her fashions because of both economy and taste. After they had identified each other and she had made it clear that he was forgiven for being a boor, he was allowed to get her a shandy while she commandeered a table no bigger than a hat and defended it against other determined Englishwomen.

"How very nice!" she exclaimed when he put the drink in front of her. "How well you look!"

He murmured something. She meant the suit, of course, which was one of those from Hire Attire and made him look like an ambassador or a very well educated Mafia lawyer.

Mrs. Bentham was carrying a brand-new plastic briefcase that bulged with papers. "I loathe business!" she cried. She opened a piece of paper on the table in front of him. "My bill."

He was paying not only for Mrs. Bentham, but also for two typists, three hundred and seven pages of photocopying, typing paper, and the plastic briefcase. "All of that is mine?" he said doubtfully.

211

"Once you pay the bill. I loathe business, don't you? It is so *cruel*!" She bent forward. "I prefer a check."

"I don't have a London account." That was not true, although it was true that he did not have a London account in the name of Rider. "I have to give you cash."

"Ah, well." She sniffed. "I hate business." She looked around them. The bar was packed. "Handing money about *looks* so bad."

Tarp took a plain piece of paper from the briefcase and folded it like an envelope, wrote her name on it, and put the money into it. He then laid the thing on the table between them. "I've added in twenty-five pounds for your transportation home."

"Oh. How very thoughtful you are, when you put your mind to it." When he looked down, the improvised envelope had vanished and she was snapping her purse shut. "They will blink the lights or ring the bell or whatever they do to end the interval at any moment!" she cried. "I must run."

"Wait." His tone stopped her. It was not often that she was stopped. "You have plenty of time. What have you found for me?"

"Everything. Within reason, I mean. The history of the *Loyal*; its mission in the South Atlantic; a complete crew roster for the year of the *Homburg* encounter. Several accounts of the *Homburg*'s sinking. Quite a nice biography of Admiral Pope-Ginna, the commanding officer. And so on. It runs to more than four hundred pages."

"You're very quick."

"That's what I'm paid to be."

She started to get up, and he detained her with a hand. "Not yet. They haven't called yet. What did you find about the *Homburg*?"

"Not as much, of course. Most of that would be in Germany, I daresay. But I did find a recently unclassified document that was circulated in 1944. It was sent to the *Loyal*, in fact. The first lord had reason to believe that the *Homburg* was carrying Nazi gold to South America, as well as some important Nazi officials."

"How much gold?"

"It's in my report. About a hundred and fifty million pounds sterling—by today's debased value, I mean."

The bell rang. He felt her tense. "What Nazi officials?"

"That I couldn't find. 'Certain civilians,' is all it said. Some of that is still classified."

"Can you get at it?"

Her professional expertise had been challenged. "Mr. Rider, I know the Official Secrets Act better than the people who now enforce it. I do believe that *I* can 'get at' something that was classified in 1944."

"Do, then."

She stood up. Someone bumped her from behind, and a look of martyrdom attached itself to her face. "*Do* you mind?" she bellowed over her shoulder. Several people looked guilty. She turned back to Tarp. "Call me tomorrow evening. I really *must* go."

To say that she faded into the mob would be wrong; rather, she parted it. She was a big woman.

Tarp sat at the small table until the bar was empty. He finished the whiskey.

"Want another?" the woman at the bar said. She smiled at him. He thought of what it would be like to linger over another drink there, to respond to that smile. Was she offering more than the whiskey? He supposed it might be fun to find out. "No, thanks," he said.

The briefcase was heavy. He admired Mrs. Bentham's strength as he walked out of the theater and looked for a cab. A light rain was falling now, barely more than a mist, but it made taxis hard to find. At last he gave up and found an underground station and rode out to where he had left the rented car. He put the briefcase into the back and drove up to Bloomsbury, where he parked it as close as he could to the phone booth where Jenny Barnwell would call.

The telephone jingled at one minute past ten.

"Well?"

"It's me, who else? Got your message, obviously. What's on?"

"How's my Belgian friend?"

"Very quiet. Carries a gun, you know that? I don't like messing with people carry guns; they're troublemakers. Like you. What's this call about, anyway? I could be boogying right now, if it weren't for you."

"Boogie tomorrow. Bring my friend to the same place where we met last night. Then I've got a job for you."

"Oh, Christ! There goes my whole bleeding evening!"

"Naturally he'll pay as if he'd stayed the night."

"Naturally. You think money solves everything, don't you! Bloody fucking American, that's all you are. Violence and money, that's all you people know."

"I need a car, Jenny."

"What, you want me to steal a car!"

"No, rent or borrow. Got to have good papers. For about a week. I'll pay well."

"It isn't quite the time of day for the car rentals, chum. Still, I know some people. Take me a couple hours, you know."

"No longer. I'm in a hurry."

"Oh, naturally. All right, I'll get a car. Doesn't have to be fancy, does it? You ain't visiting the Queen Mum."

"No. Something nondescript."

"Oh, just my line. Swell. All right, gimme two hours, I'll pick up your pal and meet you at the Rose. Midnight. No, make it half after. Okay?"

"Okay."

Tarp had backtracked mentally through the days in England and had tried to find if there had been any way by which MI-5 could know the number of the car he was driving or the name under which he had rented it. In the end it seemed too risky to go on using it. If Matthiessen's people caught up with him now, they would take him. Rattled by the disaster in the passage, they would be looking for a scapegoat. A former Agency man with a fake passport and a Moscow tie-in would make a lovely diversion for them.

He dropped the rental car at the all-night space of a rental agency and carried the loaded briefcase back to his hotel. He spent three-quarters of an hour going through Mrs. Bentham's work, then separated a dozen or so pages that he needed and put the rest back into the plastic briefcase. Paying his bill, to the astonishment of the owner, who was ready for bed, he dropped the briefcase into the dumpster behind a restaurant and then went to the underground and found his slow way to Hire Attire which was deserted and dark. He left the bloody and torn clothes with the clean ones in a bag with a note: "Please hold until called for. Some cleaning may be in order. Black."

It was cold. The rain had turned to intermittent sleet. He wore a turtleneck and a heavy sweater and the tweed jacket wit its wet sleeve, and still he was cold. His leg hurt. He was tired. He thought of Johnnie Carrington and found a telephone. Grimes Hospital did not want to put him through to anybody, but after much pleading on his part a resident came on.

"I'd like to inquire about Mr. Carrington."

"Uh, which Carrington is that?"

"John Carrington."

"Who is this?"

"How is Mr. Carrington?"

"I'll have to have your name, sir. It's regulations."

Tarp thought he was being stalled. *Matthiessen,* he thought, and he hung up. *Matthiessen's not going to save his public ass at my expense.* Matthiessen would deplore Carrington's injury, but he could be grateful that it gave him a possible way of locating Carrington's renegade American friend.

Renegade. That had been Repin's word. Not so very long ago. Last night, in fact. In the noodle restuarant. It seemed an age.

He walked for five blocks in case MI-5 were quicker at tracing telephone calls than they were supposed to be, and he let two taxis go by before he waved one over and fell into it. It had taken twenty-two minutes to let three cabs go by, and he was wet and shivering.

"Dreadful night," the driver said cheerfully.

"A bit."

"Where to, then?"

"Camberwell New Road."

The driver turned and looked him over, then slowly pushed over his flag. "Not a very bright spot, this time of night," he said dubiously.

"I'm not going to rob you." Tarp dropped two bills on the front seat. "I'm too cold."

The pink word *Rose* burned its mysterious way against the rawness of the night. Tarp paid the driver and then paid him more to sit there. Many minutes later a pair of headlights slowed as they came past going the other way, then did a U-turn and came up behind.

"Keep your motor running," Tarp said.

"I got no intention of turning it off. What's up?"

"Just checking to make sure it's my friend."

Tarp waited until he recognized the slim figure of Jenny

Barnwell. Then he paid the driver for the fourth time that night and climbed out.

"You're late," he said accusingly.

"Of course I'm late!" Barnwell said. Tarp looked into the car. Repin was sitting back there, smiling happily. He looked warm and pleased with himself.

"What's he so happy about?"

"He taught Sara how to make brioche. She give him a couple dozen and a big kiss."

"Who's Sara?"

"Never you mind."

The car was a big old Humber with an engine that could have powered a truck. Tarp walked around it, still shivering a little but needing to inspect it. It was solid, well cared for. "You did well," he said.

"God, don't give me a word of praise! Don't say I did something up to snuff! Christ, I'll croak from the shock if you approve!"

"Get in."

"Bloody well right. You're driving me back to the club. Well, you don't expect me to walk, do you?"

They sat in the front seat together. Rose cast its pink glow over their hands. Repin leaned forward, munching a brioche. There was a warm smell of milky coffee.

"Sara?" Tarp said.

"Yes, Sara," Repin said. "Is very nice little lady."

Barnwell sneered. "Some Belgian!"

Tarp handed him two pages from the sheets that Mrs. Bentham had given him. He pointed with a slightly quivering finger. "I want you to track down these people. There are nineteen of them."

"Holy Christ. They aren't dangerous, are they?"

"I doubt it. They'll be pretty old, most of them. A lot of them will be dead."

Barnwell peered at the paper. The light from the car's ceiling was absurdly dim. " 'Navigation officers and ratings, H.M.S *Loyal.*' Wot's this now?"

"Just find them. I want to talk to some of them."

"That's all I do, find them?"

"That's all."

"You're paying?"

"That's right."

Jenny bobbed his head. "Well, that's not so bad, then."

He dropped Barnwell outside his club and turned the big car around. It was a pleasure to drive, with lots of reserve power and an affinity for the road on turns.

"Can you spare some of Sara's coffee?" Tarp said.

Repin maneuvered himself into the front seat and reached back for a sack and plastic cups and a huge Thermos bottle. "Is my pleasure."

"Who's Sara?"

"Very nice, very large English female. Ask no questions."

"All right." Tarp took a cup of the sweet, milky coffee.

"Where do we go now?" Repin said. He held up a brioche. It was half a day old, but it was delicious, just faintly salty from the butter.

"France. There's a truck ferry from Folkstone at four."

"You look bad. Trouble?"

"Much trouble." He pointed the car toward the bridges and began to tell Repin about the day.

CHAPTER 25

The telephoned instructions from Paris took them through a village that was nothing more than two lines of gray houses along the road, one a store and one a cafe, past a gasoline station sitting by itself two hundred yards beyond the last building, past a seventeenth-century farmhouse with windowless walls up tight against the road. They were fifteen miles inland from the Pas-de-Calais coast. In the overcast, the land looked like rock covered with gray moss, bumpy and grudging and as if nothing could ever put down roots into it.

The roads got smaller and rougher. The last two hundred yards was a rough, stony track up a hill between tough little oak trees that somehow clung to the surface as if they had been glued there. At the end of the track was a tumbledown stone farmhouse, and behind it were three even more dilapidated barns arranged in a U. They and the house were all collapsing into what had been the barnyard. There was a silent old man already in the cold house, and a younger woman with frightened eyes. Tarp thought she might be his daughter, a stick of a woman with the shrinking posture of a dog that has been kicked. She looked at the big old Humber and at Repin and at Tarp with hostile eyes.

"Are you the caretaker?" Tarp said in French to the old man.

"Yes." The old man looked at the car and the ground and at Tarp. "You are the monsieur?"

"Have you got your instructions?"

He shrugged. He looked around himself, as if for witnesses. "I am not a servant."

"Who takes care of food?"

He jerked his head. "She does. She is all right." He said it as if Tarp had said the woman was not all right.

"Where do you sleep?"

"Downstairs. In the back."

"And her?"

"With me, with me, what do you think?"

"Who is in charge?"

The old man looked at the woman. She looked as if she were going to cry. "Who is in charge?" Tarp said again.

"You are, monsieur."

"Good. Do not forget it." He looked down the rutted track as a Fiat with two French security men in it appeared. "And these?"

"They stay at the next farm." The old man spat. "Filth."

Tarp touched the woman's arm. When he took his hand away, she covered the place as if he had burned her. "Get us something to eat," he said.

"What?"

"Bread, eggs. Cheese. Whatever there is. Coffee."

"There is no coffee," she said.

"Buy some."

She stared at him. "Where?"

The old man stepped between them. "We are not from around here. We were brought in. We are not experts on the neighborhood. We are not responsible for buying."

"You are now," Tarp said. "Go buy coffee, sugar, jam. *Now*. If you do not know where to buy such things within an hour, I will kick your ass from here to the end of that road."

The old man tried to look him in the eye but could not, so he turned aside and spat. He had been a big man who had probably used his size to bully people as he now bullied the woman, but now his muscle had all gone slack and his bigness was mere weight. The two security men had gotten out of the Fiat and were watching the scene, enjoying it; the old man glanced at them and muttered, "Filth."

Tarp lowered his voice. "You are old," he said. "It would be unfair of me to hurt you." He put his mouth very close to the old ear, which was filled with dark hairs. "Do not force me to be unfair. I would feel very bad if I had to do something to you, because I am so much younger and stronger.'' He put his left hand on the man's jaw and turned the head so that their eyes met. ''But I am the kind of man who would do it. Eh?''

The head jerked. Tarp relaxed his hold. ''Good. Go buy some food.'' He turned toward the two security men, who were smiling cruelly. Tarp walked the few yards to them. There was a puddle in the road and he stepped over it, feeling his shoe sink into the ring of mud on the far side. ''We are going to be a family here,'' he said. ''I hope it will not be unpleasant.''

''Why should it be unpleasant?'' one of them said. He had wide, childlike eyes, plump cheeks, and not much chin. His cheeks were permanently flushed, and, perhaps because he knew he looked so boyish, he wore a huge mustache.

''So that we understand each other,'' Tarp said quietly. ''I am in charge here. You are not my jailers.''

The other man, who was also young but who had a clipped dark beard and looked older, said, ''We know our job.''

''Good. When is the Cuban woman coming?''

''Maybe tomorrow.''

''Good. And Laforet?''

He shrugged.

''I need to talk to Laforet. Is there a telephone?''

''In the village.''

''But you have communications.''

The man shrugged again. Tarp decided not to press it just then. ''There will be coffee,'' he said. He went inside and looked over the house, which had been empty for months. There was very little furniture. Downstairs was a kitchen with an enormous wood range; a large room that took up most of the ground floor; and a very small room with wallpaper, as if it had had aspirations toward being a parlor. Upstairs there were four small bedrooms. Repin had already commandeered one that had a wooden bedstead in it with a mattress but no bedclothes. A new sleeping bag lay rolled on the bed. Repin picked it up, dropped it. ''I lived better in Indochina,'' he said disgustedly.

''You lived like a prince in Indochina.''

''Only some of the time. This place stinks.''

''It needs airing out.''

Tarp picked a room for himself. Like Repin's, it had a new

sleeping bag on the bed. One of the other rooms had had a hospital bed moved into it for Juana.

Tarp went downstairs again and found the frightened woman coming into the kitchen from the back with five eggs in her hands, which she carried cupped against her belly like a woman in a medieval painting. As if to emphasize the freshness of the eggs, a chicken cackled outside, and then a cockerel jumped up into the open window and strutted. The woman with the eggs stood looking at it; Tarp looked at them both. The picture that they made seemed ancient and full of symbols, but he could not understand them because he was so tired or because he was alienated from them.

He slept most of the day, then woke when the sound of a helicopter passed close overhead and went toward the village. Some minutes later he heard the voice of one of the guards, calling up the stairs, "The chief is coming!"

Tarp smelled coffee and something wonderful, full of onions and perhaps chicken. He rolled out of the sleeping bag and went downstairs carrying his shoes. The woman had built a fire in the range and there was a huge pot there, cooking. There were chicken feathers on the floor and a little dried blood on the windowsill. Tarp was wearing the same clothes he had driven from London in and the trousers they had given him in Paris after the attack in the restaurant. "Hot water," he said to the woman. She stared at him. "To shave."

"Ah."

The only running water came from a tap in the kitchen. The toilet was a separate stone privy next to one of the barns, with a stone urinal through which water always ran and a filthy flush toilet that had a tank high above and a chain pull. Tarp told himself that it would have to be cleaned and went back into the kitchen. "What is your name?" he said to the woman as she filled a black iron kettle from the tap.

"Therese."

"Are you the old man's wife?"

"He is my stepfather."

He took a small pan of hot water upstairs and borrowed a razor from Repin, who had provided for himself in London. Repin carried a scuffed leather case that he had brought with him from the doomed aircraft, and Tarp supposed that he had the makings of a new life in it: currency, perhaps some gold;

somewhere sewn into the lining or the handle, a strip of microfilm that he could use to bargain for freedom and security. Repin was a survivor.

His room was small. Half of it had a sloping ceiling. A single window opened outward on a view of the privy roof and the collapsing barns. The bed was high; in a corner was the squat washstand where he stood to shave. Against the only other wall was a massive wardrobe that was black as if from charring. He stripped, gathered the dirty clothes into a bundle, put on the trousers and the shoes, and went down again to the kitchen.

"Wash these," he said, handing her the clothes. "Then dry them over the stove. Quickly. They are all I have."

She looked at his bare torso. He had a long scar that seemed to fascinate her. She put the dirty clothes into the zinc-covered sink and went out the back and came in again with an old jersey that was frayed and faded but as soft as cashmere from much washing. She held it out to him.

"Thank you."

He pulled it over his head. When he pulled it down from his eyes, he found that she was still looking at him, her hands cradled in front of her belly as if she were waiting for him to put more eggs into them.

"If I had flour, I would make bread," she said.

"Tell the old man to buy flour."

"I do not tell him anything." She turned her face away, and he saw the shadow of a bruise high up near her pale hair.

"I will tell him, then."

He went to the door as the guards' Fiat came up the stony road. Laforet got out, looking Parisian and governmental, his shoes too delicate for the hard ground, his suit inappropriate but beautiful. He wore no hat but had on black gloves, and he carried a dark-gray coat over his arm. He looked out of place and too solemn, like the minister of a small country forced to negotiate its surrender in the mud of a battlefield.

"So here you are," he said, giving Tarp his left hand. "Leave us," he said over his shoulder to the guards. He looked around the big downstairs room. Laforet was an urbanite. He actively disliked the country; he had often said so. The stone floors and the thick whitewashed walls were not to him picturesque, but unsanitary. "Where can we talk?"

"I brought somebody with me."

"So I heard. Is it Repin?"

"Yes."

"So he is not dead. How like him. Well, you and I must talk; I cannot deal directly with Repin. You understand."

Tarp led him into the small room with the wallpaper. It had big, hard chairs and a painted cupboard that was locked.

"Therese!" Tarp called. She appeared almost instantly. "Is there wine?"

She was trying not to look at Laforet, as if he terrified her. "From the village," she said.

"Bring it."

It came in a bottle twice the size of an ordinary one, without a label. There must be a place in the village, he knew, where you took your own bottle to have it filled from a barrel. She put down two stemmed beer glasses and hurried out.

"That looks like dreadful stuff," Laforet said.

Tarp smiled. "You must bring your own next time." The wine was rough, strong, almost black. Tarp liked its coarseness, and Laforet drank it without complaint.

"So," Laforet said. "This is becoming very complex."

"I know."

"First you, then the woman, now Repin." Laforet took his gloves off the table and put them on his coat, which he had folded on the seat of a chair. "Your sanctuary is becoming a commune, my friend."

"I couldn't leave him in London. They tried to kill me there."

"There, too?"

"Something has gone wrong there. It smells. The whole thing smells." He told him quickly about the meeting with Matthiessen and the shooting of Johnnie Carrington. "It smells," he said again.

"It does, indeed." Laforet sipped the wine, which he seemed to like better and better. For all his elegance, Laforet was honest in his tastes. Tarp had a flash of memory: Laforet bending over a jungle pool that was green with scum, drinking, raising a face then rimmed with golden beard, saying, "Nectar!" They had been on the run for four days, looking for the montagnards to hide them. Now the beard was gone, the hair was silver, but he still could take nectar on its own terms. "I must hold Repin here," he said now.

"He'll have something to bargain with, I'm sure."

"He won't be pleased. He won't thank you for bringing him here."

"I don't care about his thanks."

"You have an idea?"

Tarp poured more wine. "Moscow thinks he's dead."

"Not for much longer."

"No. Let's put out a story that Repin is in England."

"London will deny it."

"So?"

Laforet tapped his lower lip. "I don't want them looking for him here. This arrangement is very much disapproved of by part of my department; nastiness would be a gift to people who want to get me out. I want things here to stay quiet. Beautifully quiet." He sipped. "Well, we will try saying that we have heard that Repin is in London." He crossed his legs and bent sideways to take a cigarette case from his side pocket. "About the Cuban woman."

"Yes."

"She is KGB, as you know. Her father is a translator in the Fifth Department. Spanish, a leftover from their civil war. You know all that? He was in the gulag, did you know that, too? Oh, yes; he was a singer, and he sang a song about Stalin. He doesn't sing anymore. But he's not a dissident; we have nothing on him in that direction. The daughter has been in Cuba for four years. Nothing on her, either. I would assume she works for the Eleventh Department."

"Have you talked to her yet?"

Laforet closed the cigarette case with an audible snap. "One of my people interviewed her. She's quite heavily sedated. Nothing worth repeating." He gave Tarp a brief, sad smile. "She asked how you were."

"Can she be a double?"

"Of course. But we have very little in Havana, my friend; Cuba is not our area of interest. Of course, there have always been rumors. Castro is unpredictable, to say the least. When Khruschev had the confrontation over the missiles twenty years ago, we thought it a logical time for Moscow to set up a machinery that was not known to the Cubans themselves. On the other hand, Castro has been maddeningly independent sometimes, especially in the midseventies, and we don't know how far he may have gone in getting rid of KGB probes. We did get a Caribbean defector, curiously, about seven years ago who said in passing that she had heard that the Cuban KGB had been infiltrated by a different wing of the KGB. That was provocative. We turned it over to the Americans, and naturally we never heard anything more about it.''

"I think somebody in Moscow may have planted his own people there."

Laforet lighted the cigarette and inhaled deeply. "Don't you think it's time you told me about it?" he said.

Tarp hesitated. "Do we have a deal?"

Laforet lowered his head, his eyes almost closed. "We do." He raised his eyebrows as his head came up. "But please, no more people to share your sanctuary."

Tarp told him about Maxudov and the plutonium. He was thorough and it took time. When it was done he said, "I think you ought to get in touch with 'Mr. Smith.' "

"Washington and Paris are not close these days."

"It isn't official."

"Very well. Are you going to Moscow?"

"Yes. I've got to have a way in."

"I think I can help there. When?"

"A few days. I've got to tie up loose ends."

"This business of the German ship?"

"Partly, yes."

Laforet paused, then shook his head. "The connection is not there."

"Not yet."

"Ah, well."

"I need a secure telephone to call my contacts in London, and I need the hardware to talk to my data bank."

"I shall take you back to Paris with me."

"I'll need clothes."

"I noticed."

CHAPTER 26

Mrs. Bentham had "some papers" for him, and Jenny Barnwell was "working on something." Access to his computer from a Parisian terminal was more difficult than he had expected, and it was after midnight before the printer began to hum in the chic and soulless computer center that Laforet had borrowed for him. He was almost alone in a room that was oppressive in its insistence that all machines, all humans, all ideas were interchangeable.

"Mr. Smith" and Hacker had both been supplying information, but the sum of what they had given was not much. The biographies of the KGB officials whose names Repin had given him on the *Scipio* were no more revealing than if they had come from a popular magazine; there were contradictions, vast holes. There was even some confusion as to which departments of the KGB they headed.

The materials on Juaquin Schneider were more complete and, he supposed, more accurate. Yet when he had studied them he was impressed by what was not there instead of by what was. He queried the data bank but got no further answers. At first he focused on a single question: Where did Juaquin Schneider get the money when he emerged in the nineteen fifties? Then, as he went over and over the pages of mostly irrelevant material that had been given him, another question surfaced: Who was Juaquin Schneider's wife?

There was, to be sure, a figure with a name: Nazdia Becker. There was a marriage date: 1949. There were some details: Jewish, born in Hungary, refugee; brilliant biochemist, holder of several patents that Schneider Agri-Chem had turned to great profit. But where had she been educated—and when? How, Tarp wondered, had she gotten to Argentina? What was her birth date? She had died in 1971—but of what?

At three o'clock Tarp turned the machines off and lay down on the cot that had been provided for him. If he dreamed, he remembered nothing. At midmorning he flew to the farm, landed at the security guards' house two hundred yards away, and walked across a muddy field. The Fiat was in the lane; the Humber was parked under a twisted apple tree, and there was a new Citroen close to the house.

"Too many cars," he said to the guards. "They attract attention."

"One of them's yours."

"Whose is the Citroen?"

"Nurse. They're sending the Cuban woman up today."

He started toward the house. The bearded man grinned. "The old man's drunk. Watch out for him. He's bad."

Therese came to the kitchen doorway. "I have made bread," she said without prelude as he crossed the big room toward the stair.

"Is there cheese?"

"He bought cheese in the village. It is from Denmark. In a can. He thinks it is comical." She stared at him. "He is drunk."

"He'll regret it."

Repin was upstairs, surrounded by newspapers that the guards had bought for him. On the window ledge were the last crumbs of the brioches. "I have been watching birds," he said. He was wearing glasses with gold rims that made him look severe. "This is a very boring place. The birds are the most interesting thing here." He jerked his head. "Except maybe that one." Tarp looked out and saw the old man asleep on a mound of rotted hay. "When are you going to Moscow?"

"Soon. I need more information. From London."

"Why do you need information from London so you can go to Moscow?"

"I think they're two ends of the same stick. I'd like to understand at least one end."

"You still think it smells?"

"Rotten."

"You think I have lied to you?"

"It occurred to me, Repin, but I can't think of why you should. No, it doesn't smell because it's wrong; it smells because I don't understand it. You brought it to me as a simple matter of a man in Dzerzhinsky Square. But it's not a man in Dzerzhinsky Square. It's Buenos Aires and maybe London. *And* Dzerzhinsky Square."

Repin eyed him over the tops of the glasses. "Moscow cares only about Dzerzhinsky Square."

"Fuck Moscow."

"Mm." Repin went back to the paper. "Better men than you have tried."

Tarp went down and filled a bucket at the kitchen tap and dumped it over the old man. He groaned and rolled down the pile of moldy hay and lay with one shoulder and an arm in an ice-rimmed puddle. His eyes were open, however. Tarp bent over him. "This is the warning. I only give one warning. Stay sober or you're out." When he went back into the kitchen, Therese was there. "Does he hit you?" he asked.

"Sometimes."

Tarp put the bucket under the window where he had found it. "Tell him I will hit him once for each time he hits you. I can hit harder than he can. If he gives you trouble, tell me."

"And if you aren't here?"

"Tell the other man."

"The Russian?"

"Yes, the Russian."

"Is he a nice man?"

"Better than the one you've got."

She nodded. "He liked my bread. He said he would teach me to make brioche."

Tarp nodded. Repin planned to do more than watch birds, he thought.

He put in a call from the other house to Jenny Barnwell, whose return call came two hours later. He had found somebody, he told Tarp—a petty officer who had been on the navigation bridge during the *Homburg* engagement. The man lived in a village sixty miles south of London in the Weald.

"I'm on my way."

He drove the Humber to the ferry at Calais and arrived at Dover late that night. There was a guest house open near the castle. He was on the road again at dawn and in London for a late breakfast. He picked up the dark suit from Hire Attire and got a chauffeur's cap and what he hoped was Barnwell's size in a dark coat. Mr. McCann was severe with him. He thought that Tarp was very hard on his clothes.

Jenny was waiting under the Rose. Tarp paid him and then asked him about the man in the Weald.

"Harry Gossens. He retired from the navy in seventy-five, been puttering around his roses or some such stuff ever since."

"You're sure he's alive?"

"He was yesterday. I telephoned him to ask if he wanted to buy an encyclopedia."

"That was bright."

"I used to sell encyclopedias, don't be so quick to criticize!"

"I never thought of you as a man of letters. What'd he sound like?"

"Like a nice old duffer, know what I mean? Lonely, I'd say. Was glad to talk to me, even about the encyclopedias. Almost bought one, the poor sod; I had to persuade him not to. Wife died four years ago of the big C; he's up with bad circulation of the extremities and don't get about much, he says. Practically bedridden."

"You're sure he's the right one."

"Well, I couldn't come right out and ask him if he was the Harry Gossens that was on the *Loyal,* now could I? That would rather have queered whatever lie you're going to tell him, wouldn't it? But he's the Harry Gossens that's getting the pension check for Harry Gossens, Royal Navy retired, number aught seven seven five eleven fifty-one."

"Jenny, I underestimated you. You have resources."

"Christ, a compliment! It must be about to rain solid gold suppositories. A compliment from the original hard case! Oh, Mum, can I write it down in my commonplace book?"

Tarp handed him the coat and the hat. "Be a chauffeur."

Barnwell looked at the clothes with disgust. "I should of known. First the pat on the head, then the shove into the pismire. A bloody servant!"

Tarp sat in back while Barnwell, now in the rather ill-fitting chauffeur's costume, drove him down to Mrs. Bentham's in Croyden. She peered out through impeccable curtains to see what chauffeured eminence had driven up; recognizing Tarp as her Mr. Rider, she was so grand that he had trouble making sense out of her. She had one thing for him: a list of the German civilians on the *Homburg*.

"Still classified, Mr. Rider! And publication of these names would involve us both in a technical violation of the act. You are warned."

"And the names?"

"Three scientists, a banker, an engineer, and four others who were either diplomats or military men *incognito*. Some of them were easy to identify, but some I simply haven't had time to track down. Shall I persist?"

"Please do."

"I didn't really find a *great deal*, I'm afraid. These were highly secretive people, you know. One librarian suggested that I might do better on the other side of the Iron Curtain. They seem to have been active there during the Nazis' heydays."

"Perhaps I'd better go there to look, then. Thank you so much."

They drove south and then east, through the far suburbs of London, past one of the reservoirs where boats were being painted, as if spring were really almost there, and into the rising country above the Downs. The narrow road plunged downhill and then up again, always twisting, and there were deep woods and gullies that looked as dark and secretive as they must have when the Romans had found Britons smelting iron here. Harry Gossens's village was a wriggling cross of two roads lined on each side with brick houses with a pub at the end of each arm as if to mark the limit. It occupied only the top of a hill; on all four sides the roads plunged down into more of the Weald's wooded gloom.

"Ask at the post office store," Tarp said.

"Oh, la, just like a bloody capitalist. I ain't really your chauffeur, you know, ducks."

"Ask at the store, Jenny."

Harry Gossens lived in an attached house in a row of four behind the church, as if they had once been almshouses or even a school. The house looked clean and cared for, the small front yard given the excessive care of someone with not enough to do. Tarp rang and then waited a long, long time while the sounds of painful shuffling came toward him through the house.

"Yes?"

Harry Gossens was bent. His head was twisted a little to the left and his neck seemed unable to support it so that it hung forward. He had been a tall man when he stood straight.

"Mr. Gossens? Mr. Gossens, my name is Matthew Rider and I'm an author. I'm writing a book on one of your country's great ships. I wonder if you can help me with some questions about HMS *Loyal*?"

Mr. Gossens seldom closed his mouth. It made a constant, soft, interrogative circle at the bottom of his face, as if life had become so puzzling to him that he would never get enough answers to justify closing it. "I—I'm sorry." He stared at Tarp. "I don't hear well. You said your name is Rider?"

"Yes, Matthew Rider. I'm a writer." He had meant to say author, because "Rider the writer" sounded funny. "I'm writing a book on the *Loyal*."

"The *Loyal*." Gossens considered that, gazing down at Tarp's shoes. "A book, you say?"

"Yes, a book. About the *Loyal*." Tarp had a story ready—that he had written several letters to Gossens and received no answer; that perhaps the naval office had given him the wrong address.

"Come in, come in," Gossens said surprisingly. He gave a kind of ghastly chuckle. "No point in heating the whole outdoors, as my father used to say. Would your, um, young man care to come in?"

Tarp looked back toward the Humber, where Jenny was slumped against the fender. "No," he said decisively.

They drank tea and ate a dark, heavy cake thick with fruit and some rather stale scones and a paste of mashed sardines. Gossens rustled this up by banging on the wall, a noise that brought the woman from the next house, who, he explained, "took care of him." She came in twice a day and in emergencies like this one. "And the church is very good. Very good."

"I'm sure."

"Very good. Hot meals. Very good." Mr. Gossens was a religious man. A Bible and a crucifix and two religious pictures were very prominent. He was not a dedicated navy man, as it turned out: he had joined the navy on the day Churchill had been made first lord in 1939, purely out of patriotism and a sure instinct for greatness. He had stayed in for thirty-six years because there was nothing he would rather have done. Now, his house had not a memento of those days.

"I had hoped you might be able to help me with the encounter with the *Prinz von Homburg*," Tarp said.

"There was a terrible thing, now."

"Was it?"

"Terrible. So cold. I was snug in the navigation section, you know, not even having to go up to shoot readings, but those poor fellows out on the decks! We had ice on the ship as thick as—as I don't know what. It was terrible. I think often about those poor Germans in the water, and us not able to help them. I pray about that still."

"Why couldn't you help them?"

"It was dark, and there was ice. It was quite peculiar. We'd broken out of the ice that afternoon, I remember it very clearly; there we were all of a sudden with open ocean. Oh, I was so glad to see it! Though you'd have died in minutes if you'd gone over, you know. Still, it looked so much more—more *natural* than the ice. We'd been trailing an icebreaker for two days, you know, with *Homburg* up ahead out of range, they said. It was terrible. The men used to come down from the deck watches with their faces frozen, some of them. They lost toes, fingers. I hate the cold, I always have. It was terrible."

"You came out of the ice into the open ocean *before* you sank the *Homburg*?"

Gossens chuckled. "Oh, I didn't sink the *Homburg*. On a big ship, you know, Mr., um, Rider, you're ever so far away, and the guns go bang, and then by and by somebody says you've made a hit. There we were in the navigation section, closed in with charts and readings and gauges, you know, we might as well have been in London, I used to say. What was your question, sir? I'm so sorry. . . . Ah, about the ice! Yes, we came out. That was why the navigation officers were so confused."

"Because of the ice?"

"The water. We'd been proceeding mostly by dead reckoning—that's a form of educated guessing—because we had no electronics down there, no Loran or any of that; and the weather was simply constant fog and cloud and snow, we hadn't shot a star in days. Taken a reading, I mean—do you understand celestial navigation? It's steering by the stars in very mathematical fashion. Well, we couldn't do that. And dead reckoning had us deep in the ice, you know, and then we broke through into the open ocean, and the navigation officer and His Holiness—that was Admiral Pope-Ginna, we called him His Holiness; you see the pun, of course—you aren't Roman Catholic, are you? I meant no offense—no, no, dear me. . . . Where was I? Oh, there was quite a set-to. His Holiness was both ship's captain and flag officer, and so his ship's navigation was the example for the force. Well, we seemed to be scores of miles from where dead reckoning had us. There was a great row. Then one of our airplanes sighted the *Homburg* in the ice. It was sheer luck, they said. You know. War's half luck, I think. Or God's will, and we call it luck because we're blind. Are you a religious man, Mr. Rider?"

"I'm afraid not."

"Ah. You should be afraid indeed. No offense. 'If the righteous know fear, what shall be in the hearts of the sinful and the ignorant?' No offense."

"How did they resolve the navigational problem?"

"Well, there was the battle, you see. We went right into battle formation, flank speed, off in a direction where the *Homburg* wasn't supposed to have been, until the seaplane saw it. Then, they said, they got it on the radar and the guns started. It was night by then. Such a night as it was! I went up on deck for a moment, thinking to see something. Guns roaring, black as a cat's belly, snow coming down, and somewhere off there was something they were supposed to be shooting at."

"Did you know when they sank the *Homburg*?"

"Well, we heard something of it. A hit, and so on. But as for sinking, you know, a capital ship doesn't go down like a hammer you've dropped in the water. Some of them take days. The *Homburg* went quickly, as big ships go. It was gone by the morning, I mean."

"And did you pick up survivors?"

Gossens was silent. "Too few. Too few."

"Why?"

Gossens breathed heavily through his mouth. "They told us there were many, many icebergs. There was great fear we'd strike on one. That is not an idle fear down there, Mr. Rider. We did stay in the area another day and a night. But . . ." His voice trailed off. "Poor chaps. Even if they were Germans."

He looked appealingly at Tarp. "Do you believe the Germans are terrible men?"

"Some of them were then. Not the ones who died down there, I suppose. Not most of them."

Gossens sighed. He was tiring, Tarp saw. Yet he was younger in years than Repin. It was important to Tarp to tie down the matter of the ship's position as closely as possible. "About the navigational row."

"Yes. Terrible row. Yes."

"How did they settle it?"

"They settled it by His Holiness telling them what the position was to be, *that's* how they settled it! He was a splendid leader, Pope-Ginna. Men liked him. I always liked him, as much as a rating can like an admiral. But he could be a holy terror, too. What we heard was that he'd called the navigation officers of every ship in his force for a conference—and indeed, we had 'em coming over in the breeches buoy, murderous thing to do in those seas—and a fellow who had been there taking notes said he took everybody's dead reckoning estimate and compared them all and then told them what the position was, as coming from the flagship. They could like it or lump it— meaning they could file official protest to the flag log if they wanted. You can imagine how many takers they had. Actually, I believe there were hearings after we returned to Port Stanley, but the real row was over. His Holiness had his way, I believe—as was only right and proper, of course."

"And did you have to go through the ice again *after* you sank the *Homburg*?"

Gossens stared at him. His eyes were as round as his mouth. "Yes, as a matter of fact, we did. It was very peculiar."

"As if you'd been in a lake of open water surrounded by the ice."

"Yes. That's just what it was like. But that's fanciful."

Tarp smiled and rose to go. "Well, writers are fanciful people. Thank you so much."

Gossens had been delighted for the company, but now he was glad to see Tarp go, because he was tired. Age had come down to that paradox for him.

"Enjoy your tea, Mr. Rockefeller?" Barnwell said as he drove them away from the town.

"As a matter of fact, I did."

"I bloody near froze my ass off. Never gave a thought to me, I suppose."

"You could have gone to a pub."

"I *did* go to a pub! Christ, you didn't even notice I was gone! It's lovely to be a negligible human being, believe me, just lovely! Christ, you're a specimen." He pounded the wheel. "How was the old poop?"

"As a matter of fact, he wanted to ask you in."

"Yeah, see? See? There are some genuine human beings left in the world! Not that I ever meet them, naturally. Or work for any of them!" His eyes met Tarp's in the rearview mirror. Tarp said nothing, making Barnwell's mood even worse.

"Drop me at Gatwick," he said as they came to the highway.

"Oh, very good, my lord."

"And take the car back wherever you got it."

"Oh, *thank* you, my lord!"

He flew out of Gatwick on a shuttle to Lille and, instead of going on to the farm, spent the night there. Deep fatigue had settled over him on the flight, and with it the depression that makes all things seem pointless. He wanted to believe that what he was doing was worthwhile, and so he sought sleep.

CHAPTER 27

He picked up a car in Lille in the morning and drove down toward the coast with nothing in his belly but black coffee. He was no more hopeful than he had been the night before. He knew it was time to go to Moscow, and he felt as if he were holding nothing in his hands but strands like the slime of fish, which slipped through and broke and were gone.

He left the car at the gate and walked up the stony road. One of the security guards was standing by a copse of trees seventy yards away and waved languidly, but there was no other greeting. Tarp went to the kitchen and found fresh-baked bread and some of the cheese; he ate the bread and cheese standing by a window set up high in the kitchen wall. Therese came in and watched him, more as if he were some domesticated animal she had been set to watch than a human being. Without looking at her he said, "Has the other woman come?"

"The beautiful one?" she said without envy.

"I suppose."

"Yes. She is upstairs." Her canine eyes watched him as he finished the food and drank a cup of bitter coffee that she put down for him. He went by her and up the stairs, noticing that Repin's room was empty and that the fourth room had belongings scattered all over it, clothes and medical instruments and stupid popular magazines, all the signs of the nurse's occupation. Juana's door was closed, and he knocked and then went in, finding her in the high, rather old hospital bed, with an IV bottle hanging in a rack beside her. The nurse was sitting in a chair with one of the mindless magazines. "Leave us," Tarp said; she started to resist but he said it again in the same inflexible tone and she left them.

Tarp looked at Juana. Her left eye was covered with a bandage that should have looked rakish but that looked dangerous because it suggested that so much of her head was injured; her left arm was taped up against her lower ribs, and the long gash along the shoulder was heavily bandaged, with a tube coming from it to drain the worst of the wound. Her short-cropped punk-rock hairdo stood up above her bandage like a cockerel's tail.

"I didn't betray you," she said quietly.

"I never thought you did."

"Of course you did." She didn't open her mouth very far. He saw that she had lost a tooth in front. "Somebody betrayed me," she murmured.

"Who?"

"Somebody who wanted to kill us. Don't you think?" He sat down on the bed on her right side and held her hand. She did not respond much. "It was awful," she said. "All those people."

"You saved me," he said. He was not sure it was true, but it was true enough. He breathed heavily. "Why did you come?"

"I love you."

"You hardly know me."

"I know." She turned her face to the left; her right shoulder made an effort to shrug.

"Did you have a message for me?"

"Of course!" In her anger, she turned back to face him.

"What was it?"

She looked away again. "I am not really Cuban."

"I know."

"You do? Yes, of course. I forget things now. The doctor says that will pass. My father is Spanish. My mother is African. I grew up in Moscow. When I was sixteen, they said they wanted to send me to a special school; it would help my father, they said. He was in the camps then. For revisionism. I went to the school and became a technician in intelligence; then I was recruited for fieldwork. My father was home by then. They sent me to Havana, which Moscow does not trust very much."

"I know."

"I report to a man named Sandor." She rolled her head back to look at him. "You are *not* KGB, are you?"

"No."

"You lied to me. Lied and lied. For a long time I didn't believe you. Then, in the safe house in Havana, I believed you. Now I don't believe you."

"I'm not KGB. I'm not anything. I'm working for the man you saw me bow to at the ballet. He is working for Andropov."

"I don't believe you."

"No."

She breathed in and out. "But I love you. I reported to a man named Sandor. He reports through channels to the Eleventh Department of the First Directorate—that is—"

"I know."

"All right, you know. Kepel reports that way, too. That means that there are two channels reporting the same thing to Moscow, so there is a way of cross-checking. I was trying to find out about plutonium, as you asked me. Back when I believed you." She stroked his hand with two fingers, then pulled them away. "I had sometimes a—relationship with a scientist at the academy." She twisted her head so that she could look up at him. She searched his face for a response. "You're a stone, aren't you?" she said bitterly.

"What did you find out from your scientist?"

She waited, gave the one-shouldered shrug again. "A woman who ran errands for Sandor came to me and told me she knew something I ought to know. She said that she had been ordered from Moscow to help me with the plutonium investigation. I said I didn't know what she meant. She said, 'You know, your tall friend in the KGB.' So I let her talk. I knew she was a fake. Or thought I did. She told me that two submarines had docked in Cuba and unloaded plutonium at the small base near Guantánamo."

"How was she supposed to know this?"

"She didn't say."

"She knew you'd been with me in Havana?"

"Of course, what else? Sandor had found me out somehow. So he fed me this information, I suppose on orders from above someplace. So I talked to my scientist that night. I slept with him. See how much I love you? I love you so much I sleep with other men for you." The right side of her mouth smiled bitterly. "There is no plutonium in Cuba. He says it categorically, and I believe him."

"Would he know?"

"Of course."

"He could lie to you."

"I suppose. Anyway, that was my message: there is no plutonium in Cuba, and the line to the First Directorate is corrupt. I knew it was corrupt when the woman gave me the false information and now I know it is corrupt because they followed me to Paris so they could kill you. And me." She touched his hand again. "That is what I carried my rose for." Her eye was full of tears. "I was so happy when I saw you!"

He looked at her, at the bandages and the tube and the lost tooth. "You shouldn't have come," he said unkindly. "It was stupid. You were almost killed."

"Wasn't my message worth it at all?"

"No. Not at all." He was very angry and the anger poured out. "You could have sent it through the line we set up. You brought it because you wanted to indulge yourself. You did it for yourself." He stood up. "Now look at you."

She wept. After a while he apologized for being cruel to her. He kissed the side of her mouth that wasn't bruised. "I'm going away soon," he said. "You're to stay here and get better."

"Are they going to interrogate me?"

"Some. Nothing deep. They're all right."

"When will you come back?"

"When I'm done."

"Where are you going?"

"Never mind."

"You're going to Moscow. Aren't you?"

He kissed her again. "You get better."

Late that afternoon the helicopter came over the house and Laforet appeared a few minutes after. He visited briefly with Juana and Repin, like a schoolmaster checking on the sick ones in his infirmary, and then he came to sit with Tarp in the wall-papered room. He threw down his hat and his gloves and sat rather heavily, showing the fatigue of overwork. "I have some bad news for you. You want to hear it first?"

"Of course."

"Your friend Carrington lost his left arm. Just above the elbow."

Tarp thought about Johnnie, who seemed so young and so

silly and who ran at life so very seriously. "I'm sorry. Thanks, Jules."

"He will be all right, they say. He is young; he will bounce back."

They sat quietly, thinking about what it meant to bounce back from the loss of a limb. Therese came in with wine and a rough paté and bread and hurried out.

"I'm done in England," Tarp said. "You might go on checking on the *Homburg* business."

"I've been in touch with your Mr. Smith. I shall ask him, too."

"If you can check in Germany, so much the better."

Again, a silence fell. Laforet put a little of the paté on the bread and ate a very small bite as if suspicious of it. He nodded approvingly and ate a much bigger bite. He sat back. "Well? What now?"

"Moscow."

"When?"

"Now."

Laforet looked down at his pant leg. He smoothed it, straightened the crease. "If you mean it, I can have you on the way in two hours."

"Now."

Laforet snapped his head up and gave him a dazzling smile. "Good. Good luck."

CHAPTER 28

The house on Podgornyi Street had been built late in the nineteenth century and had been intended to display the solidity of a Russian middle class that did know it was moribund. Now it was a warehouse for a primary school, perhaps scheduled for demolition the next time the city government made a lurch forward. An elderly couple lived in two rooms at the back, their windows covered with rags so that only a sliver of light spilled out over the thin and melting snow. In the rest of the house painted boards covered the windows and the rooms were filled with child-sized school desks, maps of the world that no longer showed what the world was like, and gymnasium equipment that was too clumsy-looking to interest the children of the new age.

"I am looking for a ticket to *The Seagull*," he had said at the kitchen door. Repin had told him that it would not matter how he used the code word *seagull*. The old woman had looked at him resentfully; then, without a word but frowning terribly, she had pulled the door a few inches wider to indicate he could come in. Tarp heard her whispering fiercely while he waited in a damp entry that smelled of earth and the sour cabbage that was cooking.

The old man had put his head into the gap of the inner door and looked him over and then disappeared. More whispering, and then he had come and told Tarp to come in. The old woman had gone into their other room—too angry, Tarp thought, to face him.

"Are you hungry?" the old man demanded. He was in his

241

seventies, or he had suffered enough to look that age. He was dirty, too—obviously a man who had simply given up trying to keep clean.

"I could eat, yes."

The old man put down a plate of cabbage soup and a big piece of dark bread. It was like a stage version of a Russian meal.

"You see how we have to live," he said.

Tarp believed that they had been made nonpersons because of some crime. They were lucky to have even this—two rooms, the stove, food—and he knew that they must have them for some other reason than their good fortune. They were probably informers, recruited after the legal punishment for their crime, put in this place to live out their lives as purveyors of gossip. They would be working for the Moscow police or the local Party secretary or even the Fifth Directorate. Probably the last, Tarp thought, because it would explain how Repin knew about them and had some kind of leverage on them.

"It has been a long time, you understand," the old man said, as if he followed Tarp's thoughts.

"You need money?"

The old man brightened. He had an evil, cynical, entirely corrupted grin. "Always. You know the situation."

Tarp did not know, but he pretended to. He put a little money on the table. The old man all but sneered. "It takes many drops to fill a bottle," he said. Tarp shook his head. He did not want them to appear suddenly rich and start other people asking questions.

The old man took the money and put it up under his heavy sweater in a pocket so high that he had to bend over in a contortion that looked as if he were scratching his own back. When he straightened, he had that dreadful grin again. "You want vodka?" he said.

"A little."

"You pay by the drink here."

"All right."

He opened a cupboard and took down a bottle. There were other bottles behind it. *His bank,* Tarp thought. *The family fortune.*

"I got a nephew in the black market," the man said. He squinted at Tarp. "You're not after black marketeers?"

"Not my line."

"Since Andropov, you know, you can't trust anybody. We're all to be saints, he thinks." He poured three glasses of vodka. "Jews? You after Jews?"

"Mind your own business."

They had been told that the people who came to them from time to time with the code word *seagull* were clandestine operatives of the Fifth Directorate, who, for unexplained reasons, were working unknown to the Fifth Directorate itself—a Byzantine complexity of double-dealing that only a society haunted by deception could believe.

"Varya," the old man bawled. He had filled the glasses to their brims, so that a mound of liquid rose above each. "Varya! Vodka."

She shuffled in, wearing felt slippers and a man's overcoat over a wool skirt. She had been crying. They drank the vodka in an almost ceremonial way. *Welcome to Moscow.*

The old man wanted to refill Tarp's glass and settle down to serious drinking, but Tarp covered it and stood up. "What do you do?" he said. "During the day?"

The old man hedged, finally allowed that he picked through trash containers in the streets.

"You know the statue of Gogol?" Tarp said. "Near the power station?"

"Gogol the playwright?"

"Are there two Gogols?"

"Near a power station?"

"Do you or don't you?"

"I guess I do."

"I want you to go there tomorrow."

The old man looked stunned. "It's half across Moscow!"

"You'll be paid."

The old woman showed Tarp where he would sleep, a filthy space the size of a closet with one small electric bulb in its ceiling for both heat and light. "You want blankets?" she said.

"Of course." He guessed the temperature in the room to be about fifty.

She shuffled into their bedroom, banged some doors, then appeared loaded down with ancient comforters, seemingly more than he would ever need. She opened her arms when she got near him; bedclothes cascaded to the floor in a pile. She turned around and went back into the bedroom and closed the door.

Tarp put several of the comforters under him, the rest on top. He slept in the long underwear he had worn from France. In the middle of the night he felt movement on his legs, then itching. He had a small flashlight, and in its beam he saw fleas. He stripped, then sat in the cold, cracking the shiny brown blood-suckers between his fingernails. They were still slow because of the cold, but he got tired of it, and he put out his light and went to sleep. He even smiled a little, feeling the low hum of tension in himself that always came when things were moving. He imagined himself face-to-face with Maxudov, and he fell asleep.

In the morning he marked up a copy of *Novy Mir,* following the code he had worked out with Repin, handed it to the old man, and told him where to leave it near the Gogol statue.

"Then what do I do?"

"Come home. Pick up rubbish. As you wish."

"I don't wait by Gogol?"

"Certainly not." The man was wearing two overcoats over his sweaters and a torn leather helmet of the kind that aviators used to wear. "I will know if you do not do exactly as I want. You know what will happen if you do it wrong?"

The old man licked his lips. "Yes."

"Good."

The next day he sent him to a suburban railway station to look for a message in the restroom. There was none; Tarp had not really expected one yet. The day after, however, the old man had his awful grin on when he came in the door. He handed Tarp a crumpled sheet of newspaper. "It came, it came!" he crowed.

"What came?"

"The message, the message you have been waiting for!"

"You are an idiot."

The message was stark—three words indicated by needle pricks five words after those that mattered: *Yes Where When.* Tarp's first message had been picked up by a French cutout who had passed it to an Italian who had sent it through two So-viet entrepreneurs; the reply had come through a channel al-most as tortuous. Tarp marked up another copy of *Novy Mir* and sent the old man back to Gogol. He sat quietly in the old house, feeling the hum of suppressed excitement but showing nothing, content to smell the sour smell, to listen to the rats in the walls. After he sent off the second message his tension increased, because now he was sitting like the bait in a trap. Now they knew where he was, and if they wanted, they could make him vanish the way magicians caused things to vanish in stories.

At twilight of the next day a van backed into the untended lot behind the house. Tarp was sitting in the kitchen, which was the only warm room. He heard the engine as the driver gunned it up over the curb; the old man and woman heard it, too, and they went to a window and tried to look through the rags.

"It's a school van," the woman said, "it says so."

"This has never happened before," the man said. He looked tearful, almost sentimental, like the sad clowns that bad painters make pictures of; Tarp knew that he was frightened.

A door slammed.

"Somebody's coming!" the old woman cried, and she ran into the middle of the kitchen.

"Let them in," Tarp said.

"No!" She began to whisper to herself. Tarp remembered the same sound when he had arrived.

There was a bold knock at the door.

"Open it," Tarp said.

The old woman tottered to the door. It took her a long time to unwrap the chain and to take down the wood props that they used for security.

When the door was open a man pushed past her without haste and came into the kitchen. He looked around with professional caution. He had drawn a pistol, a 9mm Makorov, a big, powerful weapon. Two other men came in behind him, similarly armed.

"Are you Tarp?" the first one said in Russian.

"Yes."

If they were going to kill him, he thought, they would not do it here. They would take him somewhere outside the city, out on the still frozen ground of a forest.

The man looked around again. He was in his midthirties, one of those sleek, rather round-faced men who seem good-looking because they take care of themselves. He even smelled good; Tarp caught his scent over the smells of the kitchen and the rats.

He was probably from the Guards Directorate, a hand-picked and utterly loyal gunman.

"This place won't do," the man said. "It stinks." He walked out of the room, moving the old man out of the way with the same ease and the same lack of interest with which he might have moved a curtain. The old man was looking at Tarp with hatred; next to him, the old woman was sobbing. Tarp was the only one sitting down.

He heard a jingle of keys and then the sound of a door, then hollow footsteps from that part of the house where the school things were stored. The footsteps got softer and then louder; doors banged; once, something fell and the old man flinched. After ten minutes the sleek man came back; he had put his gun away. He picked up a rag from the wooden sink and wiped his hands on it, hating the rag as much as the dirt. "We'll use a room in there," he said. "I left the light on so you'd know which one. Get to it."

The other men went past him and disappeared. The round-faced man, who had been wearing a fur hat like the one in which Brezhnev had so often been photographed, put the hat on the broken kitchen table and pulled up a chair. He unbuttoned his heavy cloth coat and let it fall open. Tarp and the round-faced man sat quietly as noises came from the other part of the house; the old man fidgeted.

"Sit over there," the round-faced man said. He looked at a bench against the far wall; the old couple almost ran to sit on it. "I have vodka," the old man said, as if he had been waiting to be spoken to.

"No."

The old woman clutched his arm and wept.

Twenty minutes later one of the men came back and hunted until he found the remains of a broom. He came back a few minutes later with a piece of cardboard covered with trash, and he threw it and the trash and the broom out into the yard.

"You want to look?" he said.

The round-faced man stood up. "Stay here," he ordered. He was gone only a short time; when he came back he said, "It still stinks. Fix it." One man went to the van and fetched a string bag in which Tarp could see aerosol cans and plastic bottles. By and by a more pleasant odor, spiced and piney, reached him from the other part of the house.

"You want to look now?"

Again the round-faced man went out, leaving the other as a guard; coming back, he said, "Tell them it's ready," and his subordinates and the string bag of cleaning materials disappeared.

They sat in the kitchen for two hours. Tarp made his mind blank, as he had done when he had been captured years before and kept with nothing to do for weeks. Thinking was no help now, so it was best to cleanse the mind. The time passed as if it were the tick of a clock, from which he awoke rested and at ease.

The round-faced man had stood up. "In five minutes," he said to Tarp, "you must be ready. You understand?"

"Yes."

"Do you need to toilet?"

"No."

"Walk ahead of me. First, I must search you."

They walked into the other part of the house. The cold was awesome there. He could smell old wood and mildew and the pine scent. There were overhead lights in the corridor and in one room; the corridor was lined with school desks that had come out of the room, which had been swept and wiped and polished. The floor was glossy with it. The ceiling fixture had been made for four bulbs to swing on short chains, but only one socket had a bulb in it; on the floor was a plain desk lamp with a frayed cord, alight and turned up to shine into the room.

Tarp and the round-faced man stood because there were no chairs. The room encouraged stiffness. It had been bullyingly formal once, a symbol of somebody's propriety and uprightness, angular and without prettiness. It was a room in which humiliated young men were meant to ask stiff-necked fathers for their daughters' hands, a room in which the priest was to be received for calls.

A car drew up. It had a big, throaty engine. Doors thudded. Tarp could hear no voices, but he heard feet on a stone walk. The round-faced man stood straighter and checked his tie and his fly, then stepped toward the doorway. There were footsteps in the corridor as several people approached. One figure went past the doorway without looking in, and then a second figure came to it, paused, looked in, and entered.

It was Andropov.

He was so tall that he had a habitual stoop, as if the world's doorways had not been made large enough for him. He was taller than Tarp. He was both professorial and menacing, as if, in his struggle upward for the supreme power of the organization that was both the source of Soviet control and its greatest sickness, he had coupled the intelligence of the academic with the ruthlessness of the gangster. He wore gold-rimmed glasses and a well-made suit, although it fit him as if he had lost weight recently. He was at that age where most men retire and where a few begin the last desperate clawing up the glass mountain of power. He had almost feminine eyes, but familiarity with him showed that not modesty but secretiveness explained them. His lips were full, the nasolabial folds defined, faintly Semitic; in all, he was handsome, intellectual, imposing, weary.

The round-faced man from the Guards quivered from the tension of being in the same room with him. Andropov did not even seem to notice him; one glance took in the stiff room, the poor light, Tarp. He wore no hat, but his long hands were gloved; he took a step into the room, then whirled, drawing the glove from his right hand with his left almost as if it were not a hand but a weapon he was taking from a sheath. He thrust the hand toward Tarp; he took only Tarp's fingers, let go instantly. He took another step, turned profile. The round-faced man went to the door and stood there with his back to them.

"Repin sent you?" Andropov said in excellent English.

"Yes."

"You have been slow getting here."

"Yes."

Andropov removed his other glove and put both of them on the mantel. "I have ten minutes," he said. He put his back to the empty fireplace. "What is it you want?"

"I want information." When Andropov said nothing, Tarp took his silence for permission to continue. "I want the files of the people who are suspected. I want help with a related matter. And I need to know, for form's sake: Is it you?"

Even in the bad light Andropov's face seemed to lengthen, to grow paler. "No." He tipped his head back slowly and looked Tarp over. In the light from the lamp on the floor, his eyes looked Oriental.

"That leaves six possibilities."

"Five. Galusha died of a stroke on Monday." He stated it as fact, allowing no objections.

"Five, then." Tarp's tension was gone. He felt now a great sense of well-being. "Can two of them be working together?"

"I do not think so, no. I think we would know about that."

"Repin wanted me to talk to Telyegin first."

"Good. Telyegin is dying, you know. Maybe dying men are most likely to be honest."

"Or deceptive. Dying men have nothing to lose."

"Have you ever died?"

Tarp let the irony pass. It was the one clear sign that Andropov disliked him—or, perhaps, disliked this process and all it implied.

"Will you tell about them?"

"Very briefly."

"Telyegin."

Andropov looked away, as if to gather thought. He and Telyegin were old rivals. Andropov seemed unsentimental, but that was vastly different from being unemotional. "Telyegin," he said, drawing the name out. "Old. Pitiless. Wily. A European, not an Oriental. A Stalinist. His work is his life."

"Strisz?"

"Strisz is very intelligent. A deal-maker. He tells jokes, perhaps out of nervousness." Andropov did not seem to approve of the jokes. "A very promising early career."

"Beranyi?"

"Quite young. Ambitious. Difficult—stubborn in the way he insists upon first principles. Yet, oddly, a risk-taker. Difficult."

"Falomin?"

"A man of his time—a brilliant manager. The opposite of Beranyi. Sometimes he gives the impression that he could as easily manage a movie house or a tractor factory as the Jewish program. He has an unfortunate wife."

Tarp waited for more. Nothing came. "Mensenyi."

Andropov looked at him. He saw something that made him decide to be frank. "A clown. He has already been promoted above his proper level, because of political maneuvering. He will be demoted . . ." He hesitated. "Soon."

"Clowns can be dangerous."

"I did not rule him out."

"You are convinced that one of the five is Maxudov?"

Andropov narrowed his eyes. "I *require* that one of these five be Maxudov." He let that sink in. He might as well have said, I am not turning my government upside-down even for this. He had already decided how the matter was to be contained: these five or nobody. It would be very hard on all five five of them if Tarp could not prove that one was Maxudov, because all five would be forever suspect. In fact, they would not last long. Nor would Tarp.

Andropov's right hand moved to the gloves. Seeing the movement, Tarp said quickly, "There have been four attempts to kill me. There was the crash of Repin's plane. The manner of them suggests some—incoherence. More than one person, perhaps."

"I cannot accept that there is more than one."

"Might somebody else be exploiting it—maybe knowing something, planning to come forward when no solution is found, to benefit from being a hero?"

"Ambition is not unknown in Moscow," Andropov said. "But I advise you, do not look for complex solutions."

"What if it is a complex situation?"

"Then give me a simple solution to it." Andropov took his gloves, and, putting them on, became businesslike. "I want the man who calls himself Maxudov, and I want the plutonium. That seems quite simple. If there are complications . . ." He shook his head.

"Maxudov may have colleagues in other countries."

"I want the man who calls himself Maxudov, and I want the plutonium." He stood with his gloved hands by his sides. The room seemed encased in ice, dead with cold. "I will help you with information and I will not oppose you on any of those little grounds that would normally arise because you are a foreigner. But I remain above it all. Do not expect to communicate with me again. You will be given the means to communicate with appropriate authorities. All of that. Now, before I go: What more do you want from me?"

"I must talk to the others."

"Of course. Telyegin first, you said. Good; I will arrange it, and the others. Their files? I will give the matter to an assistant; naturally, there will be censorship. You mentioned a 'related matter.' What is that?"

"Some German records from the Second World War."

"I do not see how they relate. However, talk to my assistant about it. I will have the request examined; if it makes sense, you will have it. Now I must go."

They shook hands again. "If you succeed, you can have a good life here. I would personally be grateful to you." He seemed to say it as a formality.

"I have made other arrangements."

Andropov's eyes hooded over. "So be it. If you do not succeed . . ."

"Then no arrangements will be necessary."

"Yes." Andropov started for the door. The round-faced man darted out of his way, and the tall figure swept out, turning sharply to the left in the corridor and collecting lesser men around him as he passed.

CHAPTER 29

The next morning early an unmarked truck came and took the old couple away. They had been given thirty minutes to pack up what they wanted.

"Where are we going?" the old woman asked. She was crying again.

"I don't know, Mama," the round-faced man said. "It can't be worse than this, can it?"

He said it without rancor and certainly without any particular pleasure in their pain; yet Tarp winced at this reminder of the system with which he was working. He did not like the old man and woman; he was glad to see them go; but their own lives were so clearly irrelevant to a system that had other plans that he could not ignore the viciousness of it. Tarp did not believe in evil, just as he did not believe in good. He had neither faith nor readily definable politics anymore. He had given up trying to forgive human frailty in favor of overlooking it. But the offhand transplanting of the two old people was like seeing a huge, ugly eye open in what had been an empty sky, seeing it blink, and seeing it disappear again. The eye, like the log that is really an alligator, like the snake that appears under the foot, was obscene, and it made individual existence a pathetic lie.

The round-faced man brought in an exterminator, who sprayed white liquid over the floors where the old people had lived, while another man carried out armloads of their rags and trash, their pathetic belongings that they had guarded with chains and bars, and burned them. When darkness fell that night, the rooms smelled better and there was more space and the fleas were dead, and they might as well have ceased to exist. It was little consolation to Tarp to say that, being what he was, being the man he was with the past he had lived (*How many old couples did I move out of their homes in Viet Nam?*), he was implicated in the obscenity whether he actively helped the KGB root out its Maxudov or not. There *was* no consolation for being what he was—such was the executioner's creed, the torturer's creed, the agent's creed. The only consolation in any of it was knowing that, unlike the old man and woman, he would never go without a struggle, and that was not a consolation of morals but of emotions as elemental as the ape's grunt.

A woman came from Andropov's staff and listened to his requests and went away; a day later the files began to come. She came with them. What Tarp was allowed to see was heavily censored, as if these were files that had already been combed for sensitive material, yet the woman looked over every page before he could read it. The materials that he had requested on the German civilians aboard the *Prinz von Homburg* "were in the process of research," she said. He found Russian governmental jargon as difficult to follow as American.

Eugen Telyegin was a dying man. Andropov had been quite right about that. Telyegin was "of that generation," as they said, meaning the ones who had fought in the October Revolution. He had been only fifteen then, but he had fought; he had lived through that first terrible winter close to Lenin, perhaps favored because of his youth by the ideological purists who liked his receptive mind. Tarp got this from the file, from photocopies of letters and newspaper stories from those days.

Telyegin received him in the downstairs room of a *dacha* outside the city. A car had come for Tarp in the evening and had taken him to a drab apartment in a block of drab apartments; next morning he was driven out to the *dacha*. Telyegin was in a wheelchair that had been placed between two electric heaters. An armchair had been placed for Tarp opposite him but too far from the electric coils to benefit from the heat.

Telyegin had inoperable cancer. That was in his file, too. It had begun in his lower bowel and it had spread. He had been given six months to live, but that had been two years before, and there were reports of his temporary remissions, as if the body were urged back to life by his commitment to his work. Now, nobody knew when he would die, but he was dying.

Yet his eyes were eager, like the eyes of a young man on the way up. When he could lift his voice above a tired whisper, he was passionate.

"I have not betrayed the Party," he hissed at Tarp. "Not the Party, not the nation, not the service." That little effort tired him. "This is an offense to my whole life." His was a bitter whisper. He struck his chest weakly with a mittened hand. He was wearing a fur-lined coat, a thick scarf, boots, a fur hat. "They should have waited until I was dead to insult me with somebody like you."

"I am very sorry," Tarp said. He meant it. He did not like offending this old man, who, in his way, was as defenseless as the couple had been.

"You!" Breath sighed between his yellow lips in an exhalation of disgust. "Keep your being sorry. You—I know who *you* are." He glared. "*I* never took money to serve the enemies of my people!"

But Tarp could not be moved that way. "You know why we are here."

"Oh, yes, *Comrade* Andropov told me. *Comrade* Andropov, who was in short pants when I took a bullet in the leg from a White."

"You know why we are here."

"Yes, yes." Telyegin sank into the clothes. He had a narrow head, which the disease had reduced to pure skull. Chemotherapy had taken his hair. He looked like a baby bird in a nest. "Well, do your filthy work."

"There have been thefts of plutonium."

"I know all that. Skip all that. My time is short. Plutonium, submarines, Maxudov—it's all shit. It isn't me. What do you think, that I would confess to you even if I was Maxudov?" His mouth moved and a sound like a cat's sickness came from the throat. He was laughing. "Did they think I would make a sentimental gesture because I am dying and save them trouble? Maybe, if I confess to crimes I didn't do, they will give me a hero's burial because I saved them so much trouble."

Tarp asked about three periods in Telyegin's life, two when he had worked in departments with Central American connections, the third when he had for six months been posted in London. The questions and the answers both seemed pointless; what he always heard was the old man's hatred.

"You could have set up a network in Cuba and Central America," Tarp said after half an hour of wrangling. The old man was getting weak by then.

"So?"

"Maxudov set up a network in those places."

"Maxudov isn't me."

"He could be."

The eyes merely stared at him as if the face were too weary to show expression.

"Who do you think it is, then?" Tarp pleaded.

A long silence. Then, with a malice that pierced through the weariness, Telyegin said, "Comrade Andropov?"

"It is not Andropov."

"You mean, even if it is Andropov, it is not Andropov." He made the ghastly noise that was laughter again. "What has a Cuban network to do with anything?"

"Maxudov tried to kill me in Cuba."

"Good for him." The clothes stirred. "I know who Maxudov is," he whispered.

"Who?"

"He is a character in a book. Did you know that?" The eyes were malicious and gleeful when they saw that Tarp did not know. "Not too bright, are you? Uncultured, yes. Maxudov is a character in a novel. Nobody reads it. It's a piece of shit. Of course nobody reads it in America—no money in it." He wanted to laugh, but the words had taken his energy. He sat there, gathering his strength, his breath wheezing over the hum of the electric heaters. "In the *Theatrical Novel* of Bulgakov. The character of Maxudov. That is who Maxudov is."

Tarp felt that he had been checkmated. "I am not interested in novels," he said lamely.

"There is also a character named Strisz in the novel. You find that interesting?"

"Do you think that Strisz is Maxudov?"

"I don't know. I don't care." He closed his eyes. He looked like the corpse of a king. "Sixty-four years of service, a devoted Chekist, a full colonel, and I wind up being asked stupid questions by an American. If I had the strength, I'd puke."

Tarp got to his feet. He tried to say something human, even

something as simple as "Thank you" or "Good-bye," but the old man's fury was palpable, and he refused any gesture. Before Tarp got out of the room, however, he heard a sound, and he turned to see Telyegin's eyes open and glaring at him. He had been husbanding his energy for a last statement, and it came in a voice that must have been the voice men had heard in his good days, powerful and deep. "I hope you die this way," he said. "I hope they all die this way."

Tarp got into the back of the car without knowing what he was doing. He was shaken by that rage and that curse. He could not answer when the guards spoke to him.

"I am not Maxudov. Do you think I really could be Maxudov? Do you think I could really be stupid enough to use a name from a book in which my real name appears? I do not know this novel; I'm not a great reader, especially of fiction, which usually bores me, but . . . do you think I would be so stupid?"

Strisz was in his fifties and prosperous-looking. Andropov had called him "too social," and indeed there was something both amiable and sociable in his wide face, as if he were eager to entertain. He looked well fed, more Scandinavian or Dutch than Russian, without the high cheekbones that made many Russians' eyes look small.

"Some men would pick such a name because they would think themselves clever, because nobody would believe they would be so stupid. Some men would take the risk to enjoy a secret feeling of being smarter than their enemies," Tarp answered.

"Oh, people would believe that I could do a stupid thing! I have a record of doing stupid things. You've seen my file." He laughed. He seemed absurdly relaxed for such a situation. He seemed guileless, and Tarp believed that no one was guileless.

"If you are not Maxudov, why do you think somebody has used that name?"

"It's rather witty, isn't it? A character from a Russian novel, and none of the Russians who are tearing around worrying about it recognizes the name. That's rather witty."

"It's a fairly obscure novel."

"Have you read it?"

"I glanced through it. Maxudov is the narrator—a stand-in

for the author, Bulgakov. He was under KGB surveillance at the time.''

"You see? That's witty.''

"You believe in taking a psychological approach to Maxudov?''

"Well, psychology is often more productive than beatings, which is what some of my colleagues prefer. Naming no names, of course.'' He opened a drawer in the desk behind which he sat. It was not his desk, but he seemed curious about what was in it. They were in an office of an annex of the municipal offices—a space borrowed for the purpose by Strisz and as anonymous, for him, as the *dacha* where Tarp had met Telyegin.

"Do you know Russia?'' Strisz was saying.

"Does anybody know Russia?''

Strisz laughed and made a face. His face was very lively, always showing emotional play. Tarp had to resist liking him, and he guessed that Strisz knew the effect he was having. He was a man whom it was easy to like, and it may have been for that, too, that Andropov had seemed to distrust him.

"I mean, do you know us well enough to figure us out?''

"I don't know.''

"It's a little thick, you know, bringing in a capitalist to find a Soviet traitor. I suggested a Chinese, but that was taken as a joke.'' He made another face. "Far too much of what I say is taken as a joke.''

"You have had only two foreign postings, is that right?'' Tarp said severely. Strisz would recognize the tone—that of the serious man returning to business, rejecting amiability.

Strisz sighed. "Only two, yes. Bulgaria and Hungary. As you must know already.''

"You have never been to Cuba? To Argentina? To England?'' Strisz shook his head right through all the questions. It amused him to do so.

"You were passed over for promotion last year.''

"I remember.''

"Three years ago you asked for a transfer.''

"And was refused, yes.''

"Why the transfer?''

"Because I am an ambitious man.'' He raised his eyebrows as if to say, Surprise, surprise! "I asked to be switched to satellite communications training for one year and then to be given a suitable post in the Eighth Directorate. Am I saying too much?'' He pretended to be worried. ''Am I violating security, telling you this?''

''The Eighth Directorate is satellite and electronic communications. I believe that's already known in Washington.''

''A Soviet citizen can be arrested for discussing these things with a foreigner. Are you really a foreigner? How do I know you're not a Ukrainian in disguise? Ukrainians are the very devil for disguises. I may be one, in fact—this may be a false face I'm wearing.''

''Why did you want the transfer?''

''Because my post in the First Chief Directorate is a beautiful dead end. Do you think the future of communism lies in the reports of agents planted in the Warsaw Pact countries and Cuba? I doubt it—really, I doubt it. Satellite communications, on the other hand—there, an ambitious man could have a good time.'' For a moment his face was open, as if he were asking Tarp to understand him as a man. It could have been part of his act. ''I'm still young as these things go—the Soviet Union is a country of young workers and old leaders, as you may have noticed. Twenty years as head of the Eleventh Department doesn't much excite me; twenty years scrambling to the head of First Chief Directorate does.''

''You would have to take an inferior post.''

''I have faith in my own abilities.''

''That sounds like something that Maxudov might say.''

''Now who's indulging in psychology?''

Strisz was a good subject for interrogations. He was, as Andropov had said, intelligent, but he was also strong-willed. ''Look here,'' Tarp said, trying to sound hard but not unfriendly. ''The man I want set up a clandestine network in Cuba, I'm sure of it. That took time and it took inside knowledge. You're the ideal man for that. You have the opportunity, the contacts—I'm sure you have rewards you can hand out—you know the KGB presence there because you're in charge of it. All right—on that basis, you are Maxudov.'' He held up his hand as Strisz got ready to say something. ''However, I'm also looking for a man who seems to have set up something much cruder in London.''

''Same man?'' Strisz said conversationally. He might have

been listening politely to a story about a not very interesting acquaintance.

"Perhaps. Logic would say so." Tarp leaned back. "But I don't think you're the man who tried to kill me in London."

Strisz smiled a little painfully. "Did I try to kill you in Cuba?"

"That could certainly be."

"And who stole the plutonium."

"Yes, and who blew up Repin and that aircraft. Did you ever see those dancers?"

"They weren't from Moscow."

"They were very young. Good-looking, vital."

"Are you trying to shame me?"

"Maxudov is beyond shame."

"Well, surprisingly, you *do* shame me. Amazing, yes? I'm amazed myself. I don't like death. I don't like violence. I've never been involved in wet work. I am an *intelligence officer*. I am fascinated by the collection and analysis of facts. The other side of the business . . ." He seemed sincere. "It is evil. Do you believe me?"

"You seem very believable. But Maxudov will always seem believable." Tarp stood up. "I may want to talk to you again."

"But do you believe me?"

Tarp looked at him. He knew that nobody who had risen this high could be simple or simply fun-loving or really open. He thought of Juana's bandaged head and the huge gash on her shoulder. He thought of the dancers in Havana. He thought of the old man lying in his blood in the Paris restaurant. He thought of Johnnie Carrington without his arm. "No, I don't believe you," he said. "If you really thought you hated violence, and you stayed in this business, you would be so self-deluded you would be a lunatic. You aren't a self-deluded man." He gathered up his papers and his coat and the Astrakhan hat he had been provided. "Neither is Maxudov."

Konstantin Mensenyi met him in a park. Their cars were thirty yards apart on the wet, narrow road, the drivers inside with their newspapers while the two men walked across a field on which melting snow lay in a pierced crust that stood on the tips of the grass like lace. The firs that stood around the field were black in the gloom of the dense cloud.

Mensenyi was grossly fat—double-chinned, blubber-lipped. Tarp disliked him on sight, then scolded himself for deserting any attempt at objectivity.

"I protest," Mensenyi began. "I am making my protest formally, to the general secretary. It is bad enough to be suspected of the worst crime of the century, but it is unspeakable that they should bring me face-to-face with a man like you."

"Your department is Latin America?" Tarp said coldly.

"Did you hear what I said just now?" Mensenyi had a rather high voice. The fat and the high pitch made him seem a eunuch, but his file mentioned a wife and five children and a problem with a girl who had been a maid in the house.

"Your protest is noted and I think you are wise to make it formally to the secretary-general. Is your department Latin America?"

"You know it is."

"Including Cuba?"

"You know the answer to that, too."

"I'd prefer to hear it from you."

"Bah. Very well. Cuba is not in my department except in cases where there is overlap."

"Argentina?"

"Argentina, yes."

"You managed the transfer of intelligence materials to the Argentinians during the Falklands war?"

"That is not relevant."

"It is relevant if I make it relevant. Answer the question."

"I protest. I will put this in my written protest as a breach of security. The answer is yes—note what sort of grief you may have caused yourself by acquiring classified data!"

"Did you receive a reprimand from the director for your conduct of intelligence during the Falklands war?"

Mensenyi grunted, then stopped. He looked around them, as if to make sure they were in the very center of the lace-covered field. "A letter was put in my file," he said softly.

"You used a courier sometimes whom you called Penguin."

"Code name Penguin, yes, yes. What has this to do with anything?"

"Penguin made four trips to the Soviet Union in the last three years."

Mensenyi stared at him. He breathed partly through his

mouth; his nose was thickened above the nostrils as if from adenoids. "Well, what if he did?"

"Three of them came immediately after three of the plutonium thefts."

"I—" Mensenyi breathed heavily and then puffed out his cheeks. "The dates of the thefts are not known. Surely. Are they?"

"Putting two and two together, Comrade—the sailing dates of certain submarines—yes, that is known well enough. What have you to say about this coincidence?"

"It is a coincidence, what else? Ask Penguin, if you think you have made such a brilliant analysis! Eh? Go ahead!"

"Give me the identity of Penguin, and I will."

Mensenyi contrived to look very sly. "Oh, no. That is *very* highly classified. No, no, you don't trick me that way." He stabbed a short, gloved finger into Tarp's chest. "If you want to know that, *you* go to the general secretary."

Andropov had called Mensenyi a clown. He struck Tarp as more of an ox, a stubborn, almost immovable dullard. In fact, he reminded Tarp of Hacker, the CIA turncoat.

"You have made five trips to the West since 1971," Tarp said. "England twice, France twice. Canada once."

"What of it?"

"What was the purpose?"

"I was meeting with very important people from the other side."

"Yes, that's what the file says. What were the real reasons?"

"The file reasons are the real reasons!"

"There are very few good reasons for a department head's leaving Moscow."

"I was not department head until 1977."

"Your last trip was to London in 1981."

Mensenyi set his fleshy jaw. His cheeks, mottled with red from the raw, wet breeze, looked like slabs of meat. "I brought out an English agent who was going to be exposed."

"England is not in your area."

"I was ordered to bring him out."

"You were ordered to bring him out because you begged to do so. It's all in the file."

Mensenyi's face became ugly. "He was an old friend."

"You make a hobby, do you, of running agents in areas not your own?"

"I do whatever I can to help the nation, the Party, and world communism. I have always cultivated foreigners. I understand the foreign mentality. I have performed valuable service, turning foreigners to good use."

"You've also imported a remarkable collection of foreign art objects and consumer goods. You've even once been the object of an investigation into a black market food shop run for the diplomatic community in Moscow."

"I explained all that satisfactorily," Mensenyi said hoarsely. "It was to entrap foreigners."

"And turn a profit."

"I turned all profit over to the state!"

"After the investigation began."

"Bad timing! I was guilty of bad timing!"

Andropov had been right. The man was a clown.

Tarp ran quickly through the dates of the foreign visits, his contacts in the nuclear industry, his proximity on two occasions to the home port of the submarines at Murmansk. Mensenyi was sweating despite the wind. "You have nothing!" he shouted. He was in rage, or pretending to be. "I am innocent! I am not Maxudov! I am a thousand times better man than you!"

"Have you read Bulgakov's *Theatrical Novel*?"

"What?"

"I may want to talk to you again in a few days."

"Wait— See here . . ." Mensenyi put a gloved paw on his arm. "You're finished?"

"Yes."

"Well . . ." The blubber lips quivered. "See here, you don't seem to be a stupid man. Nor unsophisticated. Tell me the truth. Do you know who Maxudov is?"

Tarp removed the hand from his arm. "I may want to talk to you again in a few days."

"Yes, but see here . . ." He pulled at Tarp's sleeve. "This can't be easy for you. I understand that. You have to forgive my outbursts; I'm a man of short temper. It comes of having principles. Innocent men are often like that. But see here . . . a man like you, what happens to you when this is over? I understand the foreign mentality. I mean, I know what ambition is in the West. In Moscow, a man of your stature would be wealthy.

You deserve that—eh? Here you are, working in the highest, the *very highest* echelons of the service, who knows, maybe even the Presidium is consulting with you. And what will your reward be? You maybe ought to be giving some thought to your own future, do you follow me? After this is over, maybe?"

Tarp pushed the hand away roughly this time. "Not interested."

"I beg your pardon?"

"Not interested. You know what that means—Comrade."

It had been a clumsy attempt at a bribe. Maybe it had been an intentionally clumsy one, so that later Mensenyi could deny that he had meant it. He would say that he had been laying a trap, and in fact he probably was. "Already above his proper level," Andropov had said, and he had been right. Tarp thought of the stupid people all over the world who had risen too high in intelligence because of political shrewdness or luck or influence. They made it much more dangerous than it already was.

They walked back toward the cars, Mensenyi keeping a couple of yards' distance between them. Still, when they were fifty feet from the road and at the bottom of a steep bank leading up to it, he came closer. "See here," he said, "there's no reason why you would say anything to implicate me."

"No?"

"I've been cooperative. Let me make a gesture to prove how cooperative I am. I'll tell you who Penguin is." Tarp was a step or two up the bank and so was looking down at him. The broad, sweaty face was turned up in appeal. "It's an Englishman. His name is Pope-Ginna. That's classified."

"I'll make a note of it."

Josef Falomin waited for him at the end of a long baroque gallery in a museum of second-rate paintings. The building looked like a minor palace that the Bolsheviks had overlooked; closed until after World War Two, it had been used to house some of the overflow from other museums as Moscow modernized itself. There was an elderly guard at the gallery entrance and, across an echoing and domed corridor, an Oriental group with an Intourist guide. Otherwise the building seemed as deserted as if its owners had just been grabbed and shot by the Reds.

A hard-faced young Mongol was standing next to Falomin. Falomin was in his sixties, big-chested, stolid, ruddy as if he ate too much and took long walks to make up for it. He had watched Tarp as he had come down the long gallery under half-naked Renaissance goddesses and leering satyrs, between over-stuffed sofas and panels made gaudy with too much gilt. Falomin, his hands crossed in front of him, looked as immovable as a tank. When Tarp was close, the young man, who was standing in profile to Tarp, held out a hand toward him, palm up. "This is the American," he said.

Falomin stood on ceremony. A formal introduction, no less.

"I am Tarp."

"This is Comrade Falomin."

Tarp held out his hand, which was ignored.

"I will now leave you," the young man said. His shoes clacked on the marble floor long after he had turned into the corridor.

"Would you like to sit?" Tarp said.

"No."

"You know why I am here."

"Of course. I have a file on you."

Tarp waited. Falomin spoke with the flat voice of a man controlling an anger. It was a humiliation for him to go through this—above all for him, who ran the department that terrorized the rest of the KGB, the diplomatic corps, and every Soviet citizen who left the frontiers.

"You are the head of Special Service Two?"

"You know I am."

"You were in London during World War Two?"

"Yes."

"Would you tell me about it?"

"I was a file clerk in the military liaison office. I maintained certain connections. Those were very disorganized days."

"You ran a network?"

"I was too young. I was a file clerk."

"But you ran agents in London."

"I had certain foreigners I kept contact with."

"Who?"

"I am sure it is in my file. The foreign so-called freedom fighters who had taken refuge in London—the Poles, the Yugo-slavs, the French."

"Did you have contact with an Englishman named Pope-Ginna?"

"I had no contact with the English." Tarp thought he had scored, however; for the first time there was an edge to Falomin's voice.

"Did you know Pope-Ginna?"

"No."

"But you had heard of him."

"Perhaps. I have some recollection of the name."

"In what connection?"

"A naval victory, I think. In a very cold place, I do remember that. Colder even than this tomb." He looked at the gallery with distaste. "It amused me at the time. The English were astonished by stories of the ice. To a Russian it seemed commonplace."

"I thought you had no contact with the English."

"In the newspapers, I meant."

"What you meant was, your English mistress was astonished."

Falomin stared at him. He blinked. It was like seeing a rock blink. "It is in my file, I suppose," he said slowly.

"You had a child in England, in fact."

"It is in the file."

"Have you ever seen her?"

"I have not left the Soviet Union since I returned in 1946."

"Isn't that odd, for a man who controls a worldwide department?"

"I don't find it odd."

Tarp was wearing a Russian overcoat, but he had no gloves. He had to keep his hands in the thick pockets, and even then his hands were cold. Outside, the sun was shining, but the museum was frigid. "You know what I am looking for," he said.

"Naturally."

"You are the perfect candidate for Maxudov, on paper. You have access to every embassy, every Soviet traveler. You have the organization to cover up a complex operation inside the Soviet Union."

Falomin still looked like a rock. "What motive have I?" he asked in the same flat voice.

"I wish I knew."

"Perhaps you would like to suggest some romance about my

daughter in England. Or perhaps her mother—love, let us say. Is that what you want to suggest?''

"No."

"No." Falomin looked smug. "In fact, all that has been thoroughly checked. Yes? My old mistress has been dead for eleven years; my daughter married a professor and went to Australia in 1967. There is no romance. What is my motive, then?''

"Power."

Falomin looked contemptuous. "Don't talk about things you cannot possibly understand. It is a very American habit. You do not understand power. I respect you—I know your background, and I respect you—but I know that you are not a creature of the pack. You are a lone wolf. The creature alone does not understand power. Except his own power, and perhaps in that I envy you, for I have no chance at that. But real power is found only in the pack. Not alone. I am a wolf, too. We are all wolves here. When a wolf gets old or sick, the other wolves turn on him and eat him. Every wolf I eat increases my own power. Until one day I will be eaten. But do not tell me that I have made myself Maxudov in order to increase my power. Maxudov is outside the pack, like you.''

"Maxudov is a loner?"

"If he is one of us, he left the pack or was driven from it. That is Maxudov.''

"That's an interesting idea."

Tarp asked questions about plutonium and about submarines. Falomin had a very wide general knowledge and he seemed quite willing to talk. He was either very confident or very daring. The questions quickly became routine. When Tarp stopped to think, Falomin said, "Why did you ask me about the English admiral?''

"That's my business."

"I have another recollection of the name. He was adviser to the Argentine government when we sold it a submarine.''

"That wouldn't seem to fall under your responsibility."

"Oh, I know many things that don't fall under my official responsibility. Every wolf in the pack does.''

"What else do you know about Pope-Ginna?"

"I may have a report on him somewhere."

"I'd like to see it."

"Only if the order comes from the director."

"Why tell me about it, then?"

"To show you that I am a wolf." Falomin unclasped his hands, took Tarp's right arm in a powerful grip, and started to walk him up the long gallery. "I am not Maxudov. I am insulted that they think I could be, but I put up with these things; it is part of life. However, I am telling you I am not Maxudov, and I will not be made to feel guilty because I keep a lot of information to myself. Now, your time is up. I told the general secretary how much time I would give you, and your time is up. Leave me alone."

They stopped at the door. Tarp put out his hand again, and this time Falomin took it. "You were wrong about me," Tarp said.

"I would be very surprised if I was."

"I am not a wolf. In Alaska the Eskimos dip a knife in blood and freeze the knife, hilt down, in the ice. A wolf comes along and begins to lick the blood; he cuts his tongue on the knife, and then he licks up his own blood, because it is so cold that he does not know he has cut himself. Soon, he cannot stand. Other wolves come along and eat him. While they are eating, the Eskimos shoot the wolves." He looked at Falomin, unsmiling. "I am not a lone wolf. I am a lone Eskimo."

"And Maxudov is a very smart wolf. I think he knows all those tricks."

CHAPTER 30

Beranyi was the last on the list. Tarp expected him to be the toughest, although he wondered really what he had gotten from any of them. All would deny being Maxudov to their graves. He could hope to keep pressure on them all, perhaps, and so force the one to do something revealing or stupid.

"Your next interview will come for you at five," the round-faced Guards man told him.

"Like the ghost of Christmas yet to come."

"What is that?"

"Charles Dickens. You don't read the *Christmas Carol*?"

"Charles Dickens, of course. *The Cricket on the Hearth*. It is a classic production of the Art Theatre. I took my daughter to see it."

"In the *Christmas Carol*, a man waits for visitors he doesn't really want to see. They keep coming at stated times. They're more or less ghosts."

"Ah."

"My visitors are not ghosts."

"No." He laughed.

The last ones would take him somewhere to meet Beranyi. *Saving the best for last.* He wondered if it had been Beranyi's insistence, or if they had drawn straws, or if there was some protocol at work he knew nothing of.

When he heard a car Tarp got up and began to dress. The days were warmer, but when dark came it was cold again. He put on the heavy overcoat, a wool scarf. "I still need gloves," he said.

The Guards man snapped his fingers. "I knew I forgot something! Tomorrow, Comrade."

"Maybe I won't need them." Tarp went out and found two men in the yard behind the old house. One was Oriental, probably Mongol; he looked distrustfully at Tarp. The other man looked like an American stage cop—beefy, middle-aged, red as if from drink. He looked tough and capable, the kind it would be better to run from than fight; with a ten-yard lead you could wear him out in a block, but if he ever caught you he'd commit murder.

"We were going to knock," the big one said.

"I saved you the trouble. Let's go."

They looked him over, then studied his identification. They produced their own. They were identified as guards attached permanently to Department V. *Nice people.*

"Let's go," he said again.

They were using yet another dark sedan that they had pulled up under the trees. There was a driver in front, and the two guards got in on each side of him in the back. Tarp suspected Beranyi of having chosen them for their looks in order to shake him before the interview began.

They drove with that disdain for ordinary traffic laws that often marks policemen. It was dusk. Lights were on everywhere. There were deep pools of slush along the roads, and people stepped back as they roared along, trying to avoid the ice water that splashed shoulder high. They would be standing there, trying to wipe the water and the dirty ice from their clothes, muttering about bigshots and Party favoritism; would they have understood if they had known he was American? Being good Soviet citizens, they probably would have the sense not to try to understand.

It was only when they passed the Dzerzhinsky statue that Tarp understood they were headed for KGB headquarters itself. He was surprised. Beranyi was proving to be the only one audacious enough or secure enough to meet him on home ground. The others had felt a diffidence about being seen where, presumably, they were most themselves.

The car turned into the wide entrance from the square and drove along between two buildings, turned again and went through a small parking lot in which Tarp could see the white blurs of signs reserving each space. The driver flashed the lights and a door opened upward, exactly like a suburban American garage door. Beyond it was a tunnel through part of an older building, and, at the far end, a courtyard that looked black in the near darkness. The driver spun the wheel and brought the car to a stop in a reserved space next to a gloomy and ancient doorway.

Tarp had not seen it before, but he knew what it was by instinct: the old Lubyanka Prison.

Going right to the source.

The four of them, two in front, one in back with Tarp, walked through the doorway and along a brick corridor where the four sets of feet gave off noises that rang in a way to jangle the nerves. They stopped at a doorway above which a red bulb glowed; when one man knocked, a grill opened, somebody said something. The door opened and a green bulb went on.

The driver stayed behind. Tarp and the two men who had ridden in the back with him crossed a metal grating as, behind them, the heavy steel door thudded shut. There were metal doors on each side now, then a metal stairway that seemed to plunge down into an open well in the building. They directed him downward.

I've bought it, Tarp thought.

Beranyi was proving even more audacious than he had guessed. Beranyi was going to take control.

The metal stairway led to a concrete floor at the bottom of a large open area two stories high. Doors opened from it at each level. High up were lights in factory shades, but their light was inadequate. Any light would have been inadequate.

The Mongol had a key to one of the doors.

Inside was a room with a tile floor and white tiles running up the walls to head height. In the center of the room was a round drain with a pierced metal cover, and the floor sloped slightly to it from all four walls.

The mongol went in. He beckoned to Tarp.

Tarp started to speak. "I—"

The beefy one hit him from behind between the shoulders, knocking the breath out of him and sending him forward and down. He caught himself, but, clumsy in the heavy overcoat, he stumbled; another blow put him inside the tiled room. The Mongol swung his right hand, in which Tarp glimpsed something long and dark; it struck his head with a thud like the closing of a door. It was a leather sap, weighted with bird shot to deliver a crushing blow without breaking the skin.

"Strip," the beefy one said.

"I protest," he had time to say before they hit him again. The beefy one locked his arms behind him and the Mongol opened the overcoat and broke three ribs with a kick. Tarp tried to kick back and gave it up after a punch in the groin. He was sensible enough that he was in the hands of two experts, and fighting them would be futile.

They stripped him and went away with the clothes. They came back after half an hour and beat him again. Tarp was afraid that one of the broken ribs would puncture a lung and he covered his chest, and they began to work on his back and kidneys. One of them, in swinging him around, hit his mouth, and they both stopped and looked worriedly at his upper lip.

"Is he bleeding?"

"Mostly inside the mouth."

"I missed. The fucker ducked."

"It was stupid."

"You saw it. He ducked."

"They won't like it."

They pounded his back with lead-filled, phallic-looking saps and then left him again.

Two hours later he was moved to a cell on the level above. When he did not move fast enough, they beat his back and buttocks. The flesh there, already bruised, was excruciatingly tender.

He was alone in the prison, so far as he could tell. There might have been thirty cells around the central opening, but he heard no sounds and never saw another person. It had been reserved entirely for him, he supposed. There would be no record of his having been there and no witnesses except the absolutely essential, probably absolutely loyal few.

The cell was cold. There was an iron cot with a thin mattress but no bedclothes. In the corner was a water tap and, below it, a three-by-six-inch hole in the concrete—the toilet. There was no window, but high up in the wall opposite the steel door was a metal grate. In the middle of the ceiling were three light bulbs covered with a basket of metal mesh, like the lights in an old gymnasium. The walls were scarred and painted over so much that the once square holes in the gratings were almost round and partly closed. It was a very old part of the Lubyanka, probably a very historic part, in which some very good people had died.

He tried wrapping himself in the mattress, but it was sewn to the cot with wire. He lay on it and shivered.

Beranyi. It seemed disappointingly clear. *Beranyi, all the time.* He wondered if he had been set up in some way by all of them, to give the appearance of an investigation that would end with his disappearance. Perhaps the word was already out in Moscow that he had disappeared. *Where?* Where did people disappear in Moscow? A thousand places. Anywhere. Or maybe it was Beranyi working all by himself, audacious enough to say that one of the others had done it and Tarp had never reached him. *I sent my car to get him, Beranyi might say; he was already gone. We were going to discuss this terrible Maxudov business like civilized men over supper at the Slavansky Bazaar. The Guards men at the house said a car came for him, pretending to be from me. Not mine, of course. Thugs. Criminals hired for the purpose.* And so on.

Well, at least I didn't destabilize the new regime. "Mr. Smith" will be relieved.

The door opened and three men came in, the two who had been beating him and a slender man with glasses.

"He's a doctor," the Mongol said. "He's going to examine you."

The doctor probed quickly, deftly. Like many medical men who go into the service of the doomed—prisons, the military—he looked a little defeated. Perhaps he had an ethos, and self-hatred was defeating him. When he prodded the cracked ribs and Tarp cried out, he showed no sympathy. He made notes.

"Twenty minutes," he said.

They took him down to the tiled room and beat him again. When the doctor came in, Tarp was lying with his face almost on the metal drain cover. There was a smear of blood along the floor where he had pulled his right cheek, trying to get up.

"You have made him bleed," the doctor said. "Do you never do as you are told?" He put an astringent on the cut and examined Tarp again. Tarp wanted to ask how he was doing, but he knew he would get no answer.

"Take him upstairs."

He hobbled along, holding himself up on the iron railings, as if he were making his way along a pair of parallel bars. He had been kicked in the right thigh and he had trouble walking now. One of them hit his buttocks with the sap to make him go faster.

The doctor told him to lie down on the cot, and then he began to fill a syringe. "For the pain," he said.

Tarp knew better than that. The other two had to hold him. He felt the contents of the syringe go into the muscle, stinging and spreading. Twenty minutes later he was having trouble breathing.

Perhaps it had looked like an opportunity to try out a new biological agent. His nose was so filled he could not breathe through it; his sinuses pounded; his chest felt small and dry and he could never draw enough air into it. His body temperature fell and he thought that he was losing his strength and his will. When he tried to get up so he could go to the corner and relieve himself, he could not stand.

"Take him to room seven."

Tarp had been asleep. His nightmares had been dreadful, filled with an omnipotent, many armed Maxudov. He looked up at the doctor with hunted eyes. The doctor did not look into his eyes but put a stethoscope to his chest instead. Tarp could not feel its cold touch. He wanted to say that he could not breathe, but his mouth was dry and his tongue was thick and unusable.

"Don't make him go too fast. The heart is weak now."

They almost had to carry him. He was shivering. Twice he nearly fell, and only their hands under his arms kept him from going down. Their faces loomed horribly at him like things from dreams, all eyes and wrinkled foreheads. He understood after he had thought about it for a while that they were wearing surgical masks.

He had to go up one flight of metal stairs and down a corridor. There was a room there with a varnished door. Inside were a wood desk and five wood chairs. There was a recorder's machine on a small table and a typewriter on the desk, but nobody was there to use them. There was no telephone. The walls were bare of decoration, painted mustard below and brown above shoulder height. It was like a room where people had to wait for state employees to process papers for mundane things like auto licenses. The banality of evil.

There was a short man standing in the room. He had curly

gray hair and a dark, almost black mustache. He wore an almost black suit whose tightness suggested powerful shoulders and the beginning of a belly. His nose had a bump below the bridge and another at the end between broadly flared nostrils, below which were very deep nasolabial folds so that he always looked as if he detected a bad smell. He could have been a New York cabdriver or a Paris union organizer, but he was Mikhail Beranyi, the chief of Department V.

"Put him in a chair."

Tarp felt himself pushed to the right. His supports left him and he sank down, to find himself sitting in a straight wood chair.

The doctor muttered something and showed Beranyi a piece of paper. Next he handed him a surgical mask, which he helped him to tie behind his head. Beranyi made a gesture with his hand, and the others left the room.

"Tell me your name," he said.

Tarp tried to speak. No sound wanted to form in his throat. "Ta—" He took a breath. "Tarp." He shivered violently.

"Tell me in Russian why you are in Moscow."

Beranyi was simply trying to find if he could talk and think. He knew all these answers, as Tarp had known the answers to so many of the questions he had asked the others.

"I came—to—look for—look for—" He had to swallow. He sucked air in, trying to fill his burning lungs. "Maxudov. Stolen plutonium."

"Good. I am Beranyi. You have already guessed that. You wanted to meet with me; well, we meet. I am not like the others, you see. I do not choose to tell you anything. Instead, I choose that you tell me. Once you have told me things, you will be quite safe. But you understand your position here. You are alone. You can hardly walk; you are very sick. If you do not work with me, you will be beaten. And there are worse things, to be sure." He passed his right hand over his cheek, making a scratchy sound that Tarp associated with not shaving. Maybe it was late in the day, or even night. "Tell me now in Russian that you understand."

"I understand."

"Good. Now, we begin."

He pulled a chair closer and sat down, taking a dingy notebook from a pocket as he did so. He uncapped a plastic pen. He took a pair of plastic-rimmed glasses from a case and put them on. "Begin with Telyegin. You saw him when, please?"

"Telyegin?" He had to concentrate fiercely to remember who Telyegin was. *Old man in the wheelchair. He hated me. In the* dacha. *Yes, that one.* He began to talk, the words disjointed and his voice hoarse, but Beranyi paid no attention to his condition. He made notes. Tarp shook so badly sometimes that he thought he would fall out of the chair. Beranyi called the others into the room and said, "Do something with him, he keeps falling." The Mongol put a chair on each side of Tarp and draped his arms over them so that they supported him. Beranyi jerked his head and the man left.

"Feodor Strisz next. That is correct, is it not—Strisz next?"

Tarp fought for air and could manage only panting breaths. His head was down on his chest. His arms were shaking on the chairbacks, yet there was a film of sweat matting the hair on his chest and belly, as if he had been rubbed with grease.

Beranyi went on. He would let Tarp talk until he ran out of voice; then he would backtrack and ask a question from another direction. The character named Strisz in the *Theatrical Novel*— who had brought that up? Why? Did Strisz laugh then? Did Strisz mention Cuba? What did he say? Why did he say that? What was his tone of voice?

Tarp woke up in his cell. He did not remember it ending, but here he was. *Maybe I just stopped. Maybe I died.*

He was not shivering now; in fact, he was hot. He had new pains across his shoulders that were not the result of the beating, but of fever.

Tarp put a foot on the floor, then a hand, and then he let himself down and crawled to the corner. He squatted over the hole, smelling the sickness of his body. There was no paper, no towel. He slowly raised his left hand to the faucet above him, only to find that he lacked the strength to turn it on. He gave up and crawled back to the iron cot but had to lie next to it on the floor because he could not get up on it.

This isn't fatal, he told himself. *This is some kind of flu. They do ads about it on television. Everybody gets it.* He knew that that was not quite true. He had never been this sick. *Common ailment. Keeps doctors in business. Keeps doctors' wives in fur coats. Keeps doctors in the Republican party. Without flu, doctors would have to go on welfare. Very common.* What he had was not common, but it might become so if the Soviets used it as an ABC agent. Perhaps they would try it out in Afghanistan or Southeast Asia, where respiratory infections really cut a swath. *Take two aspirin and go to bed.* He looked up at the underside of the bed he couldn't get into.

This is the preliminary. When I'm weak enough, he'll go after me with chemicals. Sodium pentathol, maybe. The trouble with the chemicals that made people talk was that they also made some people crazy or silly or mute with depression—or dead. *I know what my choices are.* It would have been romantic to think of it as a battle of wills with Beranyi, but all the will that he had he needed simply to stay sane.

The one thing he could do was fence off some of what he knew. Perhaps he could protect Repin. Perhaps he could keep Pope-Ginna to himself. It seemed important still to keep the Argentine part of it—Schneider, Pope-Ginna, the *Prinz von Homburg*—separate and to keep it, if possible, from the Soviets. Unless Beranyi were Maxudov, in which case he would be learning only what he already knew. *Or would he?* Even in his fever, that made him concentrate. *What if Maxudov doesn't know about them?*

He would protect Jules Laforet somehow. And Hacker, because he would be no use at all once the Soviets learned he had been turned back.

And the amenities at the New Monroe. I don't think I want Beranyi staying there.

He concocted a reality. In his invented reality, Repin was dead in the wreckage of the Aeroflot plane; Hacker was believed to be a loyal American; Jules Laforet had not figured in his work at all. He had never heard of Pope-Ginna. He thought of that for a while. He had talked to two of the others about Pope-Ginna. Maybe he could retreat to the code name Penguin and give that to Beranyi. So, in his new reality, he had heard of an agent called Penguin who was a go-between with Argentina. That, however, gave Beranyi access to the little he knew about Argentina, or it would if he were made vulnerable by chemicals and if he hadn't tied up all the loose ends. Then it became necessary to invent a recent past in which there was no Argentina. Only somebody called Penguin.

Tarp told it all to himself as if it were a story, from the moment when Repin appeared at the *Scipio*'s dock. He tried to imagine every detail. He cut events totally—Argentina, the French safe house—and made up new ones to cover the gaps in time. Places, dialogue, clothes, faces. Everything had to be right. It had to be more right, more precise, and more believable than reality. It was his revenge on Beranyi, arising from old habit and from conviction and out of an instinct for survival, for which it was necessary to hold something back.

"Take him to room seven."

Beranyi quizzed him about Mensenyi and Falomin. The routine was the same, with no chemicals used. Tarp must have looked a little better, however, because the doctor gave him another injection.

Then he was in his cell again, throwing up. There was blood in his urine. At some point—it was after his second meeting with Beranyi—he tried to escape and the two guards beat him again. Somehow one of his teeth was knocked loose. He remembered the taste of the blood and the seemingly huge, boulderlike size of the tooth in his mouth. And then a dentist was working on him. He made Tarp laugh. *I don't need a dentist; I need a mortician.* He tried to say that but he couldn't make words. The dentist shouted at him. He was not in his cell then. He was someplace clean that smelled like carbolic acid.

Then he was on the iron bed again. His cheek was swollen and there was bloody padding around the tooth. A numbness. *Novocaine. He gave me novocaine. It's* Alice in Wonderland.

"Take him downstairs."

They took him back to the tiled room. There was a metal chair in the very center, right above the drain. They put him in it and the doctor prepared another syringe.

"Count backward from one hundred, please."

He felt the chemical take him the moment the syringe went in. He was very weak, he knew. He tried to think of the Spanish word for one hundred, but he could not. But he was counting backward in Russian.

". . . four, ninety . . . ninety, ah, three, ninety . . ." A long, long silence. Then, a voice like a gong. "Ninety-two." A sense of being sucked up by a great breath, by a wind that was rushing along a corridor like the endless corridor of a baroque palace. *"Ninety-one."* He expanded as he was swept along; his body almost grazed the ornate cornices, the arches, the Roman columns that lined his way. If he touched one, he would explode. He was a balloon, a bag of blood, a tissue. He got bigger and bigger. . . .

He was laughing. Something very funny had happened. He had fallen off the chair; that was what had happened.

He was angry. His rage was like the wind in the palace; it carried him, carried the room, the men in it. He was enraged because they had killed Repin and the dancers. Those young bodies. Always the innocent first.

He was singing "Don't Cry for Me, Argentina." He was giggling.

His breathing roared like surf. His blood sang. His heartbeat was like running steps. A child running down a corridor. Heels quick as raindrops. Faster. Flying!

In the darkness his breathing came and went like breezes in the tops of trees. His heart, buried deep within him, pumped blood with the measured and cautious tread of hope.

He opened his eyes.

There was a man standing over him. The man leaned close. The man smiled.

It was Strisz.

CHAPTER 31

"Awake again?" Strisz said.

"Again?" He moved his head and became aware of a vicious headache. "Have I been awake?"

"Off and on."

"For how long?"

"You have been here two days."

Tarp rolled his head the other way. "Here" was not the Lubyanka. He could see the rails of a shiny hospital bed, an IV tube running into his right arm, which was strapped down.

"You are in a clinic," Strisz said. "One we use sometimes for special cases."

Tarp looked down over his chest, which was covered with white bedclothes, to the rail at the end of the bed and, in the very middle of the blank wall opposite, the shiny metal of a brushed-steel door frame. He was still coming back, coming a long way back, and it took him time to remember. When he remembered, his voice crackled. *"Beranyi!"*

Strisz gave him one of his intelligent, joking smiles. "Yes, Beranyi."

"Where is Beranyi?"

"Why do you ask?" Strisz was making a joke.

"Where is Beranyi?"

"Odd, that you should ask. For several days, Beranyi was asking, 'Where is this Tarp?' It seems you never appeared for your meeting with him."

Tarp was not surprised by the story. He was surprised, however, that he was alive. "How did I get here?"

Strisz leaned on the bars of the bed and looked down, the way an idle man might lean on the railing of a bridge to look at the river below. His smile was that of a man with secret knowledge and a delight in letting go of it slowly. "A prostitute in the Malkov district called the police. She said you had been drinking and abusing her and had passed out."

Tarp thought about that. "It sounds like more fun than what I was doing," he said.

"I thought that might be the case, too. Your French passport was in your clothes when the police got there. They called us. Not my section, but the Seventh Department over in Directorate Two. It took a while for the news to reach me. Actually, I heard it from Telyegin, who had a bulletin out on you through Special Investigations. We moved you here as soon as we could clear the paperwork with the cops." Strisz looked impish. "The whore gave a statement that you had paid her to tie you up and beat you with a curtain rod. She said she thought you might have some bruises."

"Not very inventive."

"Oh, being beaten by a whore is done, you know."

"Not that. The story."

"Oh? Well, if it's false, there's a tone of—may I say *bravado?*—about it. She said you had been drinking vodka for three days. She showed the police the empties. They did a blood test and you showed a high alcohol level. However, it was fairly easy to see that it had been put into the bowel."

"The part about passing out sounds convincing. I thought I was going to die." Tarp shut his eyes against the headache. When he opened them, Strisz was still there.

"What did Beranyi say?"

"You'll never guess." Strisz held up a finger, touched his nose with it as if he were a low comedian in a play. "Guess."

"I don't do guesses very well."

"Guess."

"Forget it."

Strisz looked sad. He had wanted his joke. In a flat voice he said, "Beranyi said nothing, because he went to a congress of counterintelligence specialists in Budapest the day before the whore called."

Tarp thought that over. "That seems odd."

"Oh, not at all!" Strisz's smile had returned.

"You've got something to tell me, right? You've saved the best for last."

"Exactly!" Strisz leaned even closer. He was wearing a bulky overcoat, and the material was pushed up on each side of his neck like chubby wings. "He went to Budapest—and disappeared!" Strisz straightened and his wings collapsed. "We think he did, anyway. He had an invitation to go fishing on Lake Balaton. There's some confusion about whether he actually got to the lake. *Somebody* got there and fished, somebody who looked like Beranyi, but the Hungarians aren't at all sure that it actually was Beranyi. On the other hand, it might have been. So, we've sent a team down to find out the truth."

Tarp struggled in the bed "Help me up."

"You're strapped."

"Well, unstrap me!"

"You've got an intravenous tube in your arm."

"I want to sit up!"

Strisz put two pillows behind him and Tarp was able to sit more or less upright. He felt his chin with his left hand and found a stubble that was just beginning to be long. "How long since I was supposed to have met with Beranyi?"

"This is the seventh day."

"How long has he been gone?"

"Three days."

"Christ, he could be on the moon." The room was spinning and he squeezed his eyes shut. He opened them and fixed them on Strisz to make things stand still. "Well?"

Strisz was looking glum. He shrugged. "Well?"

"All right, let me have it: what's my situation now?"

Strisz looked still glummer. Tarp accepted the possibility that Strisz might like him and might even feel sorry for him.

"Officially, you were with a whore when you should have been on a delicate mission. So, you are under official KGB detention." Strisz cleared his throat. "Unofficially, there's a panic because of Beranyi's disappearance. But under the panic, there's celebration. If he's disappeared because he's defected, then the panic will win—and I don't know what will happen to you. If, on the other hand, he arranged his own disappearance not so that he could defect but so that he could go God knows where, then . . ." Strisz beat the palm of one hand on the fist of the other. "Then he will have proved himself to be Maxu-

dov, but in a very disturbing way." He grinned. "But that is
the cause of the celebration, because if Beranyi proves himself
to be Maxudov, then the traitor is found and the worry is over.
He will be declared a traitor; we will put out a worldwide notice
on him—and you might go home."

"With thanks and a gold watch."

"Is that an American joke?"

"It has to do with what happens when people retire."

"Ah. Everyone gets a gold watch?"

"No, only people who don't need them."

"Soviet workers would be delighted with a gold watch."

"I think the sense of humor is different here."

Strisz looked troubled. "You think we lack a sense of humor?"

"What's going to happen to me? Forget humor. What's
going to happen to me?"

"The general-secretary has decided that you will be detained
until the Beranyi business is solved."

*Until it's solved. Meaning, until knowledge falls into their
laps. That could be months. Years.* "What's your role?" Tarp
said, trying to make it casual.

"Me? Oh." Strisz looked a little embarrassed. "Oh, I'm a
friend of the court, as they say in Western law."

"Well, better you than Telyegin."

"But Telyegin is fair. When he's well, I mean. For that matter, we're all fair."

Tarp looked at him. "Is that one of your jokes?"

"Certainly not. Certainly not!"

Tarp smiled. He was left unsure as to just where Strisz stood;
no doubt it had been the intention to leave him that way. He was
silent and began to think of his situation. There would be pressure now to wind the Maxudov thing up. *And that could be
good for me.* Tarp wondered about the possibilities of escaping
from the Soviet Union. *Not good. I might do something through
the French if I could find one of Laforet's people, but my
chances would be slim. There's the Gogol's statue drop.* "Is
anybody interested in what really happened to me during those
days?" he said.

"Oh, definitely. But, ah, it is not my mission to ask such
questions."

"Whose? Telyegin's? Falomin's? Mensenyi's, because of understanding of the foreign mind?"

"Two of Falomin's people are outside."

"Oh, I see. You're the warm-up act. Is that it?"

"What is 'warm-up act'?"

"I suppose everything we've said is on tape."

"There has been normal surveillance."

"I hope they get the joke about the gold watch."

For the next two days two teams of interrogators alternated in asking him the same sets of questions. The clinic seemed divided between keeping him alert enough to answer questions and sedated enough to get the sleep he needed. Still, they took the IV away the day after he woke up, and the day after that he was walking down the corridor in order to meet his interrogators there. They tried to be objective, but their questions were tinged with an incredulity that suggested they had been primed to taunt him.

"And you insist that Comrade Beranyi himself questioned you?" one of them asked for the fifth time.

"Yes."

"While you were *sick* and *injured*?" The man sounded shocked, even though he had been through it all before.

"Yes."

"How could you be sure it was Comrade Beranyi?"

"I had his file. There were seven photos of him in it. I had his physical description."

"But he did not *introduce* himself as Beranyi!"

"He used that name."

"Are you sure?"

Tarp tried to be honest. "I think he did."

"Aha! You see?"

It was pleasant in the sunroom. The Moscow sun actually shone into it, making it a warm and drowsy place. Even the repetition of the questions seemed soothing, like an old story retold by a fire.

"Have you considered," one of the investigators said, "that your story sounds like an enormous hoax?"

"Hoax?" Tarp, who had been reclining in the sun with his eyes closed, opened one eye to look.

"Suppose your story were true, but suppose these were im-

personators *pretending* to be Comrade Beranyi and these
others. Suppose the place was not the Lubyanka at all.''

"Like a play,'' Tarp said.

"Exactly!''

"You're right. It was actually the stage of the Maly Theatre.''

He closed his eyes. He heard a sharp inhalation, perhaps a
gesture of disgust. The man was young, seemingly eager; it
was a sign of what was happening in the investigation that the
ones he dealt with now were lower bureaucrats. Somebody had
decided that the way to whitewash the Maxudov affair was to
make it routine. It would be allowed to sink into the bottomless
mush of bureaucracy.

Strisz came back. The same somebody who was turning it to
routine seemed also to have decided that Strisz was to be the
"good guy'' of Tarp's world, the one who comforted and who
listened sympathetically. It was not a role that could do Strisz
himself much good, Tarp thought.

"They think they've found your Mongol guard,'' Strisz told
him. "In Balakhna.''

"Dead?''

"No, no. Quite alive. He's in the Jewish program out there.
They're going to bring him to Moscow for questioning.''

"A little strange that he's alive.''

"Well, this isn't America, you know. We aren't gangsters.
Still, yes, it's all very audacious. As if Beranyi believed we
wouldn't really care.''

*As if, in fact, he weren't Maxudov. As if he questioned me be-
cause he didn't trust me and he thought they'd understand. Or
as if he questioned me to get in ahead of me and take all the
credit for himself.* He did not say so, however. He wanted to
get out of the Soviet Union.

They brought the Mongol to the clinic that evening. Tarp was
sitting up, wearing trousers and a sweater. Two men from Special Investigations brought the man into his room.

"Is this one of the men who, you submit, assaulted you?''

Tarp looked the man over. He remained impassive, even in-
solent. "Yes,'' Tarp said.

"Are you sure?''

"Have him say something.''

One of them nudged the Mongol. "Speak.''

"What am I to say?"

Tarp ran his tongue over his injured gum. "Say, 'The fucker ducked.' "

"The fucker ducked."

"Louder."

"The fucker ducked!"

"That's the man."

The next morning Strisz brought him more clothes and a rather greasy bag of sweet poppy-seed rolls. It turned out that Strisz liked the rolls himself.

"Don't you have work to do?" Tarp said. He felt on good terms with Strisz, even good enough to make personal jokes.

"I'm doing my work."

"Was that the general secretary's decision?"

Strisz hesitated. "There was a meeting. We made some decisions."

"Who? You and the secretary?"

"No, no—at Dzerzhinsky Square. Those of who were, um, closest to this." The suspects, he meant. The foxes who had been given charge of the henhouse.

"Was the secretary there?"

"He sent a deputy."

"Telyegin? Was Telyegin there?"

"Telyegin is very ill. He went into the hospital last night."

Tarp was dressing. "These clothes almost fit. Russian factories are getting better. Why am I dressing?"

"You're being moved."

"Where?" Tarp thought of the Lubyanka, not without a tremor of fear.

"An apartment."

"You're treating me very well, I must say. Almost as well as if I were a defector."

"Frankly, the general opinion is that Beranyi was it. There's some feeling that you can be sent home. The general secretary wants to, um, send a signal to Washington that we can put our own house in order and stand by our commitments."

"I'm not much of a signal."

"Oh, yes."

"I don't work for Washington."

"You have contacts. Come, come, we're realists here. We

think it makes better public relations if we send you back in good condition.''

Tarp pulled a tie around his neck and slipped it under the shirt collar. He almost never wore ties. "And the Mongol?''

"He gave a statement during the night.''

That "during the night" made Tarp wince. He could imagine what had gone on during the night. "What did he say?''

"He substantiated your story. Anyay Special Investigations has found the cells where you were held. One of the old blocks of the Lubyanka. They'd wiped everything down, but Forensics and Evidence found two partial fingerprints on a bed frame. Yours. And a little dried blood on the underside of a drain. Your type.''

"So there is some evidence now.''

"Oh, yes. Yes. Plenty of evidence.''

Which, in Moscow, could be a help—unless it's decided that the truth will be different, in which case evidence is no help at all.

They walked down the corridor. They saw nobody; the staff were being kept safe from seeing him, in case there was trouble later. There was no checkout procedure, no formal discharge. "No bills," Tarp said aloud.

"What is that?''

"Another joke.''

"Are all your American jokes about money?''

"We have lots of jokes about sex.''

"Ah, so do we. I often find them distasteful. Do you know the one about . . .'' He told Tarp a joke that Tarp had heard when he was eleven years old.

"Yes, we have that joke, too. I find it a little distasteful.''

"Good. Then I don't have to tell you any more sex jokes.''

They stepped outdoors to a rubber matting that covered the concrete sidewalk. Water from melting ice lay in long ribbons between the raised black ribs. The air was crisp, but the sun was shining and there seemed to be reason to believe that spring would come.

"I want to show you something," Strisz said.

Tarp walked slowly because he was still weak. He wheezed when he breathed heavily, and his back and ribs were still sore.

They got into a car and Strisz murmured to the driver. For some minutes they rode in silence; then Strisz began to point out landmarks. Tarp realized that Strisz had a great love for Moscow and almost an expert's knowledge of architectural history. He also had a critic's disdain for bad architecture.

They turned into Podgornyi Street.

"Slow down at the school," Strisz said to the driver.

The car rolled quietly past the school, from which a sound of singing came. Beyond the school, where the old house should have been, there was a new gravel play area. Nothing was left of the house—not a stick, not a chunk of brick.

"That house was built in 1887," Strisz said.

Tarp was thinking of the old couple.

"Sometimes . . ." Strisz's voice faded.

Is this a warning? Tarp wondered.

They drove for another twenty minutes and then the car stopped outside a block of apartments whose bogus monumentality brought a caustic comment from Strisz. He leaned forward to the driver, putting a hand on Tarp's arm to indicate that he was not to get out yet. "Get the key from the block manager," he told the driver.

"I don't know where the office is."

"Find it, then. Idiot."

Tarp and Strisz sat together in the back of the car. The windows were partway open and the air, upon which spring had laid a very light touch, smelled good.

"Mensenyi is dead," Strisz said without looking at him. "He killed himself. I wasn't to tell you until now. Nobody knows but the upper echelon." He stopped talking and watched a girl walk past. "It's a complicating factor."

It was like being in a car on a stakeout, Tarp thought, sitting there, waiting, passing the time with talk. He had the eerie feeling that he and Strisz were partners waiting for a suspect. "When?" he said. He, too, was watching the girl.

"The night that Beranyi went to Budapest. Beranyi went to see him. We learned that afterward, of course. Mensenyi shot himself sometime that night. Actually about four in the morning, they think." Strisz dug his hands into his overcoat pockets and slumped down on his spine. "The theory is that you told Beranyi something that suggested that Mensenyi knew too much, and so he went to Mensenyi and either killed him or forced him to kill himself. What do you think of that?"

"It could be made to make sense."

"Did you tell Beranyi something about Mensenyi?"

"I don't know. I was out of my head."

"Did you think that Mensenyi was Maxudov?"

"No. Not really. But I thought he was pretty deep into some things that were going to get him into trouble. I don't think it would have been very hard for Beranyi to scare him."

"You think he knew something about Maxudov?"

"I think he knew a piece of something. I think he knew it without understanding it."

Strisz crossed his legs. He was almost lying down now. "The most popular theory is that Beranyi is Maxudov and he blackmailed Mensenyi, who had helped him in some minor way—foreign contacts, maybe. Nobody liked Mensenyi. Andropov thought he was an idiot. I used to have lunch with Mensenyi sometimes. I didn't like him, but I always found myself laughing when I was with him. We both liked jokes." He looked at Tarp, his eyes sad and troubled. "Do you believe that Beranyi is Maxudov?"

Tarp kept looking out the window, as if the suspect for whom they were waiting would emerge from the big central doorway of the apartment block. "It's easy to understand why the hierarchy believe that Beranyi is Maxudov."

Strisz managed a weak grin. "You have a fine grasp of Socialist truth. Maybe you should stay in Moscow." He wriggled into a more upright position. "It will be important to be correct in this matter."

Tarp understood why he had had the feeling that they were partners. There was a natural sympathy between them, that temptation toward friendliness. More compelling now was their isolation from power. Strisz, Tarp sensed, was being boxed in with him by rivals in the service; whether he liked it or not he was being made Tarp's ally. So, they were on a stakeout together. The suspect they were waiting for was truth.

CHAPTER 32

He was told to write a report. The report was to show that Beranyi was Maxudov. He was not told that the report was to show that Beranyi was Maxudov, but he understood quite clearly that the official truth was taking that line. Events had gotten ahead of him: he had been brought in to investigate, and now he was expected to make the investigation conform to facts it had never discovered.

The KGB team in Hungary had determined that Beranyi had reached Lake Balaton, but the man who fished there all day had been a double. Beranyi had slipped into Austria, and Strisz reported a reliable source who had seen him at the Vienna airport.

Tarp decided to write his report so that the leadership could find its own conclusions confirmed there but to try to leave enough loose ends so that they would not feel immediately vengeful if Beranyi turned up—as Tarp believed he meant to do—with the real Maxudov in hand.

He asked for Mensenyi's office files. It took a day to clear the request; then the files showed up with two guardians, one a female censor and the other a man who never identified himself but who was certainly from the KGB. Each paper had first to be studied by both of them and then, if it got by them, it was handed grudgingly to Tarp. He got about one paper in seven. The result was that his report was filled with words and phrases like "possibly," "in the case that," "if," and "should a complete search of the files show." In a sense, however, Soviet secrecy worked in his favor, for it became their fault and not his own that so much was conjectural.

He asked for a Russian dictionary. His colloquial Russian was not up to the confusions of official jargon.

The agent named Penguin was mentioned in Mensenyi's files. In each case the code name was blacked out by one of the censors, but he could tell from context who was meant. He was able to learn, for example, that he had been active in the Argentine acquisition of a whiskey-class submarine in Murmansk, refitted for polar research. There were other references that showed a blacked-out agent in Murmansk and Moscow during the period when Maxudov had been most active. It was this information, he believed, that Mensenyi had held but not understood. Somehow, Beranyi must have puzzled it out—and then killed Mensenyi.

And now Beranyi is out there looking for Pope-Ginna. But he did not mention that idea in his report.

"I'd like a typist," he told Strisz.

"Of course." Strisz looked at him quizzically. "A pretty one? I mean—do you want a woman? You know what I mean. A *woman*?"

Tarp thought of Juana. "No," he said.

"We have some very sexy typists."

"Save them for the leadership."

He got a heavily censored transcript of the interrogations of the submarine captain who had been caught by the Swedes. Many of the pages had more black than white on them and were almost illegible. There was testimony of the crew, too. Tarp read it all and found only one statement of some interest, that of a sailor who had been on a previous mission with the same captain to the South Atlantic.

"No, there was nothing unusual. Maybe one thing. Tubes four and eight, that happened before, treating them different. With Captain (name deleted), yes. No, there was no radioactivity I ever heard about. We never check for that on the (deleted) boats. We were a night maneuver in Operation (deleted) and we blew air out of tubes four and eight. No, not in the (deleted) or in (deleted) waters. No, we were south of Station (deleted). Tubes four and eight. Yes, only air. Yes, that is a funny thing."

Not in the what? Not in the Baltic? Not in Swedish waters? Maybe south of the rendezvous station in the South Atlantic?

"The committee believes Beranyi is in Sweden."

"What committee is that?"

"The Committee on Inter-Departmental Unity." Strisz looked sheepish. "Those of us who began all this, plus the general secretary's deputy, plus some people from Investigation."

"Ah, the Committee for the Protection of Hens."

"What?"

"The committee the foxes always form. Never mind. Why would Beranyi be in Sweden?"

"Because that is where we think the plutonium went."

"Why?"

"Because that is where the submarine went aground."

"And what would the Swedes do with plutonium?"

"Make bombs."

"The Swedes have trouble even getting nuclear power plants past their people. The nuclear freeze is very strong in Sweden."

"The committee believes that is a front."

"And what are the Swedes going to do with the bombs? Attack Denmark?"

"Sell them. Israel, South Africa, Brazil."

"Israel and South Africa can make their own bombs, and Brazil has made its own weapons-grade plutonium in a lab. Which Sweden could also do, if it chose. The money the Swedes might get for nuclear bombs is peanuts to what they can get for conventional industrial production. The idea is crazy."

"Not if the leadership accepts it." Strisz cleared his throat. "Anyway, there is a strong feeling against the Swedes just now. They are so smug, you know?"

In nine days he had the report done. He was much less outspoken about the Swedish theory than he had been to Strisz, and he left open the possibility that the plutonium had gone to Cuba or farther south. The typist packed up her metal table and her copy of an IBM electric and went away; the censors departed. For two days Tarp paced back and forth in the hot little apartment. He read Gogol, did exercises, cooked for himself from the lavish stock of foods that had been supplied to him. He ran twice a day.

Late on the second day the censor returned. With her was not the same KGB overseer, but a gray-haired man in a worn raincoat who was not even introduced.

"I have another file," the woman said. "You must sign."

"I've finished my report."

"I was told that you were to see it. It was on a different requisition number, you know."

The man watched him write his signature, and then the two of them waited. "We must take it back," the woman said.

"Ah." He opened the file. There were only two pieces of paper in it—one, in his own handwriting, the list of names he had asked to have checked against the German World War Two records; he had forgotten it. The other was a computer printout in a very open dot-matrix format.

FAHNER, GUSTAV. BIOCHEMIST, DIRECTOR, INSTITUTE FOR SCIENTIFIC ADVANCEMENT. SPECIALTY: GENETIC RESEARCH. PRINCIPAL AUTHOR OF THE NOTORIOUS 'SUPER-GENE THEORY' OF CAUCASIAN SUPERIORITY. PREWAR RESEARCH IN MENDELIAN DISTRIBUTION NOTEWORTHY. BELIEVED RESPONSIBLE FOR EXPERIMENTATION ON LIVING FETUSES, 1943-44, DRESDEN GYNECOLOGICAL HOSPITAL BUT RECORDS DESTROYED. KILLED, 1944, PRINZ VON HOMBURG.

There were other names, but nothing in the details about them seemed relevant. Separate from the list of those supplied to him by Mrs. Bentham was a single name that he had added himself.

BECKER, NAZDIA. b. MISKOLC, HUNGARY 1927. d. BUCHENWALD, 1943.

"Thank you," he said to the woman. He handed her the file.

"You must sign again."

"Of course."

"You made no notes?"

"As I said, my report is completed."

She and the man went away. Tarp began pacing around the apartment again. *How many Hungarian Nazdia Beckers could there be? It isn't a Hungarian name, so there can't have been many.*

Late on the third day Strisz came to the apartment. He had been staying away, perhaps to get his own work done, perhaps to be discreetly out of the picture if the leadership rejected the report. He seemed elated.

"Your report has been accepted!"

"Good." Tarp was cooking rice with canned mushrooms

and fresh yogurt, and steamed cabbage with sesame seeds. "I'm going to eat. Would you join me?"

"It smells good!" Strisz threw his coat over a chair and rubbed his hands together. "It smells delicious, in fact. What is it?"

Tarp told him. Strisz stopped rubbing his hands together. "How can you eat like that? Where is the meat?"

"Meat is for capitalists."

"Meat is for men!" Strisz picked at the rice, then began to eat it and the cabbage with some interest. "Not bad." Tarp poured vodka for him and set out coarse black pepper. Strisz shook pepper into a glass and poured in vodka. "Very good, in fact." He drank off the vodka.

"About the report," Tarp said.

"Yes? Is there bread? Ah, there—yes, good! The report?"

"What did they say?"

"You live very well here, Tarp. Very well. You are comfortable, yes?"

"Comfortable, yes. It seems contradictory to have canned mushrooms when I know they're not available in the stores."

"That is a privilege. A perquisite. Because you are an honored guest."

"Because I'm a temporary member of the upper class in this classless society, you mean. What about the report?"

Strisz swallowed and had to clear his throat. His eyes were shiny with tears because he had swallowed too much at one time. "How would you like to go on living in this apartment as an honored guest of the people?"

"Not much. Do I have a choice?"

"Of course!"

"What about the report?"

"It was accepted. It was approved. Between you and me, if I could write reports like that, I'd have a much larger office than I have." Strisz mopped up yogurt and mushroom juice with dark bread. "Telyegin says you ought to get the Korilenko medal."

"What's the Korilenko medal?"

"They just created it. For service to the State in extraordinary circumstances."

"I don't collect medals. I thought Telyegin was in the hospital."

"He's out again. He was at the committee today. He's like that, up and down."

"Are they going to let me go?"

Strisz chewed the bread. He made a humming sound several times. "Mm. Mmm. Mmm." He poured more vodka. "Andropov likes you," he said.

"Are they going to let me go?"

"Well." Strisz tossed down the vodka and then sat back, arms folded. "You have two choices. One, stay in Moscow, you will get the medal, this apartment, any job you want that doesn't offend security. We would assist in making your personal life very pleasant—bring to Moscow the Cuban woman you met in Havana, for example—a boat and a beach house in summer, and so on. Or, two—you can leave in four hours on the Aeroflot to Berlin. From there, you would be on your own."

Tarp looked at him very unpleasantly. "What about the other hundred and twenty-five thousand in gold?"

"As the plutonium has not been found, and Beranyi is still missing . . ." Strisz looked embarrassed. "The committee did not feel that, um, another payment was justified."

"Until I find Beranyi and the plutonium?"

"No. I am very sorry, Tarp. Personally, I am humiliated. The case is closed. Whether you stay in Moscow or not."

"They want to bury it."

"Yes."

Tarp's face became ugly. "What are the rules if I go?"

"I do not understand."

"When do I become a target?"

Strisz touched a fleck of mushroom with a finger. He lifted the finger to his mouth and licked it. "I do not know."

"Who's taking over Department Five from Beranyi?"

Strisz's mouth turned down as if he were going to cry. "Falomin."

"Falomin!" Tarp shot to his feet. "They put a former suspect in charge of the death squad! Do you know how long I'll last out there? I won't get out of the East Berlin terminal!" He was shouting. Strisz looked as if he had been slapped. *"Mokrie dela!"* Tarp cried. "It's so wet you could swim in it!"

He reached the window in two strides and stood there staring down like a statue of one of the crazier saints staring down from a pedestal at the dark street three floors below. His face was contorted with anger, and on the sill his fists beat slowly. He heard Strisz push back his chair and cross the room to him. Strisz put a hand on his shoulder. "Stay in Moscow," he said softly. He sounded sad, but his was not the sadness of a man who felt that his country had betrayed a friend; he was a loyal Communist, a tough administrator of an oppressive bureau, a pragmatist. His sadness came from a perception of friendship threatened. "Stay in Moscow. Tomorrow, the ceremony will be in a private reception room of the Kremlin. Take your medal. There will be two of you. It will be a great honor. These things never work out perfectly; only children think they will. You're a man of the world. Life can be good here—it *can*; Americans mock us, but Russia is a wonderful land! Join us. You can be just the same as if you were wealthy in the West."

"It isn't the same." Tarp exhaled heavily and steam formed on a windowpane. "I have a place in Maine. Spring is coming."

"Every man loves the ground he first got dirty on, eh?" Strisz patted Tarp's shoulder. "There is a joke about that, but I won't tell it. Ah, well. I knew you wouldn't, you know. I'm sorry." They looked at each other in the glass of the window, but it was so dark that the meeting of eyes was uncertain. "I will miss you."

Tarp went on looking at the street. There were two men leaning on a car down there. If he went out, they would follow him. It would always be like that if he stayed. "Who else is getting the medal?" he said idly, trying to lower the temperature of the conversation.

Strisz chuckled. "The Penguin. Remember? He's in your report."

"I'd think he'd be contaminated from having worked with Mensenyi."

"Well . . . there is that, yes. After he gets the medal, he's going into the country for the weekend with some of Falomin's people."

It would always be like that, too. Weekend interrogations because you had the bad luck to get into the files of a loser. At another level, Tarp was thinking, *Pope-Ginna's in Moscow. What does that mean?*

"I want to see Andropov." He had let his voice heat up again. It sounded imperious.

"That's impossible."

"Before I make this decision, I want to see Andropov."

"But you can't." Strisz was truly shocked. "Nobody does," he said lamely.

"One of the British spies who got busted last year testified that he'd had dinner with Andropov. It was a great honor, he said. I'm entitled to a great honr. Ten minutes is all I need."

Strisz sagged. "I'll see what I can do."

"No. Not good enough."

Strisz became a little angry at that himself.

"You're a good man, Strisz," Tarp said. "I like you. I think you're my friend. But you've given up. That's why you won't go any higher in the service. It's your sense of humor—you have too much good sense to be really ruthless. I don't. I'm angry now and I'm making a demand. *You must get me to see Andropov!* If you don't, I will withdraw my report and I'll write another that will show that Beranyi is not Maxudov. And you know what a mess that will make."

Strisz unfolded his arms and wiped his face with a pocket handkerchief. "You are going to ruin everything," he said bitterly.

"What is 'everything'? It's a fiction. Yes, I can ruin the fiction." Tarp lowered his voice. "*You* know we don't have the truth yet. You know that Maxudov may still be in Moscow."

"Andropov will be very angry."

"I'll take that chance."

Strisz picked up his overcoat. He put it on slowly, as if he were an old man. He buttoned it with care and then picked up his hat. Only then did he look again at Tarp, and, shaking his head, he left the apartment.

CHAPTER 33

There is an antechamber off the Great Hall of the People that is used by those going into the hall from the dignitaries' end. In it are armchairs and a coatroom and, often, a bar. Beyond the antechamber is a very small room paneled in Circassian walnut and furnished in impeccable modern furniture from the factory at Kem, where Finnish craftsmen who were on the wrong side of the boundary when the Karelian A.S.S.R. was created make Scandinavian furniture for the new Socialist aristocracy. This room is used by the general secretary, as a certain room in St. Peter's is used by the pope, for private rest before an important appearance.

It was in this room that Tarp waited. "The secretary-general will have four minutes only," an intense, spectacled young man had said. He had seemed anguished by those four minutes, as if they had been cut out of his own flesh instead of Andropov's appointment schedule. "You must wait here and not leave this room! You must be ready to speak instantly when he asks you! Do you understand?" Tarp had said yes and the young man had gone away, looking even less satisfied with the arrangement than when he had come in. Later, security men had examined both the room and Tarp. Later still, the door opened suddenly and Andropov's tall figure filled the doorway. He glanced at Tarp, spoke to somebody outside too low to be heard, and came in. The door closed behind him as if he were a wizard who could control such things with spells.

"I did not think to see you again," Andropov said mildly.

He looked bemused, like a busy man with other things on his mind. "What is it you want?"

"I want a chance to stay alive. I want to be put secretly on a different flight to the West."

"You got me here for that?"

"Don't you want the truth about Maxudov?"

Andropov was looking down at his hands, already thinking about something else. "I am satisfied that we have the truth," he said. He took a single sheet of paper from an inner pocket and began to read it.

"Would you be dissatisfied if I found something different?"

"You do not think it is Beranyi?"

"I don't have the facts. Comrade Secretary, the facts will come out sooner or later. If one of the Western intelligence services finds that it was not Beranyi, they will use it against you. They will try to humiliate you. If it is not Beranyi, there will be trouble. Great trouble. And if it is not Beranyi—Maxudov is still one of you."

"You chose not to stay in Moscow?"

"If I return to the West, I will be killed by Department Five. If I stay in Moscow, I will live, at least for a little while. Is that a choice, to stay alive? Not a very flattering reason for me to choose Moscow."

Andropov raised his head; his heavy-lidded eyes looked sleepy. "Moscow will survive not being flattered by you, I suppose."

Tarp could feel the man's attention slipping away from him. "Comrade Secretary, I am not asking for much! Let me leave the Soviet Union safely, and I will abide by the contract I made with Repin! And I would expect you to abide by it, as well."

Andropov looked down at the paper again, and Tarp thought he had lost him. Andropov said, however, with real curiosity, "Why do you so much want the truth? Is it for the money?"

"It's what I set out to do."

Andropov looked piercingly at him. His eyes flicked back and forth between Tarp's eyes. "You mean—you are a craftsman," he said after some seconds of this examination. "Now I understand." He shifted his weight and looked at the door, his concentration already moving toward the Great Hall. "Very well. Tell my assistant how you want to leave the country."

"Thank you, Comrade Secretary."

"But naturally, I will accept the committee's recommendation that this case is closed. Unless you find differently very quickly, our arrangement is ended."

He went out quickly. Tarp saw him pause by another man and bend his head to say a few words. The other man glanced toward Tarp. Andropov moved away, and there was a general motion to follow him among figures scattered around the antechamber. Then, as a door opened somewhere out of sight, a patter of applause began and swelled and became a sound like rain.

The man beckoned him. Tarp went into the antechamber. The room was empty except for the two of them, with that air of suspended time that comes when a great deal of activity has been ended abruptly. Smoke was still rising from a cigar that had been left in an ashtray; half-filled glasses stood on small tables and even on the floor.

"We are to go at once," the man said.

"All right."

"We go straight to the airport. His orders."

"Fine."

"We'll check the flights when we get there."

Tarp was driven out of Moscow in his Russian suit and shoes and sweater, without going back to his apartment, without speaking again to Strisz. It was late in the day and the sky was darkening, and many cars moved with their headlights on. As they passed the Gorky statue, a few flakes of wet snow began to fall. The river was running free of ice in the middle. *Like the pond in Maine by now.* He wondered if it was ice-free yet.

There was a girl on a corner where the car stopped for traffic. She wore a raincoat too light for the season and she looked harried by her life, by petty annoyances and perhaps by the huge annoyance of trying to be happy. She was pretty and intelligent-looking, fair and yet somehow like Juana. Their eyes met. She did not smile, but she did not look away. *An unhappy woman, but a realist.* The car moved slowly forward and he turned his head to watch her. *Good-bye, Moscow.*

He thought they might drive him into the country and kill him. He had little trust in Andropov's word. He remembered Hungary too well—1956, and promises that were broken, and a Russian ambassador who was now the general secretary. When they were waiting in a badly heated room at the airport, he thought that Falomin's men might come in and take him. Then they ran out to the aircraft after the stairs had been pulled away and ducked under the huge body and went up the emergency after-stair. He ran up three at a time, feeling the stair bend under him. He and two security men sat in a row of three seats at the back, behind a beige curtain so the other passengers could not see them.

One of the men handed him his French passport, his other French papers, and his credit card. The other had four hundred dollars in deutsch marks.

"We didn't have time to change the money," he said.

I hope you didn't have time to change anything else, either.

They flew to Helsinki. Tarp got off alone, looking for the ones who would be waiting to kill him. He put distance between himself and other people, suspecting knives, syringes. He looked far ahead down Helsinki's sterile passages, looking for the terrorist who had been sent to kill him.

He got on the first flight out and went to Malmo, where he rented a car and drove through the black night of the Swedish winter, watching behind him for headlights that never appeared.

Good-bye, Moscow.

CHAPTER 34

She stirred in his arms and murmured something in Spanish. Lying awake, he had been thinking of Moscow, and the slurred Spanish had sounded alien to him. She had been sleeping heavily, keeping contact with him as if, even in sleep, she wanted assurance that he was alive.

He had come up the road to the farmhouse on foot after two days in Paris with Laforet and "Mr. Smith," and he had seen her walking at an angle to the road, her eyes on the ground, her shoulders slumped. Something had made her look up—perhaps a peripheral sense of his movement on the road—and, seeing him, she had straightened and then had begun to run. She ran coltishly, like an adolescent who runs for the joy of it, and she had wrapped herself around him and wept.

They had made love. She laughed, then wept again. It was late afternoon then; they had gone down to eat with the others. Tarp had spoken quickly to Repin. Then he and Juana had gone upstairs again and made love. Tarp wanted to warn her off him, to make her pull back from what she called love, but she laughed at him. They went to sleep entwined and sated. He slept for four hours and then lay awake.

He had been thinking of Strisz. The Soviet's career would not go well now, for, having arranged Tarp's meeting with Andropov, he had put himself outside the circle of the cooperative ones and of the good assistants who kept such unpleasantness from their chief. Strisz might become a likely candidate for turning when he realized that his career would go no further.

"Don't go away," she said in Spanish. This time he understood her. He rolled on his back and she held him with a bare arm and leg. "Did you hear me?" she said.

"I thought you were asleep."

"I don't talk in my sleep. Do I?" Her hair had grown long over her ears and at the back of her neck, but the mass of it along the top of her head still stood up in a cock's crest of black, spread now over his left arm and shoulder. He ran his fingers lightly over her healed wound. He had seen it in the light, livid and disfiguring.

"Don't you ever sleep?" she said.

"Of course."

"I felt you awake."

"You did not; you were sleeping like a rock."

"I was awake a lot."

The rectangle of the window was a warm gray. He could make out the shape of the armoire, the black hole of the door.

"What are we going to do now?" she said.

"It's very complicated."

"Tell me about Moscow."

"Not just now." He stroked her arm. "Laforet is coming today. We're all going to talk. Plan."

"Repin, too?"

"Of course. You got along with Repin?"

"Oh, yes." He could tell from her voice that she was smiling. "He makes up wonderful compliments, did you know that? He is a great flatterer. Of women, I mean."

"Did he try to get you into bed?"

"No, he told me I was only for looking at. He is sleeping with Therese."

"What about the old man—Therese's stepfather?"

"The old man is gone. Repin broke his arm." She raised herself so she could look at him in the dim light. "At least that is what Therese and I think. Repin was out in the field and the old man went after him with a pick—you know, for working in the earth?—and they went behind the hill, and then the old man came back without the pick, and his arm was broken. So the guards took him away. Now Therese sleeps in Repin's room."

Tarp thought about Therese, who seemed to have been handed from one man to the other like something won in a contest. "What does Therese say?"

"She says she is going back to the Soviet Union with Repin."

Tarp's mind begin to work forward toward what must be done next. He was surprised, then, when he heard her voice, for he had forgotten her. "I have been thinking," she was saying. "Are you listening?"

"Of course."

"I had time to think, these weeks. I love you, and part of me wants that to be my whole life. But . . . I cannot be that indulgent. Can I? I have a responsibility. I am healed now, strong again. I must work."

"You want to go back to Cuba?"

She was silent for a while. "I don't want to leave you. But I must do my work in the world. Does that sound stupid?"

"No. Laforet will send you back, I think. Or—you can work with us."

"Us. Who is us? I cannot work against my conscience, against my beliefs. I *believe* in socialism."

"I think you can work with us and still believe. Until this business is over. Then . . ." He kissed her shoulder.

"I know, I know."

At six-thirty he heard Therese moving in the kitchen. He pulled on clothes and went down. She was building up the fire. Her face looked fuller, he thought. She pointed her chin toward a coffeepot. "That's from last night. *He* likes his coffee fresh in the morning."

"And his bread?" He touched the coffeepot, found it hot, reached for a cup.

"Of course."

"We will have two visitors this morning."

"From Paris?"

"Never mind from where. They will be here all day; one of them may spend the night. Make sure there's enough food."

"I was going to make cassoulet. For those types who guard us, too." She drew herself up straight. She was wearing only a knee-length white slip; her feet were bare, big, heavily marked with calluses and broken nails. Her tiny breasts did not even show behind the fabric of the slip. She seemed confident now. "I can go to the village and buy more food if you give me money."

"All right. One of the visitors is bringing wine." He poured a second cup of coffee for Juana. "Are you happy with him?"

"He is good to me." She threw a small chunk of wood into the range and dropped the lid with a clang, then stood quite straight again, hands on hips. "I want to go with him back to his country. Can you fix that?"

"You know where he's from?"

"Of course."

"It's a hard country."

"Wherever I have been, it's a hard country."

He picked up the two cups of coffee, looked at her. "I'll see what I can do."

At midmorning he heard the helicopter come in from the southeast and pass near the farmyard to land at the other house. Ten minutes later a Citroen sedan came swaying up the rutted road with one of the French security men at the wheel; behind it came a new Renault with several American Secret Service men. Tarp breathed deeply of the air, which was warmer and earthier than the air of Moscow; he took several steps forward and met them as they got out of the car.

"I brought the wine," Laforet said, and he started to instruct the guard about the handling of the cases. He turned back to Tarp. "You don't mind?"

"Not at all. You two are getting along, are you?"

"Just great, just great." "Mr. Smith" clapped Tarp on the arm. "He plays a mean game of tennis. Beat the pants off me. I've got a return match at golf if we ever get on a course." He went back and spoke to the Secret Service men, and their car backed down the road fifty yards and then they fanned out to surround the house.

Laforet came to Tarp and said in a low voice, "It looks all right. I think both sides will cooperate."

"Good. The ship?"

"I think it's arranged. *He* thinks it is."

They settled in the central room of the tumbledown house—Laforet, the former president, Tarp, Repin, and Juana. Therese was sent to the other house and the guards waited outside, French and Americans ringing the house, each group with its own communications, distrustful.

Laforet said, with the authority that comes from chairing hundreds of committees, "Who will start?"

"I will," Tarp said. The former president seemed to make no objection. "What language?" Tarp said.

They settled on Spanish.

"Does everybody know everybody?"

"I believe I know Mr. Smith from somewhere," Repin said wickedly.

"Maybe we know some of the same people," the former president said. He was not much amused.

"Professional acquaintances, no doubt," Repin said.

Tarp cut them off. Without prologue, he told them what had happened in Moscow.

"Beranyi is still missing," he said when he was done. "He hasn't turned up in any reports reaching the intelligence services. Therefore, we still don't know for sure who Maxudov is and we still don't have the stolen plutonium. However, we do have some other things. All that Moscow cares about now is a clean case. But some other things have come up. They center on a man named Pope-Ginna. He's English, resident in Argentina. He commanded a British ship in World War Two, and he's connected with the Argentine purchase of a submarine from the Soviet Union, with Juaquin Schneider in Buenos Aires, and with the KGB as a go-between during the Falklands war."

Repin interrupted. "What is the connection with Maxudov, please?"

"Maxudov stole plutonium in the Soviet Union and sent it out by submarine. He sent it somewhere for a reason. I don't think we paid enough attention to the reason. It wasn't a one-way arrangement, I believe; it was an exchange. A barter, a sale."

"For money?" Repin said.

"No, not money. Something else."

"What?"

"I don't know yet. But Pope-Ginna, I think, was the means of payment. What we call a 'bag man' in American politics."

"You think he took something into the Soviet Union every time he went there?"

"I'm not sure that it was every time. But there were four trips that came very soon after the first four thefts, and I think those were payoffs, yes." He glanced at Laforet. "Jules is checking to see if he went to London on the same trips. We think there's a London connection.''

"To do what?"

"I don't know."

Repin pushed his lips forward, wrinkled his nose, cocked his head. "It sounds very fishy to me, my friend." He watched Tarp with his head tilted like a sharp-eyed bird's. "What are you thinking?"

"I'm thinking that we've been going after Maxudov from the wrong end of the stick. Now I'm going after what he was buying, not what he was selling."

Repin narrowed his eyes. He looked at Juana, than at "Mr. Smith." He sat back and nodded once, as if to say that he was a reasonable man who was willing to listen to the whole tale.

Laforet cleared his throat. "I have been checking into certain new facts that have been brought to my attention in the last two days," he said rather formally. "These do not fall nicely into the kind of coherence that one would like for them to have. Nevertheless, they are provocative in their outline, and, subject to further investigation—which is going forward even while we talk, let me say—I think they justify a certain course of action that we shall discuss shortly." He looked at each of them. He rather enjoyed the spotlight and certainly was used to it. And dressed for it.

"One must go back to World War Two for some of this. In the last year of the war, a German ship was sunk near the Antarctic by the cruiser under this Pope-Ginna's command. On board the German ship were millions in gold that have never been recovered—never, one would have said, until this investigation began. It has always been thought that the gold was simply part of the German hoard intended as a fallback in case of a German defeat. However, also on board that ship were certain German civilians—again, until very recently, believed to be a lucky few sent ahead to set up the machinery for a Nazi enclave. The destination was believed to be—and still is—Argentina.

"For our purposes, the only person of note on board that ship was a biochemist named Gustav Fahner. He is of interest to us because we now believe that some of Fahner's work has shown up in the enormously profitable enterprises of this Juaquin Schneider—a generation later, in Argentina. What is the connection?'' Laforet shrugged. ''One could say coincidence. One could say knowledge of some sort—there were survivors of the German sinking, although they were few and none of them, so far as we know, was Fahner. Or one could say that Schneider had gained access to Fahner's research, which, one would believe, was on board the *Prinz von Homburg* when Pope-Ginna sank it.''

''Divers?'' Repin said. He looked at Tarp. ''Is that possible?''

''I'm having somebody look into it. Go ahead, Jules.''

Laforet smiled. ''I have been made the expositor of a great deal of work that is not my own; most of this comes from Tarp, of course. Where am I? Ah, the possibility of research records on the ship. Yes. So, one postulates a connection between Schneider and the *Prinz von Homburg*. There are other correspondences—the emergence of Schneider himself from obscurity as a newly rich man in the nineteen fifties; his rather sudden appearance as an entrepreneur in biochemicals. His marriage. Yes, his marriage.'' Laforet again glanced at each of them, and, taking a paper from a case at his feet, he turned a little sideways so as to catch the light from a window.

''All sources available to us have Schneider marrying a woman named Nazdia Becker in July, 1949. The bride was a Jewess, born in Hungary in 1927, a refugee from the Nazis who had made her way to England and then to Argentina.'' He turned back to them. ''The only difficulty with this, as Tarp discovered in Moscow and as we have subsequently confirmed in Germany, is that the only Nazdia Becker who matches the birth date and Hungarian background even remotely died in Buchenwald in 1943.''

''Somebody used the identity,'' the former president said.

''Precisely.''

''Who?'' Juana asked.

''Who, indeed?'' Laforet paused for effect. ''Gustav Fahner had a daughter,'' he said softly. He consulted his sheet of paper again. ''Ilse Fahner, born Leipzig, 1925. Date and place of death unknown. May have accompanied her father on the ill-fated voyage of the *Prinz von Homburg*.''

''Schneider married Fahner's daughter?'' Repin said.

''Possibly.''

Tarp leaned forward. ''Fahner's daughter would have known

what was on the *Homburg*. She may also have known her father's research; the woman Schneider married became a very gifted biochemist. Jules is trying to find out now if Ilse Fahner was already a scientist before the *Homburg* sinking. But if she survived the sinking, then she would have had access to information and possibly to money—to Argentine accounts already set up. We're trying to check that now.''

''How would she have gotten the Jewish girl's identity?'' Juana said.

''She would have brought it with her. That would have been a fairly simple precaution. So, let's say she survived—she's pulled from the water by a British crew; she's carrying the papers of a Hungarian girl; she's returned to England—''

''Pope-Ginna,'' Repin said. ''Of course. Pope-Ginna!''

Tarp nodded. ''That's what I think.''

''He is the arranger! How does he know who she really is? We do not know; no matter. What does he want? The money, probably—yes? Hundreds of millions in gold, not so bad. And he is an admiral, a naval hero—he can help the girl with her identity, make a place for her, fend off questions.'' He frowned. ''But that is not enough, surely.''

Tarp nodded. ''Correct. Pope-Ginna knew something nobody else did. *He knew where the* Homburg *was.*''

He told them about the *polynya* and the confusion over the ships' positions when the *Homburg* was sunk. ''Pope-Ginna knew that there was open water in the ice, and he knew what the real position was. It's my guess that it all happened without his control, and he simply put it together and saw where things could lead. I'd think that the catalyst was discovering who the girl really was—suddenly understanding that a colossal piece of luck had come his way. It doesn't really matter when he saw it. After the *Homburg* went down and before he filed the final report in London. Plenty of time, I think. Plenty of time.''

They were all silent, not looking at each other. ''And Schneider?'' Laforet said after they had sat that way for a time. ''What of Schneider?''

''I don't know,'' Tarp said softly. ''But I'm going to find out.''

''How?''

''I'm going to go look at the *Prinz von Homburg*.''

Juana's voice was very controlled, very professional. "Under the ice?"

"It isn't under the ice now. The *polynya* is open. Mr. Smith?"

The former president produced several photographs. "These are satellite photos. The only one we've got that goes over the area. It's fall down there, so it's getting colder, not warmer, so it looks like the hole is closing. Still, you can see it." He handed the photographs around. From the altitude of the satellite, the *polynya* looked small—an uneven black mark in a white surface. In the last photo, taken only five days before, it was smaller than in the other two.

"The ship is under that spot?" she said.

"Not quite," Tarp said quickly. "Just off the left-hand edge, I think. I'm estimating from what a man in England told me. He was in the *polynya* in 1944, at a time of year when it would have been at its biggest. Jules is having somebody look through the admiralty records to see if any of the other ships' logs from Pope-Ginna's force show a different position, even one that was later corrected. The officially accepted position is two hundred miles from here, which is much too far."

Laforet had put the tips of his slender fingers together as he sat cross-legged in the hard chair. "The Argentinians began to show an interest in undersea research in the middle nineteen fifties—about the time Pope-Ginna emigrated to Argentina and Schneider first began to make a splash as an industrialist. France has always been a world leader in the field, of course; it was hardly an accident that they came to us for a submersible. Not a submarine, but a two-man deep-diver. It was purely a private undertaking on both sides—an Argentine consortium buying from Recherches Maritimes of Marseilles. I've had people looking into this for two weeks now. They bought a used submersible with a very limited range and a depth capacity of two hundred meters. It could not have been used by itself to reach the *Homburg*; however, carried on a submarine that surfaced in the *polynya*, it could probably have explored the wreckage. Actually bringing materials out of the wreckage would have taken divers."

"In that cold?" the former president said. "Poor guys!"

"The *polynya* is there because the water's warmer than the ice. Something's causing it to form every few years in the warm season. I don't think cold would have been much more a problem than if they were working at that depth anywhere.''

"Still," the former president said wonderingly, "that's a remarkable damned operation!"

"It's an involved operation. Especially in the fifties. But the goal made it worthwhile. It would have taken cooperation from the navy, or at least from the sub commander and his crew. A plane, probably, to check on the *polynya* before going in. Hired divers. But it was a lot of money. You can subvert a lot of people with that much money.''

Repin was scowling. "But what has this to do with the price of cabbages in Moscow? This is all history. I am interested in Soviet plutonium, not in Argentine gold.''

Tarp spoke very carefully. ''Pope-Ginna was the adviser on a the purchase of a refitted Soviet submarine in the midseventies. That could have been when the contact with Maxudov was made. It may have been his idea, not Maxudov's, to deliver the plutonium by submarine. I believe that the delivery was made underwater down toward the Antarctic drift ice.'' He met Repin's skeptical eyes. ''And picked up by submarine, I suspect. And taken to a very safe storage.''

Laforet linked his fingers over one knee. ''In 1978, the same Argentinian consortium took delivery of a French-made deep-sea habitat. They have been developed out of the technology used in ocean drilling platforms and are intended for research where divers spend rather long periods of time actually living at depth. We don't know what the Argentinians did with the habitat.'' He uncrossed his legs and smiled around the group. ''Is anyone hungry? I think it is time for something to eat.''

Tarp watched them as they ate. There was the bread that Therese had made, crusty, golden on its outside; Danish butter; and two cheeses. Laforet had brought wines that would have suited a diplomatic dinner and that had the effect of suiting Repin as well. They had not come together as a group, and Tarp purposely held back from taking any of them aside. Laforet and ''Mr. Smith'' were already compatible and tended to gravitate together; Juana headed for Tarp; and Repin looked as if his suspicion of the American president and his resentment of his French captor would keep him isolated. It took a question from Laforet about the wine, however, to make him a third with the two older men. They remained suspicious of each other, but they used the wine as a medium through which to reach and test each other.

"Are you really going there?" Juana murmured to him. "Under the ice?"

"Yes. It's actually safer than some other diving I've done."

"It makes me sick in my stomach to think about it."

"That's because you're thinking about the ice. Don't think of the ice. Anyway, I'll have the best equipment going."

"How? From where?"

Tarp nodded toward the three older men, who, at Laforet's insistence, were opening a different wine so they might compare it. "Them."

She looked down at the floor. Her crest of black hair nodded in front of him like a plume. "What of me?" she said.

"You have a more dangerous job. If you'll do it."

"*More* dangerous!" She almost laughed. "Where am I to go—the *North* Pole?"

"Buenos Aires."

He took her hand and moved toward the others. With a far greater concentration than they had shown to the matter of the *Homburg* and its passengers, they were, all three, standing with half-full wineglasses just under their noses, inhaling. They might have been practicing some obscure religion, so intense and so odd were they. Tarp stopped and squeezed Juana's hand, and they stood there and listened to the deeply serious, strange things that men say about wines. Shaking his head, Tarp led her to the kitchen, where they made coffee and she uncovered a tray of sweet pastries that Therese had somehow concocted.

"Repin will do very well with her," Juana said. "She is a good, good woman for him."

Tarp thought of the Lubyanka, of Moscow's cold, of the girl he had seen on the corner as he was being driven out of the city. "Maybe," he said. When they went back in, "Mr. Smith" was asking Repin if he ever played golf, and Repin was saying that he did not, but he admired American poker.

"Gentlemen," Tarp said. Repin and the former president had been speaking English; Tarp stayed in that language. "Can we return to business now?"

"*Revenons à nos moutons,*" Laforet murmured.

"To the matter," Repin said in Spanish. They all sat in the

same chairs they had sat in before, as people invariably do; Tarp and Juana put the pastries and the coffee on the floor in the middle of the group. When a silence had fallen, Laforet, a small cup and saucer held in his hands like a votive lamp, said, "The French undersea vessel *Vairon* was in the Red Sea day before yesterday. It is a deep-diving submersible with a range of forty miles and a maximum safe depth of three hundred meters and will carry three people. Two nights ago, it was brought ashore and trucked to the military airfield at Tokar. Yesterday, an American C-one thirty aircraft picked it up and flew it to Cape Town, South Africa. Mr. Smith?"

The former president hurried to finish a tart, and, brushing his fingers free of crumbs, he said, "One of America's more cooperative oil companies has a high-speed tanker called the *Global Clipper* that was supposed to start around the Cape for Lagos several days ago. For reasons I won't go into, the chairman of the board persuaded the captain to turn around and head for Cape Town. Estimated time of arrival is after midnight, tonight."

Laforet stirred his coffee and then cleared his throat. "Tonight, two superheavy Hirondelle XP-seventeen helicopters will fly from their base in Cameroon to Cape Town and one will go aboard the *Global Clipper* as soon as possible. The ship, with the research vessel and one helicopter, will sail at once for the Antarctic." He looked at Tarp.

"I'm leaving for Cape Town at seven tonight." He looked at Juana, who was pale but expressionless; Repin, on the other hand, seemed agitated. "The second chopper will fly me out to the *Global Clipper* and will stay aboard. We hope to be off the drift ice in four days. From there, I intend to have the choppers transport the *Vairon* to the *polynya*."

Juana said coldly, "And I am to go to Buenos Aires? On whose authority, please?"

Laforet took another sheet of paper from his case and handed it to "Mr. Smith," who handed it to Juana. "You will want to confirm this, of course."

She frowned as she read it. She looked not at Tarp, but at the former president. "I thought your government and mine were not in communication."

He cleared his throat. "This was kind of special," he said.

Talking to her seemed to embarrass him. She shrugged. "Well, I am going to Buenos Aires, then."

"And me?" Repin said. His agitation had given way to a fierce control. "What about me? What am I supposed to do—sit here with my French nursies and play patty-cake?"

Tarp smiled grimly. "I want you to go to Moscow."

"Ah." Repin grinned back. "Well, that is better than sitting in this cold house. At least in Moscow, there is vodka." He clapped his hands together. "Of course, I will be killed as soon as I get there, but that is still better than sitting here getting French bruises on my backside. No offense, Monsieur Sous-Ministre!"

"Naturally," Laforet murmured.

"You're going in clandestinely," Tarp said. "Once you're in, can you get together a team of people to help you do something?"

"What am I to do?"

"Pope-Ginna is having an interview with some of your former colleagues in the country. I think they'll go easy on him, and then they'll let him go. I want you to be ready to snatch him. If they won't let him leave the Soviet Union, I want you to grab him and bring him out. If they let him go, I want you to put somebody on the plane with him and I want you to take him the first chance you get. Can you do it?"

Repin was quiet. The old lips came forward in that familiar expression that looked as if he were going to spit. "Naturally," he said. He sipped the wine and savored it in his mouth with a new gusto.

"You'll have to cover the disappearance once you've got him. We don't want to warn either Maxudov or Buenos Aires. You'll have to take him very quickly and very quietly and then you'll need a cover story. If it's outside the Soviet Union, I think you can get away with a heart attack—that means buying off a doctor and a hospital. Then you'll bring him where we can talk."

"Where?"

"Maybe the ship. We'll see."

Repin nodded happily. He could not hide his delight. When he looked at "Mr. Smith" he nodded again and held up a finger as if to say, *Aha, you see!* "How do I get in?" he said.

Laforet was extricating a cigarette from his case. "I believe that will be my responsibility. Through Ho Chi Minh City."

"That is good. That is very, very good." Repin's little eyes were almost hidden as he grinned widely. "How soon?"

"One hour. We could have you on your way sooner, but I assume you will wish to prepare yourself."

"Thank you, Monsieur Sous-Ministre." Only Tarp knew that the two men had once been enemies, although neither had seen the other before. They had been on opposite sides until Dien Bien Phu had fallen. Laforet had lost; Repin had won. Laforet had said "Ho Chi Minh City" as if he had mentioned Paris or Chicago, not the city that had been Saigon, the Paris of Southeast Asia. Now, Repin became gracious. "Might I have one of your cigarettes?" he said.

"They are *sobranies,*" Laforet answered. He held out his case. "I find that as I get older, my tastes become more Russian."

Repin took a cigarette and their eyes met. "We Russians have much to learn from you—wine, for example." He accepted a light and the two men were quiet.

Tarp stood up. "I understand there's a packet for each of us in one of the cars. It will give contacts and codes. We're routing through a French network for purposes of efficiency. Repin, I'm sorry, but we've cut Moscow out on this part because I think Maxudov's still there and I think we have to act as if the whole Moscow system is corrupted. Now, let me say that both the French and the American involvements in this operation are very delicate and very deniable. Both countries are in it so that a bigger mess won't result, but neither one is in it officially. Repin, if we bring this off, I'm to tell you that the Soviet leadership is to be reminded forcefully of both countries' cooperation in pulling its ass out of the fire. Juana, the same thing goes for you in Cuba. Now, let me remind you all that the British are not in this one in any way, and any offer that seems to originate with the Brits is to be taken as a trap. They chose to stay out—I won't speculate as to why just yet—and so they are to be treated as outsiders. Is that clear to everybody?"

They all nodded.

"We'll be getting limited intelligence from Paris and less from Washington, and no tactical support from either. No wet work, that means. No hands-on help. You're on your own."

He looked around the room. "All right?" Juana looked grim, Repin impatient. The former president seemed to have discovered that it was a very serious business indeed. "Let's go," Tarp said.

He caught up with Repin at the door. "The French woman wants to go with you," he said.

"Not this time."

"No, not this time. But she wants to go back with you when you go for good. What are you going to tell her now?"

"What do we ever tell them? 'I'll see you when I come back.' Eh?"

Later, he was in the upstairs room with Juana, holding her for an instant. He was ready to leave; she was waiting for the helicopter that would start her toward Buenos Aires.

"Be careful," she whispered into his shoulder.

"And you," he said. Half-jokingly he murmured, "When will I see you again?"

"I'll see you when I come back," she said. In the weeks that he had been gone, her love had changed. It was mature now and it had been put into a large context—that of her own life, her own commitment. She was excited by her part in what was happening, and she would see him when she came back.

CHAPTER 35

The tanker's bow rose with a wave and then seemed to hang there as if cantilevered over the wave, as if it might break in half; then the midsection rose, then the stern, and it was as if the entire vessel had been levitated magically, free suddenly of the water that had dragged at it like glue; and then the bow started down, ponderous as a bull's head going down under the cape. There was an explosion of water around it, and the bow disappeared and came up again, white water streaming from it like drool from a mouth.

"Christ," the man with Tarp said.

"Well?"

"Christ, what weather."

The stern was starting down into the trough. The tanker looked like a football field sliding downhill.

"It's cold, yes."

"Cold! Jesus, Tarp, it's *cold*!"

The sea came on in long swells as if it were on rollers, a dirty gray-green carpet over which they lurched like something in a fun house. The wind had been blowing for a day and a night, straight into their teeth.

"Are they going to make it?"

They were looking at the tiny French submersible that sat a third of the way along the deck. Overhead, the two huge helicopters kept pace with the ship, one of them trailing the cable with which it would try to transport the *Vairon*.

It was shaped like an egg. Isolated on the empty deck, it seemed puny, although it was in fact as big as a compact car,

316

with room inside for two people, even for three on a trip like this one, when it had been stripped of some of its gear. There were three ports forward and a cluster of booms amidships that looked a little like a conning tower. Around its bow were powerful lights, and, retracted now, a pair of jointed arms that were controlled from inside.

The submersible's pilot had been standing to their left on the deck. Now he moved toward them.

"Alors," he said sourly. *"L'oeuf se crasse, eh?"*

"What'd he say?" the man with Tarp said. He was Gance, a good diver but a poor linguist.

"He said they're almost ready."

"He doesn't sound too happy about it."

"He thinks they're going to drop it."

The man behind them sucked in his breath as the cable tightened between the helicopter and the submersible. Something happened on the deck and men started to wave their arms, and he hissed, *"Oh, la,"* and began to make a sound in his throat like eh-eh-eh-eh-eh.

"They got it aboard all right, what the hell," Gance said.

"They didn't use the chopper."

"Christ, no, they used a big crane. It was doodle-zip the way they did it, like lifting a suitcase."

"That thing's heavy."

"Christ, these big choppers haul tanks around. What the hell, it's a piece of cake. Of course, they're French."

The man behind them started to hum. It sounded like a wail.

"Don't look," Tarp said to him in French.

"Eh-eh-eh—that's easy to say."

"Go have breakfast. They'll be hours yet."

"Eh, when they drop my egg, I want to see it crack." His face was very red from the cold. He had grizzled hair that was plastered down by a black watch cap; on his cheeks, the hairs of silver stubble gleamed like little nails. "That's my child, that thing," he said. He did a little dance on the steel deck because he was cold and tense.

Gance looked sideways at Tarp. "Christ, tell him to cool it, will you?" he said.

Tarp turned to the pilot. "My friend says it will go well."

"No offense, but your friend does not know shit from shoe polish. Does he speak French?"

"No."

"Shit from shoe polish, I say it again."

"He meant well."

"Eh!" He jerked his head toward the helicopters. "So do those morons."

There was an iceberg off to their right, sitting majestically in the waves like an island; ahead there was a band of silver where the drift ice met the clouded sky. "That little egg has to travel a long way on the cable, my friend."

"Five hours, I know," Tarp said.

"Has it ever been done?"

"They say they've done it with a truck. They say they can do it."

"Eh, of course they do. Morons."

Coils of plastic lay around the submersible on the deck. They formed an inflatable collar that had been jury-rigged from a boom designed to contain oil spills. If the helicopters actually got the *Vairon* to the open water inside the drift ice, the collar would stabilize it while Tarp and the others boarded. The pilot believed it might flip over or take on enough water to sink in rough seas. Tarp thought he was a neurotic fussbudget, but he was willing to concede that the man knew more about it than he did.

The men on the deck hurried away from the submersible again. The helicopter's motors got louder. One of the men waved. The helicopter seemed to grow as the noise of its engines rose to a roar, but the submersible clung to the deck.

"Holy God," the pilot muttered.

"Go, go," Gance chanted to himself. "Go, you mother, go."

The *Vairon* lifted suddenly, easily, and seemed to spring ten yards into the air. Tarp glanced at the Frenchman, who had his lower lip caught firmly between his front teeth. His cap was wadded in his fists.

"Ooop, allez-*oop*!" he was saying.

A cheer carried down the deck to them like a scrap of paper on the wind.

"*Go*, you mother!"

The white egg was moving into the sky and pulling ahead of the ship. When it was several hundred yards up, it leveled, hung there like a spider on a strand of its own web. Then the egg and the chopper began to move slowly toward the silver horizon.

"Hey!" Gance was shouting. "Hey, man, hey, man, hey, how about that, man!" He was pounding the Frenchman on the shoulder. The pilot, still capless, was nodding his head and smiling, shrugging and pouting out his lower lip, bouncing up and down on his toes. He shook his cap in a gesture of victory.

"Not bad for morons," Tarp said to him.

"If they don't drop it now."

"How about a brandy all around?" He looked at Gance. "Brandy?"

"Hey, you're talking, man. I thought you didn't touch it when you were diving."

"We've got hours and hours. Let's go below."

Gance grinned at the Frenchman. "Brandy, Pierre? Huh? *Vous comprendi*, brandy?"

"Brandy, *oui, cognac*."

"Pierre, you're okay."

"*Qu'est-ci qu'il a dit?*"

"He says you're a good man."

"Why does he call me Pierre?"

"He can't pronounce your name."

"My name is Jean-Marie."

"I know, but he can't get the sounds right."

Three-quarters of an hour later they climbed into the second helicopter, which had returned from flying watchdog on the first one. The tanker would keep station where it was, its captain refusing to go closer to the ice. If the weather cleared, a Russian satellite would pick it up, and Tarp wanted to move quickly.

The chopper was as big inside as a bus. With only the three of them and their gear, it felt as big as a church. Gance began checking over the special suits he had brought. Surrounded now by the tools of his craft, he was content. He even whistled, but the sound was lost in the noise.

Tarp looked down. The tanker was far behind. He could see a dozen icebergs; ahead, they seemed to merge into a solid mass.

Jean-Marie was sprawled against one wall. He was doing something with a calculator.

"What's that?" Tarp shouted.

"Figuring battery consumption!"

"You've figured it twice before!"

"I like to be sure!"

Tarp moved back to Gance, who was checking the seals between a helmet and a suit. "Looks like a spaceman without the spaceman!" Tarp shouted.

"Beautiful stuff! Beautiful! Four hundred feet in this mother! Beautiful!"

Tarp had heard it all on the tanker. They had been four days together. If the *Prinz von Homburg* lay below three hundred and sixty feet, it would be beyond them; if it lay more than twenty miles from the *polynya,* they would not be able to reach it and return. He pinched the material of the suit that Gance was working on. It felt like very thick rubber with a nylon surface. It felt fragile. Tarp disliked the idea of deep diving in a self-contained suit; yet this was a state-of-the-art unit developed from NASA's experience in space. There was no way to go after the *Homburg* in scuba gear and no way to go after it with umbilically connected equipment.

"We won't have much room in the sub with these suits on!"

"I know!" Gance seemed pleased by the idea. Tarp moved to Jean-Marie and shouted, "We won't have much room with those suits!"

Jean-Marie looked at the suit that was spread out on the floor. "You won't have any," he said, and he went back to his calculator.

But they had already been in the submersible with the suits on. There was virtually no room, it was true; Tarp had simply been venting his own concern about it. They had already found that they had to enter the *Vairon* in a definite order, Jean-Marie first; once inside, there was no changing places.

Tarp watched the drift ice flow beneath them. The icebergs had given way to a vast blue-gray field that was marked with black lines like rivers and canals. There were crevices and ridges, miniature mountain ranges of ice, and cracks wide enough to take a big ship into.

A cold desert, he thought. *A very tough place to die.* Yet they had seen whales that morning, and he knew there were organisms that lived in the water and even in the ice itself. *Man is the alien here. Man is the soft one. Very fragile.* He looked again at the suit, which, spread on the chopper floor, looked manlike but two-dimensional. *Very fragile.*

They caught up with the other aircraft and kept pace with it for half an hour. The two pilots chatted. Tarp's swung below the other and looked at the cable and the *Vairon*. Satisfied, it surged ahead. They reached the edge of the *polynya* and Tarp stationed himself behind the pilot. They swung west and began to drop sonar buoys.

The chopper turned above a point of ice that jutted into open water. There were black dots on the ice.

"Petrol!" he shouted. They had brought in fuel the day before.

The satellite will spot that, Tarp thought. *As soon as the clouds lift.*

They dropped more buoys and swung northeast. The pilot pointed. "We dropped them over there yesterday. No response."

He moved over the open water and placed three deep-water probes, which would sink to a predetermined depth and send back pulses from a floating antenna.

"How thick is the ice?" Tarp shouted.

The pilot made a face. "Near the edge, eight meters! Farther into the ice field—eighty meters, maybe."

"Is that from the sounders?"

The pilot nodded. "It is like a dome. No ice in the middle, then very thin ice, then it gets thicker. Like a dome of water under the ice."

They dropped three more deep probes, then headed back toward the point and met the other helicopter as it approached the *polynya*. Below them, whitecaps flashed like lights on the dark water. Tarp moved into the cavernous midsection and found the other two still occupied with their work. He moved again restlessly to the cabin.

"He has a chart," the pilot said, nodding at the navigator, who sat behind him and to the right. Charts were spread on a table; electronic gear surrounded him on three sides.

"We are here," the navigator said. He seemed like a boy to Tarp. He touched a penciled map. "There are the probes. These lines are echo bars—they are clarified by a computer that adjusts for distance and so on. The red lines are ten-meter depths—of ice, not water. The very dark line is the edge of the ice.''

"He said it's dome-shaped."

"Like a dome, yes. A very uneven dome. Like a cave."

"Any sign of metal yet?"

"Nothing. But we're out of range of some sounders yet."

They flew on. There was radio chatter. The pilot called Tarp forward. "The other aircraft is burning up fuel because of the load! If we don't find anything soon, we have to put the vessel into the water. Then we'll refuel and put out more probes!"

Tarp grimaced. Once the submersible was in the water, getting it out again would be very difficult, perhaps impossible. It was hoped that, if they had to scuttle it, they would have found the *Homburg* first. If, however, it was put into the water miles from where the *Homburg* lay, and it then had to traverse those miles under its own power, they would lose time and the Russian satellite might track them.

They flew on. Minutes passed. The pilot shook his head. Fifteen minutes more.

"Eh, the sweetheart," Tarp heard the navigator say. The boy looked up with a beatific smile on his face. *"Voilà,"* he said.

"You've got it?"

The grinning kid fiddled with a dial and a high-pitched *ping!* sounded above the engine noise. "Metal!" he cried. "Lots of lovely metal!"

"Big enough to be a ship?"

"Absolutely! A *big* ship!" His voice rose. "A German cruiser, at least!"

He turned the gain up still more. The sonar return was like an enormous tuning fork in the throbbing space. "It's got a German accent!" he shouted happily.

CHAPTER 36

In wet suits they jumped from the helicopter to the water thirty yards from the submersible. It floated in its disorderly rings of inflated tubing like an egg surrounded by sausage.

Tarp hit the water first and felt it like a thrill of excitement, as if the cold were a pulse along his nerves instead of something outside his own body. The wet suit seemed first colder, then warm, and he reached the surface already looking for the vessel. He swam toward it, welcoming movement as the second and astonishing shock of the cold reached him. The *Vairon* rose on a wave and disappeared, its collar moving supplely with the water like a raft of grasses.

He could not pull himself up on the slippery tubing, which collapsed under him because it was not fully inflated; he had to find one of the lines that bound the long boom into coils and slide up and over with its help until he could get a foothold in the yielding mass. Supporting himself against the white side of the sub, he watched Gance grasp a line on the other side. Beyond him, Jean-Marie was swimming toward the collar.

Gance heaved himself up and began to tear off his flippers. "Cold, man. I mean, that's cold." An iceberg about the size of a suburban house floated a hundred yards away, and he pointed at it.

"Let's get this thing under as soon as we can!" Tarp shouted. "Those clouds are going to break up soon!" The wind blew into his mouth and almost choked him. Jean-Marie was pulling himself up on the collar. *"Vite, vite!"* Tarp shouted at him.

Jean-Marie was lying on his belly on the soft collar. He looked up at Tarp with great disgust, pulled himself to a sitting position, and slowly began to take off his flippers.

Tarp grinned. *"Pas si vite?"* he shouted.

Jean-Marie nodded. He clambered up the rows of the collar and began to undo the entrance hatch. "We make haste slowly," he said. "*I* am the captain now."

Tarp and Gance worked to loosen the collar. They had hoped to open it into one large ring that would serve as a protective boom for the submersible in the waves, most of all when they tried to reattach the cable for the return to the tanker.

"No way we're gonna move this mother," Gance said. "You can't budge this stuff. It's like soft concrete."

Tarp signaled a line down from the chopper. They attached it to an end of the boom and the aircraft pulled it away from the *Vairon*, then changed course and pulled another section free.

"He is moving us!" Jean-Marie shouted.

"It can't be helped!"

Tarp and Gance pushed the next coil of tubing free, and Gance put his fins on again and went into the water to reattach the cable close to the submersible. Another ring straightened, and then *Vairon* was enclosed in a single layer, the rest curving behind like the tail of a comma.

"Enough!" Jean-Marie shouted.

"We have to attach the ends!"

Jean-Marie disappeared down the hatch. Tarp put on fins again, bracing himself for the water and then welcoming it when he was in it. They reattached the cable and saw the tubing pulled into a circle, with the *Vairon* spinning slowly at the other end as the last coil opened. When the ends were joined, however, the egg floated within the protective ring of yellow tubing. They pulled themselves aboard the vessel.

"Cold," Tarp said to Gance.

"My ass it is!"

"I didn't think that would work."

"I *knew* it wouldn't! How come it did?"

Gance signaled to the helicopter and one of the free-dive suits started down. It looked like a big corpse being lowered. *Like Frankenstein's monster. It died on the ice.* Spray blew from the whitecaps, beyond which chunks of ice rolled like rudderless ships. He thought briefly of the crewmen of the *Hom-*

burg, trying to swim here. It was not a thought to dwell on. His teeth were chattering as he stood in the wind. It was warmer in the water, given the wet suit for protection.

Gance detached the suit while Tarp held it by the feet, and the cable snaked up to the chopper. Gance braced himself between the *Vairon* and the boom and began to work his way into the suit.

"This isn't the way you were meant to get into these mothers, Tarp!"

"I know!"

"They got special racks for these mothers at La Jolla. You walked into them, no shit! With an attendant! Christ, I'm freezing. They didn't mean you to wear a wet suit in the thing, either!"

"Here comes the other one."

Gance looked ready for a space walk. He lashed his helmet to one of *Vairon*'s booms and moved to help Tarp with the second suit.

Tarp found the suit deadening. He had had it on three times, and he was still not used to it. He loved the freedom of scuba; this suit was like a walking prison. There was a necessary trade-off between freedom and safety; especially out of the water, the suit was ponderous, with both chestpack and backpack, and the clumsiness of a multilayer fabric that would be inflated between the layers with compressed air.

"Let's go."

Tarp climbed up the metal steps that led to the hatch, undogged it, and swung it open. The effort of getting above the hatch in the suit had him panting. He looked at Gance in disgust.

"Piece of cake!" Gance shouted.

"Right."

Tarp went down the hatchway with an inch to spare on each side. When he crouched inside the *Vairon* he was surrounded by instruments on every side. He reached up the hatchway for his helmet, took it and then Gance's, and moved one shuffling step forward and one to the right to squeeze himself into the crewman's chair. Gance came down the ladder and fastened the hatch behind him, then turned slowly with his arms held at his sides and wedged himself into the deck space between Tarp and Jean-Marie.

"Ready?" Jean-Marie said.

"When you are."

The pilot flipped four switches above his head and watched a row of lights that told him that they were watertight. *"Allons,"* he said.

It was very quiet. After the helicopter and the wind, the dive was like a dream. There was no sensation of descent, but merely the end of the rise and fall of the waves. The light beyond the ports changed from silver to gray to green, and they were under the water.

Tarp went over the final sonar readings on the table in front of him. Two of the depth probes had picked up echoes from the mass of metal that he hoped was the *Homburg,* eleven miles west under the ice. The ice was thirty-seven meters thick there and the metal mass lay at about seventy meters on an undersea ridge running roughly north-northeast. The bottom dropped away from it toward the *polynya.*

"Sonar on," Jean-Marie said in a singsong voice. "Check."

"Picture," Tarp said.

On his screen was a computer simulation of the bottom and the ice ahead of them, made from composite signals of a coned forward sonar and two side-lookers.

"Switching to scan."

A more conventional sonar circle appeared. The metal mass appeared as a bright pulse just inside the screen's edge at thirty-five degrees.

"Distance?"

"Nineteen point three kilometers."

"Check."

The hum of the engines filled the space. As they went deeper there was a gurgling, as if they were being swallowed by an enormous belly.

"Pressure?"

"Two point seven."

Tarp saw water in the floor of the submersible and he opened his mouth to shout, then realized the water was from his own suit. *I'm spooked. I'd have liked a test dive in this thing.*

Gance was watching over Jean-Marie's shoulder intently, his tongue stuck out a little between his lips. His face was sweating.

"We are under the ice, my friends. Descending."

"Depth?"

"Thirty meters."

Tarp switched to the computer composite of the sonar scans. The ice roof above them was uneven, exactly like the roof of a cave, as the helicopter navigator had said, and, although its average level was well above them, it reached down toward them with long fingers.

"I'm taking it twenty meters lower."

The electric motors hummed. It was black outside the ports.

"Anything to see out there?" Gance said.

"No. Anyway, he's saving power." Jean-Marie touched a control. "The outside temperature is rising, Tarp."

Figures began to move across a fluid crystal display.

"What are those?" Gance said.

"Temperature and depth."

"Dieu!"

"What is it?"

"Heavy current. Very heavy. It wants to take us north. *Merde.*"

"Can't you overcome it?"

"Of course, but it takes fuel. *Merde, merde. Eh-eh-eh . . .*"

Tarp itched. He knew that he was going to be uncomfortably hot soon. His skin would be wrinkling, turning white. *Bad planning. Done too quickly.* He looked down at Gance, who held up a thumb and grinned. *Good for him.*

He made his mind smooth, smooth as the surface of the *Vairon*. A white plain, curving to infinity. Featureless. Timeless. Without concerns.

"One kilometer," he heard Jean-Marie say.

Tarp tightened the sonar scan to three kilometers, and there was their target, big and bright and dead ahead.

Temperature 6° C . . . profondeur 63m. . . .

"Why's the temperature going up?" Gance whispered.

"Maybe thermal activity on the bottom. Whatever it is causes the *polynya* to form."

"What's this, then, Hot Springs, Antarctica?"

"Why not?"

Tarp shifted to French. "How are the currents?"

"Very rough."

"Thermals, I think."

"I think so, too. Maybe moving in a circle that forms the *pol-*

ynya. When you get out there, it's going to be like moving in a heavy wind."

He switched the sonar picture down to a six-hundred-meter scan. The metal mass was a bright line almost eighty degrees long. In composite simulation, it was possible to see its height, even the elevation on one side that could be a superstructure.

"If it's the ship, we're coming in on one quarter," Jean-Marie said. "Looks as if she may lie on her side somewhat."

"Can you veer off and approach dead on the beam?"

"Of course."

The image shifted and lengthened and took up most of the screen's midline. Above it the fainter signals from the ice were enhanced by the computer into a tracery of lines that curved above the heavier image of the target.

"It's certainly big enough, Tarp."

"I know."

The sonar separated out three distinct features rising from the large horizontal mass.

"What's the direction of the current?"

"Quartering from left to right from our bow."

Tarp looked at Gance, who gave the thumbs-up sign again. Jean-Marie turned and looked at him. *"Eh bien?"*

"Take it in."

When they were a hundred meters away, the lights went on. The ports changed from black to opalescent green. Jean-Marie switched the interior lights off, and they found themselves looking into a swirl of brilliance.

"We will see nothing until we are right on it," Jean-Marie said. "This is going to be tricky in this current."

The *Vairon* slowed. Tarp waited for what seemed many minutes.

"There!" It was Gance who saw it first. "See it?"

Tarp saw the window change color from green to a mottled green-brown. He looked at it, trying to get some sense of scale. "Stop!" he cried.

"I stopped some time ago, my friend."

"What are we looking at?"

"The *Prinz von Homburg,* I hope."

Tarp was leaning forward over the navigation table to get closer to the port. Now he saw something move beyond it. *"What's that?"*

"I am putting one of the arms out. Calm yourself."

The arm was jointed like a dentist's drill. Eighteen feet long, it could be fitted with a wide variety of tools; now it held a powerful lamp. Tarp watched it unfold in the green glow of *Vairon*'s lights, uncannily like a living thing. The lamp at its end came on.

Tarp saw rivets. Then the edge of a steel plate. The arm moved slowly. Jagged metal. A hole. More plating. Steel cable like plaited hair.

"We will never see it whole," Jean-Marie said. "I haven't the light."

"I want to do a circuit around it."

"As you like. But I have only six hours of fuel left."

"How long to get us back?"

"Two hours."

"With the current?"

"Eh, maybe we could ride the current. I don't know. I don't want to count on it."

"All right, let's start searching."

"*Bon.* What are we looking for?"

"A habitat, I think. We'll know when we find it."

They found it in the lee of the *Homburg*'s stern, in an anomaly of the ocean bottom where there was protection from the current. There, sheltered like a house protecting itself under a mountain, the steel structure stood on three pylons anchored to the ocean floor. The main part stood twelve feet above the bottom, a flattened sphere protected by the darkness and the depth.

"What is it?" Gance said.

"You know what it is."

"Yeah, but here! It's a sea lab. Is there anybody in there now?"

"Let's find out."

He touched Jean-Marie's shoulder. "We're going out."

Jean-Marie was looking at the structure. "It's eerie, you know?" he said.

"Why?"

"I spent two months in one in the Indian Ocean. Down only sixty feet. But still . . ." He shrugged. "Like finding your mother's picture in somebody else's pocket."

"Is it exactly like the one you were in?"

"Mm, no. But very close. I recognize the pylon structure. That is a French-made *ambience marine* all right. There will be an entrance underneath, in the middle—you go up into an airlock. If somebody is inside, the airlock may be closed. The airlock is a cylinder, with all the controls on the wall. But where do you suppose the power comes from? An *ambience marine* uses a lot of power."

"The thermals would be my guess. Maybe heat exchange, maybe some kind of windmill."

Jean-Marie moved his head in approval. "That is quite an achievement, that thing out there. Do you know that?"

"I know."

"Look, my friend—I know that thing; I can go out there and—"

"Absolutely not. You're in charge of the *Vairon*; I'm in charge of the mission. You have to get us back."

Tarp and Gance helped each other with the helmets; then each turned on the suits' systems and checked for leaks and malfunctions. Readouts appeared inside the helmet itself, just above the transparent face plate. The suit became noisy with its work, even as the body is. Tarp equalized the pressure between suit and cabin and felt the suit thicken as it pressurized. He took a belt of tools from a rack and buckled it on and then a cylindrical carrier that held the things he had hoped to be able to use—camera, radioactive test gear.

Tarp pointed with a gloved thumb toward the airlock. Gance nodded.

He entered the tubular airlock headfirst. The cylinder followed. He slid forward to the far end and heard, like a distant drumbeat, the closing of the watertight door behind him.

Like a torpedo in a tube. He worked a hand lamp free of the belt and shone it on the controls. He and Gance had run this time after time while the the *Vairon* sat on the tanker's deck. *Seals. Closure. Warning. Water. Red light; that's good. Filled. Check suit. Good. Hatch. Green light. Go.*

He shone the light on the hatch that was only inches from his face plate and pressed a button, then pushed on the hatch. It opened into blackness.

Like a baby.

The umbilical was just outside the hatch so that it could be attached as he left the airlock. Tarp felt the current on his arm as he reached for the cord. He fastened it to his belt and slowly pulled himself out, exiting headfirst into darkness.

The suit crushed against him but held; it was a little like wearing waders in fast water. This was the suit's natural environment, and it felt both lighter and more flexible. The noise of the undersea current was louder than the noises of the suit; he could hear the cavitation of *Vairon*'s propellers as they held her steady. He thought of the whales he had seen from the tanker. They were at home here, while he was so alien that only this curious suit, which carried a tiny pod of his own environment, protected him.

The airlock opened and Gance's light appeared. His hand followed, grasped his umbilical. Seconds later he was sliding out, borne into the cold water.

They worked their way forward, clipping the umbilicals to rings welded to *Vairon*'s hull as they moved. When he reached the bow Tarp signaled to Gance to stay there, and he began to make his way forward along the flexible arm. The steel members were as thick as his wrists, slippery, white as bone in the brilliance of the light. He could hardly bend at all. He tried moving on the side of the arm from which the current flowed, but it pushed the suit so tight against the metal he could hardly move, and he slid back and went to the outside, feeling it try to sweep his feet away. Behind him Gance paid out the umbilical, without which he would sail into the void like an astronaut untethered from his vehicle.

He moved into the lee of the *Homburg* ten feet from the first pylon. The current buffeted him less there. Five feet from the pylon he was able to keep his feet with ease, and when he reached the structure itself he was able to let himself slowly down the metal rungs he found there, using only his hands. As he left the *Vairon*'s skeletal arm it followed him, shining its light in a circle that seemed to protect him.

There were handholds set into the ocean floor. He had no need for them, the suit's weighted feet keeping him upright, but he guessed that there must be times when the currents here made it impossible to walk. Still, he moved slowly, careful of his slight negative buoyancy.

At the center of the triangle formed by the pylons, as Jean-Marie had said, was a steel ladder. It rose into a cylinder that projected down from the floor of the habitat itself. The hatch was open.

He climbed, using only his hands.

There were six rungs up to the hatch. He pulled himself inside and shone his light around. The cylinder, now filled with water, was about four feet across, with the hatch in the middle of its floor. Tarp tugged at his umbilical but got no response because the current tore at it too vigorously for Gance to feel the pulse. He detached it from his belt and fastened it outside the hatch.

There were controls on the cylinder wall. Their markings were painted on the white metal in Spanish, but there was a brass plate below them that read *Agence Maritime Française*.

He closed the hatch and worked the control that emptied it. Compressed air forced the water out from top to bottom. As the cylinder began to empty, bright lights came on.

Seventy seconds later he was standing in an air-filled, white-walled cylinder with only a small puddle of seawater on its floor. Steel rungs rose to a hatch in the habitat floor above him.

Clumsily, he climbed.

CHAPTER 37

Always, afterward, he would wonder what it had sounded like inside the habitat. Its special noises never reached him through the helmet, except like the distant and garbled conversations overheard on a telephone line. Unsure of what the environment inside the habitat contained, he left his seals closed, balancing the suit's and the environmental pressure and finding them almost the same. He imagined that the steel bubble creaked as ships creak, that its support systems made noises as his own did. He supposed that the current that swept down from the decks of the *Homburg* carried sounds, perhaps even something that sounded like the cries of men. But he never heard them, and to him the habitat under the Antarctic ice would always be a place of silence.

It was shaped like an Edam cheese. The entry tube went right up through its center, like the hole in a doughnut, its upper level a second airlock for entry into the space itself. It, like most other systems he was to find, was redundant, to assure that the environment would be as safe and stable as was possible.

The door from the cylinder into the habitat was like a ship's, so low that he had to stoop, hard as that was to do in the semirigid suit. The door closed with a wheel, like a safe's. White light flooded the space as he stepped out; above his head a display gave him the temperature, pressure, and air quality inside.

The habitat was divided into four sections connected by a narrow corridor that circled the core. The corridor itself hardly permitted him to move because of its narrowness, and it was so

333

low that his helmet grazed fittings that projected down from the ceiling. Everything was labeled, and he supposed that the place was used by new crews often, for whom the signs would be their salvation. The corridor curved tightly around to his right as he emerged from the core; the wedge-spaced rooms were on his left, each entered by a watertight door. First was a living space—two rooms, each seven feet by about six, the first a sleeping room for two people and the second a combined galley and lounge. Much had been learned from space research about packaging and arrangement. Two people could have survived there for weeks, he thought.

He took three clumsy steps along the corridor and opened the second door. Inside was a room larger than the combination of the first two and more severely wedge-shaped. The ceiling was a featureless surface of light that made the whole room bright and sterile-looking. A table ran the length of the wall on his right, its plastic surface gleaming like ice. Above it were three CRT monitors and banks of instruments, while down the center of the room was a bank of gray cabinets and a computer terminal of considerable power. The first nine feet of the left-hand wall were taken up with banks of small doors made of brushed steel, each about the size of a book. Beyond the doors were another steel table and another bank of instruments.

Tarp moved cautiously down the room. The surfaces were immaculate. There was none of the clutter of the working laboratory—no notes, no cigarette butts, no discarded wad of computer paper. Whoever came here performed a task and then left, leaving nothing behind.

On one table was a rack of closed-end tubes a little like those that some cigars come in; they were made of steel and lined with foam.

The computer hardware was American. Tarp took a screwdriver from his belt and pressed a key with it because his gloved hands were too clumsy, and the monitor glowed and announced itself ready.

Tarp tried several languages on it, but there was no response. He wondered if anybody would bother with an access code in such a protected place.

Tarp tried the name Maxudov on it, and Schneider, and the names of the men left back in Moscow; he tried the word plutonium. The computer was mute.

Tarp went out, careful not to touch the corners of the tables with the suit for fear of damaging it, and he turned left to the next of the rooms.

Like Bluebeard's castle.

The third was the control room. It was narrow and irregular, as if it had been intruded upon by other spaces and by the machinery it was meant to govern. Its walls had sprouted gauges and wheels and buttons, and the ceiling was festooned with instruments that flashed bright messages. He found a bank of meters that recorded the state of the capsule's power supply; he found others that showed six parallel readings of heat measurement, probably from six heat exchangers. Others measured the current that flowed so brutally beyond the metal skin. Somewhere out there in the blackness a unit was extracting oxygen and storing it for the habitat's use.

One part of the space was set aside for meters that recorded the conditions inside the habitat itself. There, above a desk, he found a bank of shiny dials set into bands of metal, all alike, all clean and precise. Their great drawback was that they all looked alike, packed into too small a space; looking at them, Tarp found it difficult to keep his focus on any one. They danced in the vision. Their operator must have found them as daunting as Tarp did, for half of them had been labeled with a black marker whose sometimes smudged letters were distinctly at odds with the glitter of the panel.

Tarp leaned forward until his helmet almost touched the dials. The black pen had marked a number of the dials with *occ*; three were labeled with the whole word, *occupado*.

Good. But what's occupied?

The marker had put numbers on most of the dials that had *occ—L443, L447, X271*.

He found one dial that was labeled *MAX*.

Above it to the right was another labeled *JB*.

And at the bottom on the left-hand side was one with an understandable Spanish word: *GAUCHO*.

Tarp clumped back to the laboratory and looked at the bank of doors, verifying that there were forty-eight of them just as there were forty-eight of the dials. *MAX* was the fourth from the top in the third row. The doors were locked, but not against theft; it took only a tool like an allen wrench to open them. He took one from his belt, tried it, found it too large; took the next size and screwed open the lock and the door swung out.

Pale-green light glowed from within the cavity behind the door. In its glow a white plastic rack looked like dyed ivory. It held three glass tubes fitted with rubber diaphragms for use with a syringe. A fluid like heavy, slightly pink cream filled each of the phials.

He did not have time to open all the doors. He opened half a dozen at random, finding phials of fluid in each, varying in color, seemingly in viscosity. Labels with cryptic identifications were attached to each. The two that corresponded to the dials marked *GAUCHO* and *JB* were much like that marked *MAX*. The phials were the same in all; all fitted snugly into the cigarlike tubes on the worktable.

Tarp left the boxes open and went out into the corridor again. He was oppressively hot in the suit, and the effort of walking in it was beginning to tire him. He plodded on past the control room to the last of the doors. Marked REFRIGERATED STORAGE, it had a triple-safe system of lights and buttons that prevented its being opened accidentally. CLOSE DOOR AFTER ENTERING, the last light read, but he stepped in and left the door open.

Like the other rooms, this one was bathed in white light. A fine matting of white frost lay in stripes along the wall opposite the door, marking the location of pipes that carried the freezing medium. Between the pipes were banks of rectangles with handles, like the fronts of file drawers. Everything was scrupulously clean. Unable to feel the cold, he felt as if he were watching a film of this frozen place: in the film, his massive, gloved hand reached up, grasped a drawer handle, and pulled it toward him.

The drawer contained racks of test tubes. Again there were the cryptic labels, the fluids. Many of these were brightly colored, however, as if they had been stained. Part of the drawer held microscope slides. In the deepest corner were stacks of round glass dishes with a brown medium on the bottom and, spread across many, an uneven growth that looked like mold.

The second drawer was empty.

And the third.

He began to pull the drawers faster. They were eight feet long, like mortuary drawers, but he needed to open them only a quarter of their length to see what they held; finding one empty, he pushed it without much force and it would slide gently closed on its machined bearing. After six drawers he was impatient to be done, and he yanked open the seventh and had his gloved palm already flat against it to close it again before he had even taken in what it contained.

It was not empty, however.

It looked like a supermarket case in which a pinkish substance had been stored in heavy gauge plastic bags. Each was about the size of a pair of shoes. Stacked neatly in the drawer, two to a row, sixteen rows long, they looked neat and rather pedestrian. Ice crystals unevenly masked their contents. Tarp had to lean very close. It was like looking at the rusted skin of the *Prinz von Homburg* and trying to make sense of what was seen. Now he looked and tried to puzzle out these shapes—a curving gray pinkness, a bulge. *A hand?* But such a very small hand.

A baby's hand.

He looked at another bag.

Not quite a baby. A fetus.

He stepped back.

He had seen quite a number of corpses. Few had nauseated him. For a moment, however, these did, and he turned away and steadied himself. Then he turned around and deliberately opened the drawer as far as it would go and looked in. *Neat rows of bagged and frozen, miniature human beings. Neatly labeled.*

He took a very deep breath of the stale-smelling air of the suit, then closed the drawer and began to open the rest. There were two more drawers of the same sort. Then one that held five dead dogs. Then one that contained seventeen hearts, not, he thought, human.

The last drawer held a full-size human adult.

The body, like the fetuses, was in a plastic bag. Ice obscured much of the nude torso, but the area over the face was clear as if it had been already scraped clean for him. He had no trouble puzzling out what this mass of waxy skin, this blotched pallor, this slightly mangled shape was. It was a man's head, and he knew the man.

It was Beranyi.

He took the camera from the carrying cylinder and went from

room to room methodically, trying to get enough coverage of each to show what the habitat was like. An integral flash blinked with each exposure. Grim now, he worked quickly, ignoring the headache and the muscles that objected to the weight and the poor balance of the cumbersome suit. He shot the bank of small doors and the phials; he shot the controls from four angles; he shot the freezer room, then one drawer of the fetuses, and Beranyi. He took three pictures of Beranyi. He wanted there to be no doubt. He wanted anyone who saw the pictures to see that Beranyi was dead and that he had died the brutal death of torture.

Tarp packed the camera into the carrying cylinder again and then put in eight of the phials from the storage boxes and the hard discs from the computer. He put in all the phials from the box marked *MAX* and two each from *GAUCHO* and *JB,* and one chosen at random from the others. Each went first into one of the metal tubes, then into the cylinder until there was no room for any more of them. He snapped the locks on the carrying case and moved to the core of the habitat, locking the watertight doors behind him.

Three minutes later he placed the carrying case into the claw of *Vairon*'s left arm, and then, despite his fatigue and the warnings from the displays inside his helmet, he signaled Gance closer. He could just make out the shape of Gance's face behind the thick plate of his helmet. *Like a baby in a plastic bag.*

Tarp shuffled across the ocean floor below the habitat toward the legs of a steel structure set behind the flattened sphere. He flashed his hand light over it, then motioned *Vairon* and its light closer. The brighter light showed something like an oversized wine rack, and, in the openings, eight bulbous canisters with Russian markings.

CHAPTER 38

He watched the helicopter lower the *Vairon* to the tanker's deck, and then he went below, no longer patient with the anguished twistings of Jean-Marie; the Frenchman had stood beside him, his body contorted by the tension of watching the submersible lowered in. Hands in the pockets of his heavy coat, he had jerked his head and his shoulders at every motion of the egg. *Vairon* had been slightly damaged getting it out of the *polynya,* and Jean-Marie had flown back almost in tears, staring as it dangled off center from the cable.

"Not on the ice, not on the ice, not on the ice . . ." he kept repeating. He had told Tarp that he would rather they had left it in the *polynya* where there was a chance of recovering it, even if it sank. Tarp had ordered it lifted out, however, despite some damage; now it had come to rest again on the tanker's deck—one arm broken, a boom sheared off, but without damage to the hull. "Eh-eh-eh-eh . . ." he could hear as he left the rail.

The capsules that contained the plutonium had been flown back in the second chopper and had been stored in one of the tanker's forward compartments. There they were nestled in improvised racks and the compartment had been flooded.

"Man, you're nuts to stay up on that deck." Gance was in the wardroom with coffee, a beer, and a steak. "It is *cold* up there!" He waved at a chair. "How's my friend Pierre doing?"

"Being a pain in the neck."

"Comm says there's message traffic for you. You want to eat first? The beef is great stuff. The best. You hungry?"

"Later."

He went to Communications and was handed a clipboard with a single sheet of paper on it. He sighed, then took it to a cubicle and read it.

FOUND PRESENT FOR YOU MEXICO CITY. RUBIN.

Meaning that Repin's got Pope-Ginna. He wrote a reply:

PLEASE GIFT WRAP AND DELIVER IN PERSON. LOVE, BLACK.

He took another sheet and wrote out a message to "Mr. Smith":

BUY.

The single word would be enough. It meant that they had succeeded.

Tarp went along a passage toward his cabin and found himself stumbling over a raised doorsill. He wanted a hot shower and sleep, he knew; he had been promising them to himself since he had climbed back into *Vairon*'s airlock. But he was disoriented, not merely by fatigue and by the enormous strain of the work under the ice: he was deeply disturbed by what he had seen in the habitat. It was not the fact of the fetuses. He was not sentimental about either life or birth. It was the appalling efficiency of it all, its ruthless *cleanliness,* which was always an expression of what was supposed to be best and most rational about humans. If cleanliness was next to godliness, then science, with its devotion to pure states and sterile environments, should have been almost holy. What he had seen in the habitat, however, suggested that those things could as easily be the attributes of evil. Hell might be as clean as an operating room.

He had the plutonium and he thought he knew who Maxudov was, but he felt profoundly dirtied.

One of the big helicopters brought Repin and Pope-Ginna out from Cape Town two days later. Gance had gone with the chopper's inward flight, taking with him two of the phials from the habitat and the name of a biologist who would analyze the contents.

When the big chopper was visible against the dense gray sky on its return flight, Tarp went above-decks and waited near the improvised landing pad. It was warmer on the deck now, but there was a drizzle that the ship's motion whipped into a stinging spray. Not cheerful weather.

He had readied a space for Pope-Ginna's arrival—a forward anchor locker that he had had emptied of all its gear. It was trapezoidal, uniformly gray, noisy with the vibration of the engines. Entered from above, it was eleven feet from deck to overhead, its only light the portable lamps that had been rigged from winch lines up above. When a man stood on the floor of that space, he knew he was a prisoner, an outcast in a steel shell.

Repin came out of the chopper like an athlete bursting from the stadium tunnel. He was wearing a new alpaca overcoat and a black hat that was so stylish he looked operatic. On his hands were gloves of leather as thin and flexible as rubber.

"So!" Repin was smiling gleefully. "So!" He looked questioningly at Tarp. "So, my friend?"

"I got the plutonium."

Repin clapped him on both arms. "Ha-ha!" He looked up into Tarp's grim face. "But that should please you, Tarp!"

"It does."

"No, it does not."

Tarp shook his head, pulled away from Repin's grasp. "Where is he?" They were shouting over the sound of the dying helicopter rotors.

"He is very slow old man. Almost as old as me." Repin laughed again.

Tarp led Repin away from the helicopter pad toward the superstructure. "Is he on the chopper?"

"Of course, of course!" Repin turned a triumphant face toward the aircraft, whose rotors were almost still. "He comes out now, you see? He is very sick old man."

Two crewmen were struggling to bring their burden out of the helicopter. It looked like a body bag to Tarp.

"Sedated?"

"I hired a doctor in Mexico City." He clasped his hands in front of him. "A healthy climate, Mexico City. Very enjoyable. Cuban cigars, good drink, *very* pretty girls. . . ." He sniffed as if he were smelling that air and not the mist of the South Atlantic.

"How long before he'll come around?"

"I have an ampoule of something if we want to wake him up. Otherwise, several hours."

Tarp frowned. "I want him healthy," he growled.

Repin looked coldly at him. "Do you, now," he said in a chilly British voice.

"I want him so he can talk."

"He will talk."

"Has he talked already?"

"I know better than to do that. I am not an amateur."

Pope-Ginna was in a sleeping bag, his face a pink circle in the hood at the top. As he was carried by them, his eyes blinked slowly, unseeingly.

"Compartment A-twenty-seven!" Tarp shouted at the seamen as they came close. They nodded. They already knew.

Tarp took Repin's arm and led him along the narrow and slippery gangway that flanked the huge deck. The metal surface was crisscrossed with cast-in steel ribs, but there was still danger of sliding on the wet surface. Repin grabbed the rail and looked around at Tarp. "I do not like the water much!" he shouted. The ship rose and his weight shifted suddenly; Tarp put out a hand and started him toward a ladder.

He had requisitioned a vacant suite behind the captain's, one kept for executives and guests of the oil company that owned the tanker. It was luxurious, and Repin, stepping into it, seemed to forget the discomfort of the deck.

"For me?" He beamed.

"And Pope-Ginna, when he's done talking."

There were two rooms, a private bath, a serving galley. It was like a very, very good hotel. "I should have brought Therese," Repin said, looking into the galley. He glanced at Tarp. "No, I did not take her to Mexico."

"I didn't say you did."

"I know how suspicious you are." Repin laid his beautiful hat on a polished table and tossed his beautiful gloves into it. "Now Repin pretends he is very important man, appropriate to this suite, yes? Yes. Repin will be manager of oil cartel. So, to business!" He slapped his hands together. "So, you got the plutonium. You are very remarkable. Very remarkable. Where is it now?"

"On board."

"Is radioactive?"

"Barely."

"So." Repin nodded several times. "So." He looked out a

port that had been made square like the window of a building. There was nothing to be seen but gray sea, and yet he looked and looked. "So now I can go back to Moscow."

"We don't have Maxudov yet."

"You think you will find him?"

"I hope so. He isn't Beranyi, I'm sure of that."

He told Repin about the habitat and about Beranyi. He showed him the photographs of the Russian. He did not mention the phials or the computer discs or the fetuses.

"What is it for, this habitat?"

"Dead storage."

Tarp was still wearing the weather jacket he had worn on the deck. He unzipped it now and took it off; as he did, Repin unbuttoned the overcoat and stood with it swept back behind his arms. "Why?"

"To hide things."

"What things? Plutonium? Bodies?"

"Yes. Those things. Some other things, too."

"What?"

Tarp shook his head. "Part of it's a laboratory. It looks as if it's used for one stage of a process. The final stage, that would make sense. Everything's brought in; I don't think that much actual work is done in the habitat. I think that it's meant as a safe repository—surrounded by a very hostile environment. There were some experimental specimens there, in locked boxes that were kept at a constant thirty-one degrees Celsius. Outside the habitat it was six degrees; ten miles away it was one degree. It's a good place to put something that's unstable and potentially dangerous."

Repin narrowed his eyes.

"What kind of something?"

There was coffee in a shiny vacuum bottle. Tarp poured himself some and handed the bottle to Repin. "Something alive."

He looked at Repin over the rim of the cup. Repin poured, replaced the bottle's top with great care. "You are being mysterious."

"Not intentionally. I brought back a sample of something. I'm having it analyzed. You remember the message in your man's pocket in Havana—about Schneider and about a doctor who ran an abortion clinic?" Tarp sipped the coffee and set the cup down. "Whatever is there in the habitat, I think it uses research on fetuses. Gustav Fahner had used fetuses in research in Germany." He touched the saucer, tapped the side of the cup with a fingernail. "I don't like it."

"You're sure it's Beranyi?"

"It's Beranyi all right."

"But he isn't Maxudov."

"I don't believe so."

"But do you *know* so? How does being dead prove anything? He could be Maxudov and be dead—ah?"

"We'll find out from Pope-Ginna. Maybe." Tarp poured more coffee. "This is a dirty business."

"That is not news."

"No, no, not what we're doing. What went on in that sea lab. A filthy business. There were little boxes in the wall—a sickly green light inside them, and test tubes of stuff that looked like . . ." He shook his head. "Like something you'd find in a boil. And the fetuses. I know in my bones what it means: it's Fahner's work, being done in a new way and a new place. It's that Nazi shit come back to make us filthy again."

Repin looked at him with great sympathy. In a low voice he said, "The Nazis did not invent evil, my friend. But they taught your country what it is. For that, ironically, the world should perhaps be grateful."

"For what, for learning how to live with filth?"

"For learning to live with the rest of us in the real world."

"In order to be real, does it have to be filthy?"

Repin smiled, mostly to himself. He took Tarp's cup from him as if Tarp were a sick man and put it down next to the vacuum bottle. "I envy you your idealism," he said simply. He clapped his hands together. "Come, come—this is no good for you and me! We have work. Let's work!"

Tarp zipped the jacket. "Let's see what Pope-Ginna can tell us."

They started out. Repin glanced into the bedroom, then, unable to resist it, darted in. Tarp saw him bending over the bed. Seconds later he was back. "Real percale sheets," he said. "Very nice. Very seductive, capitalism. At the top, I mean."

Tarp remained matter-of-fact. "Funny, that's just what your friends in Moscow tried to tell me about communism."

Repin was pushing the fingers of the thin gloves down over his own fingers. "But it is true, of course. Everything is seductive at the top. Morals aside, I mean—always, morals aside. One could live happily with any system—morals aside—if one could live at the top . . . eh?"

CHAPTER 39

Pope-Ginna was still swaddled in the sleeping bag. He had been put on the floor of the empty chain locker, and from above he looked like a caterpillar that had crawled into the rivet-studded compartment and died there—soft, small, wrinkled. Up close the pink face looked ill, blue-gray under the eyes and along the unshaven chin, the lips almost brown. When Tarp leaned close he realized that Pope-Ginna had worn false teeth and that now they were missing.

"What happened to his teeth?"

"In my pocket. The doctor feared he would swallow them."

"All right, let's wake him up."

Tarp unzipped the bag and Repin busied himself with a small plastic kit, then straddled the plump pile and lifted a white arm. Pope-Ginna was naked inside the bag. Repin straightened and let the arm drop. "Fifteen minutes," he said, his face red from bending over.

"Cold in here," Tarp said.

"Good." Repin bent again and felt for a pulse. "We don't want to kill him," he said.

They pulled the bag off the limp old man and laid him down on the metal floor. Pope-Ginna had a pendant belly and a small, sad, flaccid scrotum below gray pubic hair. In his prime, his hair had been red or blond, and the hair on his arms and legs still looked coppery, but the skin was gray-white. He had started to show goose bumps and to shiver.

"He's coming around."

"Stand up," Repin said some minutes later. "Please." Pope-Ginna was awake and shuddering with cold.

"I can't." It was an old man's whine.

"Get up," Tarp rasped. "We don't care whether you can or not."

Interrogation had many variations, but it was always cruel, and its basic pattern was sadistic: bully and victim, predator and prey. The interrogator used fear; it underlay all his other tools—guile, surprise, entrapment. Unless the interrogator was careful, this great advantage could be turned against him, for sometimes the victim was able to make the victimizer guilty for it. Tarp was trying to be very careful.

Pope-Ginna was trying to get up. The ship was just then moving up into a wave, and he was pushing himself up on his hands and feet, just getting his knees off the vibrating metal plates when it started down again and he lost his balance and fell heavily. He yelped with pain. When he looked up at them there was blood on his forehead where he had struck it on a rivet.

"Get up," Tarp said.

"No."

"Get up."

"I can't. I won't."

"Get up."

They went 'round and 'round. Pope-Ginna was made to understand that he would get nothing until they were satisfied, and their satisfaction could not begin until he got up. No food, no clothes, no warmth. At last he crawled into a corner and got up by bracing himself against the walls and then leaning there. Tarp remembered his time in the Lubyanka, and he winced inwardly, knowing how those cold plates felt under that old skin.

Tarp was the bully, Repin the nurse. As Tarp became harsher, Repin became comforter and confidant to the Englishman. He may have felt some real sympathy because of their age. Perhaps he was simply a good actor.

"I don't want him to do this to you," Repin was murmuring. He and Pope-Ginna were in the corner, while Tarp had backed away as far as he could and turned his back. "This is very bad place for you," Repin said.

"Tell him to let me go."

"I cannot. You tell him what he wants to know. Is only way."

"I don't know you. Who are you?"

"Tell him, please. Is only way."

"I don't know anything."

"You are old man. Like me. At our age, what is important, but that we be comfortable? Eh? Tell him what he wants, and I can take you back to your life."

Pope-Ginna was disoriented and physically weak. He had been with the KGB interrogators before he had left the Soviet Union. They would have been very easy on him, but the experience would have told. "Are you going to kill me?" he said in a small, frightened voice.

"Is a very bad situation, this. Make it easy."

Pope-Ginna hugged himself. "I know *him*," he said. "I met him in Buenos Aires. I never did anything to him. Why is he doing this?"

"Tell him what he wants to know."

"I'm seventy-nine years old. I'm an old man," he whined.

"Yes. Yes." Repin's voice was very soft. His accent had gotten thicker, and to Tarp he sounded like an actor playing a Russian, perhaps in something slow and sad by Chekhov. "Yes, you are old." He sounded very kind. "An old man." He was not touching Pope-Ginna, but he was very close. "I tell you something about old men: we do not want to die, either. Yes?"

"I don't want to die. No." Pope-Ginna hugged himself and shivered. "I'm not going to die."

Tarp stood in front of him and pushed Repin away. "Look at yourself!" He sneered at the old man. "You ought to be damned well ashamed. Look at yourself!"

"Give me my clothes."

"If your men could see you now! They worshiped you—damn well worshiped you! And look at you. They called you 'His Holiness.' They would have walked through fire for you. And look at you! And you're a traitor."

"Oh, no."

"A damned traitor!" Tarp's shouted voice came back to him from the steel walls like the banging of a drum. "You sold them out!"

"No."

"No? Then what did you do?"

"It had nothing to do with—I didn't. I'm a loyal subject. I am. How dare you! I am decorated, a much decorated flag officer of—"

"Traitor."

They kept at it for two hours. Tarp left to relieve himself, came back to find Repin walking Pope-Ginna up and down, sheltering him in his overcoat. Repin left the old man when Tarp came down the ladder and Tarp began to bully him again. *This is awful,* he was thinking. *This is dirty. The poor old sonofabitch.*

It ended with Pope-Ginna sitting splay-legged against the hull with Repin's overcoat wrapped around him. Repin sat next to him while Tarp paced up and down only inches from the bare old feet, a small tape recorder whirring in an inner pocket.

"How did it start? Well? It started with the *Homburg,* didn't it? Didn't it? *Well, didn't it?*"

"Yes." A voice like a sigh, a surrender.

"Tell me about it."

A very long pause. The old voice gathered strength, as if the memory itself brought sustenance. "I had HMS *Loyal.* And the pickets—"

"I know all that. Cut that."

The old faced winced and tears came to his eyes. "I did, I was the flag officer of an attack force. I was!" He paused for breath and shivered. "London ordered me to hunt the *Prinz von Homburg.* Coming south of Cape Town into the South Atlantic."

"Why?"

"London wasn't sure."

"Why?"

He hesitated, then panted, "It was most secret."

"Tell me."

The old man looked to Repin for help, but Repin shook his head. In a flat voice, Pope-Ginna said, "There was an intelligence report she was carrying gold. Millions. There was talk of setting up a Nazi state in Argentina. Oh, God, I'm so cold."

"You'll get warm when you finish. Go on."

There was another, longer pause, but it turned out be the last one. It was as if he had opened a door that had been closed for a generation; now that it was open, he flung it wide.

"The order was very clear: seek out and sink. The Nazis were not to be allowed a refuge anywhere on earth. The *Homburg* was well south. I knew she would be. They'd tried to track her by air from South Africa but had lost her. Weather. Tried to sink her twice as she came down the coast, but no good. So it was up to me. I sent out aircraft 'round the clock. Took my force out of Port Stanley and headed southeast. My staff said I was mad. Said I was sure to lose her. But I had to take the risk. I'd—botched a job earlier. Done well in my war, but—in forty-three I'd lost some ships I oughtn't have. So they'd posted me down to the Falklands and the *Loyal*. She was old. Not much doing down there. Running submarine patrols. It was my chance. See?"

He was telling the story straight to Repin, as if Tarp were not there, and Repin was listening sympathetically. "Yes. You were quite right."

"So I took my force out. *Loyal* carried two seaplanes. Launched from catapults; that's the way we did things then. Land in the water, get picked up by a crane. Gave me some air surveillance, you see? We looked and looked. And we found the *Homburg* on the eighth day. Incredibly farther south than London thought. Almost in the drift ice. Been hiding there. Sitting, looking for fog banks. Lots of floating ice to confuse radar. Terrible chance the German was taking, but it was the best one. He took a risk, I took a risk. See?

"So I went right after him. It was a chase. Hell of a chase. *Loyal* was slower but had bigger guns. One of my destroyers got in a hit with a torpedo, damaged his steering, I think. Then it was only a matter of time. We chased her right into the ice. Icebergs, I mean, in among the icebergs. Ice pack." His voice faded.

"Is that what you mean, Admiral? You're sure? Just among the *icebergs*?" Tarp made his voice threatening. "You don't want to lie to me."

Pope-Ginna sighed. "Into the *ice*. He had two icebreakers. I had two. In the drift ice, there are—like rivers, veins of water— you can get a big ship in, but . . . You can tear the bottom out, too. I lost one destroyer to the ice. Then . . ."

He looked up at Tarp. He sounded hopeless. "We came out into open water. I'd never heard of such a thing. A sea of open water inside the drift ice. Incredible. You *have* to believe me.

Really, I'm not lying! Really." He appealed to Repin. "Please believe me."

"But it never went into your report."

"No. I— At first, I didn't want to be thought wrong. It was almost night when we broke through. I sent out a plane. He saw how much open water there was. And he saw the *Homburg*. That was the big thing. You see, my officers . . . Many of us believed we'd come out of the drift ice entirely. Got our bearings wrong and come out into open water. See? I was very excited. I knew my career was in balance. So I put on speed to get in range. Got *Homburg* dead to rights on radar, not much floating ice there—ice behind her, no place to hide. Like a shooting gallery. We pounded her for two hours." He licked his lips. "Sank her."

"And lied about her position."

"I—" He licked his lips again and appealed to Repin. "I didn't *lie*. There was confusion. About the location. My navigation officer was sure we were north of the icĕ, thought he'd made some terrible boner. He said to me, 'I've botched the dead reckoning.' His very words. Really! 'You'll have my bars for it, Admiral, but I've made some terrible error.' His words. Not mine. Didn't make them up."

"When did you decide to lie about the position?"

"I didn't *lie*. I—exaggerated some errors."

"How far?"

"About three hundred miles."

"Because of the gold?"

Pope-Ginna looked at him in anguish. "When the *Homburg* was going down, I happened to see a sonar report. The depth was not what I expected. It was very uneven there. Volcanic, I think now. And it flashed through my head, 'That's submarine depth. Divers could get down there all right.' And I thought about the gold."

"How did you plan to get it?"

"I didn't, I didn't! I just saw the—possibility. I mean, I had done what I had been ordered. 'Seek out and sink.' I'd prevented the Nazis from using that gold to set up a refuge. It was a triumph! Don't you understand? Nobody cared about the gold then. It was—it was *mine*! Don't you see? By any law— salvage, the laws of war—the laws of privateering, the captain's share . . .'' He sounded addled. "It was *mine*." He turned to Repin. "You see that, don't you?"

"Of course. Of course."

"I deserved something. The war was as good as over, I knew that. I wouldn't get another command; there wasn't time. The big boys would remember I'd made a mistake—meaning that in peacetime I wouldn't get to the top, not really to the top. You know. I wasn't one of *them*—you know? Wrong family, wrong schools. So, I wasn't going to the top. It'd be a medal and a 'Thanks, my boy,' and that would be it. So I *deserved* the gold."

"Were there survivors from the *Homburg*?"

"Yes." Pope-Ginna sagged again. "Not enough." His white chest rose and fell quickly with his breathing. "Poor devils. It was awful."

"Did you examine the survivors?"

"When we got back to port, yes. The usual."

"Did they know about the gold?"

"No. None of them. We only picked up two officers above the rank of ensign. Both in gunnery. No, the gold was *mine*."

He seemed to be wandering off a little. Tarp waited and then said, "Any civilians?"

"Hmm?" It was as if Pope-Ginna had been dreaming in front of a fire.

"Any civilians?"

"One."

"German?"

"A little Jewish girl." He blinked rapidly and seemed to come awake. "Is that important?"

"Wasn't it important to you?"

"She married Jock Schneider. I was very surprised when they told me. It was she made the connection. I was sitting in the bar of the Hurlingham Club, looking out over the golf course—you know—and she was there. She and Jock had been married a while. You know. And she said, 'You saved my life,' or something like that. I thought she meant because I'd bought her a drink. And she said, 'You saved my life. I was on the *Homburg*.' It made no sense to me."

"You mean that you never saw her between the sinking of the *Homburg* and her marriage to Juaquin Schneider?"

"No. Oh, maybe I saw her. In Stanley. Who knows? Young girl, you know."

"What was a Jewish girl doing on a Nazi cruiser?"

"God knows."

"You never asked?"

"Asked? Why would I ask?"

"After you knew she was Schneider's wife?"

Pope-Ginna's face, which had been drawn and sickly, took on a frightened look. "You never asked questions about something that belonged to Jock. Things happened to people who— It wasn't a good idea. Although God knows, my life would have been easier if I had asked some questions." To Tarp's astonishment he began to sob. Tarp looked at Repin and with a frown tried to ask if they should stop; Repin gave a slight shake to his head and made a pushing motion with one hand where Pope-Ginna could not see it.

"All right, cut that," Tarp said cruelly. "Get back to your tale."

"I'm trying, I'm trying." He put his face in his hands. "Oh, this is awful." He seemed unable to stop weeping. Tarp knew the state he was in and wanted to stop, but again Repin made the pushing motion.

"I said that's enough! Go back to your story, damn you! After the war. What about after the war?"

Pope-Ginna wiped his eyes, wiped his hands on the sleeves of the alpaca overcoat. "I went into submarines," he mumbled. "I thought it would help with the gold if I—"

"Skip that! I know all that."

"I'm only trying to do it right," the old man said, his eyes filling again.

"Go to the Argentine business."

"Why are you asking me this if you already know?"

"Go to the Argentine business."

Pope-Ginna was unable to look straight at Tarp's eyes; his glance moved quickly past Tarp's face, back to his shoulders, to his chin, down to the floor. It settled in the end on some featureless place near the ceiling, and the old man stared at it—his forehead wrinkled, his eyes screwed up—as if getting from the memory of Schneider's wife to that slightly earlier time took great effort. "I retired from the navy in 1952," he said slowly. He went on looking at the far wall. "It had been quite as I expected—no real chance at the top. They kept it all for themselves. All the 'right' people. Their clubs and all that. By then I knew how to get at the gold, though. I'd got that from the Royal Navy, in the end. If *Homburg* had stayed where I'd sunk her, I knew how to get the gold. Then I could bloody well buy a title if I wanted one. That's how things are done, anyway.'' His eyes snapped abruptly toward Repin. ''That's how things are done!''

Repin nodded as if something wise had been said.

''I had some money, of course. I wasn't a fool about money, after all. A few investments. A couple of pals, you might as well know, who let me in on things in exchange for, you know, introductions and a good word here and there. And I'd turned that money 'round and invested it in the Argentine, see? Because I knew I'd have to go after the *Homburg* from the Argentine. It had to be done in secret and far from British eyes, so that ruled out the Falklands or South Georgia. Anyway, the Argentines love secrecy. They understand it. I'd invested money there—lots of British interests in the Argentine back then, lots. Visited three times before I retired. Looked about. Met some fellows. Saw how it could be done.

''Funny thing happened then. When I retired, chap from MI-six called on me, Captain Somebody-or-other, didn't use his right name, I suppose, asked me what I was going to do. Go to the Argentine, I said, try to make a bundle. Oh, good, this fellow said, would you mind having a look 'round for us while you're there? Just keep an eye on the navy down there. Right-o, I said. They provided some introductions to Argentine naval people, said it would get me started, and I said fine, right, absolutely. Loyal Briton glad to help the mother country.

''I was having a laugh, of course. There they were, helping me out. And there I was, keeping *my* secrets. Oh, well. These things happen. I mean, I did what they wanted. Actually, I did it as well as anybody could have. My little bit of spying.

''So I went to the Argentine. The navy contacts led to me being taken on as a consultant in submarines. All on the up-and-up, quite public, and so on. At the same time I got in with a few fellows in their navy who were looking for a good thing. And they introduced me to Jock.''

''Schneider?'' Tarp said.

''Yes, of course, Jock Schneider.'' Pope-Ginna sounded exasperated. "He'd just made his first bundle. Rapacious bloody kite, he was. Not rich the way he is now, but rich. The long and the short of it was we formed a company, about six of us. For marine research, we said. I'd told them enough so they knew what the stakes were. Jock put up the capital—there were some fairly high bribes to be paid. The navy supplied the manpower and the equipment, through my friends." He merely glanced past Tarp and still would not look directly at him. "It was 1959 by now. Everything took so much longer than I thought." He turned to Repin. "If you want to do things fast, you have to work alone. I couldn't work alone. Not enough money. That's the bad luck that's haunted me all my life—not enough money."

Tarp wondered at the man's enduring resentments, which probably went back to his young manhood. They still seemed to drive him. "And you found the *Homburg*," he said.

"Yes. After more years. The ice just wouldn't open! It had been open in fifty-eight, but we weren't ready. Then there were all these years when the open water just didn't appear. It was maddening. Some of my friends thought I was diddling them. There were some bad scenes. Jock was pretty ugly about it. But it all worked out in sixty-three."

"You found it."

"Oh, yes."

"And the gold."

"Oh, yes."

"How much?"

Pope-Ginna hesitated. "Enough for everybody."

"How much?"

"In dollars? In the dollars of those days—a quarter of a billion. Something like that. It took me three trips—three years, that means—and I lost five divers. But I got it. We divided it. I didn't resent dividing it. Even though it was all mine. I mean, for sinking the *Homburg*." His face darkened. "Jock took too much, though. The financier always does. Eh? He does nothing but put up the cash, and then he claims the lion's share."

"What happened then?"

"I was rich. I invested mine, bought an *estancia*, my place in B.A.—the lot. I was *rich*."

"And Maxudov?"

Silence. Pope-Ginna seemed disoriented again, as if these

jumps from subject to subject and from period to period were too wide for him. "That's another matter," he said to Repin.

"Tell me," Tarp said.

"I daren't."

"Tell me."

"Please, no." Pope-Ginna pulled the coat tight about him, his voice a whine.

"I'll help you. You've made six or seven trips to the Soviet Union. You oversaw the refitting of a Soviet submarine for the Argentines. A man who calls himself Maxudov used you as the go-between in a deal that sent plutonium to the South Atlantic. The Soviets just gave you a medal. Now, tell me."

Pope-Ginna opened his mouth and then closed it, doing this three times before he finally found the words that he wanted to speak. "They eased me out of the company we'd formed. After I'd brought back all the gold. Jock was behind it, but I think his wife was even farther behind him. I mean, I think she pushed him to it. To get me out. I didn't much care; it was over, as far as I was concerned. But they kept the company going, built it up on marine research and so on. I didn't think much about it. You know. I heard some things—experimenting with undersea habitats, all that. I reported them to MI-six; I'd kept that contact. Made trips to England every year; I was spreading a little cash around over there, one eye on the Honors List. I have my vanity. Well, early in the seventies—it was nineteen seventy-one, actually—a man named Carlson came to see me. German. German-Argentine, I mean, family been there a couple of generations. It was a bad time down there, the death squads very active, a lot of political mess. And he said, "You're going to do something for me and some friends of mine." He called me Admiral. Very polite. But he threatened me. *Really* threatened me. I was to be the front for a political group that was pushing some navy officers into power. There was a lot of rigmarole— secret signals, meetings, plans. I always worked through this fellow Carlson. Got my orders from him, and so on. Go to Marseilles. Go to Murmansk. Do this, do that."

"And you did it."

"You damned well bet I did. That's why I'm alive today."

"Who was behind it?"

Pope-Ginna dared to look at him. "I always thought it was Jock."

"But you never knew?"

"Never. And I never asked, either." He glanced at Repin and mumbled, "Better not to ask some things."

"And so you started making the trips to Russia."

"Yes. You're quite right about those. I kept London informed, more or less. Not completely. Carlson seemed to know about my MI-six connection, and he told me what to say and what to leave out. Yes, I advised on the fitting-up of a submarine. For 'research,' it was said, but it was a much better version of the sort of gear I'd used in going after the *Homburg*'s gold. Divers' ports, a tunnel attachment to mate with another craft or a sea lab, a deck-mounted submersible. Cargo space. Lots of cargo space, very unusual for a submarine."

"What was it for?"

"I asked no questions." He looked away at the place beyond Tarp again. "I asked no questions." He sighed. "Carlson was killed by one of the death squads. After that, my contacts were always by telephone. Get a call, leave the house, find a coinbox, call a number—all that. Spy stuff. The first call, he threatened me. I—"

"He?"

"The voice."

"Who was it?"

"I don't know." Pope-Ginna's face crumpled up. He was going to cry again. "Really! It wasn't Jock, I know; I know Jock's voice. He said he was taking over for poor Carlson— 'poor Carlson,' that's what he said—and everything would be just as before. Then I got the instructions about the telephone calls. Really! I know it sounds . . . melodramatic. *But that's the way it happened!*" He turned to Repin almost frantically. "There are really people who do things that way!"

"I'm sure there are," Repin said kindly.

"Did you do what he said?" Tarp did not need to threaten.

"Of course!"

"Why?"

"You don't know what Argentina was like then. He talked about the death squads. About how involved I was with certain acts that had involved bribery and corruption. About how the government could freeze all my assets and jail me. That sort of thing happened every day."

"And what was it you did for this voice?"

"I, ah, delivered something in the Soviet Union."

"What?"

"A, a sort of tube thing. Like a cigar tube, really. Small, silvery tube."

"What was in it?"

"I don't know. I was told that if I looked, they'd know, and that would be the end."

"Just one?"

"No. Five altogether."

"Only in Russia?"

Pope-Ginna licked his lips. His color was dreadful and his shivering had given way to a clammy slackness of the muscles that Tarp took as a sign of hypothermia. He would have to be made warm very soon. "In London, too," Pope-Ginna said.

"And where else?"

"That was all. Moscow and London. I swear."

"How was it done?"

"I flew to London. I'd make a telephone call. Then I'd leave one of the tubes in a place. Then I'd wait for a telephone call and then I'd go to Moscow. Same thing there—telephone, and then drop off the tube. That was all. That was my part."

"Were there code names?"

"Yes."

"What were they?"

"In Moscow, Maxudov. In London, John Bull."

MAX and JB. The little boxes in the habitat. And there was a third, labeled GAUCHO. "Just those two?"

"Yes, I swear. That's all. Please, don't you believe me? Please. *Please?* Aren't you satisfied?"

Tarp looked at Repin, who nodded. "Satisfied for now," Tarp said. He started up the ladder.

CHAPTER 40

"You are believing him, my friend?"

"I don't know yet. How is he today?"

"He cries a little, like a bride. He did not want me to leave, he said."

"Did he tell you anything else?"

"His wife, she died in 1964, he said. Her heart."

"I'll have it checked. Anything more about Schneider or his wife?"

"Not today. You are checking on the death of Schneider's wife?"

"I'm waiting to hear from Juana."

They lay at anchor in a small bay north of Cape Town. Trees and grassland of a remarkable freshness (or so it seemed after the days near the ice) came almost to the water's edge; in the middle of the crescent lay a small town, the metal roofs of the pink-and-brown houses like mirrors in the sun. The *Global Clipper* seemed out of proportion to the neat bay and to the two military landing craft that lay quietly at anchor halfway between it and the town.

"Is peaceful," Repin said. He was wearing an open shirt and one of the ubiquitous cloth military hats that appear everywhere in Africa.

"You don't like peaceful scenes?"

"Not so much when American marines take up the foreground."

"Only a small part of the foreground."

Repin laughed. "American marines cannot take up a small

part, my friend. To a Russian eye, they fill the space." Repin was eating a mango by peeling sections and then eating the lush fruit off the palm-sized pit. It was messy, and he seemed to enjoy it that way. "Mr. Smith is coming soon?" he said guilelessly.

"He wants to be here in time to see the marines hit the beach."

"Ha, ha-ha. Is funny expression, 'hit the beach.' " Repin hit the rail with a fist as if to demonstrate.

"No, you don't say that in Russian, do you?"

A small boat put out from the town and curved toward the landing craft. The water was very still and very blue, and the boat cut through it neatly. A flock of pelicans took off and skimmed low and dropped down again.

"Those pelicans had better get ready for a busy day tomorrow," Tarp said.

"Soldiers playing games." Repin did not sound contemptuous, but sad. He threw the big mango pit into the water and licked his fingers. " 'War games.' Nice expression. 'Hit the beach. War games.' Funny business, language."

A little helicopter buzzed over the low brown hills that lay beyond the town. It came very fast, then slowed as it passed over the town and its single dock, then came out toward the landing craft and circled them. After one pass it came toward the tanker.

"Here comes Mr. Smith."

Repin grunted. On the tanker's deck men were running toward the helicopter pad. Otherwise the deck was empty, the submersible already off-loaded and the big French choppers gone.

The former president stepped down to the deck with a smile and a wave, still like a politician, and spent a few seconds being introduced to the ship's captain. He was wearing bush clothes and he looked tanned and healthy and rich.

He also looked pleased with himself. As he shook hands with them his mouth spread into a grin; his eyes were bright even behind the big sunglasses he was wearing and he seemed very pleased indeed. "I'm supposed to be up at Okavango looking at elephants!" he shouted as they left the pad. "Couple of newsmen even chased up there after me, I hear!"

"You like going incognito."

He laughed. "Maybe. Maybe. Yeah, I guess I like it. Well, what's the word?"

Tarp took him to Repin's suite, which had been checked for bugs and judged secure. "Mr. Smith" lay back in an armchair with his hat on a table in front of him, still with the sunglasses on, and waited to hear about the plutonium.

"We got it, that's all."

"I know you got it! You sent me the report. Where was it?"

"Where we thought it would be." Tarp looked at Repin. "We're ready to move on to the next step, sir."

"Oh, just like that? You guys don't waste any time, do you!"

"It was our agreement, Mr. Smith," Repin said carefully, "that priority was to be given to the return of the plutonium to the Soviet government. I am sure you remember that."

The former president stared at him. He had wanted to be told a good story about finding the plutonium, and he was not very happy at being denied it. He tugged at his bush jacket. "Yeah, that was our agreement. I didn't realize there was so much of a hurry about it."

"We have some more to do," Tarp said carefully. "You remember, sir, you thought it important that we help Moscow out with this and then remind them that we did so. I believe it's your move, sir."

"Huh?"

Repin was sitting at the former president's right. "Contact has to be made with Andropov personally," he said. "No other way. That, I hope, is your specialty, Mr. Smith."

"Huh? Oh, I see! Oh. Hmm." He looked from one to the other of them. His big jaw was cocked to one side as if he had a cigarette holder clamped between his teeth. "You want me to go to Moscow and tell him you've found his stuff. Is that it?"

Repin smiled. "Very nice."

"It'll take time to set up. I've never found the Kremlin very quick, you know."

"They can be quick," Repin said.

The former president looked unhappy. "I sort of hoped we'd all have a chance to relax here tonight and, you know, talk."

Tarp tried to be diplomatic. "I believe Laforet could arrange to have you meet privately with Andropov as soon as you arrive, sir."

"You mean I'd miss the marine landing here, too?"

"I think you'll just have time for that, sir. It's on for one hour from now. I think that would just give you time to make the noon flight. If you make your connections, you could talk to Andropov over breakfast. Laforet's got the schedule made."

"I was going to do it through Washington."

"No, sir."

"Huh? Oh, I get it. Right. We weren't going to ask for that kind of support. Okay. Okay. I fly to Moscow, I meet with Mr. Andropov—pardon me, but the irony of me going out of my way to make sure that the Kremlin gets back its plutonium is pretty strong—and then?"

"Moscow will arrange the transfer," Repin murmured. He sounded almost kind, as if he did not want to offend the former president with too ironic a truth. "Your marines come aboard this ship tomorrow, I believe."

Tarp nodded. "Mock takeover of friendly tanker. That's the story for public consumption. 'Rehearsal for possibility of Mideast crisis,' and so on. They'll stay aboard to guard the plutonium until the Soviets arrange a transfer."

"How are they gonna do that, anyway?" The former president squinted up at Tarp, who was standing.

"By submarine, at night, would be my suggestion. It isn't really our business, sir."

"Huh? Gee, I'd sure want to know. Don't you guys ever get curious?"

Like Repin, Tarp was feeling kind. "It's usually better not to know."

"Security?"

"Yes, and—other people screw things up sometimes. It's better not to know, once your part is over."

The former president thought about that. He did not seem to like it very much. "I'd rather carry it right through myself. All the way."

Tarp smiled. "Yes, sir, so would we. But we don't get that chance, as a rule." Their eyes met. Tarp was thinking about Viet Nam, and he suspected that perhaps "Mr. Smith" was, too.

"Now, sir, about Moscow: some arrangements will have to be made for us."

"For you?"

"Yes, sir—we're going back in. We're going after Maxudov."

"You know who he is?"

Tarp hesitated, and Repin said, "We know how to find him."

Tarp sat down opposite the former president. "You'll be given a code and a contact through Laforet. Everything's got to be kept very, very tight. Maxudov mustn't get a hint of what's happened. You're to be very forthright with Andropov and you've got to get him to be forthright with you. If he's already kissed this thing off, he's got to tell you. Then we'll have to know if they've had this ship on satellite surveillance, and if they have if they've made anything of it. However, as things stand now, we don't think that Maxudov knew where the plutonium was, so we don't think he's going to be spooked even if he knows that this ship was down there."

"At least you hope so."

"Yes, sir. Then we need a secure route into the Soviet Union and we need security in Moscow. Repin's supposed to be dead, but Maxudov must know by now that he isn't. So it's better if we're not seen. The KGB will have a blanket over all legal means of entry, and we have no way of knowing how much of that goes right to Maxudov. Therefore, we have to have another way in—military aircraft would be best, with no KGB or political officers involved. That'll have to come straight from Andropov through the air force. Got that?"

"Got it."

"Tell Andropov we're going to flush Maxudov out. We're to have complete control of the operation, or we won't play. However, he'll probably want to put surveillance on the three suspects, using agents who are completely outside the usual state apparatus."

"Can he do that?"

Repin closed his eyes, owllike, and opened them slowly. "He can do that."

"We'll require a safe house when we reach Moscow. A car, something nondescript that can go anywhere—special plates, but not too special. A trustworthy driver. Somebody from the guards is okay if Andropov personally will vouch for him."

"Weapons," Repin said.

Tarp glanced at him. "You think?"

"Weapons." Repin thudded the tip of his right index finger on the table next to "Mr. Smith's" hat. "Definitely. You go to catch a tiger, you carry things to kill tigers." He looked at the former president. "Pistols."

"You guys are something," he said.

"*Big* pistols," Repin said. "This will not be nice work."

"Okay." He looked toward Tarp. "You'll run through this with me again?"

"Indeed I will, sir. Several times."

The famous smile appeared. He seemed to have forgiven them for missing his story. "Sounds good," he said, slapping the arms of his chair. "Sounds good!"

They went up on deck and ran it again and again, until a marine colonel came aboard to take the former president to the landing craft. He delighted him by buckling an issue .45 around his waist and telling him that he would be riding the second boat in. Beaming, the former president went down the ladder to the boat, and as it started away from the tanker, he turned and gave Tarp and Repin a crisp, happy military salute.

"You think he will remember it all?" Repin said as they leaned on the rail. "Our lives depend on that man doing it all just right."

"He ran the United States for four years, Repin."

"*Da*—and look at the United States!"

The marine detachment came aboard next morning when the sun was barely clear of the dry hills behind the bay. A sweet-scented land breeze was still blowing, causing a ripple on the water as their craft came across. Tarp inhaled the faintly spicy odor of the land and waited for them. They came up the ladder on the run, weapons ready but not loaded, and then Tarp and the captain took the marine commander on a tour of the *Global Clipper*. He knew nothing of either Maxudov or the plutonium, but he knew that he was supposed to secure the ship and everything on it.

"You understand that this part of the operation is not a mock-up, Captain?" Tarp said.

"You bet." He wasn't yet thirty, but he had that hard-nosed, humorless look that made for authority. "That's live ammo those guys are carrying."

Tarp had noticed. Still, he hoped they would have no cause to load it into their weapons.

He went to Repin's suite, where Pope-Ginna, in borrowed pajamas, was sitting with an enormous breakfast spread around him. Repin was dressed but unshaven, and his face was puffy with sleep.

Pope-Ginna always flinched now when he saw Tarp. He seemed comfortable with Repin, but he could not restrain his distaste for Tarp; like a dog who has been kicked, he was always shy of a certain kind of boot. Still, he managed a smile and said vaguely, "Grapefruit?"

"I'll have a papaw." Like Repin, he relished the fresh fruit. He began to peel it. "Do you feel ready to travel, Admiral?" he said easily.

Pope-Ginna's face tightened again; his response to Tarp had become a tic. "Where to?" He tried to say it rather gaily, as if it were a joke. In a bright, very false voice, he said, "I didn't bring my resort clothes," and laughed and looked from one to the other of them.

"There's something that has to be done. Some telephone calls to make. In London."

"I see."

Pope-Ginna licked his lips and sat back from the table and looked at Repin, who said smoothly, "Admiral Pope-Ginna may be concerned, perhaps, about security people in Britain. About what maybe is said to them."

"People might think the wrong thing," Pope-Ginna said quickly. "If they were told only about—you know. About the *Homburg*. The general run of people wouldn't understand about my, my *role* in the, ah, big picture. With MI-six, I mean. And during the Falklands crisis."

"Yes." Tarp ate a slice of the papaw. "I'll arrange for you to give a statement to British security, but not on British soil, Admiral. You can make whatever deal with them you like. That's not my business. I want you to make some phone calls."

"Yes. I see. Well . . . I don't have much choice, I suppose."

"None at all."

"Whom am I to telephone?"

"John Bull."

"Ah. Hmm. Yes, I see." He looked appealingly at Repin

and then turned to Tarp. "I don't want to be pushed out someplace where Jock can do whatever he likes with me! Do you understand? That may sound cowardly, but—it's the truth. I don't want to make your telephone call and then be . . . abandoned."

"You won't be abandoned."

"If you just chuck me back to Argentina, you know, I won't last a day. Not a day. Jock's a very powerful man."

"There's no plan to send you back to Argentina just yet. You could probably stay in England, for that matter. Never go back. You can make a deal with the British, I'm sure."

"My money's in Argentina," Pope-Ginna said thinly.

"You could live comfortably in England, I imagine."

Pope-Ginna seemed to shrink. "Comfortably, yes. But I wouldn't be *rich*."

"You wouldn't be dead, either."

After many seconds of silent thought, Pope-Ginna joined his hands on the table and said, "I will do whatever is necessary. But I really have to return to Argentina. I demand it. In my own time, in my own way, I have a score to settle there."

Tarp wiped his fingers on a napkin. "We leave in two hours."

The sunshine was thin and without warmth in France, and the earth looked as if it might never let a seed sprout in it again. The views around the farmhouse were all of the bleak kinds of landscape that had taken all the romance out of farming in the paintings of the late nineteenth century: black, gray, and brown, and above them a sky of watery blue.

Tarp was sitting in the other farmhouse, where the French security guards lived, and he could just see the roofs of the tumbledown farm from where he sat. He had a telephone and a scrambler, and he was trying to talk to Juana for the first time in many days, trying to forget the sharp presence of her and to make sense of the half-garbled, inhuman sounds that came out of the scrambler.

"I cannot understand!" he shouted into the telephone. "Repeat!"

"Schneider's wife!" Her voice sounded faraway and not at all like her.

"Yes, I got that. Schneider's wife!"

"Was killed in an auto accident. Understand?"

"Yes! Got it. Any chance it was anything but an accident?"

"What?"

"Was it an accident?"

"The police said so. But Kinsella says the police would say anything they were paid to say."

"Could it have been murder?"

"Kinsella says yes."

She had made contact with Kinsella in Buenos Aires almost immediately. Kinsella was part of an intelligence cell that was trying to bring the air force to power in the ruling military junta; above all, Juana told him, the navy was their prime enemy.

"Anything new on Schneider?"

"I'm checking the men you call his 'butlers.' His body-guards." The line had cleared, and, although the voice still did not sound like hers, it was at least understandable. "Is there anything else?"

"Yes! Check the code name Gaucho. See what you can find."

"All right. Anything else?"

"No!"

"Yes!"

"What?"

"I love you!"

Tarp was embarrassed. "Good," he said lamely, and hung up. He sat and looked at the instrument, hating it, as people must have been hating it since the day it became the means for putting a man and a woman into the illusion of communication.

"Done, monsieur?" the communications man said. He reached for the unit.

"Yes, thank you." The man mumbled something; Tarp slipped out of the chair. He hesitated in the doorway, looking over a muddy yard where cars had left watery ruts, feeling in himself the opposing pulls of the desire for action and the desire for this woman. The telephone call was an annoyance, for it reminded him of her without making him close to her; it intensified the pull without allowing him to yield to it. Given that impasse, he let himself yield to the desire for action. He breathed deeply, looked once around the cheerless landscape, and then launched himself into it as if he meant to do battle with it. As perhaps he did, for he marched over the field with enormous strides, his rubber boots sucking up great gobs of mud that he ignored in his eagerness to get to the place where action started.

He came to the rocky track and started up it, passing the place where he had found Juana the first day after he had come back from Moscow. There was nobody there now; the place looked deserted. As he came closer, however, a hatless man in a long overcoat came out and stood waiting for him.

"Mr. Carrington's been looking for you, sir."

"I was at the other house."

"Yes, sir."

Tarp started for the door and the man stepped aside, then came along behind him. Tarp held the door, but the man shook his head. "I'm to wait outside, thank you."

"Right."

The house was cold. There was no fire in the kitchen now; Therese was in Paris with Repin. The guards had turned on an utterly useless electric heater in the main room.

Johnnie Carrington was standing near the heater. He looked taller and thinner; the left sleeve of his dark overcoat was empty. His face had a new acidity to it, and Tarp thought of what Repin had said about Hitler and evil—*learning to live with the rest of us in the real world.* It was slightly sad to see it in Johnnie Carrington, who had been young and who was young no longer.

"All set?" Tarp said brusquely, being very businesslike as if it were the means to make them both less conscious of the maimed arm.

"Yes, I think so." He passed his hand over his face. "The admiral's reading over the typescript of our little agreement. He's terribly cautious. I suppose it's natural." He looked down and away from Tarp. Tarp thought that he looked as he would for the next twenty years or so—handsome, slender, rather worn out by his service. Women would find him more attractive now, he thought, not less. "Will there never be an end to this, do you think? The leaks, the double agents. Men who sell out."

"It's human weakness."

"Whatever happened to human strength?" He smiled wanly, as if embarrassed by that rather Victorian question.

"Tired, Johnnie?"

"Very. See here, I don't want this one getting away, Tarp. I won't have another bolt for Moscow!"

"I don't think this one will do that. Anyway, we won't give him the chance."

"We'd damned well better not. I can't afford to be a fool twice."

Pope-Ginna came in then, and after him a male stenographer, who passed right through the room and out of the house, snapping the lid on a portable typewriter as he went. Pope-Ginna looked pleased with himself, although he showed the usual tic when he looked at Tarp. It seemed unfair that he should look relieved and Carrington should look burdened, but that was what had happened—the burden of knowledge had passed from one to the other.

Tarp cleared his throat. "I'd like to go through it once more, Admiral."

"Certainly."

"Each time you contacted Maxudov, you first called John Bull in London, is that right?"

"Yes, that's right."

"Did you think that John Bull then contacted Maxudov immediately?"

Pope-Ginna hesitated, and Carrington looked sharply at him. "I always thought there was contact. I'm not at all sure it was immediate. It seemed to me that . . ."

"Well?"

"You people are the experts at this sort of thing, but it seemed to me that Maxudov was in the sort of situation where he'd want as much confirmation as possible. So that my call to him in Moscow didn't simply come out of the blue."

"But you never said anything to John Bull about Maxudov?"

"Oh, no. I just did as I was told—made the telephone call—three, actually, the series of three. Then I waited two days and flew to Moscow. Always after two days. That was part of the system."

Tarp looked at Carrington. "So John Bull didn't flag Maxudov until after he got his own payoff, I suspect."

"Yes, looks like."

"Let's do it, Johnnie."

"I agree."

"Ordinarily, you could go slow, but time's very important to us. They'll get scared soon. I've got to move."

Carrington looked at his watch. "There's still time today. Three hours between the first two calls, isn't it?"

"Yes. Exactly three hours."

"To a machine at the other end."

"An answering device, yes."

Carrington swung toward Tarp. "He can make the first call from here; we'll be in England for the second one."

Tarp touched Pope-Ginna's arm, and the old man's face twisted quickly in its tic. "Don't screw us up, Admiral," he said. "Do it exactly right, or else. If we don't get our man—you've bought it."

"I understand. Perfectly." The old eyes, which Tarp had once thought merry but which now looked anxious, flicked from one to another. "I have to know what was playing at the Barbican Theatre last night. That was the identification signal."

"We'll find that out. Let's go."

"Good."

Tarp breathed deeply. *Action.*

The third telephone call was placed from a kiosk on the Embankment, an arrangement insisted upon by John Bull so that he could make visual confirmation that it was Pope-Ginna calling. That meant that the quarry was there somewhere, in a taxi or walking a dog or watching through binoculars from a window. There were three MI-5 people near the telephone so that Pope-Ginna could not make a run for it if such a thing was in his head, while Tarp and Carrington waited well out of sight in a taxicab, an MI-5 car behind them with three more officers in it.

"Will he bolt, do you think?" Carrington said.

"John Bull? Why should he? It all looks right."

"The admiral."

"No, I doubt it. You've promised him everything but a knighthood."

"I don't care about him. Although he is a bit of a swine, I suppose. Lying about that ship, and so on."

A bit of a swine. That seemed to sum it up—the dilution of moral outrage down to a faintly disapproving tolerance. *In an-*

*other generation, Hitler will be a bit of swine. Stalin, too.
Beria.*

"Here comes the admiral. He didn't bolt, you see."

Pope-Ginna passed them without acknowledgment and went
on along the Embankment, crossed the street, and turned toward the city. They picked him up a block away.

"Problems?"

"None. Just like always." He seemed very pleased with
himself. It was often like that. After years of duplicity, the
straightforward act became a cause for self-congratulation.

They drove southeast out of the metropolitan tangle and into
rolling green countryside, where the late afternoon sun broke
through and the clouds looked as if their tops had been gilded
for the occasion. They passed the gate of a military installation,
where a little village of tents had been put up where they could
not be ignored by anyone driving on the main road or turning
into the gate. As the car slowed for a turning vehicle, a line of
women were forming across the road into the base. They wore
raincoats and plastic rain bonnets, and they were carrying signs
and other objects. Tarp saw the words *No More Missiles.*

"What's that?" Tarp said.

Carrington was on the side nearest them. "A protest," he
said.

"Of what?" Pope-Ginna, on the far side, said. He seemed
not to understand any of it.

Carrington put his hand above his eyes and looked out at the
women with his face close to the glass. "Nuclear missiles," he
said.

"Whatever are they carrying?"

"Signs. Photographs."

"Photographs! Of what?"

Again, he had to peer under his hand. They had passed now,
and he had to turn to look.

"Children," he said.

On the outskirts of Rochester, Pope-Ginna directed the driver
through smaller streets until they reached a new business building, where he directed them down into its underground garage.

"The tube goes on the second steel rafter over there," the admiral said. He pointed along the rows of steel girders that held
up the ceiling. Already the garage was beginning to empty as
businessmen headed home at the end of the day.

"He'll be here soon," Tarp said. "It's a good time. Nobody would notice." He turned to Carrington. "You're sure he didn't follow us?"

"My people saw no one. I had a third car several miles back. They're to take the admiral with them now."

"Okay. He must always come late enough that the admiral never gets a look at him."

Tarp waited with Carrington while Pope-Ginna was taken to another unmarked car and driven away. Tarp saw his old face as a blur in the rear window as the car disappeared up the ramp of the garage. Only when it was gone did he walk toward the place where the tube was to be hidden and take the tube from an inner pocket. "I didn't want him to see this," he said to Carrington as he put it in place.

"Obviously he's seen them before."

"Yes. But he doesn't know that I have."

Carrington put a man in a car at each exit of the garage, and then Tarp and Carrington and another MI-5 man waited in a janitor's closet that had only one window the size of a playing card.

"Are you armed?" Carrington said.

"No. I didn't think you'd want me to be."

"I'd only have had to take it away, yes. We're armed." Tarp was thinking of the last time Carrington had been around guns. His people had been armed then, too.

"Here he comes," Carrington whispered.

"How can you tell?"

Carrington smiled wanly. "I know the car."

Tarp watched a maroon BMW coast down the ramp and turn into an empty space. Two men were standing at the rear of a Renault sedan, and the driver of the BMW waited for them to leave. After two minutes, however, they had still made no move to go, and the driver got out of his car with elaborate casualness and made his way slowly along the oily concrete between the cars.

It was Ramsey Matthiessen, the man who had given Tarp the lecture at Prong's and Carrington's superior at MI-5.

"Wait until he has the tube," Carrington said.

"I know."

"We must have his fingerprints on it and the photo of him taking it."

"I know."

Tarp watched Matthiessen stroll toward the hiding place. He stopped and tied his shoe. As he straightened, the two men who had been talking with such vitality raised their hands in almost military salutes and jumped into their cars; engines roared, and the smell of exhaust grew stronger. Then, with waves and grins and blasts from their horns, they pretended to lunge at each other with the vehicles and then went up the ramp and were gone. Matthiessen watched them go, for some reason with a smile on his unhealthy face. Only then did he go to the hiding place and take down the tube. He slipped it into a pocket and turned back.

Tarp let Carrington go ahead of him as they moved between Matthiessen and his car. He saw them at once. He gave Carrington an odd smile, almost of condescension, but he could not keep the smile up when he looked at Tarp. "I'd rather it was almost anybody than you," he said to Tarp.

"Keep your hands where we can see them," Carrington said briskly. "The entrances are blocked. We are armed."

Matthiessen's face seemed to darken and the discolored pouches under his eyes looked purple. "I won't give any trouble," he said. He glanced at Carrington's empty sleeve. "I always knew I'd be—" His grin turned sickly, yet he seemed genuinely amused. "We all say the same thing in this spot, don't we."

"I'm very sorry, Ramsey." Carrington went close to Matthiessen. "Ramsey Matthiessen, I charge you with violation of your oath of fidelity to Her Majesty and her government; I charge you with crimes grave and heinous; I warn you that anything you say at this time may be used against you when these matters are brought before a magistrate. I suggest you engage counsel at once." His voice fell for the last sentence, becoming conversational and almost intimate.

"I know how it goes, Carrington," Matthiessen said with artificial weariness, trying to recover some of the supercilious *hauteur* that had marked his behavior in office. One of the MI-5 men came down from the entrance to their right and began to search Matthiessen, murmuring his apologies but going ahead resolutely. "I don't have a gun, you fool," Matthiessen said with contempt.

The man used white tissue to extract the tube, which he wrapped in clear plastic. Matthiessen watched it hungrily.

"There's nothing in it this time," Tarp said.

Matthiessen looked at him with hatred.

"I suppose they're for your wife?"

Matthiessen looked at him with hatred. Matthiessen's wife had multiple sclerosis. "I think if you'll cooperate with some information, you'll be able to go on taking care of her."

"That's despicable."

"Yes." Tarp looked back without expression. "I'm a bit of a swine."

It was still afternoon in the eastern United States, and Tarp was able to put through a call from Carrington's office to a biological researcher in New Jersey. It was to her that Gance had taken the phials Tarp had given him.

"What's in them, then?" Tarp said when the necessary greetings were done.

"I haven't *really* done a job on them yet." The woman had a remarkably nasal voice, and *really* sounded like the screeching of brakes.

"Do you have any idea?"

"Oh, sure. It's a live virus vaccine of some kind. *Was* a live virus vaccine; it was mostly dead when it got to me. The temp is very critical. *Real* critical. Actually, you sent me two samples and they were different. Different viruses. Different structure, you know? Do you know viruses?"

"Not at all."

"Well, I won't go into all that. Actually, I'm pretty puzzled by some of it. *Really* oddball stuff in some ways. You know anything about the background of this stuff?"

Tarp thought of the habitat, the drawers, the dead fetuses. "I suspect there was some genetic doctoring done."

"*Yeah!* Now that would resolve just a *lot* of problems!" She began to talk in technical jargon Tarp could not understand, and he interrupted her and said, "Would there be a reason to experiment with such a vaccine on—live human beings?"

She thought about that. "Well, if you were *really* out to lick one of the big ones—cancer and like that—on an individual basis, you could be trying to turn on an individual's immune system with stuff like this. Do you follow me? What I mean is, not go for something that would work on just anybody, but tailor it to the individual and his/her immune system. You follow?"

"Yes."

"And then you'd do a lot of testing to make sure you weren't going to get a reaction for the same reason. Like organ-transplant syndrome. You follow?"

"I think so."

"And you'd want to find a way to test on individuals just like your individual; I mean, with the same genetic fingerprint. Except it would be very dangerous for your individuals, you follow? You could *kill* people."

"Yes, I see."

"Could you fill me in on this stuff and where it came from, Mr. Tarp? I mean, it's *real* strange stuff. And very unique. Could you give me some background?"

"No, I'm afraid I couldn't. Thank you."

"There's lots more I haven't said."

"Yes, I'll take a written report. Later. That's enough for now. . . ."

Matthiessen told them that he had served for more than two years as the go-between for Buenos Aires and Moscow, signaling Maxudov when Pope-Ginna was in London and ready to make a delivery; at the same time, he placed a call to Buenos Aires and left a message with an answering machine.

It was well after midnight when he had gone through it. Tarp had come in only toward the end, when most of it was clear and Matthiessen's dislike for him would not get in the way.

"Did you order the attempt to kill me in London?" Tarp said.

"Certainly not. I was told to keep track of you if I could, and when the meeting was set up at Prong's, I passed that along."

"To whom?"

Matthiessen hesitated. He looked at Carrington, who was lying on a sofa, awake but tired out. "A telephone number in London. I've already given all of that."

"We're checking it," Carrington said from the couch. "It's probably long since abandoned. "They were in an office in the MI-5 annex, which was rather rundown and whose seediness suggested that it belonged to a firm of not very respectable lawyers.

"Do you know who Maxudov is?" Tarp said to Matthiessen.

"Certainly not."

"Do you know whom you were dealing with in Buenos Aires?"

"Never."

"How was the arrangement set up?"

"The offer—if one may call it an offer—came through an intermediary. A Swiss at a clinic where I'd taken Marjorie—my wife—for treatment when her symptoms first appeared."

"Did he set it up?"

"No. Somebody else, here in London. A Bulgarian. I've given all this to Carrington."

"He has, Tarp." Carrington's voice came from his stretched-out form like a voice from sleep. "It's all in the transcript. We're after the fellow now, but it was more than two years ago and we think he's left London."

"All right. You passed Maxudov's messages to Buenos Aires?"

"Yes."

"Did you know what was involved?"

"Never."

"Did you suspect?"

"I wasn't interested. Didn't want to know. Sorry."

"All right. The last message you sent from Maxudov to Buenos Aires. Was it different from the others?"

Matthiessen was both tired and jumpy from missing his evening ration of alcohol. "Yes!" he snapped.

"How?"

"It was longer."

"Was it coded?"

"Yes."

"Did you understand the code?"

Matthiessen hesitated. "I'd worked some of it out. It was very simpleminded."

"What was the message about?"

"It was about Beranyi. Something about his going to Buenos Aires, and he was to count as a shipment."

"All right. Will you send a message to Maxudov for us?"

Matthiessen still had the self-confidence to sneer, "Out of

the goodness of my heart? Never!'' He bent toward Carrington. "Is this to be part of our arrangement?"

Sepulchrally, Carrington's voice entered the room. "Yes." His eyes were closed now.

"Then I'll send your damned message."

"You are to tell Maxudov that another payment is coming because the last shipment was so valuable."

"I don't *care* what the message is. 'The *line* is immaterial'!"

"Then I want you to send a message to Buenos Aires."

"Oh, *do* you!"

Carrington swung his legs to the floor and sat up; he rubbed his eyes and muttered, "Don't be rude, Ramsey; it's so pointless." Already he had asserted himself. Matthiessen's treason moved him up a notch in the MI-5 pecking order; his getting credit for the discovery might move him into Matthiessen's job. "I must have some tea, I think. There's got to be a porter about, doesn't there?"

"Dial five," Matthiessen said blandly. His acid smile returned. "Sorry. I've used this place so often, myself."

Carrington stood up. "I've been instructed to tell you, Tarp, that the government will now cooperate with you on what's left of your Moscow venture. The tilt in the other direction, it seems, was in good part Ramsey's doing, anyway. We've made an arrangement with Ramsey, which, if everything he says checks out, will allow him to resign without public prejudice and to withdraw from public life to take care of his wife. That assumes, of course, that his dealings with Moscow were limited strictly to this Maxudov thing."

"They were," Matthiessen said.

Carrington ignored him. "And it assumes that you will not press the matter of the attack on you here in London—press his involvement in it, I mean."

Tarp thought about Carrington's arm and about the dead man in the passage. He looked at Matthiessen. "Was it worth it?" he said.

Matthiessen's lip curled, merely from habit. "I would have done much more to help my wife," he said.

"*Did* it help her?"

Matthiessen hesitated. "For a few weeks, after each injection, she was better." He could not keep the roughness of emotion out of his voice. It was the first time that Tarp had really believed in the depth of this unlikable man's love for the woman for whom he had traded his career and what, for lack of a better word, Tarp thought of as his honor.

Repin was waiting for him at the farmhouse. He had messages from Andropov and from "Mr. Smith." "We go," he said. He was grim.

Tarp told him what had happened in England, but Repin seemed to listen with only half an ear. For him it was Moscow and the Soviet traitor that mattered.

They left within an hour by helicopter. They would go to Paris, to the Seychelles, to Oman, and to Syria. There, a Soviet military jet would be waiting for them.

CHAPTER 41

There was a Russian Fiat waiting for them in Moscow. Behind the wheel was a heavyset, thirtyish man who said his name was Gorchakov and who produced papers to identify himself as a major in the Guards. On the seat beside him were three boxes the size of reams of letter paper, each so crammed that the top was held on with rubber bands. *Files on our three possibilities.*

Repin walked around the car, inspecting it. His shoes crunched on bits of stone that had worked out of the asphalt. The day was wet but springlike, and he had opened his alpaca coat to get cool. "I don't like that license very much," Repin said to the guards major in Russian.

"Why not?"

"Too easy to remember."

The major sighed. He reminded Tarp of policemen he had known—intelligent, unimaginative, unable to put himself into the worries of others. Repin was quite right, Tarp thought: there should be nothing distinctive about the car.

"I'll have it changed," Gorchakov said.

"Good."

A car came out to the military airport from Moscow and they lost an hour while a new plate was put on. During that time Repin and the major found they disliked each other. They had too many antipathies—old-young, Stalinist-modernist, Guards-Operations. Repin became very busy with the files. Tarp realized for the first time that Repin was nervous.

They drove into an area of small factories and dumps and wooden shacks that looked like badly made dollhouses; Tarp could not orient himself. He saw the ugly buildings of the university rising beyond what looked like a mountain of mud, but he could still not place where he was. Repin seemed unconcerned. Repin purported to dislike Moscow and therefore to know nothing about it.

They parked in the submanager's space of a bicycle-wheel factory, and Repin went inside with Gorchakov, who came out only seconds later as if he were afraid that Tarp would steal the car. Watching his eyes, Tarp knew that he was worried about the files and not about the car. He had probably not been told that Tarp had seen these same files some weeks before.

"He's making a telephone call," Gorchakov said.

"Of course." Repin had a tape recording of Pope-Ginna.

They sat without speaking. Gorchakov lighted a Russian cigarette and held it out the window as if he knew that Tarp disliked it. *He's had my file, too,* Tarp thought. This kind of intimate prying was Repin's justification for hating Moscow. "You fart in Moscow, they make a note in Dzerzhinsky Square," Repin had told him. "You fart in Tiflis, people ask you how you are." It was only a joke, of course, because there were informers in Tiflis, too, but Moscow was the center and therefore the focus of Repin's distaste for his own system, now that he was one of the victims instead of one of the managers of it.

Repin came out and nodded curtly, then got into the back of the Fiat with Tarp.

"Ready?" Gorchakov said.

"We are ready to be driven, if that is what you mean."

"Where?"

"Next we go to the Children's Park."

"This is where it starts?"

"Maybe."

Gorchakov reached under his seat and took out two boxes one at a time and handed them back. There was a 9mm Makarov in each one with a full clip and an unopened box of cartridges.

"Are you armed?" Repin said to the major.

"Of course."

They drove past more factories as a light rain began to fall; then they crossed the river and the rain stopped and a bright spot showed in the clouds where the sun was trying to stab through. As they turned through the gates of the Children's Park, pale light and pale shadows appeared on the ground as if projected from underneath.

The car park was almost empty.

"Can you see the tree from here?" Repin said.

"I wouldn't think so," Tarp muttered. "Not if he's smart."

"Well, we know he's smart. An oak on a knoll above the carousel, Pope-Ginna said."

"The carousel must be over there where the kids' rides are."

Repin grabbed the back of Gorchakov's seat and pulled himself forward. "We're going to walk." He might have been threatening the major.

"Please don't let the pistols show."

Repin looked at the back of Gorchakov's head, then at Tarp, his nostrils lifted in disgust. "Come on," he said. He got out awkwardly because the Fiat was small and his overcoat confined him.

They found the oak tree. It had an iron bench around it, as Pope-Ginna had said it would, and six feet off the ground there was a hole where a branch had fallen off and the ants had eaten the heart of the wood.

"Radio working?"

Repin took a small black box from his pocket. He pressed a red button and a red light glowed. He nodded, took from the other pocket one of the cigarlike tubes from the habitat. It had been fitted in Paris with a transmitter so they could track it after it was picked up.

"And if he doesn't come?"

"He?"

"Maxudov."

"He will come. Maybe not directly, but we will find him. If not this way, then another."

They waited at the top of a slope from which they could watch both the oak tree and the car park. Gorchakov said that he had another car at the far side of the park in case Maxudov went in that direction, but Tarp never saw it. The day grew warmer and brighter; at two in the afternoon the sun came out in full and he felt suddenly that he was not in Moscow but in Boston, on the Common on an April day. Children appeared as if on cue, like a crowd in an opera; a few young people strolled among the trees. Tarp felt sleepy, but Repin stood tensely, his eyes fixed on the tree and the hole where the tube lay. He had the intensity of the end of a hunt, which Tarp did not yet feel.

At half-past three, a woman and a little boy began to play near the tree. The child was about four. The woman, who seemed to be his nurse, was in her early twenties and very fair.

"Do you think?" Repin said.

"Good cover, the kid. Maybe."

"Colossal ass on her. Shit, yes, look at that!"

The woman and the little boy had been rolling a ball back and forth. The woman sat on the bench by the tree and rolled the ball from there, and then she bounced it high to the child and he chased after it, and while he was running and shrieking, the woman quickly stood on the iron bench and reached up to the hole and got down again.

"Just like that."

It had taken only a few seconds. She was still holding the tube in her hand when she sat down, and only when the little boy came lumbering back with the ball did she open her purse and push it inside.

"The bitch." Repin seemed to hate her for playing a part in this. "Using a kid."

"It isn't the first time."

"Shut up."

Repin turned on the tracking device and moved it back and forth as the blond woman and the child moved across their field of vision. The box gave out a groaning noise when it pointed toward her and then faded when it moved away. A green crystal display showed numbers—5 when it was pointed directly at her. 0 when it was all the way off.

"They're coming this way. Let's move."

They went obliquely up the slope, coming around behind their own car from a screen of firs. Gorchakov looked bored but did not seem surprised to have them come behind him. There were other cars in the parking area, most of them clean and shiny, the status symbols of the upper bureaucracy.

"Well?" Gorchakov said when they got in.

"It's been picked up." Repin seemed to grudge him that much information.

"And?"

"Coming this way. A woman and a kid."

"Coming back to her car, probably."

Repin grunted. He swung the black box and it registered 4, and then the little boy tottered to the edge of the graveled parking area and fell down and began to howl. The woman came after him. Her coat was slung over her shoulders like a cape; under it, her gray wool dress, which was probably meant to look severe, looked provocative because of her body.

"I know her," Gorchakov said.

"What?"

"She's Falomin's mistress. The boy is his. And hers."

Repin pulled himself upright again with the help of the seatback. "Are you sure?"

"Of course." Gorchakov leafed through one of the boxes on the seat. His eyes moved back and forth between the woman and the files. "She's supposed to be the kid's nurse. He's supposed to be Falomin's brother's kid. But it's his, and so is she. There." He handed a photograph over the backs of the seats. It was a greatly enlarged picture of the blond woman and Falomin, both in casual clothes somewhere in the sun where it had been warm and there had been a lake or ocean and they had had to squint.

"She travels in style," Gorchakov said. The young woman was lifting the boy into the back of a chauffeur-driven Volga.

"Has she still got the tube?"

"Yes."

They followed the sedan toward the diplomatic section, even turning on Tchaikovsky Street and going right past the American embassy, to Tarp's rather grim amusement. On they went into smaller streets lined with handsome buildings like small Renaissance palaces from before the revolution, then into a still narrower side street where the sedan parked in front of a handsome wrought-iron gate with gilt spearheads along the top. Gorchakov drove on past, turned the corner, and stopped.

"Well?" Repin said.

"That's an apartment block. A lot of foreigners. I can go back to see where she's gone."

"All right. But if they take off . . ."

"Then you'll sit here until I get back! I have the keys. Don't worry; the other car is in the next street.'' Gorchakov said something on his radio and scrambled out.

He walked like a man trying to find where he was in a strange part of town, his head lifted as if to look for signs. He was not a bad-looking man, and in his leather overcoat he looked prosperous.

''Who is Major Gorchakov, do you suppose?'' Tarp said.

''One of Andropov's personals.''

'' 'Personals'?''

''Bodyguards. He seems to know a lot. Andropov may keep his own surveillance on his friends.'' Repin moved the black box. ''The signal is not very good here. Too many buildings.''

''I don't believe it's Falomin. Do you?''

''I can't get the damned signal!''

''Andropov said that Falomin had an 'unfortunate wife.' Is she ill? Is he like Matthiessen?''

Repin got out of the car and walked to the corner. He stood with his back to the street down which the sedan waited. Then, after two minutes, the sedan passed him and went up a hill and around a curve. Repin did not move until it was out of sight, and then he hurried back to the Fiat.

''She's dropped it someplace. It isn't in the car, but she is.''

''And Gorchakov?''

''The signal is weak, but at least it's readable. The tube is back there in that building.''

''What about Gorchakov?''

''What? Oh, he's coming, I suppose. We have to wait here some more. Who cares about Gorchakov?''

The major came back and the car sagged under him. He slammed the door too hard and turned all the way around to look at them. ''I think she's left it with a man named Czerny. I didn't see her do it; that's a guess. Take your finder down there and you can check for sure. But I think it's Czerny because I saw her coming from his stairway.''

''Who's Czerny?'' Tarp said.

''He's supposed to be an artist. Actually, he runs a shop for people from the foreign embassies. In his apartment—food, textiles, fine wines—if you can pay his prices, and in Western currency, Czerny can get it for you.''

''It sounds illegal.''

"It is. But he has friends."

"Like Mensenyi?"

"Yes, like Mensenyi." Gorchakov looked into his eyes for a second. "Actually, Czerny performs a service of a sort. It's a way of keeping an eye on a lot of foreigners."

Tarp held his hand out toward Repin. "My turn," he said. "They've seen you once." He strolled down the street and in through the wrought-iron gates, walked around the spare, beautiful courtyard beyond it, and found a stairwell where the signal was strongest. On the second floor above, by a brass plate in a door marked Czerny, the signal was strongest of all. Tarp thought of going in, then thought better of it and went back to the car.

"It's in Czerny's all right. It's a good drop. Somebody'll come in to buy something, he'll wrap the tube with it, and away it will go. Another cutout, is my guess. A foreigner this time."

"Shall I pick up the woman?" Gorchakov said. "Falomin's dolly?"

"Not yet."

"Is it Falomin?" Gorchakov said. It was the first sign he had given that he knew the case in its details. Tarp and Repin both looked at him and then at each other, and he turned away, aware that he had overstepped a line.

"Well?" Tarp said.

Repin jabbed a finger at Gorchakov's back. "There must be a tap on Czerny's telephone."

"What if there is?"

"He'll make a call now that he has the tube. It has to be done that way. He'll call; somebody will come and get it."

"We'd never get it in time. Czerny's low priority. It goes on tape, somebody types it up, next week it will be in a file someplace. It's not a live tap."

"We can go up," Tarp said, "and stay out of sight in Czerny's apartment."

"No!" Repin was almost violent. "Maxudov will have him terrorized. Czerny will be more afraid of Maxudov than of us. He will give a signal. Mark me, Maxudov has something on him—a relative in the gulag, maybe. No. We do not show ourselves."

Gorchakov got out and looked down the street and came

back. "Maybe I can put the car in the courtyard just up the street. It's the rear of one of the embassies, but they'll cooperate. Let me move the car and then I'll see about leaving it." He looked at Tarp. "It will cost some money."

"That's all right."

They parked next to a steel trash container, a row of smaller trash bins at their rear bumper like guards. Repin complained that the black box's signal was no good, but they were now in a place from which they could watch the approach to the gate.

Several cars passed along the narrow street. A few parked, but the black box did not respond, and they were sure the tube had not moved. In the dusk just after five o'clock, however, a small car pulled up opposite them and a man got out and hurried toward the gated courtyard.

"He looks like he needs the *pissoir*," Tarp said, using the French word.

"Maybe he's the cutout."

"And maybe he's got a small bladder."

But when the man came back the tube came with him. The black box's whine changed to a groan and the numbers went up as he jumped into his car and flicked on the lights before starting the motor. Repin grinned. "He was nervous." He laughed.

"Last lap?" Tarp said as Gorchakov started the car.

"Maybe. Maybe." Repin laughed again and they pulled out into the street and saw the taillights of the other car disappearing around the curve. Gorchakov followed slowly and turned his own lights off as they topped a rise where they could have been seen from the other car. It was far ahead but moving slowly.

"Easy to follow," Gorchakov said.

"Too easy?"

"No, he's just being careful. It's got diplomatic markings, that car. Italian. Your Maxudov has friends everywhere."

Gorchakov gave an order on his radio and waited until another car pulled in behind them before he turned off on a cross street. They drove parallel to the other's route for six blocks and then pulled in behind again and the other car turned off.

"He's heading for the Kremlin," Gorchakov said. He laughed nervously. "Maybe he's going to deliver it by hand."

Repin looked dyspeptically at Tarp.

"Maybe he's going to give it to Comrade—" Gorchakov started to say.

"Shut up," Repin growled.

Gorchakov shrugged himself deeper into his coat. He began to take his frustration out on the car, which seemed to find more bumps now. It was almost dark. Steering too fast around a corner, Gorchakov almost missed seeing a drunk who stepped into his path; both Tarp and Repin cried out, and the major wrenched the wheel just in time to miss the shambling figure.

"His own fault!" Gorchakov shouted. "It would have been his fault if I'd killed him! These pieces of excrement that infest the streets, they keep the government liquor industry in business and they're the shame of our society! It would have been better if I'd killed him, the—"

"Shut up," Repin muttered.

"I didn't see him!" Gorchakov said sharply. "He could have ruined everything."

"Exactly."

After that, Gorchakov drove more slowly. Tarp thought they had lost the other car, but the major somehow kept it in sight in spite of the drunk and his own anger, and he almost got too close to it as it dawdled along by a crowded sidewalk. They were two lanes over but almost abreast, and Tarp saw the driver in silhouette, gripping the wheel very tightly and sitting up straight. *Nervous. Really nervous.* The man did not look at them. He was more worried about where he was going than who might also be going there.

His destination was Red Square. He had not gone to it by a direct route, no doubt because he had been told to drive randomly. Still, the vast open space was certainly where he had been heading. *So now he must feel better.* The square looked cold, like the icefields over which the winds blew without regard to spring. There was little movement now—cars, a trickle of pedestrians near St. Basil's. Far away down the square, a row of huge banners were lighted with spotlights, yet from this distance they seemed too small to be read.

"What a place," Gorchakov groaned.

"Daring," Repin said. Red Square was a good place to sell dollars or blue jeans, but it did seem a remarkable place for this sort of operation. "Well, we wait." Repin was still watching the diplomatic car's lights by the Kremlin wall.

"I can't wait here very long," Gorchakov said.

"Turn off your lights."

"The Moscow police watch the square all the time now. I don't have an arrangement with them for this business."

"I will take care of the Moscow police. Turn off your lights!"

Repin fiddled with the black box. The signal was strong, and when the other car pulled away from the wall, there was no doubt that the tube had been left behind.

"In the wall?" Tarp said.

"Probably. Too dark to see."

"I can't stay here," Gorchakov said.

"Yes, you can."

"No, I cannot!"

"Get out the tools and pretend you're changing a tire. We wait here."

Gorchakov turned around in the driver's seat so he could confront Repin. He looked first at Tarp, appealing to him as if he were a neutral observer, and then he turned his full attention on the old man. "If the police come, they will make trouble. They are trying to clean up the black market in the square; they have lots of spirit, you know? If I pretend to have a breakdown, they will have a truck here in minutes. If I claim official privilege, they have to log it. Then your Maxudov may hear about it."

"Who says?"

"If I was Maxudov, it's the first precaution I would take. How much trouble do you think he would have bribing somebody at Police Central?"

Both men were stubborn, and they might even have enjoyed this kind of clash if Repin had not been so committed to what he was doing. Gorchakov was still angry about the drunk, however, and Repin was losing his objectivity as he feared it all might slip away from them.

"How about bringing in a cover?" Tarp said. Both men looked at him with the suspicion that two people who have been looking for a fight give to the peacemaker. "A repair vehicle, something like that."

There was a moment's pause in the hostilities. "This isn't New York," Gorchakov said sarcastically.

"We don't tear up Red Square once a week," Repin added, as if he and Gorchakov had been rehearsing the response to such a stupid suggestion.

"We may be here all night," Tarp said. "It's to Maxudov's advantage to wait. But some kind of cover shouldn't be impossible."

"No time," Repin said.

"Of course there's time," Gorchakov said as if his pride had been touched. "We have a special office for that kind of work."

"How soon?" Tarp said.

"An hour at the longest. Less."

Tarp looked at Repin. "Well?"

Gorchakov said, more reasonably now that Tarp seemed to be with him, "It's a good idea. Really, the city cops will be here anytime." He gave Repin an apologetic smile. "Good old Moscow, eh?"

Repin looked at each of them, shrugged as if he were being outvoted by idiots. "All right."

Tarp put his hand out to open the door. "We'll walk. You take the car and arrange the cover." He jerked his head at Repin. "It's still early; we can walk around the square and not look suspicious. The tourists are still out."

Repin's lips made the sucking motions Tarp had learned to recognize, as if he had a cough drop in his mouth; he was covering inner indecision. "You've got the French passport. I have an Intourist ID. That is all right for the police. You're a foreigner, I'm watching over you. You wanted to see Red Square by night." He sighed. "It will be a nice scene if the cops stop us and find these cannons. Let's go."

"I'll be quick," Gorchakov said.

Repin said dryly, "Of course you will."

They walked slowly around the enormous square, stating where they could watch the place in the wall where the tube had been left. It was colder. Repin put one hand through the crook of Tarp's arm. "I'm hungry," Repin said. Later he muttered, "This gun feels like a rock." They walked in silence. A car pulled even with them. "Police," Repin muttered. It did not stop, however, but accelerated and headed for the far end of the square. "If we go around again, they will stop us," Repin said. "We look as if we're waiting for somebody to make us an offer for dollars. Walk slower."

Forty-one minutes after Gorchakov had left them, a heavy van appeared where the twenty-foot-high banners were illuminated and began to cruise slowly by them. It stopped; men got out and began to erect a scaffolding.

"For us?" Tarp said. They were nearing the end of their round and he was very nervous about the police now.

"And about time," Repin said. When they walked to the van, Gorchakov was waiting. He grinned triumphantly. "Well?" he said.

"It's pretty obvious," Repin said. "Maxudov's no fool."

"Neither am I." Gorchakov's good humor was restored. He was one of those men who are quickly angered and who as quickly cool. "A backdated work order has been filed with the Department of Municipal Improvement; a permission chit is in the basket at Police Central, exactly where it should be in the pile if it had been dropped in three days ago. The cops here in the square have been reminded that banner replacement has been on the schedule since Tuesday because the vice-premier of Indonesia is coming to town and the motorcade passes this way."

"The Guards keep an eye on Red Square, too," Repin said. He jerked his head toward the Kremlin. "Maxudov may keep track of what goes on here through the Guards' office."

Gorchakov's smile became a little stiff. "I thought of that. I sealed off Guards' operation center before I did anything else. On the general secretary's orders."

"Sealed off?"

"I called in my own people. If anybody at Guards' operation center tries to warn Maxudov about the van and the banner changings, we'll intercept the message and stop it. Aren't you two hungry? I brought food from a canteen. You can't stand out here and not be hungry."

They stood around the van, eating salty ham and potatoes and dark bread. Repin was quieter, but Tarp knew that he was still serious when he refused a drink. After another hour a motorcycle stopped next to them and a young man in blue jeans and western boots got off. He handed Gorchakov a brown envelope and drove off again with that gutsy roar that motorcyclists everywhere seem to love.

"Well?"

Gorchakov was reading a blue message paper. "Just after I put my people in, the duty commander called and said he wanted to monitor all activities in Red Square." He made a popping sound with his lips. "I suppose he's Maxudov's man. The little man who made the drop by the wall must have made a phone call; then the duty commander was called."

"So?" Repin said.

"Awkward."

"Has he been told about this van?"

"No. We intercepted the report." Gorchakov made the popping sound again. "Awkward. He's a lieutenant-colonel. You two better be right."

Repin grunted. "We're right."

Repin and Tarp took turns watching the place where the tube had been left. There were binoculars, but Tarp found them more trouble than help. Mostly, he and Repin walked up and down by the van, both watching. Gorchakov stayed behind the wheel. A police car stopped and Gorchakov leaned down and joked with the men inside. Tarp watched them, understanding that boisterous, slightly nervous camaraderie of men in the same work under different bosses, at the same time allies and rivals. After some minutes the laughter stopped and the talk became serious. Then Gorchakov saluted; the policeman at the wheel waved, and the car pulled away.

"He wanted to know if it was going to be a wet night," Gorchakov said. "He knows me. I said it might be a little damp but he was to mind his own business."

"Will he?"

"Oh, yes. He wants a promotion. I told him I'd try to do something if he proved he could keep his mouth shut."

It was two in the morning before anything happened. Gorchakov was almost asleep. They had moved the van three times so that the work crew could change the huge banners. Tarp was leaning against the front of the vehicle, wanting sleep; Repin was standing a few feet out toward the square, staring down toward the wall.

A pair of automobile headlights appeared far down the square. Repin looked at them, then back into the shadow of the truck. The car drove into the square and stopped. Then, very deliberately, it turned and came slowly toward them.

"Behind the van!" Repin hissed. He pushed Tarp ahead of him. "Down!" he shouted at Gorchakov.

The Guards major was rubbing his eyes. When Tarp got around to the far side of the van, he opened the door and reached up and grabbed the shoulder of Gorchakov's coat. *"Down!"* he said as he pulled the stocky Russian to the seat.

The car came on slowly, the way the police cars did, with a ponderous self-confidence. It almost stopped with its head-lights shining on the van before it turned and went by them, and Tarp, looking past the fender, saw the pale shape of a face at the rear window as somebody studied the workmen.

"You think?" he said to Repin.

"Maybe."

"There's more than one."

"I expected that. In fact, there are four."

"All right. Let's get ready."

He went around the back of the van and came up on the driver's side. The other car was visible only as a pair of red lights, still moving slowly. Tarp opened the door and got in, motioning Gorchakov into the middle.

"What are you doing?" the Guards major objected.

"Making sure you stay noninvolved."

Repin was already getting in the other side. The black box was in one hand, the red light shining like an eye; he had the big pistol in the other. "I want your gun, Major," Repin said.

"What?"

Repin reached into his leather coat and took the pistol out. Tarp ran his hands over the man's ankles and calves. "You're making a terrible mistake!" Gorchakov said.

"It's for your own good," Tarp growled. "This was the arrangement."

The tube was in the wall diagonally across the square, a hundred yards away. The other car had made its turn at the corner to their right and was now moving slowly along the wall in which the tube was hidden. Tarp started the engine and the van rolled forward.

At that moment the other car's lights went off.

Tarp needed no other evidence. He slammed the van into gear and stepped on the accelerator and the tires squealed. The van bolted and their heads snapped back, and then they were hurtling across the square in the darkness. He felt the tires strike a low curb, bounce over it, and rush on. He was driving one-handed because of the big pistol. Gorchakov had both hands up on the dash to brace himself.

Reflected light from the sky made the car a black blot against the darkness of the wall. He thought he saw movement near it. The car was parked well away from the wall itself and thirty yards back from the place where the tube lay, giving the men in the car an unlimited field of fire if they needed it.

Repin ducked as they came close. He had seen something that Tarp had not.

The windshield dissolved.

Tarp cut the van across the front of the car, his own right side missing it only by inches. As they passed it he heard two thuds against the van's right side, but Gorchakov was shouting, "Go on, go on!" There were more thuds. *My God, this thing's armored,* Tarp was thinking as he spun the wheel. *They're using silencers and this is an armored car.* He sensed that Repin was flinching low on his side and Gorchakov was doing something to his face as he hit the brake and wrenched the wheel around; the van went into a skid just past the car and went on skidding over slick paving stones, careening toward the wall in a controlled spin until the right rear end hit the Kremlin Wall with a stolid boom like the closing of a vault. Then he accelerated again and the van leaped away from the wall, and he brought it to a stop between the dark shape of a man up by the wall, on Repin's side, and the car and the men with the guns, on his.

Then Repin was out of the van and Tarp had his own door open. A door on the passenger side of the car started to open and Tarp fired three times, the Makarov going off in the constricted space of the van with an ear-bursting loudness.

The car lurched suddenly forward and turned to its left to go around him and get at Repin.

Tarp stood on the accelerator, and the van rammed into the car just behind the right front wheel.

The two vehicles accelerated over the pavement of the

square, locked together. Tarp could hear the screech of metal and the heartbeat thud of a blown tire. A trail of sparks spattered along the pavement where broken metal dragged.

His door had slammed shut again. He rolled the window down and then put the Makarov out in his left hand and fired down into the car's roof until the gun was empty, but the car was still trying to escape the grip of the van, and he knew that the driver was still alive. He looked wildly into the cab of the van, thinking he might somehow reload the Makarov, and he saw Gorchakov reaching under the driver's seat and coming up with a shiny mass of metal in his hand. For an instant Tarp thought it was over: Gorchakov was holding a .44 magnum revolver, a gun so big it made the Makarov look like a toy.

Without a word Gorchakov handed him the pistol.

Tarp put two shots through the car's roof and two into its engine block. The sound of the engine changed and then began to mount toward a runaway whine, and then the van was dragging the car instead of keeping pace with it. Tarp took his foot from the accelerator and let both vehicles come to a stop.

Tarp jumped from the right side of the car with Gorchakov holding the door. He came more slowly around the rear of the two vehicles, and as he passed the rear window of the car there was a shot and he fired twice and the big magnum rounds crashed into the sheet metal and there was no more shooting. The man behind the wheel of the car was dying. Tarp reached in and turned off the ignition. He could smell burned rubber and hot metal, and in the silence after the engine stopped he heard two men trying to breathe, dying.

Tarp sprinted across the square. A red light was blinking on top of the van already, planted up there by Gorchakov. Far away, the lights of two cars came on; at the other end of the square the lights on the banners were bright and brave, but the scaffolding was empty of workmen.

There was one figure standing by the wall. There was a puddle of darkness on the ground nearby and a vague, small shape of a lighter color where an ungloved hand lay like a flower.

Tarp slowed, walked a few steps, stopped, the magnum held ready.

"Repin?"

"Well?"

"Is it Telyegin?"

"Of course."

Tarp walked slowly to him and looked down at the twisted body. It looked thin and without bulk, a pile of sticks with a coat thrown over it.

"Did he say anything?" Tarp said carefully.

"What would he have said?" Repin's voice was very thin, as if his throat were constricted.

"You were friends. I thought he might have said something."

Repin's face was lighted by the oncoming cars, and the flashing red on top of the van caught one eye and vanished, as if the eye had given him a red wink. "Being friends never entered into it," Repin said.

Falomin was subdued by the discovery that his young mistress had been Maxudov's probe, but he did his job well. He interrogated Tarp for two hours and Repin for one. He was no more cordial, no more giving than he had been that day in the museum, but he was certainly more respectful.

"So." Falomin stood and leaned on the plain metal table that stood between them. It was almost dawn. "So. Are you satisfied, then?"

"Me?" Tarp touched his chest.

"Yes. The official business is over. Here, just among the three of us . . ." Besides the two of them and Repin, there were two male KGB officers and a woman from the Guards; they did not seem to exist for Falomin. "Are you satisfied?"

"That Telyegin was Maxudov? Of course."

"How did you know?" Falomin threw back his head and waited for the answer as if he already knew it.

"His was the body in Red Square."

Falomin scowled. The flippant answer made him angry; he wanted admittance to the circle of those who had caught Maxudov. *The circle of the blessed.* Tarp smiled. *Some blessing.*

"And he did it for this medicine?"

"He did it so he could live a little longer, yes."

"Madness. Just madness. It proves what I have been saying for years. We don't retire these men early enough. Well, it's a lesson to us. Eh? A lesson. Too much sympathy for the sick can be dangerous to one's health!'' He laughed. Repin stared at him. Repin owed him nothing now. Repin owed nobody in Moscow anything anymore; he had wiped out any errors he had ever committed. He had become their creditor, in fact.

But Falomin could not let it go. He wanted them to share it with him, somehow, anyhow. "So, how do you feel now?'' he said.

Tarp looked up at him. "Dirty,'' he said. "Dirty. This is the dirtiest business I was ever in.''

Seconds later Falomin shook their hands and went out, and the two men went out after him. Now Falomin's turn would come—the interrogation in the country about his mistress and his child.

There were papers to sign and two junior officers to talk to briefly, and then they sat mindlessly in a waiting room for twenty minutes, and then they were allowed to go. They were led along corridors into a comfortable sitting room, and minutes later they were standing in the sunshine of the early morning with Strisz.

"You are going directly to the airport,'' Repin said. "Me, too.''

"They can't wait to get rid of us.''

"We are an embarrassment.'' Repin laughed and slapped his hands together. "It is very satisfying, being an embarrassment!''

Strisz managed to look both official and friendly. "Your money is to be paid over in London.''

"I'm counting on it.''

They walked toward three waiting cars. Tarp saw a spear of green tipped with dark red the color of a fire-darkened brick, thrusting out of the dark wetness of a flower bed. Beyond it an old man was slowly raking the winter's detritus from the earth.

"You did well,'' Tarp said, shaking hands with Repin.

The old man narrowed his eyes. "*You* did well,'' he said. "I enjoyed our fishing trip. We must go fishing again sometime. Now, I am going home to Tiflis, where I am going to sleep for three days, and then I am going to wake up to the smell of French bread and fresh coffee and brioche.'' Tired as he was, he strutted like a rooster. "My Frenchwoman is only waiting for the word.''

When he was gone, Strisz and Tarp stood together, both a little embarrassed. "Thank Gorchakov for me," Tarp said. "I never saw him after the shooting stopped."

"The general secretary is very grateful for what you've done," Strisz said awkwardly. "He wished me to say that if there is anything else you would like, he would certainly be happy to oblige you."

Tarp smiled, but not very pleasantly. He was tired. "Tell him I'd like to meet Raoul Wallenberg."

Strisz was shocked. "Not funny!" he said.

Tarp touched his arm by way of good-bye. "Not meant to be."

CHAPTER 42

Tarp flew to Paris and slept for twelve hours and then went to the farm. The place was empty and lifeless, although spring had touched the earth around it. A weed was sprouting in the rotted hay where the old man had lain drunk, and there was a film of green in the trees. His was the only car in the rutted yard now; he slept in the kitchen because it was warm and ate out of cans.

He spoke twice to Juana by telephone and once to Kinsella, and then when he had arranged matters in Buenos Aires he talked to Johnnie Carrington. His last day at the farm Laforet flew in, and Tarp told him everything and gave him four of the phials from the habitat. "Your people may find something there. It may be useful."

"We are very interested in the habitat itself," Laforet said almost languidly.

"So are 'Mr. Smith's' people. You'd better hurry."

"And this Pope-Ginna, and this Schneider—what of them?"

"That's what I do next."

He flew to London. Johnnie Carrington met him at Heathrow and walked him to one of the VIP lounges.

"We've booked him a seat on a flight that goes in forty minutes. Mexico City nonstop, then Buenos Aires."

"Was he pleased?"

"He seemed delighted."

"He didn't want to stay in England?"

"He seems to feel that he belongs in Argentina. He hasn't much patriotism, you know."

"He hasn't much of anything, except self-serving."

They chatted for a few minutes, and then Pope-Ginna was led in by two MI-5 men. He looked very chipper—quite as Tarp had first seen him, Dickensian and merry, clearly happy to be heading again for Argentina. Tarp excused himself and went out of the lounge to speak to somebody waiting there, then went back in in time to hear Pope-Ginna saying, "Never again, my young friend—never again!" He put his brown-flecked hand over his chest. "I shall never delve in international intrigue again!"

"You never know," Tarp said, coming behind him.

"Aha, there you are! There, there, there you are!" Pope-Ginna's tic had vanished and he seemed able to face Tarp squarely. "I believe, you know, Mr. Tarp, I probably owe you an apology—and perhaps a hearty thank-you—now that it's over."

"Is it over?" Tarp said.

Pope-Ginna laughed; the laugh was boisterous, but the tic appeared, only for an instant. Over his shoulder Tarp was watching three people who had entered the lounge.

"There's somebody I want you to meet," Tarp said. He took Pope-Ginna's arm and turned him around and started to walk him down the long, narrow room. Partway along, Pope-Ginna moved as if he wanted to escape the grip and not go with him, but Tarp would not let him go.

"I think you know Juaquin Schneider," Tarp said, standing before a man in a wheelchair. Behind the chair was a beautiful woman who might have been the invalid's nurse. "Juana Marino," Tarp said easily. He nodded at the man with her. "Jaime Kinsella, of the Argentine air force."

Pope-Ginna needed a moment to try to pull it off, but he made a good effort. "Well, Jock!" he said very loudly, his voice going up too much in pitch. "What a hell of a coincidence!"

"Don't touch me," Schneider said. He pulled back a little as Pope-Ginna's hand came toward him.

"Well, you needn't take the high-and-mighty with me, Jock!" Pope-Ginna bellowed. He laughed. He swung about to Tarp and said, "I told you how our millionaire friend behaves, Mr. Tarp!" He looked a little wildly at Tarp, then back at Juana and Kinsella. "I don't know these people, Jock! Where are, uh—Fleming, and—Voerdreck—and . . ."

Schneider fixed him with a look of sheer hatred. His small face, which Tarp had found effeminate before, looked demonic. "Your boys won't be here, for once."

"M-my . . ." The laughter faded in Pope-Ginna's throat. "See here," he said to Tarp, ."I demand to know what the hell's going on!"

"Why, this is your farewell delegation, Admiral—seeing you off to Argentina. Señor Schneider and Señor Kinsella want you to know how welcome you'll be when you get back there. Now that Señ or Schneider is no longer surrounded by the mercenaries you used to guard him, he has some very strong ideas of what sort of welcome you ought to have."

A terrible smile lighted Schneider's face. "Yes! And Mr. Tarp himself—Monsieur Selous, as I know him—said it best: *Is the death squad the purpose of wealth?*"

"I don't understand this at all," Pope-Ginna said in a strangled, small voice.

"Oh," Juana said in rapid Spanish, "it is not at all complicated, Admiral Pope-Ginna. It was complicated to find out, but it is not complicated to understand. Señor Kinsella and I have found it quite easy to understand, with the help of Señor Carrington here in England. Put most simply of all—it is you!" She came around the wheelchair, smiling beautifully. "It was always you. *You* found out who Nazdia Becker really was. *You* paid to bring her to England and to continue her training in science. Was she your mistress, ever? Was she? Well—*you* sent her to Argentina to marry Señor Schneider, who was nobody then. You have lied so much. You lied when you said Schneider was rich when you first met him; oh, no, he was a very poor young man looking for a way to be rich. And you married him to Nazdia Becker—or the woman who called herself that—and then you and she could legally get at the German money in Argentina that had been left in her father's name. I have seen the bank records, Admiral. I have nine signed statements."

Pope-Ginna was staring at Tarp. The tic came and went. "I could deny this," he said in an uninflected voice. "But I wouldn't di-dignify it with a denial."

"*You* were the one who wanted the habitat, Admiral." Her voice went on, measured and accusing. "*You* arranged the death of Juaquin Schneider's wife; one of your 'boys' told us how it was done. *You* made Schneider a virtual prisoner, blackmailing him with the vaccine that his own wife had discovered.''

Tarp looked at Schneider. "You *are* Gaucho, aren't you?''
Schneider glared at Pope-Ginna. "I am."

Tarp touched Pope-Ginna's shoulder. "And it was you who invented Maxudov. For a long time, I thought that Maxudov was somebody who had gone looking for a way to sell plutonium. I had the wrong end of the stick. It really began with somebody who wanted to *buy* plutonium—you! And you found your man when you were arranging the purchase of the submarine. A soviet KGB bigwig who was dying of cancer.'' Tarp shook his head. "You turned a man with the only thing that nobody else could promise him—a few more months of life.''

Pope-Ginna gave up trying to deny. "He took it willingly,'' he said. "The whole Maxudov business was his invention. Not mine.''

"You made him a traitor.''

"I told him what I wanted, and I told him what he would get in return. How he did it was his business.'' He drew himself up—the first time Tarp could remember his ever asserting himself with that gesture. "What difference does it make? I got what I wanted and now it will be used in the way that I intended.''

"The plutonium is back in Russia. I didn't tell you that before, Admiral. For a while, I thought perhaps it really was Schneider who was behind it, and not you—but of course it wasn't.'' He looked down at Schneider. "It *was* you who passed us the message in Havana, wasn't it?''

Schneider lowered his head. "It was.''

"I don't believe you!'' Pope Ginna rasped. "The plutonium is not back in Russia! It can't be!''

Tarp heard Carrington's voice behind him intoning the formula. "Anthony Marcus Aurelius Pope-Ginna, I charge you with crimes most grave and heinous against the Crown and against the government. Let me warn you that anything you say—''

Pope-Ginna brushed past Carrington as if the words meant nothing. "I don't believe, I say. Did you hear me? I don't believe you!''

"I was in the habitat, Admiral. I took the plutonium off.''

The old man stared at him, his mouth working. "You couldn't have."

"Shall I repeat the charge?" Carrington murmured.

"What? *What?* Oh, don't bother me!"

"Admiral Pope-Ginna, you're under arrest. Don't you understand?"

"Don't bother me! Can't you understand plain English? Doesn't anybody here understand me? What is going on!"

Three of Carrington's men appeared and took Pope-Ginna by the arms. He still seemed not to care about them, not even to have noticed them. Instead he turned on Schneider and Kinsella.

"You idiots!" he said in his slightly accented Spanish. "You pathetic idiots! Another year and I could have had forty atomic warheads and we could have blown the British Navy out of the water—*and you started the Malvinas war too soon!*"

They led him out, white-faced, muttering to himself. Carrington introduced himself to Kinsella and to Schneider, then pulled up a chair and began to explain the kind of statement he hoped to get from them. Tarp knew it would be a long, difficult process, for already Schneider was talking about a lawyer and Kinsella would say only that his work was done.

Tarp took Juana aside. She was wearing a turtleneck that hid her scar, and, except for a small depression in the skin high on her left cheekbone, she looked unmarked. "You did wonderfully," he said.

"What happens now?"

"They'll take depositions, testimony. It will take weeks. They'll want statements from you, too."

"Weeks?"

"At least. You'll have to stay in England, I'm afraid."

"With you?"

"I was thinking that might be a good idea, yes."

"Yes."

"Yes."

"Yes."

There was still snow in the deepest part of the woods, but the ice had gone out of the rivers and ponds, and the winter-bound animals prowled again at night. He had found bear tracks in the soft mud along the bank of a stream, and in the mornings the badger that lived at the edge of his clearing came as far as his door for crusts. He took the old canoe out of its storage and put it on the pond and coaxed the first brook trout up from the depths; and in the deep pool below the biggest rock in the river, he took a landlocked salmon on the fly just at dusk.

He spent the days at the computer console, studying the discs from the habitat. There was much there that he did not understand about genetic research and viruses, but there was a lot in there he did understand that had been gotten from Beranyi just before he'd died. He took it all in and filed it carefully in his data banks, where it would serve him well.

He awoke in the mornings while it was still dark. Outside the big window the sky was dull red above the black treetops. The room was cold. He moved quickly, naked, feeding the wood stove, making coffee. One morning he pressed a switch on the console and the screen glowed, and the grid of his security system appeared. He pulled on blue jeans and a sweater, and he was reaching for a cup when a light began to blink rapidly in the upper right-hand corner of the CRT.

Bogeys, he thought. *At the river. Early risers.*

He slipped his feet into canvas boots and took a pistol from a drawer, then went out through a trap in the cabin floor. The air had bite, and the wind that shook the trees was cool. Above, the sky was lighter, and a sparrow was singing as the woods woke.

He made his way to the riverbank. When he got there the sun was just appearing over the hills on the other side, and its first brightness struck on a shiny piece of metal on a tree limb near him. Tarp hung back behind a massive pine and looked at it. There was a long strip of red ribbon and then, below it, a disc of silver.

Bogey's been and gone, he thought.

He took it from the limb and held it in his hand. It was a medal as big as the bottom of a coffee cup. On one side was a man's head in deep relief, on the other the hammer and sickle and a quotation from Lenin in Cyrillic characters. Below it were his name and the date and *For service to the struggle for the people.*

Tarp looked up and down the riverbank. He knew that somebody was watching out there, probably from the other side of the river.

He threw the medal as high and as far as he could. It went up, glinting in the morning sun, trailing its ribbon-like blood, and then turned over and arched down and down and fell with an inaudible splash in the deep, swirling water where he had caught the salmon, where it sank at once and was gone.

Then Tarp turned his back and went toward the cabin for breakfast.